THE
LOCUSTS
HAVE NO
KING

THE
LOCUSTS
HAVE NO
KING

BY

Dawn Powell

WITH

AN INTRODUCTION

BY JOHN GUARE

Yarrow Press • New York
1990

The Publishers wish to thank
Jacqueline Miller Rice for her assistance
and for her dedication to the works
and memory of Dawn Powell.

The Locusts Have No King
was first published in 1948.

Library of Congress Cataloging-in-Publication Data
Powell, Dawn.
The locusts have no king.
Originally published: New York : Scribner, 1948.
1. Title.
PS3531.0936L6 1990   813'.52   89-24924
ISBN 1–878274–00–7 (pbk.)

Printed in the United States of America
Cover design by Richard Eckersley

Cover photograph: Josef Breitenbach.
Radio City. 1942.
Copyright © The Estate of Josef Breitenbach.
Courtesy Peter C. Jones, Inc., New York.

Yarrow Press
225 Lafayette Street
New York,
New York 10012

CONTENTS

INTRODUCTION

In 1987 Gore Vidal wrote an essay for *The New York Review of Books* on a novelist named Dawn Powell. Who? She wrote novels that Edmund Wilson described in 1962 as being "among the most amusing being written, and in this respect quite on a level with those of Anthony Powell, Evelyn Waugh, and Muriel Spark."

I read a lot; I pride myself on reading. I wrote a play called *Bosoms and Neglect* in which two people fall in love, linked only by a shared devotion to reading neglected writers. You shouldn't quote your own work, but the girl in my play says a neglected author is not one you choose to neglect.

I went on a hunt.

Powell's books were neither in print nor in the library. Vidal mentioned a 1934 play called *Jig Saw*. The New York Public Library at Lincoln Center had a copy. It's the typical play of a novelist: the author's voice commenting on the action is missing. The evils of naturalism. Charming but lacks a guiding voice. I asked a friend of mine on the Dramatists Guild about Dawn Powell. "Yes, I knew her slightly. She lived under the burden of being known as the second Dorothy Parker."

I found thirteen references to Powell in Edmund Wilson's diaries of the thirties (she doesn't make it into the forties). A typical entry: "Dawn Powell's knock-down-and-drag-out party."

I went to the *New York Times* and read her obituary (unsigned) before I read her work. It's dated 16 November 1965 and is the lead obit of the day: "Dawn Powell, Novelist, Is Dead: Author of Witty, Satirical Books. Middle Class Was the Object of Her Stinging Fiction—13 Books Published." A candid photograph of a plump woman in a stylish veil looking off in the near distance with a naughty grin accompanies the following: Born in Mount Gilead, Ohio, 28 November 1897. Mother died early; stepmother burned her early stories. Ran away with thirty cents earned as a berry picker. Married, had one child, a son, and lived and worked in Greenwich Village over the course of her life at 35 East Ninth Street and 95 Christopher Street.

The obit goes on: "The victims of her satire were of the middle class, and this did not add to her popularity. 'You both confuse and anger people if you satirize the middle class,' Powell had said. 'It is considered jolly and good-humored to point out the oddities of the poor or of the rich, but I go outside the rules with my stuff because I can't help believing that the middle class is funny, too.'"

And finally:"There will be no funeral service at Miss Powell's request."

The other people who shared Powell's obit page that day were:

Louis J. Fink, Insurance Man, 80. "Selling life insurance," Mr. Fink said, "is like playing good music on a fine instrument. Both stem from the heart. If the time ever comes that I lose interest in the lives and hopes of people, I'd no longer be able to write a large amount of insurance."

Sister Claudia, 97, Sister of Charity nurse to famous people: Fiorello La Guardia, Admiral Byrd, Babe Ruth, Jimmy Walker, and Al Smith.

William Martin, 71, Gathered Weather Data for 50 Years. "He received no salary for his weather activities."

Did Powell orchestrate the people who'd share her day of death?

I finally read my first Dawn Powell. *The Locusts Have No King.*

I loved it.

In this novel a literary light observes that the hero's new book on the Middle Ages could use a foreword. "It struck me," says the dean of the League of Cultural Foundations, "that a foreword in a popular vein might help a little to put it over." Frederick, the hero, is mystified and embarrassed by this offer as he feels his work doesn't need a foreword, but if it will help sell the new book. . . . He murmurs his thanks "evasively."

I'm sure Dawn Powell would feel much the same way; but the

thirties and forties of her world ("New York is not the same city it was, being overrun now with Americans," she said in 1947) belong now to our Middle Ages. All the same, if a foreword helps this shockingly out-of-print author, then I leap into the fray for her.

I don't want to tell you the plot of this book in one of those forewords where the over-anxious fan spells out in joy-numbing detail the events of the book you're about to read. I'll restrain my enthusiasm and let the 1948 dust jacket have the following say: "Frederick Olliver, scholar and recluse, emerges from his medieval research one night in the autumn of 1945 to find New York a strange and terrifying city, the peace now being celebrated, as sinister and barbaric as the Dark Ages he has just left."

But doesn't that sound more like *Double Indemnity*, more like a Fritz Lang *Woman in the Window* hurling an innocent man to the film noir wolves of fate? Yet this is the writer Edmund Wilson described as writing novels that are "more than merely funny; they are full of psychological insights that are at once sympathetic and cynical, and they have episodes that are rather macabre, which seem to represent an all-but-embitterment . . . one can always be sure that some sudden new comic idea will give a twist to the situation, which has seemed to be irretrievably uncomfortable, and introduce an arbitrary element that will give to the proceedings a touch of ballet."

When T. S. Eliot said the plot is merely the piece of meat the burglar throws the watchdog to distract him, he could have been writing about Powell in a mask with a bag of swag tossing Alpo to the Dobermans.

On 30 December 1947, Powell wrote this to a British publisher:

> . . . my novels are based on the fantastic designs made by real human beings earnestly laboring to maladjust themselves to fate. There are no principles for them to prove—they may disobey the law of gravity as they please. My characters are not slaves to an author's propaganda. I give them their heads. They furnish their own nooses.

I met Jacqueline Miller Rice, who is the executor of Dawn Powell's estate and was her friend. "I was much younger," Rice said, "but so incorporated into her world by her. If you knew Dawn Powell, you didn't need to know anyone else. . . . If people said she was another Dorothy Parker, she'd hit them. Dawn was a Village person. Not an Algonquin person, even though Benchley adored her. As did Edmund Wilson, Hemingway, Malcolm Cowley, and Gerald and Sara Murphy. People came to her. She told me once, 'Never go anywhere you're not wanted.'. . .

"Dawn didn't think politically. It was John Howard Lawson who brought her into the Group Theatre to do her play *Big Night*. He became one of the Hollywood Ten. But Dawn didn't care about politics. At least they weren't the main event. A year later she had a play produced by the Theatre Guild. Very establishment. And when Dos Passos went from the left to the right, that made no difference to Dawn either. He was her friend.

"She always kept on writing, though most of her books went out of print. She had so many bad things happen to her in her life that it didn't surprise her if things didn't work out. She knew how to deny in order to survive. . . . Her son was born in 1921 severely brain-damaged. She told everyone he was 'exceptional,' keeping him at home for years with tutors in Italian and piano. She helped her husband wage a long, excruciating battle against cancer, but when it came to her own cancer, she refused surgery. We were sitting in the Jumble Shop on Waverly Place. I told her: 'I want you to live to be a mean cranky old lady with a cane.' She wouldn't listen. Her cancer could have been so easily treated. But she'd had terrible experiences with doctors, the most notable being an operation to remove a vestigial heart. . . .

"One of the last entries in her journal was about the birth of my child Hilary Dawn. When her sickness got worse in 1965, she stopped letting me bring the baby when I came over every day. She was afraid her cancer was contagious. She thought she'd caught her cancer from her husband. . . . She hid her fear and despair. She showed her best face to the world. And what a glorious face. I wake up some mornings so happy because I've dreamt that that whole world is still alive. And it's so real to me."

Without telling you the fate of the characters, I will tell you the very end of *The Locusts Have No King* because it is a brilliant summation and union of all the textures in Powell's book. If people are unfaithful, it is their own hearts that are broken. History is really something that concerns the lower classes. People like to look at their loved ones while sitting at mirrors gazing at themselves.

> . . . Frederick was idly fiddling with the bedside radio and there was a sputtering of words and confused noises.
>
> "It's the Bikini test—the atom bomb the elevator man's wife is afraid of," Frederick said.
>
> "When you hear the words —'What goes here' that will be the signal—" said the faraway voice, and suddenly Frederick was filled with fear, too. . . . In a world of destruction one must hold fast to whatever fragments of love are left, for sometimes a mosaic can be more beautiful than an unbroken pattern.

This extraordinary blend of narcissism and earned love produces a comedy and melancholy that is magically devoid of any sentimentality. At this moment, in a declaration of ironic wisdom and passionate insight, Powell transforms her New York of the forties (and nineties) into a Vienna of Strauss and von Hofmannsthal's *Der Rosenkavalier.*

The writers' organization PEN publishes a column in their bulletin searching out lost members.

Attention: PEN. Dawn Powell? Found. We're ready for her.

Read this book. Pass the word along.

JOHN GUARE, *October 1989*

THE
LOCUSTS
HAVE NO
KING

The locusts have no king,
yet go they forth
all of them by bands.

PROVERBS

1

. . . journey into the juke-box . . .

WHEREVER he went that night people insisted
on confiding in him. Perhaps some fear of his fellow-men
gleamed in the young man's intense blue eyes that made
them want to reassure him that they, too, were unarmed.
Perhaps his eager haste suggested a mission of love, so
circumstance must conspire mischievously with people to
delay him.

It began when he stepped confidently into a taxi at
Fourth and Bank, gave the address on East End Avenue,
suddenly felt in his change pocket, then in his wallet with
an expression of acute chagrin, impatiently crumpled his
hat under his arm and stepped out on the street again.
Frowning he considered Umberto's Grotto lettered in
white on a blue canopy tilted up to street level like a
tea-pot snout. He dashed down the stairs but the man
he sought had just left. While he hesitated in the doorway his taxi escaped and pudgy Umberto clutched his
lapel to lament how grievous had been the mistake of
listening to relatives, adding a garden and Muzak, and
how much happier he, being a simple man of simple
tastes, would be if only his worthless wife and children
could have fallen in the East River. A man should never
marry, said Umberto, and would gladly have revealed
more, generously offering a glass of chianti and a toast
"Salut e figli masci!" but Frederick pleaded that his
emergency would permit him to waste no time. Perhaps
he could find Murray in those spots further east, sug-

1

gested Umberto following him up the steps and making a wide gesture toward the lights beyond Sheridan Square. Pulling his topcoat around his neck, Frederick hurried out into the chilly March rain. He had lived long in the neighborhood but everything looked strange and new tonight, a little terrifying to a man just emerged from seven years' burial in the dead ages. Tonight the work was completed and it was as if he had just returned from a long voyage and must grope eagerly but a little uncertainly for the old familiar landmarks. Each block toward the bright lights seemed a century's step through a tunnel of darkness toward Lyle—and life. Names of bars mentioned by Murray flickered vaguely through his memory, and he stepped tentatively into one called the Florida.

It surprised him that everyone knew Murray. Everyone knew Murray Cahill and his nocturnal habits far better than did the man who had shared his apartment for years. This was Murray's world. In the Florida Tavern a long-nosed girl with sleek head, chin sliding into a gaunt length of black sweater and slacks, looked up at mention of the name. Her long feet in ballet slippers hooked over the rungs of the bar stool.

"Try the America's bar two blocks over and up," she suggested. "He goes there first. How about sticking around here for a while? Have a drink. I gotta talk to somebody. No? Okay, okay."

Hurrying across the street the misty golden lights made faces blur as in a dream, shine brightly for a second, then fade into a half-smile, a moustache, harlequin spectacles, wide red lips. Little dark streets waited for footsteps, invited shadows to creep back to forgotten ages; cats' eyes peered up from cellar windows, watched from sloping roofs for some signal from the hidden moon. Frederick felt like the banquet guest in the fairy-tale who took the wrong overshoes and stepped out into another age. He wondered if his disguise was adequate, if his toga showed. He wondered if the day would ever come when he would cease being the stranger, the solitary wanderer, the observer without passport or knowledge of the language. Like a shy but curious nursery child in adult wonderland, he peered into the Americas whose blue neon sign cast a warning green shadow on each new arrival. The bar was long and narrow with a juke-box glowing like hell-fire in the back, bellowing demon songs to the damned. No Murray in sight.

"Murray ought to be in the Barrel about now," said the waiter. "He doesn't get in here till around two as a rule."

"Have a drink," said a man at the bar, a bald fat man in a plaid shirt. "I think I'm being stood up but I'm waiting to make sure. She said she'd be here, but that's the way she is. This isn't the first time. You look like an intelligent guy, I'd like to ask you a question. Now I'm a married man. My wife—here, take a seat."

"I'm sorry, I'm late," Frederick apologized and hastened into the street again, darting in and out of the cafés of Rubberleg Square, so-called for the high percentage of weak-kneed pedestrians. Rough bar, fancy bar, bars with doormen, bars with sawdust floors—Murray was bound to be in one of them, but which? Frederick was astonished at the variety at first, and then at their inevitable sameness.

Wherever he went he found advertising men all weeping into their Bourbon of happy days when they were star reporters on the Providence *Journal*. They yearned to tell him their dreams and disappointments. Sometimes they were with petulant wives, who, if from the South, had been the prettiest girls in Tallahassee; if from the Middle West their folks had the biggest house in Evansville. Sometimes these men, happier by far when cub reporters than now with their twenty thousand a year, were not with wives but with stylists, camera ladies, women's-angle-women from their offices, all emotionally fulfilled by making fat salaries, wearing Delman shoes and Daché hats, and above all being out with The Office and talking shop. These were the women who had won the war, the spoils were theirs; these were the women who had found a swansdown paycheck warmer in bed than naked Cupid. Wherever he went Frederick found the new race of men and women, the victors who had won by default, who had sold a pint of Type O for the merest goldmine. Wherever he went his sobriety induced warm overtures from total strangers unable to make friends by day.

Hopefully looking around the bar of the Barrel, most regal of the neighborhood bistros, he was pounced upon by a man from the K.G.R. Advertising Agency whose tears over good old newspaper days were mingled with belligerent pride in cigarette campaigns.

"Just wait till you see what I've done with Hazelnut," the K.G.R. man boasted, detaining Frederick by the lapel. "Just a woman's hand holding a flaming match and the line 'Let Me Give You a Light.' Just that one line, mind you, but it sings. Hazelnut knows it. K.G.R. knows it. They've got to admit it. 'Let Me Give You a Light.' And the match playing like a searchlight over a pack of Hazelnut Cigarettes up in the sky. It's good, damn it, if I do say so myself."

"Excellent," Frederick said, wary as he always was with genial men, not wishing to rebuff them but dreading their intrusion.

The K.G.R. man removed his right hand from the lapel, loosened his hold on the highball glass, readjusted his foot on the rail, and swaying briefly at the loss of support transferred his grip to Frederick's reluctant hand. He smiled engagingly.

"Hi, fella. I like you. You're all right. You know what it's all about. Got a poker face but I can tell you catch. Jack, give this guy a drink. Here, fella, sit down here. I had a girl but she blew. Where'd Dodo go, Jack?"

"Thanks, I won't have any more," Frederick said, and in an effort to discourage further intimacy turned to the bartender with a stern, almost accusing voice. "Where's Murray?"

Suddenly he felt foolish. It seemed to him that customers and bartender looked up suspiciously at his haughty tone. It seemed to him they must guess at once that he was a stranger to these places, queasily dismayed by the revellers clustering around the little red piano lustily singing old songs and spilling their drinks on the colored pianist; the smell of ancient tombs and crumbling ruins must be about him; Latin footnotes and ravellings of doctors' theses must be swarming in pursuit of him like hungry moths. Prudently he said no more when the bartender, ignoring his previous protest, placed a drink before him.

"Murray's hat's still checked," said the bartender coldly. "He'll be back."

He knows, thought Frederick, that Murray's roommate doesn't belong, plays no part in the neighborhood's midnight antics; he recognizes a discreet, sober man certain never to drink except within his means, to resent amiable offers of treats and therefore not to reciprocate; here is a man unlikely to create the mirage of gaiety that impels customers to magnificent gestures; here is a man who would remember that tomorrow was Rent Day when it was his turn to buy a drink, a man who would not admit the compulsions of bar room etiquette. Here is a man who ought to get out and make room for the genuine members; maybe he speaks a dozen languages but he doesn't speak ours. "Nor understand," Frederick admitted, listening to the strange phrases fly back and forth around him.

"*The Detroit Free Press? . . . Good God, old man, then you knew Jack Huberman? . . . You did? . . . Well, I was on the Post-Dispatch by that time, then I went to Ivy Lee . . ." "What—you were with Ivy Lee? . . . I left there for J. Walter Thompson . . . what? . . . no! no! . . . Have a drink! . . . You were? . . . No! No! . . . You were? . . . Have a drink . . ."*

He turned to thank the K.G.R. man but the latter had found a more congenial attachment at the other end of

the bar, another old newspaper man now in public relations. Hazelnut campaign was forgotten in the joyful
exchange of old encounters with Huey Long, Ford; intimate anecdotes of front-page names; fond reminiscences
of the great hearts of Hearst, Howard, Munsey, Patterson,
McCormick. Frederick listened, meditating on the curious way newspaper men, despite their apprenticeship in
realities, end up convinced by their own romantic inven-
tions, respectful of the celebrities their own lies created,
teary over sob-stories they had made up themselves, doffing
their plumes reverently to whatever powers had kept
them down. The public relations man, a stout little chap
named Mooney with a trim moustache, spoke sardonically
of the prostitution of his journalistic genius, but as he
heard himself sneer at the first-water phonies whose repu-
tations he preserved, stuffed, and mounted, he was moved
to awe at his own power and its fabulous possibilities. He
might be engaged in the world's most degrading occupa-
tion but at least he was better at it than anyone else. He
called to two ladies in a booth to affirm this, both of them
high in the business world—one in Gimbel's or Altman's
department store, the other in real estate. The ladies
paused in the midst of their comparison of income-tax
to declare that Mooney was certainly the best there was,
and they only wished they had his accounts.

Mooney gratefully shook their hands and even went to
the trouble to explain that he was the soul of honesty,
refusing to touch certain large sums that clients had
placed at his disposal into which he could have dipped
without the big saps knowing the difference, but which,
in his ridiculous honesty, he never even considered touching, unless, of course, it was absolutely necessary, and in
view of how much money the particular clients had a person need really feel no compunction about rewarding his
honesty with a little extra dividend, what the hell, we're
all in business, we know what time it is. The K.G.R. man
lurched up to receive equal attention, jostled Public Relations aside to lean across the table and recount his Hazel-

nut inspiration, was so overwhelmed by their polite attention that he ordered more drinks to add to the regiment
of glasses before them, drinks consumed, drinks started,
and the drinks Public Relations had ordered; he invited
them to dance, to sit at the bar, to go up to the Blue Angel
where Arturo knew he was a person of consequence, to
visit his home in Greenwich any time, any hour of day
or night. The two men hovered over the table, vying with
each other for the approval of these splendid influential
women who were not flibbertigibbets but real guys, pals,
people. They patted the pals on the back, dropped cigarette ashes and an occasional cinder down their bosoms,
waved their drinks at perilous angles over their heads,
shouted with resounding laughter over every word even
before it had been said, were generously happy in the
pleasure their company was surely giving. Frederick
watched the innocent scene in the bar mirror, and speculated on how long this fine new friendship would last,
and what would happen if the ladies really should appear
sometime in the dead of night in Greenwich. One of the
ladies waved to him, and he bowed gratefully, since he
knew few people. Probably one of his students at the
League.

He thought of Lyle waiting for him, reproached himself for not starting out sooner. Each morning his waking
thought was "How soon will I see Lyle today?" but he
was always late; wanting wings to fly to her he must always
punish his desires with barriers of his own creation. He
had promised to meet her at the Beckleys' at ten but at
ten he had been putting the last fond period to his manuscript. Then he had been obliged to think about clothes,
an outrageous tax on the brain, to rummage for dress
shirt and silk socks. Moths had embroidered their initials
on the trousers of his dinner clothes, dress hose were in
threads, so he had to switch back to tweeds. He found
he had enough cash for his own carfare but not enough
to be an evening's guest at a millionaire's house; that
meant he had to find Murray. A burst of anger swept over

him at the sheer inconvenience of being in love with Lyle, and at the demands her group made on him. Be on time. Dress. Be discreet for these are friends of my husband. Please take home all unescorted ladies, pay for the night-cap in the fine café they select, use your breakfast money on a check-room tip, walk home when your small funds give out. All for love. All for the incurable need of seeing Lyle whenever and wherever he could. How often he had rebelled at the bondage of his love, said goodbye forever, then rushed back to her sweet forgiving arms, begging for his chains. He had refused the easy teaching job in a Southern college, all for Lyle; and now the only way he could celebrate the completion of his work was to follow her to her own world and hope for a word with her. He would know no one there and be intensely uncomfortable, all for Lyle.

"But you ought to know Ephraim Beckley better, dar-ling," she had said. "I don't expect you to like him, be-cause nobody does, but after all he is a power, grandson of one of the great publishers. You ought to have a little scientific curiosity. You can't stay in another century every minute. It will do you good, darling. Ephraim spoke of you particularly!"

Frederick professed immense gratification at the com-pliment, adding that, for his part he always enjoyed being introduced to Ephraim Beckley and considered the Beck-ley amnesia in the presence of unknowns nothing short of genius.

"But he didn't realize you had written the *Swan* es-says," Lyle said. "He probably thought it was only *Swann's Way*. He meets so many Prousts. Do come. Even if it's horrible it's something you ought to know. You do have to know the world, dear!"

So he must promise to meet her there, half annoyed and half touched by Lyle's transparent efforts to bring him out of his shell. She was always mistaking his retreat from life as loneliness that must be assuaged, or else she was chiding him for not liking people. She was wrong, he felt. People amused him, and safe in her arms he did not fear them. He wanted to be spectator, that was all, not actor; if possible he wanted a glass wall between him and other human beings and he was happy when Lyle joined him in the observation post, unhappy when she was on the other side of the glass. It made him uncomfortable when the actors addressed him, as if Myrna Loy should suddenly reach out of a moving picture to shake his hand. Still he would go where Lyle bade him, knowing he would hate it, knowing he would be unable to curb his misery at seeing her surrounded by admirers and be-longers. Above all, he would be obliged to think about money. That was the thing that was always coming be-tween himself and Lyle, the expense of being good to the rich. His own poverty never inconvenienced him; his ascetic tastes required little more than enough for dinner at Umberto's or the Chinaman's, coffee and a sandwich in Whelan's, a beer or two, a concert, a book. But no, for Lyle's sake, he must forage around trying to borrow money enough to visit or sup at some rich man's home, be pre-pared for the little accepted duties of Extra Man. "Be good to the rich." Why couldn't the rich mind their own business, divide expenses with each other, invite each other to dinner and feast on each other's fruity conversa-tion? The truth was that they feared other rich might be richer than they were, a horrid thought, for if they are not the richest, what are they? So they must have artists, scientists, economists around them to feed their bleak minds and to verify their superiority; yes, yes, they are the richest, sing hosanna, and so far as they know are leading a cultural life as well, since the finest minds have been bemused by their cellar.

He brightened at the thought of a decent supper, but suspected that the Beckleys ate well only when they were alone, so as to save the feelings of guests less fortunate. Some lonely artist might have a tantrum at sight of a whole beef from their deep freeze, and the injustice of a first-rate label on a bottle might send him sobbing to the cloak-room. One mustn't tantalize the poor. How much gayer the old Ward McAllister days must have been, when the rich really clinked, had silver sleigh bells on their streams of consciousness, and ermine diapers on their young! But today, each Mrs. Beckley had One Good Black Dress like any stenographer, and only when a dangerous law suit shook the coffers did she feel poor enough to wear all of her diamonds.

Frederick toyed for a moment with the idea of staying away from the Beckleys'. He would only document his prejudices and hurt Lyle's feelings. He would not be good to Beckley, probably would not even speak to him, curious as he was about the monster, but would lurk in some corner, contemptuously bored, impatient with Lyle for enjoying such people. He wondered if his slumbering bitterness could be merely jealousy of her professional success, since the rewards of his own work were so limited. But hers was not the kind of success he wanted, if he did want success. No, he thought, his resentment came from the way she unconsciously made his otherwise good life seem a pitiable failure. After all, he wrote what he chose in the manner he chose for a limited and highly respectful audience; he lived an independent scholar's life which was a boon in itself, and he had his love. He was far too sensible to ask that she divorce Allan and marry him. He loved solitude and Lyle next; she loved the world and him next. They told this to each other. They never mentioned Allan's invalidism or his dependence on Lyle. No, they declared their reason for not marrying (at anyone's cost) was their sensible awareness of the basic difference in their tastes. But being too reasonable to wish for complete fulfilment did not keep the denial from corroding inside you, until the constant analysis bared a torturing sense of injustice. Even in this resentful mood he could not stay away from her, must follow her to any party, be introduced again and again to people interested only in flamboyant success, be conscious of his inadequate tailoring, lack of small talk, and find himself shamed by a fretful desire for millions merely to avoid adolescent humiliation. It was as if all these people mocked him with "Thirty-six years old and no more money in his pocket than when he was twelve!"

He was considering what he would do if he didn't find Murray, when Murray came in the door. Whenever he caught sight of Murray in public he was reminded of how little they knew of each other in spite of sharing an apartment these last few years. How odd to believe the careful protection of each other's privacy complete proof of deep spiritual sympathy! Murray's tempestuous marriage had left him grayer and more stooped than his forty years warranted, but there was something boyish and sweet in his square ruddy face with its snub nose and wide, wry mouth. Frederick wondered if it was the defiant swagger and independent air that challenged women to clutter up his life. Certainly basic kindliness would not be a bait. More likely it was his passion for bars, poker, and a womanless world that drew them; perhaps he was irresistibly cruel and double-crossing in his dealings with them; borrowed their money, betrayed them marvellously with their best friends, left them crying their eyes out. The girl who came in with Murray was unknown to Frederick, but then he had met only Judy, his regular girl, and Gerda, the ex-wife.

Murray lifted eyebrows in surprise at sight of Frederick drinking and came over to inquire into the cause of such deviltry. His girl stood by an empty booth, smiling at them both with her head cocked in a determined roguishness that made Frederick nervous. He had a feeling that one kind look would have her leaping at them like a too exuberant puppy.

Murray did have cash and if that wasn't enough he would be glad to okay any checks Frederick might sign, having the sound prestige of owing a considerable sum to The Barrel. Frederick confessed to a prejudice against using credit in cafés, on his small salary; a few small bills in his wallet was all he asked.

"Mur-ray!" a voice called. "Remember me?"

"What's the idea of stealing my girl?" The K.G.R. man was slapping Murray on the back. "Where'd you two disappear?"

"The new place down the street," Murray confided. "They got a juke-box and drinks only forty cents. I was just saving money, Larry."

"Okay, but you were stealing my girl," said the K.G.R. man. "I dont mind your stealing her but why do you bring her back just when I'm having a good time? Hey, honey, come on over here."

"I don't want to sit at the bar," pouted his honey. "I want to talk to Murray. Mur-ray!"

"Ought to be a law keeping women on a leash in bars," Murray muttered to Frederick. "I swear these guys bring them in just to get rid of them. Don't get me wrong. Dodo's a nice kid, known her for years, but hell, I got other things on my mind. Tell you in a minute."

Dodo came over, finger in mouth in an attempt at little girl sulks. She was evidently proud of her extreme slenderness for her gray-striped green wool dress followed every bone and sinew snugly, and from the demure way she thrust out her high-pointed breasts you would have thought they were her own invention, exclusive with her. Even on close view her face had no distinction to warrant her obvious satisfaction with it, but then Frederick granted that he had never been a judge of beauty. That she had no misgivings as to her value was clear for she wriggled between the two friends with a spoiled, little-girl giggle.

"Why can't I meet this good-looking man, Mur-ray?" she demanded, cocking her head up invitingly. "It can't be that terrible man you live with, Mur-ray. You said he never went out."

Murray nudged Frederick.

"This is the lad, himself, Dodo. Frederick Olliver. Dodo Brennan. Larry down there brought her to dinner with me. I knew her in Baltimore. Lay off this man, Dodo, he's off to a party with big folks."

Miss Brennan put her head back, half-closing her eyes in a knowing, teasing smile that Frederick recognized as the "I - know - all - about - you - naughty - man - and - your - secrets - and - I'm - every - bit - as - smart - as - you - are - I - can - see - right - through - you - this - very - minute" look. She put out a small, elaborately manicured soft hand and laid it in his as if it were a dear little dove. Frederick was startled to find that the skin actually did have a silken feathery texture that affected him not disagreeably. She had a small, neat-featured face with tidily-pencilled green eyes, smoothly pancaked skin, low forehead, daintily chiselled nose with that half-moon flare of the nostrils that meant something or other. Her hair was black and drawn tightly back into a thick gleaming roll at the nape, a green-spangled snood with a jewelled spider comb doing hat-duty. Her complacency and the way she waved one fancy, long green glove indicated a proud conviction of being the ten best-dressed women in New York.

"You're visiting here?" Frederick asked.

"Pooh on you," she tinkled in pretended indignation. "If you mean I look like an out-of-towner, I'm living here, if you please. At the Barbizon till I find an apartment. Murray's going to find me a husband, too, aren't you Murray?"

The dear little dove stayed in his hand trustingly until Frederick placed it around the daiquiri before her. He noticed, or her careful maneuvering brought it to his attention, that her legs were gracefully slender, another matter for her private satisfaction. It struck him that he had never seen a woman so pleased with herself; this satisfaction was so tremendously out of proportion to its cause that you were attracted by it and not by the appearance itself. Conscious of his monastic tastes, his long bondage to Lyle to the exclusion of other loves, Frederick admitted that he would probably never know what the heartier males really stalked. This girl must have gotten her assurance from superior connoisseurs; she couldn't have cooked it up out of her own vanity. Instead of being just a neatly groomed, undistinguished woman as he, in his worldly inexperience thought, she must be a beauty in the eyes of most men or she would not have this manner. There was the way she stroked her slim hips and tenderly powdered her face as if they were treasures on loan to her from the royal collection; the way she smiled lovingly into her compact mirror and then back at her image full-length in the booth mirror as if "Oh you darling, you, you perfectly adorable creature, you!" Frederick felt an odd mixture of scorn and respect for this self-satisfaction. He bowed to what must be a majority taste, a little pleased at himself for actually studying any other woman but Lyle. It might be due to his curiosity about Murray's private tastes or there might be a hint that his terrible, lovely enslavement to Lyle might have an end, someday. (But how could he bear it?)

"Murray showed me things you wrote," Dodo said, both little doves encircling the daiquiri as if it was a baby's mug of milk. She grimaced. "Oh, but how dull! Really, honestly, truly, Mr. Olliver! Deadly! You're not really that serious—you're too handsome—you just can't be that awful!"

"Why not?" Murray asked. "Look here, Dodo. You could be just as awful if you put your mind to it. You only half try, that's the trouble."

Dodo thrust her chin in the air.

"I could do better than that without trying a bit," she said playfully. "Nobody wants to read all that tiresome blah about old dead people nobody ever heard of. Please, Mr. Olliver, don't do it any more, or we just can't be friends. And you do look so *darling,* doesn't he Murray?"

Frederick looked at his watch embarrassed.

"You're going to a party, you lucky you," Dodo sighed, and now the little dove hands were outrageously tweaking at his tie. "I don't see why you don't take me. You know perfectly well I'm nicer than anyone you'll see there. Come on, do take me. Look at that horrible Larry down

there; he'll talk about his old Hazelnut all night, and
Murray says he has to go someplace. I'll be all alone!
Please! Where is the party?"

"Biggest house you ever saw, honey," Murray said.
"Take your skates along. You've heard of Ephraim Beckley, haven't you?"

Well, for goodness' sake, she hoped Murray didn't think
she was a complete dunce! She may have been in New
York only a month but she could read the papers, thank
you, and what with Beckley libraries, Beckley Foundations, and Beckley stables, she guessed almost anyone
would know who Beckleys were. What was more, another
girl from her home town had met all sorts of people at a
Beckley party. By this time Dodo had both little doves
tugging at Frederick's sleeves, and as usual he had no idea
how to extricate himself. But if Lyle hadn't insisted he
come up there he would not have had to hunt for Murray,
and none of this would have happened. He looked around
for escape as Murray's little friend began jumping up and
down in a delicate, kittenish way, moaning, "Oh Frederick, if you don't take me, I'll call you Mr. Olliver! I
will so! I'm in a party mood and I don't know any parties.
The Beckleys are the dream of my life! Please."

Frederick had a fleeting picture of himself entering the
Beckley drawing-room with the bold little stranger. He
could see Lyle's astonished face knowing well his panic
before importunate ladies. He could picture Dodo running wild in the august gathering, squealing banalities,
buttonholing, flinging legs and bosom in all directions
tossed from man to man like an animated beanbag. With
a shudder, he took advantage of her momentary switch
to Murray and started for the door, as hastily as he dared.
A cab had drawn up at the curb to deliver a pair of very
young sailors and Frederick got in as they paid their fare.

"Any girls in there, champ?" one asked him with a
nod toward The Barrel entrance.

"Only one—" Frederick started to warn them, since
The Barrel could scarcely boast of any female customers

of suitable age for these hopeful youngsters, but even as he spoke a girl ran out and pushed past them into the cab. It was Dodo, merry and triumphant, giggling archly at him as she settled herself in the cab. There was nothing he could do in the face of the watching sailors but to handle the situation as Murray might have done.

"You know perfectly well you wanted me to come along," Dodo pouted at him. "You've got to take me, now don't you look so cross! That party is the dream of my life!"

"I would not want it said I deprived anyone of the dream of her life," Frederick said. He gave the address to the driver.

"I never saw anyone so mad!" Dodo cried delightedly.

"Mad with joy," Frederick corrected her, managing a gallant smile. "This seems to be my lucky night."

2

... the human dynamos ...

*I*T WAS Ephraim Beckley's father who had had
the real editorial genius to amass a fortune, but the heirs
had been shrewd investors and knew a few tricks themselves. Now that the old gentleman was gone, biographers
engaged every decade to rewrite his life (since it could not
be re-lived) had difficulty spotting any sensitivity to litera
ture in the records, his immortality as a great editor
resting, as one embittered Jewish chronicler wrote, in
"Yankee-ing" down his competitors and in making a good
thing of his associations with great authors. His collection of intimate letters from Poe, Whitman, Clyde Fitch,
Jack London, Ambrose Bierce, Frank Norris, O. Henry,
and lesser lights, had sold for a fortune. None of the
letters was witty or in the writer's best vein, running
largely—"*I must apologize for coming to your house last
week in such a deplorable state of shabbiness that your
butler was asked to dismiss me, but the truth is I must
ask again for a small sum to buy food for myself and
family. I realize you have principles about loaning money
to private individuals and cannot blame you for your
attitude on drink. I hope, however, that you will not
ignore this request as you have the others, since I am
in desperate need . . .*" etcetera.

The Poe letters, largely in this vein, sold separately for
thousands being in excellent condition and exquisite
handwriting. The Beckley offspring, with this impeccable
literary tradition, had no difficulty in placing themselves

17

in important civic and publishing positions. Soon they had their own collections of autographs—from international figures, minor and major poets, inventors, painters, all asking for loans. Having learned from Papa that a courteous reply curtailed the collection they never answered, thus sucking out four or five letters per poet and providing future profits for their own heirs. Papa had a nice sense of humor and his favorite family joke was, "If I'd given every author five dollars the first time he asked for it you children would be in the poorhouse." It was as good a slogan for success as any, and the children did not quarrel with it.

Frederick Olliver had brought his resolute companion into the Beckley house with an assumption of poise he was far from feeling. The guest of a guest had no right to bring a guest even if he had the desire. But when he caught sight of Lyle, in the midst of her admirers, and as soon as he had received his host's clammy handshake and heard him mispronounce his name he took mischievous satisfaction in unleashing a Dodo. He had a flare of annoyance at Lyle for having said "Beckley's dying to see you" when obviously Beckley had no idea who he was unless he was Olivier, the actor. Lyle had wanted him to be there to see herself in her element; she wanted him to appreciate her sacrifices in preferring him, no matter how embarrassing his own position there might be. (He was being unfair but he wanted to be.) He saw her eyebrows raise a question about Dodo but he ignored it. Let her think the incident was of his own choice. He was considering taking Dodo over to introduce her but was relieved to find the young lady had darted after a famous name in a corner and he escaped to the third floor, following the invitation of his publisher, Benedict Strafford, the only person he recognized there. Presently he was peacefully wandering around the Beckley library in the upper reaches of the house, looking at the glass cabinets of rare manuscripts, viewing the sumptuous canyons of books, the portraits of beagle-nosed

Beckleys each firmly clasping an exquisitely bound book as if to keep the artist from stealing it. Here he could forget Lyle, Dodo, and the disagreeable flavor of the entire evening for no one in this literary household had thought of the library but Strafford and himself.

Mr. Strafford, bald and bullish, sprawled in a vast white leather chair smacking his lips over a drink of his own mixing. His imperious voice and decisive manner suggested big business far more than did the pallid, whining host, although Strafford's struggles to keep in publishing savored of a reckless loyalty to Art. Strafford himself was constantly torn between respect for the praise of Frederick's work by foreign readers with convenient large estates for him to visit, and the incontrovertible fact that his sales were never over twelve hundred copies. At least, it was a relief to know that an Olliver book usually took years to perfect, and even more pleasant that the author's wants were met by weekly lectures at the League for Cultural Foundations and his essays in the *Swan Quarterly* and similar magazines. Feeling somewhat guilty every time he thought about Frederick, Mr. Strafford soothed his conscience as a fatherly publisher by offering him a room in his offices where he could write. This suited Frederick admirably, providing stenographic assistance and convenient access to a research library. He worked slowly and was glad Strafford never rushed him or made dutiful attempts at friendlier relations. They kept out of each other's way except for necessary encounters, and tonight at the Beckleys' was the first time they had met outside their business requirements. Both were astonished to discover themselves linked in the warmest friendship by mutual dislike of their host. To Strafford, his first visit to the Beckley home was a needling reminder of his own inadequacies in business. This was the way a publisher should live—country home right in New York, innumerable servants, trained nurses for distinguished diseases, buttons everywhere to turn off the radio, drawing-rooms stuffed with celebrated guests all deliciously bored, opera boxes to leave empty, the finest brandy hidden away. The pretty panorama stirred Strafford to a sense of injustice; it pointed out that here was the only decent way to live. The thought that at the age of sixty it might be too late to achieve it made him withdraw from the company to brood. The sight of Frederick gave him the first pleasure of the evening; here was his author, by George, here was someone who could testify to his power, such as it was. Frederick's feelings were similar; in Strafford he saw the only person here besides Lyle who remembered his name and respected (without quite understanding) his talents. Furthermore, say what you would about the man, he had the good taste to be a bad business man and the innocence to be civil to authors if not utterly baffled by them. The two gentlemen strolled amiably arm-in-arm away from the center of chatter, pausing to consider a huge Zorach marble mother-and-child on the landing flanked by massive urns of chrysanthemums. They examined in silence a special corridor lined with Beckley best sellers, each shelf equipped with a special light for close study of these nine-day wonders. Determined to discover the secret of success Mr. Strafford spent several minutes searching for and adjusting his reading glasses and one minute in a swift glance up and down the collection, observing tersely that every fifth one was an historical novel. Something could be learned from that, surely. A statue in evening dress turned out to be no work of art but a watchful servant who advised them they would find themselves comfortable and alone in the adjoining library, a room to be bequeathed, panelling, chandeliers, portraits, and all to a western university already negotiating to sell it. After blinking incredulously at the grandeur of the room and noting an adorable decanter of brandy on a coffee table, Mr. Strafford remarked that it was certainly a well-chosen library. Frederick replied that a "well-chosen" library usually indicated that someone, not the owner, had selected it. In the case of Beckley, he stated that the shelves would reveal his real literary attachments by being lined with United States bills. Mr. Strafford pointed to an open volume of Juvenal on the desk. Frederick replied with a shrug that the maid must have been reading it; he disagreed that any clairvoyant insight into any human being may be gained by a masterly glance at the books they leave around. Might as well judge an actor by the wigs and costumes hung in his dressing-room. Of course, as in tea-leaf reading, the truth was sometimes struck by accident. Mr. Strafford weighed this dissertation and began to fidget.

"I was just thinking of the idea anyone would get of me by a peek at my desk," he said uneasily. "Good heavens!"

"You mean you left out that little court memoir you're publishing," Frederick guessed.

Mr. Strafford shook his head. Evidently suppressing a confidence with great effort he picked up a pocket magazine that lay on the table, a silk bookmark calling attention to an article called "Ephraim Beckley, The Human Dynamo."

This served to release pent-up indignation and break down his discretion in one instant, for he pounded his fist on the quaking coffee table.

"*The* human dynamo, my eye!" he muttered hoarsely. "What about there being *two* human dynamos? Beckley isn't the only man with ideas, granted he ever had any of his own. He has the capital to get other people's brains and other people's ideas. I don't. But let me tell you I've got an idea as good as any Beckley ever had and if I had the right man for this project—Say!"

Something about the glint in Strafford's eye as he regarded him made Frederick distinctly uneasy, and the word of a new "project" as Strafford called the fancy side-line ventures into which he sometimes entered, filled him with foreboding. He was further dismayed by the sound of a reflective whistle emanating from Strafford's lips, a cheery sign that ideas of an ominous nature were bubbling within.

"What do you know about a magazine named *Haw?*" asked Strafford mysteriously.

Frederick recalled that the words "*Haw,* Periodical" were on the door of the office below Strafford's.

"That's what's on my desk this minute," Strafford burst forth. "Last twelve issues frozen. You see I own it."

"But what on earth can you do with it?" asked Frederick, astonished.

"I just decided," Strafford whispered. "Run it, begad. On the q.t. maybe. Probably bad if it got around the Strafford name was tied up in it. But, by George, that's where the money is these days. I didn't know why I bought it but sometimes I have a hunch. And just this minute it all clears up for me. I'm going to run it and you're the man that's going to help 'me with it."

"Me?"

"Why not? We understand each other. I don't want the average sort of fellow around for the job, you know, I wouldn't want the *Haw* sort. Why, this can make our fortune. You're the man, Olliver! I got a hunch."

Frederick looked at Strafford incredulously. The gentleman sat biting the end of a Beckley cigar with as much gusto as if it had been Beckley's ear, bald head thrown back, face beaming triumphantly at him.

"I mean it," said Mr. Strafford benignly. "Don't try to talk, boy, I know you're surprised. But you're it. Why, the thing'll be a sensation. On the quiet, of course."

Frederick, quite speechless, pondered the peculiar logic that had inspired his chief to consider an obscure scholar with a passionate indifference to what the public ate as the ideal assistant in this rowdy venture. Mr. Strafford's innocent idea that the undertaking might be a sensation but at the same time a dark secret further nonplussed him until he identified it as the same logic the gentleman was rumored to use in his cautious flings at sex. While Mr.

Strafford blew smoke rings dreamily at the panelled ceiling Frederick recalled the Strafford legends, of how he always took his ladies to dine on the mezzanine of the Vanderbilt where he considered himself invisible instead of to the lower dining-room where he conducted his more respectable guests. His manner on these occasions had often been remarked by acquaintances he did not see; it was so charged with sinister implications that the wonder was he was not arrested on sight. He kept his jaunty felt hat pulled down well over his eyes, coat-collar up around his ears, and he pushed the lady through the revolving doors with the veiled eagerness of a wolf about to fling her onto a perfumed bed instead of into a *petite marmite*. Clutching her arm doggedly, he hustled her to a table, pushed her into a chair in a dark corner as if he was locking her in a private bedroom. He ordered a cocktail, whispering the order to the waiter as if mixed drinking was as scandalous as mixed bathing; and after the dinner he hurried the lady out, hovering about her protectively, as if to hide her nudity from the leering crowd. His splendid air of guilt was retained all the next day at the office, and came from nothing more than the naughty fact that she was a woman and he was a man, that they were out together like other men and women, and that other men and women were probably doing mischievous things that he and she were not doing but very likely could do.

"Well?" prodded Strafford, and as Frederick was still speechless, he went on plaintively, "By George, Olliver, I'm tired of men like Beckley hooking all the plums. This is just the sort of thing he'd snap up if he knew about it. There's a mint in it."

"How did the owners happen to sell?" Frederick asked.

"Bankrupt. I got it just for taking over their debts," Mr. Strafford said with an extremely foxy leer. "Didn't have to give out a penny."

There was no use in commenting on this typically Strafford coup. When Strafford continued that he had been hung by his regard for prestige all his life and was going in from now on for Sure Things, Frederick demurred that no prestige plus a proven financial flop might not be classified as Sure Thing, Strafford brushed the objection aside as sheer modesty. Frederick didn't realize how much confidence Strafford had in him. All you needed to put the thing over was brains, and surely Frederick would admit his and Strafford's brains were superior to Beckley's.

"It's the sort of thing he's always done to pick up a quick dollar," Strafford assured him.

"I don't think it would help the firm's prestige," Frederick murmured weakly, causing Strafford to give an impetuous snort. "Isn't it just cartoon strips?"

"Of course it is! But how would Beckley have prestige except by making money? Look at your own situation. If your own books had sold half a million copies you'd have all the prestige of a Santayana. We can both make something out of this, Olliver—you'll get your prestige, alright, don't you worry about that. But I can tell you that you don't get prestige in this country with a frayed shirt-cuff. Excuse me, old man."

Very red and abashed by the slip that happened to be a true observation Mr. Strafford hastily gulped a brandy, and Frederick pulled down his coat sleeve with a wry smile.

"I know, I know," Strafford pursued, appeasingly. "You don't care about anything but getting your own book out. But the public doesn't want highbrow books now. I'm thinking of your own good, old man, in putting off publication for a while. What the public wants now is *Haw* and that book of ours, *I Was a Court Lady.* You've got to wait till the time is right. Meantime you can be polishing up the rough spots, say, but making a little money on the side. Let's say we let Miss Jones do the routine chores on *Haw*—clip stuff, paste-up, stick in a murder between jokes. All you have to do is drop down there once in a while to shape up things, look after my interests. Suppose I put you on the pay-roll at seventy-five a week. It's a snap for you and a favor to me. It means I've got somebody in there I can trust and I can keep clear of it, personally."

"I appreciate your faith in my business ability," Frederick managed to reply with due gravity, preposterous as the suggestion was, "but——"

The doors opened and Strafford held up a warning finger.

"Mum's the word on this," he whispered. "Mustn't let it out that the firm has anything to do with it. But, by George, I'll show Beckley yet. Try to see it my way, old man."

Lyle came in the door.

3

. . . the invulnerables . . .

AS SOON as Lyle sat down beside him Frederick's smouldering resentment vanished. He was ready to confess that bringing a strange girl to her friends' party had been punishment, not pleasure. No amount of cold analysis could dispel his sense of utter completeness when he was with Lyle. The corrosive thoughts which sheathed and armored him against the world melted; disarmed, he was content. Here was Lyle, and nothing else mattered. Without looking at each other, without touching, their love flowed between them and around them. Incredible that they could ever quarrel, incredible that a little while before he had felt stonily hostile towards her for no better reason than that her friends and her pleasures were not his, incredible that he should ever question this peace. Here was the rock on which all his life was built, here was love invincible, indestructible. Strafford and the whole room faded when their eyes finally met.

"We'll have a chat later, perhaps," Mr. Strafford said, vaguely aware of this, and with a courtly bow to Lyle, he strolled toward the hall. At the door he turned to give Frederick a meaning nod, finger to his lips.

"He does look like a bleached bull," Lyle murmured. "What's he like, out of the arena?"

Frederick looked away from her, longing to take her in his arms. These public encounters were torture.

"This party has brought out the tycoon in him," he tried to answer calmly. "I don't know what he's like any more. Tonight he has me baffled."

His head began to swim with the necessity for control, familiar as the demand was. Now for the clenched heart and the small talk, the interminable words that must veil their love. One of these days he would kick the screen of words aside and let the lightning strike, even, he thought desperately, at risk of it striking their love itself. He felt a blaze of anger at Lyle for demanding this endurance of him.

"It's you who baffle me tonight, dear," Lyle said. "Who is this girl you brought?"

He had forgotten Dodo completely in his anxiety to tell about his book being done. He had expected Lyle to ask the question of course, and he had intended to tell her the whole story. But now he hedged. After all, was there any reason he should not bring along insurance against being a wall-flower? Hadn't Lyle noticed that he usually stood around on one foot at her friends' parties, waiting for a word with her? Why shouldn't he show a little independence by bringing along someone to talk to him? The fact was, however, that he had left Dodo Brennan almost as soon as they arrived. At first he had been amused by her wide-eyed queries—"Not really Harry Kooney, the arranger? And my, so many countesses and everyone talking French or German! Poor little me!" Then he was mightily relieved when she forgot him in her quest for bigger game. He hoped she would forget him the rest of the evening, too, but he did not want Lyle to guess this. His terror of young women always secretly amused her. Before he could frame an answer Dodo came in, pointing a playfully accusing finger at him. He was sure Lyle guessed his discomfort; she must know he was comparing the younger woman's brassy smartness with her own soft, casual grace. He could never say whether the impression of beauty Lyle gave to him was valid or whether he was only admiring in her the memory of his own love. The pile of pale red hair reminded him of its silky softness against his own cheek; the slender white arms had been cool around his neck, the wide blond-lashed dark eyes spelled unquestioning love for him, the sulky crooked mouth remembered his. He was, he admitted, an Ephraim Beckley in his own way, gloating over his possessions because they were his, reasoning that if this object had been desired and won by such a fastidious collector as himself, then it was axiomatically priceless.

"There you are, you awful man!" Dodo cried, tweaking his ear impudently. She made a wry face at Lyle. "He brought me here and then he ran away before he even told me who people were. Is it true that somebody here wrote that play *Summer Day?*"

"Mrs. Gaynor and her husband wrote *Summer Day*" Frederick said, and motioned to Lyle. "Mrs. Gaynor. Miss Brennan."

Dodo clapped her hand over her mouth and made wide eyes. She used her face as she did her voice and the rest of her body as if this was her favorite doll and she could make it do all sorts of things. Then she put out her hand to Lyle in the sweetly respectful way a good little girl says goodnight to Mummy's friends.

"I'm so sorry I didn't know. Of course I've heard of the Gaynors but I got mixed up hearing everyone talk. I just loved *Summer Day*. I saw it twice when it opened in Baltimore."

Lyle murmured something and gave Frederick a glance he knew well enough meant a plea for escape. The next minute Dodo had drawn up a stool to Lyle and was saying, "Oh, Mrs. Gaynor, I don't see how you do it! She must be a perfect whiz, mustn't she, Frederick? All those plays! I've simply got to sit at your feet! Frederick, you tell her I really mean it. Seriously."

"She means it seriously," Frederick said, unwilling to catch Lyle's eye.

"You mustn't spoil me," Lyle said, wanting to punish him.

"But you should be spoiled! Even if you do only half the work, you deserve loads of credit."

Suddenly Dodo leaped up and impetuously straightened
Frederick's tie and flicked his sleeve with a possessive assurance. She looked over her shoulder at Lyle.

"He could be really handsome if he had the right
tailor and would smile sometimes," she said archly. "Did
you ever see such blue eyes? But, please, don't you ever
smile, Freddy?"

"Freddy," Lyle repeated under her breath.

"I have my elfin side," Frederick answered.

Dodo looked at him suspiciously.

"Pooh on you if you're trying to be clever!"

She turned her attention to the room, her eyes roving
the balcony and lofty windows, frowning at some object
that should have given a cue to its value by a price mark,
blinking hard as if to make the secret pop out.

"A man said the library alone cost a fortune," she murmured. "I don't get it."

Strafford came back in, looking devilishly complacent
with two actresses from the Gaynor play. He began to
lecture loudly on the incunabula in one cabinet, tossing
in an aside or two that hinted of easily detected forgeries
and the charming gullibility of the owner. As the ladies
moved past them, jewelled, fragrant and beautiful, tinted
porcelain faces and lacquered golden hair suggesting residence on some angel planet, they waved lightly to Lyle.
Dodo stared at them as if Fate had sent these superior
beings to tantalize her personally. Confidence in her own
charm vanished at the comparison; her little artifices
dropped from her like a shabby cloak and left her standing
forlorn, a plain fretful little woman childishly in doubt for
the first time. Frederick observing this had a rush of pity
for her bewilderment. The fleeting glimpse of something
genuine in her roused his curiosity. He watched her eyes
travel jealousy over the women, pause at each jewel. He
saw her glance back to Lyle, and at the tiny chinchilla
cape behind her on the sofa, at the jewelled vanity in her
lap. Anger blazed in the girl's face. Her hands clenched.

"I wish I had a million dollars!" she exclaimed passionately. "I wish I had ten million dollars! I—" She recovered herself quickly and finished with an apologetic murmur, "I mean so I could buy a lot of books and things."

Frederick heard Lyle smother a soft laugh but he would not share it. Lyle was invulnerable, but the stranger, like himself, was not, no matter how desperately she pretended. All these guests were Lyle's people, a success clique; there was nothing about them he liked, understood or even cared to understand. The half-a-minute revelation of the young outsider showed that she belonged with him, never with them. She was on the outside and always would be. He was sorry for her, for wanting something she could never name, and for that painful moment of doubt in her own beauty. He watched her trying to recover her saucy confidence, lighting a cigarette with lips curved in mocking, jaunty smile, eyelids lowered to hide the torment of envy they might betray.

Lyle, too, was watching Dodo curiously. She had been struck by the eyes before, thinking of the many times she had seen that expression. It was in the jealous eyes of old Southern women as they watched young debutantes dance as if here were their thieving rivals not their successors. It was in the cold, measuring eyes of a woman who makes a business of being a woman. Skeptical, hard, relentless eyes, they divide all visible assets in the rival by a thousand. If another woman is beautiful these eyes grudgingly admit that she is not ugly, no more than that; if she displays wit the eyes significantly find a wine-stain on her dress. But when the other's toilette reveals free access to a fat purse, then the eyes are unmasked and flash with righteous indignation; this is the end for which a woman is a woman. Beauty, brains, position are enviable, not in themselves, but for their purchasing power; if crutches won masculine rewards these women would break their own legs. Flaunting of luxuries was testimony to superior power over men, medals of practical victories. So Dodo's eyes flashed with bitterness as they priced the other women's trophies. When Benedict Strafford came back to the group she winked at him merrily to show the others she had valuable connections of her own there. Strafford was taken aback by the wink and looked from Dodo to the others to see if he had missed something.

"Excuse me, Olliver," he said. "I just saw Tyson Bricker in the music room."

He paused to stroke his jaw, pushing his face to left and right as if it was a rubber mask that needed adjusting. Frederick, fearing some new inspiration, waited in silence.

"Bricker was mentioning how much he liked your work in the *Swan*. Said you had classes at his League. It struck me that he might listen to you if you asked for a little boost on that Court Lady novel of ours."

"I'd love to meet Tyson Bricker." Dodo was all of asparkle once more. "He lectured at my mother's club in Baltimore once. He was marvellous! Better than Sinatra. Where is he?"

"I doubt if he'd trust my word on anything like that," Frederick said, "especially since I can't lie very well. I've barely met Bricker, and I didn't read the book."

"You could thank him for what he said about your own work," Mr. Strafford said wistfully. "Just say you're doing work for the firm now and happened to notice he had been neglecting our books. Well—never mind. It just seemed a good chance to take advantage of his interest in you. I don't quite dare approach him myself."

"I'll go along with you," Dodo offered eagerly.

Mr. Strafford looked alarmed.

"I'm sure Mr. Bricker would like that better," Lyle said.

"Dear me, no. Olliver is the only person who could carry any weight with Bricker," Mr. Strafford protested. "I don't mean to go after him in a pushing way, of course. Maybe, if you just strolled up and said 'Thanks for your good words, old fellow. Why not get together sometime for a little chat?' All the Beckley authors are at him now, no reason one of my authors shouldn't edge in."

Frederick's manifest horror evidently discouraged him for the publisher hastily changed the subject.

"Funny how you can always tell a Beckley author," he turned to Lyle. "The men always look like solid country squires—dogs, trout, good roast beef, that sort of thing; wives always pregnant in dirndls, pardon me. The women all three-name writers always crazy to wear low necks then get a bunch of tulle to cover up, saying interesting things so fast you can't hear yourself think. I'm not against them, mind, I just think it's funny how you can always spot 'em."

"Dennis Orphen looked different," Lyle said.

"That's right, he looks more like a soda jerker," Strafford granted. "The way a writer ought to look, eh, Olliver?"

Dodo was tugging at his sleeve roguishly, being very much the little-dirl-wiz-big-mans.

"Come on, let's you and I go talk to Tyson Bricker," she coaxed, pulling the publisher toward the door where he turned and waved goodbye with a helpless shrug of his shoulders.

"He was really serious about your sucking up to Tyson, wasn't he? Does he think you're the go-getter type?" Lyle asked as they left. "Or does he think that's the proper social approach?"

"This house has a strange effect on its guests," Frederick explained. "It's put Strafford into a frightful state of ambition. It's made the young lady lust for millions, and it's made me want to go home."

Why had he come, anyway, he wondered angrily? There was almost no chance of persuading her to come home with him for she was always cautious around Allan's friends.

Lyle put her hand over his, smiling ruefully. No, there was no chance.

"Is it that bad, darling? I thought you'd be amused."

"The things that amuse you usually infuriate me," Frederick said. "I can't be amused at the spectacle of an idiot like Beckley in control of so many first-rate brains. Is that so funny to you?"

Rebuffed, Lyle withdrew her hand and lifted her head stubbornly.

"Yes," she said. "I find it hilarious. And he's not an idiot, he only looks that way. It's his Uncle Hector who's the idiot. Old Hector Beckley. He's the dean of all idiots."

"He sounds like an old dear," Frederick said, eyes flashing his hurt at her silent refusal.

"He presided at the annual Beckley dinner last week," Lyle chattered, pretending not to see. "All the sons and sons' wives and grandsons. Uncle Lex, he's the bad boy, Ephraim's brother, was stinking, of course. Ephraim made everybody all get back into their uniforms, World War I and World War II, and old Hector sat at the head of the table under flags of all nations and one big Beckley flag with dates of all our wars on it. It was to show that Beckleys were only in business to help their country instead of to get rich. Hector is senile, of course, and sat playing with some chessmen and gurgling while every one read speeches to his business genius and leadership. Then he cried because he dropped his cake on the floor and they wouldn't let him pick it up. Uncle Lex tried to make everybody sing *Dearie* and *Everybody's Doing It*. Cordelay, the youngest son, refused to say a word during the whole evening. He was mad because he was too fat for his uniform but he had to wear it anyway."

"Fascinating," Frederick said. "I don't see how you lived through it."

They would quarrel, as always, not over the real thing but something, anything else.

"I'm trying to show you how really amusing they are," Lyle defended herself, flushed, rising to the bait. "Must people be in print? Does the whole living world have to be translated into book form before you will look at it? I wonder if I will ever understand you—or if I should."

"Perhaps we should be content to baffle each other," Frederick said distantly. "No use my trying to understand the Beckleys or why you always want me to meet them. I find them criminally ignorant and dangerously unfunny."

"You are so determined to have a difficult life, aren't you?" Lyle said quietly, but her cheeks flushed, as if by a slap, and betrayed her feelings. "A little courtesy, a little interest in human beings, would make everything easier for you. But you would rather have your difficulties so that you can stay bitter and oh, so misunderstood and I can stay worried about you. Does your artistic integrity require you to be rude to Tyson Bricker and Beckley, anyone who could be valuable to you? Is it a crime for me to want to help you? And how can you understand another century if you refuse to even look at your own?"

Frederick stiffened. It angered him that she should think his career was, like hers, something to be coddled by social contacts, little flattering gestures, an eager nod in the right direction. She had not even asked if he had finished his book, so he would not tell her. He was piqued, too, that she had betrayed no flicker of jealousy over his bringing another girl to the party. She accepted his love and his career as matters for her to take up when she liked, mould as she liked, dictate what terms she liked. Having coaxed him to meet her here to test again how much he desired her, she would not reward him by going home with him. She had wanted him to come in order to "contact" Bricker or Beckley—she was almost as bad as Strafford! Lyle saw his face harden and put her hand over his, pleadingly.

"You're so much better than any of them, darling, that's why," she whispered. "And you won't do anything right, that's why I love you. But it could be so easy . . ."

"I think we'd better stay in our separate corners and

not try to understand each other's business," Frederick said coldly. He was ashamed but stubbornly silent when her hand dropped from his and she drew back like a beaten child fearing another blow. She tried to smile.

"Let's go," Lyle proposed, fastening the little cape over her shoulders. "Perhaps this house does have a bad effect on all of us. I'm acting like some agent arranging a little deal. Come on."

"My place?" Frederick said, challenging her.

Lyle would not meet his eyes.

"I'm supposed to stop off at our leading lady's apartment down the block to console her. Allan asked me to. She's not 'happy in her part' after the notices, now they're on the road, are all going to Louise. After all she was the New York hit. Can you wait—or shall I telephone her instead?"

"You mustn't forget your professional interests even if I do forget mine," Frederick said, blazing as he always did at the primary importance of her work, work that bound her to her husband even more than did duty or pity. "In any case, I shall have to look after the lady I brought here."

This, he saw with mingled satisfaction and horror at his own words, had its effect. Lyle looked at him, unbelievingly.

"That Dodo girl? That Pooh-on-you girl? But she wants to stay and meet all the wonderfuls. I heard her say so. We can ask Ephraim to see that she gets home safely or dangerously, whichever she likes. No reason you should have that bother."

"It's no bother to look after an attractive twenty-year-old girl, my dear," Frederick said perversely.

Lyle's color rose.

"Imagine her being only twenty!" she said. "It usually takes a woman years to acquire that polish. Goodnight, then."

It was a triumph to disturb Lyle's poise, but he hadn't intended to carry it this far. She had walked out of the

room, head high in the air, before he could bring himself
to call her. His chest ached with love for her and his
smouldering hurt that she should always assume he was
the failure that needed her help. He had been unfair,
but she had hurt him, too. He picked up the brandy she
had left on the table and drank it. Through the open
door he heard dance music and the sound of farewells
from the hall below. He could hear a high, artificial
baby-laugh above other noise. Dodo, of course. A man
came in and started removing ash-trays and glasses, and
Frederick, feeling ashamed and defiant over his childish
scene with Lyle, followed the noise downstairs to the
music-room in the back of the house. Lyle and the actress,
Vera Cawley, had left, as had most of the Beckley regular
crowd. Only the guests other guests had brought were
staying, making the most of their first and last visit. The
mulatto pianist was holding forth on the virtues of the
Schillinger method in composition, idly improvising a
combination of the *Second Tchaikovsky Concerto* and
Two Little Girls in Blue, stopping to jot down notes.
In the glass alcove where gleaming green plants under
blue lights made evil jungle shadows on the black glass
he saw Dodo with Tyson Bricker, laughing shrilly at
Ephraim Beckley. Ephraim's hands were flapping together
behind his back like fish fins, and his wide fish mouth
was making futile efforts to join in the laughter, though
his bulging oyster-colored eyes betrayed private fury.
Dodo was poking him with her little fist and backing
him into the plants.

"Come on, Mr. Beckley, what makes you such an old
stuffy?" Dodo was gaily teasing. "My daddy's just as
good as you are but he knows how to have fun and
you don't. Why, we have bigger parties than this in
Baltimore every day, and bigger houses, too. Come on,
now, let me teach you the rhumba!"

Frederick hesitated but it was too late to retreat. Dodo
caught sight of him and shook her finger at him.

"There's that terrible Olliver man! You won't look after me but Tyson will, won't you, Tyson?"

Mr. Beckley's eyes directed a rocket of hatred around the group that landed with regrettably negative results on Dodo. He slid out of the room, locking his smile back up in the deep-freeze as he did so.

"I'll gladly look after the young lady, but I shouldn't want to scrap with Olliver," Tyson Bricker said with his gusty laugh. "How are you, old chap? Not leaving?"

"If the young lady is ready," Frederick said. "I gather that our host won't protest too much if we all leave."

The young lady, offended by Ephraim's exit, decided that she would leave if she could be taken back to the Barrel. It was only half-past one and the Barrel was wonderful then. Absolute bedlam. She insisted on the company of the arranger and the two plastic men (they were the best plastic men in the trade—Hollywood was raving over what they did with The Last Supper). As Tyson Bricker lived in Gramercy Park and as Dodo kept a firm hand on his arm they all went down to the Barrel together. Frederick was deeply thankful that Lyle could not witness his undignified finish as one of five escorts, the least important one at that.

The K.G.R. man had left for the new bar when they arrived at the Barrel, and Murray had started on his usual rounds with midnight cronies. Dodo made the arranger play a duet with the colored pianist and ordered double Scotches for everybody. The bill was handed to Frederick and the three dollars left from Murray's loan paid the tip.

"Murray will okay this," he said to the waiter as he signed for the twenty-six dollars. He had a dizzy feeling of doom, for he was desperately afraid of debt and its testimony to his practical incompetence. But after all there was that salary Strafford offered for that idiotic *Haw* job. Perhaps his incompetence was not so obvious, after all. He must be a little tight, but his head felt quite clear—strange but clear. He was glad when Dodo insisted on going to hear Roger Stearns up at the One Two Three with the Plastic Men and the arranger. She wanted Tyson to come, too, but Tyson looked doubtfully at Frederick.

"What about you, Olliver? Shall we go?"

Frederick saw that Dodo was already at the door, standing with her head on the arranger's shoulder, and her hand cuddling one Plastic Man's chin.

"Why not let them go along, and you and I have a nightcap here?" he said to Tyson, and heard himself adding genially "There are some things I'd like to talk over with you, old man."

4

. . . a dozen white shirts . . .

*N*EW YORK was a city named Frederick, Lyle thought. Walking down through the Park from the Metropolitan Museum she reflected that her pleasure in the Chinese show had been based on *his* pleasure in it; the Boat-house down yonder was nothing in itself but a spot that had amused Frederick with its fantastic night-life of shy sailors and terrifying bobby-soxers. Coming out on Fifth Avenue at Fifty-ninth she read his name into whatever she saw; down that street was the restaurant where they must go for the curried dishes he loved; further along was the motion picture house with the Italian movie he wanted to see; here was the gallery with the Marsh show he would like; here was a shop to order slipcovers for his furniture; here was the refugee shirt-maker she had recommended to him. She remembered hearing that the man had just received fresh supplies, and that he had Frederick's measurements. The excuse for making him an intimate present pleased her, and she hastened into the building and up to the little shop. It was possible to get white material soon, she was told, and she might even order a dozen. But as soon as she had made out the check, she had the familiar sinking feeling of having made a mistake. She walked down the three flights to the book-store on the first floor and wandered through it, unseeingly.

Frederick would not wear the shirts, of course. After

a few weeks, noticing the same frayed collar and cuffs, she would try to ask tactfully if he had received them and he would say, "Oh, those? Oh yes, but of course I don't need them. Much too good for my purposes. I never need anything that luxurious."

And she would have to pretend her feelings were not hurt and try to be reasonable. First, he would consider the gift a criticism of his poverty as well as of his appearance, and he was satisfied with both. He was a meticulous man, but he believed that an austere shabbiness within one's means was proper for a gentleman. Second, he would suspect that the present had been suggested by one of her friends, say a Beckley, and that would start the old bitterness—you-and-your-fine-friends and me-and-my-simple tastes. Third, she was opening herself to the wound of his chronic ingratitude. She would stay awake for nights wondering if he really loved her or anyone, if he had any capacity for feeling whatever, and why he should wish to deny her the simple joy of giving a present. She would torture herself with analysis of him, taking each virtue apart and finding its cruel base, then in the deep necessity for preserving a love without which she could not live, taking the cruelties apart and finding the noble base. Hers was the real crime—for having a flair for happiness, for being spoiled by luxury and friends, for taking good fortune as her due, surprised that anyone else should expect the same.

Supposing he did sneer at her gift. Ingratitude was not a vice. You were not compelled to give and you were not compelled to be grateful for another's pleasure in being generous. Frederick had always made it clear that he disliked being beneficiary as much as he disliked being benefactor. He had often declared his admiration for honest ruthlessness; it meant that the person knew what he wanted and went after it openly. Unselfishness, he had said, was a form of confusion. The person gave away what he was not sure of needing for himself. Later when he found he did need it, he demanded gratitude. In summer he threw away his overcoat and in winter sought gratitude. Instead of accusing himself of lack of foresight he pinned the fault on the innocent victim of his own folly.

This was the cold logical reasoning that always hurt her in her lover; his indifferent dismissal of her impulsive warm gestures, his fear of losing himself, his caution, his painful reticence. Was it reticence, or was this all there was? Granted that taciturn people through no fault of their own are always credited with deep reserves of emotion; then, as the guards hold so relentlessly for so long, the suspicion dawns that there is no feeling there at all; and they are berated for monstrous insensitivity in their later years, as if it was their crime that natural coldness was construed as controlled passion. He was sexually passionate but emotionally afraid perhaps. She must forgive that. After all, what would she do if he were reckless enough to demand she leave Allan? Yes, she was to blame there, for her bondage to Allan was not so much love or pity as work—Allan represented her work and this was her love and her necessity, which Frederick only dimly understood. He understood and disliked her discretion, but it was for the sake of their love as well as for her own self-preservation. Would she love him if his demands prevented her from writing, if his dislike for the stage obliged her to give up its gay tissue-paper people, its fantastic but dear extortions? Then there was his contempt for all her friends, begrudging her the pleasure in small things, as if it was unworthy of her to enjoy anything but his love. Yes, he was arrogant, but wait! Wasn't his arrogance a phase of the mental and personal integrity she loved? Wasn't his caution a scorn of throwing waste to the mob? As for her own "generosity," she had always had more of everything than most people. Did she ever deprive herself? No. Candidly, she believed she was capable of doing so, but sacrifice had never been required. Except the sacrifice of being unable to divorce Allan and marry Frederick. What she was sure she could never bear was what Frederick endured with such dignity—professional obscurity. She knew of no one else who accepted this fate without shrill breast-beatings, bitter envy and cries of "Unfair!" Strafford had treated him shabbily, postponing his book, doling out consolations, denying him the simple reward of critical recognition. Her heart ached for him, but whatever he suffered he would not tell or let her help. He withdrew almost slyly from her sympathy; he would not be her hurt little boy. For that matter, he would not be her true friend, either; he was lover only, an emotional gourmet selecting from her heart whatever dainty morsel that he needed, then withdrawing to his private world. But supposing he submitted to her completely, bared his wounds, begged for pity, wouldn't she despise him? Wasn't his elusiveness the secret of her gnawing disease for him? Wasn't it a challenge in its way equivalent to her own iron-barred marriage?

There were excuses for his eccentricity. There had been his mother who had squandered her own and her sons' money on gay companions, there were the gambling debts left by his older brother. Fortunately his scorn for the hollow laws of sportsmanship saved him from the silly martyrdom of making good these debts. There was his precocious childhood, one school after another, never a real home, that kept him always lonely and shy until his pride furnished armor; there was his detached curiosity about all human beings as if they were books to be studied, answers to be found by mathematical formulae. Tragic, since he had no ability to communicate with ordinary people. A farm boy on a country road nodding a greeting would freeze his tongue. As a little boy he had the feeling, he had told her once, of being under ice unable to push through or make the world hear his cry. Thinking of all of this, Lyle felt an overwhelming surge of love for him. Love was not for the virtues or vices of the beloved, but for his dear childhood, his lost desires, his memories; it was a never-slaked curiosity about that lost world, the mystery forever unsolved. Loving was partly the quest (how much of the unsolvable lost boy can I recover) and part acquisitiveness (the greed for another life to live besides my own).

Suppose she did love too much. Suppose she was the one who gave, who pursued, who made the overtures after every quarrel. There was nothing either wonderful or tragic about loving too much, any more than there was in eating too much; no need to take a Byronic bow on pure greed. This was the kind of reasoning Frederick would use, Lyle thought, and she felt happy again. It was the way she changed her thinking around with each new character in a play, trying to think like a thief, a tart, a general, an empress. It was a gift valuable in collaboration with Allan but it was actually more of a child's game than talent. Here was a toy playhouse of dolls to which she could retreat when her heart might break. Allan, constructionist, built the toy house, and she made the dolls—that was the part of her marriage she could not give up even for Frederick. Allan needed her dolls and she needed Allan's doll-house. And now she had made Frederick into one of her dolls, a doll with a dozen custom-made shirts. She set him, mentally, in several dramatic situations; she saw him as inventor too proud to sell to Industry, as monk obliged to enter worldly life to rescue fallen brother; amused with her game she tried him as high-minded reformer posing as king of the under-world, as disappointed poet turned successful thief, as aristocratic scientist turned jitterbug by empty-headed bobby-soxer. Here Lyle stopped herself with a shock of acute pain. The girl Frederick had brought to the Beck-leys'! The girl he said he had to see home! His curtness had wounded her feelings and they had parted angrily, but she had had no doubts of his fidelity. She had never had a doubt of his love. He might have been piqued

into hurting her feelings, but he never, never— —But
then she would have said it was impossible for him to have
tolerated such a silly girl; as a doll in her play she could
not deny that such a character might welcome the oddest
temptations. Lyle felt weak at the doubts crowding to
her brain. She walked to the curb, raising her hand for
a taxi, trying futilely to keep the play from unfolding in
her facile imagination. The shock of surprise last night
when she had caught sight of Frederick entering the
Beckley hall with a strange girl, a girl who clung to his
arm with a coy burlesque of stage-fright while Mrs.
Beckley made the introductions. A girl named Dodo! A
girl aglitter with artificial postures, mincing mannerisms,
lisps, pouts, goo - goo - eyes, shy smirks of oh - I'm - just -
a - little - nobody - and - you're - all - so - big - and - wonderful - I'm - scared - weally - twuly, then burgeoning
under liquor into brash insolence. She had wondered why
Frederick, who tolerated few people, had never mentioned
knowing the girl, then she had smiled, understanding that
this was one of Frederick's sardonic jokes, producing for
their mutual edification a fly in the Beckley ointment.
She had blamed herself for the final quarrel. Her possessive attitude that he could not be interested in anyone
else (newer and younger, at that!) was not flattering to
a male ego. After all, the darling was attractive, definitely
male, not so eccentric that he did not have the usual
man's aversion to being considered an open book. She
should have been clever enough to hide the fact that she
knew him by heart. Oh she did, did she? Why, she
didn't even know her invented characters by heart! They
were always doing something unexpected. What stupid
complacency was this, anyway? Her daily routine was
complicated and unpredictable, but his was unchange-
able, she had always thought. At this very minute he was
having lunch with Edwin Stalk down at the Swan Café.
Just as this crossed her mind Lyle heard her name called
and saw Edwin Stalk getting out of a taxi before her.
Stalk, editor of the *Swan*, was part of the Olliver life

she never penetrated. He couldn't be more than twenty-eight she thought, a dark, strikingly handsome lad.

"Do you want my cab, Mrs. Gaynor?"

"Thanks, yes," she said and could not resist adding, "Do you know if Mr. Olliver went back to his office? I understood him to say he was lunching with you."

"He telephoned to cancel the appointment," Stalk said, his always mournful dark eyes registering the minor social blow as if it was a death in the family. "He never breaks appointments, either, you know."

"I know," said Lyle, smiling. "But he's not too old to learn."

"I'm glad to see you," Stalk said simply, holding open the door of the cab for her and looking at her with childish admiration. "I am always glad to see you, I think."

Lyle murmured the address to the driver, so preoccupied with her thoughts she paid no heed to Stalk standing on the curb, hat in hand, watching her drive off. She did not know her lover by heart, after all, was in her mind. For all she knew he had broken the date with the *Swan* editor to lunch with Dodo. Dodo! Plot Number 486—Bobby-soxer changes stately scientist into jitter-bug! Very well, it served her right, Lyle told herself, for cutting up friends and lovers into stage dolls and walking them through her pasteboard plots. Maybe they wanted to make their own plots. Maybe she had always been so blindly sure that she had lost the capacity to observe. She huddled in the corner of the seat, drawing her furs around her, cold with strange new fears. There would surely be a message from him when she got home, but when she rushed in the hallway there was Pedro saying Mr. Gaynor wanted to go over some notes and was waiting in his bedroom. She must call Mr. Sawyer at once as to whether she could put up the visiting English star and her husband, Mr. Gaynor's masseur wanted to speak to her about a new specialist at Medical Center doing wonders with bone diseases. The *Post* wanted her

to do Allan's theatrical memoirs and awaited her call.
Mr. Beckley wanted her to reconsider the invitation to
go South. Had Mr. Olliver telephoned? No. Lyle wanted
to telephone him at once but Pedro said Mr. Gaynor was
very nervous. He had waited so long for her today. If
she would hurry right in to him, please . . .

"Of course," Lyle replied mechanically. She was not
to be allowed one moment hunting for the vanished
lover—not even if he were dead, floating face-upward
down the Hudson, unclaimed in the Morgue or Bellevue,
she thought with a fierce upsurge of rebellion, walking
toward Allan's door. For the first time it seemed to her
that she was a prisoner.

5

. . . the prisoners in great form . . .

ALLAN was sitting up in his specially designed
writing chair, which indicated he had had one of his bad
days. He always felt personally affronted by these attacks
and deliberately forced himself to sit up, work, entertain,
do everything to show he was undefeated. Visitors who
did not understand this were prone to exclaim, "Why,
Allan, you're your old self again," and Allan would smile
proudly as if Pain, overhearing, would withdraw, properly chagrined at having met its match. Deprived these
many years of the theatre, he revelled in his own theatri-
calities, affecting a bottle-green velvet house-jacket, white
scarf under his ruddy jowls giving him the appearance
of a Dickensian country squire. He was a big-shouldered,
florid man, moustache still black though his thinning hair
was iron-gray shading to wings of white above the ears,
contrasting effectively with the crooked black eyebrows
above the black, unrevealing eyes, shades, rather than
windows to the soul. It amused him, further, to have his
room with its dark oak chairs, panelled walls, and high
frost-paned windows, seem more of the taproom than bed-
chamber. "I like the idea of playing Elizabeth Barrett in
a *Student Prince* set," was his explanation. It was a matter
of pride with him to have none of the invalid look or
trappings about him, just as it had pleased him in his
younger days to be taken for a stock-broker or full-back
instead of an actor. In his presence Lyle felt herself and

often saw others wilt, as if his greed for life left no oxygen for anyone else.

Sam Flannery, for twenty years Allan's business manager, press-agent, slave and whipping boy, was sitting on the oak settle by the fireplace. He was a tidy, little man with a rosy choir-boy face, pretty blue eyes anxiously searching for rebuffs that the eager perpetual smile sought to deflect. Lyle had come to accept Flannery as one of Allan's necessities though he represented a truth she hated, that Allan would accept anyone who would toady, ridicule them though he did. Curled up gracefully on a cushion at Allan's feet was a frail wisp of a blonde whose thick, black-rimmed spectacles must have been all that kept her from blowing out the window when the door opened. A small audience, thought Lyle, resigned, but still an audience. She was sure from the set of Allan's jaw, high color and glittering eye, that he had been having one of his annual Master-Mind days, when he suddenly revolutionized their affairs, changed butchers, demanded linen inventories, planned musical revivals, insisted on financial reports, and switched the leading character in whatever they were working on from man to woman. Flannery always supported him in these brainstorms.

"Don't tell me you've decided to come home, my dear!" Allan exclaimed. "It's barely four o'clock. I'm afraid you've cut short your luncheon with the other debutantes, dear, dear! Surely not on our account, my love?"

"Not at all," Lyle answered. "I simply ran out of reefers."

"You poor child! And the other girls were mean and teased you, I suppose. But how was the meringue glacé?"

"Yummy," said Lyle. "Buffy and Booboo and Bunny and I all had four helpings with our Southern Comfort. Oh—lush!"

"Nothing like old school friendships, Flannery," Allan said, shaking his head wisely. "Same class, came out same year, engaged same week, all married in pink—bridesmaids in black, of course, very chic—same wedding-day."

"Same man," Lyle said.

It was their standard manner of masking mutual irritation and Lyle saw from the exchange of smiles between Flannery and the girl that as usual the audience thought it indicated a merry rapport between them.

"Sawyer says your first act hasn't any heart and isn't funny," said Allan.

"I say the same of Sawyer," she said. It was *her* first act when anything was wrong. She didn't care today what was the matter with the new play. All she cared about was finding out where Frederick was and if he had really taken the pooh girl to lunch.

"Oh, I forgot. This young lady is stage-struck. Marianna, is that right, my dear?" Allan waved to the girl at his feet. "Says she's planning to study ballet, voice, percussion and How to Read Fast at the League for Cultural Foundations. I've just recommended her to drop all that and give her secretarial services and her body to a playwright as the best way to get ahead. Don't you agree?"

"I've always found it worked," Lyle said.

"I knew she'd bear me out," Allan said. "Back to your notes, now, Marianna."

The girl flashed Lyle a smile of intense sweetness, and when she spoke her voice showed such cautiously refined diction as to hint of some fatal native coarseness.

"I can't type, you know. Not yet. I'm just writing in pencil what he says."

"The real trouble is her thin legs," Allan said. "Eyes too far apart, too, shoulders humped. Have to dress her in wings to hide that hump."

Lyle saw that the girl regarded this as good-natured chaffing and was blushing with pleasure. They never knew, she thought, any more than she had known when she was a stage-struck girl delighted to be object or victim of the great man's attention. Poor Marianna. Poor Allan, with his savage efforts to balance his frustrations by frustrating others.

"I've got a wonderful idea, Lyle. What about making

Martin a woman?" Allan asked, and indicated the notes on Marianna's lap with his pipe. Lyle smothered a sigh of dismay. Allan's master-mind always messed up everything. "He might like the change—eh, Flannery?"

Lyle hated the days when he chose to be funny about Flannery's homosexual leanings; they were times when his own physical difficulties galled him into taunting everyone else with their undesirableness, impotence or unnatural tastes. She knew he was suffering but today she was tired of pitying; she did not care to be even polite about his inspiration.

"Too trite. There've been hundreds of dowagers saying-damn and cracking their canes around the props," she said. "I like a good mean old man."

Allan frowned thoughtfully, then changed the subject.

"Flannery says you can get white shirts now. He said he gave you the address of a man."

Lyle looked at him blankly and then the familiar feeling of guilt came over her—not for having a lover but for always thinking of Frederick first in the matters that meant most to Allan and least to Frederick. She wondered if the tailor would even let her have more white shirts.

"Maybe Martin could be a woman, after all—someone like—well, say a female Roland Young or maybe a female Ernest Truex," she conceded, guiltily. "Yes, I see it."

"Stick to your side. I like him better an old man, now that I think of it," Allan said reflectively. "Eh, Flannery? I saw something in the paper about a birthday party at an old man's home. Some old boy's hundredth birthday. Had outlived six wives and forgot their names. Reporter asked him as an expert what he thought of a wife two-timing him and the old boy said it was a fine thing once in a while. 'Makes her more chipper round the house,' the old boy said."

Marianna and Flannery screamed inordinately at this. "True, too," Allan added. "All faithful wives are nags. Nag because they haven't had a chance to be unfaithful, or else passed it up."

"Put that in," Flannery urged. "It makes sense, doesn't it, Lyle?"

Lyle felt her face flushing.

"If it's funny and shows heart," she said.

"Flannery says we can get Schafer dough for this if we play our cards right," Allan said. "Mrs. Schafer is crazy about interesting people. They also like sailing and the Museum of Non-objective Art and lobster at Billy the Oysterman's."

"He's an awful man," Lyle said. "He has a notebook full of risqué stories and he can remember the story of his life besides. Anyway, he tells everybody 'the Gaynors are terribly overrated.' He told Sawyer so."

"We'll just have to agree with him," Allan said. "Remember what it says in *The Knights.* 'To steal, perjure yourself, and make a receiver of your rump are three essentials for climbing high.' Flannery knows that."

She could not stand his badgering Flannery any more, but Flannery's vague smile masked any resentment he might feel. He said that he was sure Lyle was mistaken about Schafer's prejudice because he was a shrewd man and therefore certainly must know that the Gaynors were the hottest bet in town, the greatest team since—since— "Beaumont and Fletcher," assisted Allan. Flannery nodded admiringly.

"Marianna, this guy knows everything in the book," he said beaming. "There isn't a reference he doesn't get. I've said it before and I'll say it again,—the Gaynors are the biggest stuff in the American theatre and they've only just got going."

Lyle hoped this flattery would stop Allan, but on the other hand she supposed Flannery was well-enough protected, having the complacent ego of the ignorant. He might be obsequious to his clients but on the outside later he would be bragging of how he had just told off the Gaynors and how he not only kept them from bollexing up their business but practically wrote their plays himself. He handled a musical star and a concert-violinist and his

reports on what he did for them indicated what he must
claim for the Gaynor success. Celebrities were kind to him
because he seemed honestly to like and deeply appreciate
their qualities, but this was not devotion but an insatiable
curiosity about their luck. He saw no superior talent in
them, merely a mysterious magnetism for luck. His violin-
ist client scoring a fabulous hit in Carnegie Hall made
him puzzle anew over the fellow's fool luck. He himself
could have done it better, if he had ever learned to play
the violin, but the thing was—how did they manage to
attract luck? That was the admirable thing. He made a
good living out of these lucky folk but he should have been
an artist. "The reason I never went in for painting is that
I'd want to do it so much better than anyone else," he
stated once. "My great ambition has always prevented me
from doing anything." Frustrated by his perfectionism he
consoled himself by circulating around favored ones un-
fettered by high ideals. He had a strong faith that luck
might be contagious and that someday he would catch it
and astound everyone by blossoming forth artist, musician,
poet laureate and movie-tycoon all in one. Until that day
he was their abject slave with a valuable knack at figures
and a soothing imperviousness to insults which made him
ideal for Allan. Lyle did not know how she could have
managed without Flannery as buffer. She needed him but
there were times when she thought it was Flannery, not
Allan's helplessness, that kept her bound to Allan. Flannery, constant reminder of the dozen different bars to
her escape.

"Can I change my clothes?" she asked. She would telephone Frederick's apartment, she thought, then Strafford's.
He'd have to be at one place or the other—he always was
on Thursdays. If he wasn't it would mean . . .

"Good God, we've been waiting for you hours while
you were probably furbishing up your rhumba at Arthur
Murrays!" Allan exclaimed impatiently. "Listen, my
beauty, we happen to have struck gold and we've got to
ride our luck while we've got it. Don't forget I was in this

business when you were in that pretty silver cradle of yours, and I know we can't let the grass grow. You can't just run around celebrating and re-arranging your laurels, you sweet child."

"Right," said Flannery. "As I was just telling that dumb soprano of mine . . ."

"Or was just wishing you could tell her," Allan laughed genially. "Never mind, Flannery, old boy, someday you can kick out your soprano and have a whole stable of tenors. Like my naïve little wife, here, with her stable of intellectuals—good God, not one of them could put her to bed. Intellectuals, but so dumb they don't know what she really wants."

"What I really want is coffee," Lyle said and went to the halldoor to call Pedro.

"Oh she doesn't know she wants it, I grant you," Allan pursued, suddenly wincing as the pain whipped his thighs, and his voice went on in a shrill gasp. "Why would a little spoiled darling from a second-string finishing school know what she wanted anyway, outside of her name in the columns and a foot on the stage? I'll tell you one thing, Flannery, any woman of my own generation would have had enough red blood in her to have given me a hundred horns by this time, and by George I'd respect them for it, I respect decent lust in a woman, yes, even in a pansy . . ."

"Personally I lust for respect," Lyle said calmly, "and coffee. Do you remember a book about a woman in love with an orchid? She used to creep out in the greenhouse at night for a rendezvous with it. Would you really like horns from an orchid—especially a green orchid so that you wouldn't know how the child would turn out? So unfair, too, when he'd start going to school and be called orchid by the other children."

Allan was distracted only for a moment. Lyle went to his bed-table and brought him the bottle of capsules, but he shook his head impatiently, angry at the assumption his sarcasm was only a pitiful defense against pain. She left it at his side, nevertheless, knowing he would take it when she pretended to look at his page of notes. His voice was calm again next time he spoke.

"I console myself in my affliction, Flannery," he said mockingly, "by the knowledge that it was my reputation and not my sexual ability that won the lady. Her martyrdom is not so amazing since the reputation at least is bigger and better than ever and fortunately she is herself in the best of health and can distribute autographs all over the town without a twinge. Isn't that fine, Flannery? Isn't that ducky, Marianna?"

"I'm getting lazy, though, Marianna," Lyle said, smiling. Poor Allan, poor Allan, oh poor Allan, she thought, her pity clutching her heart or was it her heart clutching for pity? "I want to sleep late and let somebody else run around delivering autographs. Maybe in a little closed carriage like *Rosemarie-Confiseur,* with a coachman—a green orchid in livery maybe."

"Oh Lyle, you're wonderful!" Flannery burst out in his high giggle of exaggerated appreciation. "Oh you two are in great form, today, you really ought not to waste it on Marianna and me."

"Do you hear, Allan? Flannery thinks we ought to write a play. Next he'll be suggesting we move to New York City—Greenwich Village, maybe, where all the angels live."

"Oh Lyle!" shrieked Flannery, laughter dying uncertainly as he saw Allan suddenly lie back in his chair, arm thrown wearily over his eyes. "Well, I guess I'll leave you fellows to your conference. Bye now. I'll take you down street for a sandwich, Marianna, if you're through. Maybe a drink."

"Sure. Take her. Put a little nourishment on her bones," Allan said without moving. "Wore out my energy waiting around here for Lyle, I guess."

"I'm sorry," Lyle said. "I was held up at the Museum looking up those costumes."

A lie. She was held up ordering shirts for her lover who had been having lunch with somebody else, somebody new, somebody who was not bound to a cruel duty. Somebody who could call him up whenever she chose, who wasn't afraid of her husband's reputation. Or where was he? She had to find out. She could tiptoe out now and telephone all the places he might be, just to hear his voice, just to know she was wrong. If Allan would only fall asleep —or die? . . . Die? She'd never thought such a wish, never before. . . .

Marianna was hesitating beside Allan's chair, being very much the shy child, a little frightened of the king. They always pretended to be shy, once they'd battered their way in; one needn't bother to reassure them. Without the mighty black spectacles for restraint her fair hair fell over her eyes in careful disarray, and she was standing in a manner to exaggerate her humped shoulders, now that they had been noticed.

"Here are my notes, Mr. Gaynor," she said timidly. "If you want me to come and work for you again I'll be awfully happy. Flannery knows where to find me."

The notes, Lyle observed, consisted of half a dozen words to a page written in the carefully standardized boarding-school script considered suitable to recommend Marlboro Cigarettes. Her lip curled but then she remembered the dreadful requirements of the stage, the need to act every moment, to conceal every genuine ache under a mock one. If the girl wanted a job, it was certainly wiser for her to appear artless, timid, and fey than to cry out her hunger and deep necessity.

"Marianna's alright, isn't she, Allan?" Flannery wanted to know.

"She has enough intelligence not to try to show any," Allan granted wearily, the two guests chuckling happily. "Something my dear wife has yet to learn."

After they left, Lyle poured herself coffee from the tray Pedro put on the table, and Allan sat up slowly and painfully.

"Let's go away from New York," he said abruptly. "Let's go to Mexico. I've always wanted to live in Mexico."

"I know," Lyle said, her heart dropping at the mere suggestion of being separated from Frederick. "But it might be bad for you. Oh no, we mustn't."

"The doctor says the Southwest would be fine. I might even be able to ride. I could ride through the mountains. join up with the Penitentes, maybe, offer myself for crucifixion, really enjoy myself, for once."

"You wouldn't enjoy yourself away from New York, you know that," Lyle murmured, already suffering the anguish of farewell forever to Frederick. No matter what one sacrificed there was always one more great renunciation that was demanded, the one wish that could not be granted.

"Never mind. I'll get there," Allan said. Her silence suggested to him that he may have carried his needling too far today in the glow of his appreciative audience. He seldom nagged when they were alone.

"That bastard Flannery got on my nerves today, you know," he said. "Imagine a little punk like that making a fortune out of our brains—yours more than mine, dear, I freely admit. The old bean's getting rustier and rustier. And then the little punk has to hang around boring the pants off me till you come."

"I know," she said.

Allan looked at her furtively.

"You look tired," he said solicitously. "Maybe the best thing is for you to take a little rest now so you'll be fresh. Yes, that's the idea. You run along and take a nap. We can put off this talk till later."

"Thanks, I will do that," she said.

Allan never wanted to work except before an audience, too. But she could thank him for making her fatigue his excuse. She went upstairs to her own room and dialed Frederick's apartment again. There was no answer and she was afraid to call the League or Strafford's to ask for him. Allan might someday take it into his head to listen on the extension.

6

. . . moonlight on Rubberleg Square . . .

*T*HE real night does not begin on Rubberleg
Square till stroke of twelve, the moment after all decisions
have been made and abandoned. The reformed citizens
who have cautiously stayed home reading four-dollar books
that instruct as well as entertain, and have even gone to
bed because tomorrow is a big day at the office, suddenly
rear up in their sheets, throw on their clothes once more,
and dash out for one night-cap to ward off wagon-pride.
Couples who have braved Broadway to attend a solemn
play concerning injustice out of town are smitten with an
irresistible craving for the proximity of barflies, wastrels,
crooks. The artist's model who has been doing uptown
nightclubs in her room-mate's mink has had as much
splendour as her Irish blood and whiskey content can
endure and has escaped in a taxicab to the Florida bar
downtown where her amazing hair-do and evening clothes
make a gratifying glow in the dingy room and her amorous
whim is satisfied by a genial merchant mariner more than
it would have been by the elderly broker who was her
dinner host. Here, on Rubberleg Square, the four dark
streets suddenly come to life with running feet. "BAR," in
red or blue neon lights, glows in any direction as if it was
all one will-o'-the-wisp, same bar, same Bill, Hank, Jim,
Al pushing Same-agains across the same counter. The
whisper of light love is in the air; plain women brushing
past are beautiful in veils of heavy bedroom perfume;
men's eyes darting through the mist are ruthless hunters;
hands touch accidentally, shoulders brush, smiles are

smuggled in the dark to shadowy strangers. On Eighth Street the Russian shops, Chinese shops, Mexican Craft shops, Antique Jewelry, Basketweave, Chess, Rare Print and Rare Book Shops all darken simultaneously and life begins.

Rushing from Blue Bar to Red Bar to Blue Bar two sailors support an inanimate companion, his feet dragging as their grip on each arm loosens. A gentleman in somebody else's hat balances himself carefully down the middle of the Avenue of the Americas, as if it was a slack wire; his head thrust forward like a hen's, his arms flapping, his knees buckling, he tacks from curb to curb and finally flutters into the safe cove of "BAR" like a clumsy pigeon. Another gentleman with a frozen, waxy face drags an enfeebled lady behind him by her arm; her pocketbook swings from a long strap in a wide vigorous circle and slaps passers-by with a rhythmic thud. Cats lope purposefully along the gutter, alleycat and runaway pet hunt together, shying away from doting ladies with growls of jungle hatred. Taxis slide noiselessly through the damp streets, their doors swing open; a man and woman catapult from a restaurant canopy into one of these roving love-nests, are locked in an intense embrace before the door bangs shut; the taxi speeds into midnight. From unseen cellar night-clubs comes the sound of tom-toms and hidden revelry, though if you were to penetrate one of these caves you would look in vain for gaiety; you would find a bare half-dozen unsmiling guests, a dozen frowning waiters, an unhappy orchestra. The unseen mirth must be piped in from absent proprietors, or perhaps the walls are laughter-conditioned.

This is the hour when the four Pillars of Rubberleg Square collide, astonished to see each other at the usual places. Why, hello Caraway, hello Marquette, hello Doctor, hello Rover! The idea of something for the road occurs, is pounced upon as a brilliant epigram that must be celebrated. From now till closing time the Four are inseparable, examining other bars, retracing the steps

each has taken singly before. The four Pillars know everybody, everyplace, and everything. The four Pillars are
Mr. Marquette, trim, gay, plump, an ex-postal clerk who
drinks because his wife is a lady; ("A fine thing. Look at
you, a respectable man with a bank-vice-president in the
family, staying up all night, keeping the neighbors awake
with your groans and carrying on. What would my people
say out in St. Louis? For shame!"); Dr. Zieman, lean,
hawk-faced, Van-Dyked, who gave up teaching English
literature for rum when his wife's juvenile *Wootsy, the
Bad Cricket* was compared to something or other with
the success that invariably follows any comparison; Mr.
Caraway, an old New Yorker who has been sipping away
for years at a small trust fund that permits him neither to
go very far or stay very long anywhere. Lastly there is
Rover, spit and image of the younger John Drew, up on
all stage, radio and film small talk, has influential friends
named Herman, Brock, Terry, Bogey, Jasper, and Norman
through his wife, a prominent off-stage noise named Clarice. The lives of these gentlemen seldom cross by day but
by night they unite in the business of inspecting and re-
porting on selected bars in the neighborhood. Earlier in
the evening they have found plausible errands for themselves in different blocks, and at the final round-up they
are able to piece together the activities of almost anyone
you can mention.

At the Florida bar they begin comparing notes. Someone inquires whether anyone has seen Murray Cahill
tonight. Why, yes, Marquette happened to be dashing past
Barney's at six-fifteen and caught a glimpse of him in the
bar having a double whiskey sour (no cherry) with a tall
legal-looking chap in a London gray snap brim, bow-tie,
ruptured duck on lapel. Being in a hurry Marquette could
not tell whether it was a friend from his O.W.I. days or
a bar stranger. Caraway saw him around eight at the
Lafayette having onion soup and a ham sandwich reading
the sport page of the *Telegram* all alone. He said hello,
that was all, then paid his check ($3.40, so he must have

had a couple of drinks too), made a local call in the phone booth on the way out, probably what he came in for, because he was never a Lafayette man. Last Caraway saw of him was standing on the corner just as that K.G.R. advertising man who always buys drinks all around came along with some cutie and the three went up the street together.

Is that a fact! Dr. Zieman, for his part, on his way to the lending library for a reserved copy of *I Was a Court Lady* as an antidote for *Wootsy* had seen the advertising men and the girl draped around the pianist in the Barrel all singing *Chickery Chick*. No sign of Murray, but he might have been in the boys' room or out with that Polish girl of his only he never took her out. At this point, a square-set lady in a good Brooks Brothers tweed suit comes into the Florida with the harassed air of someone called in at the last moment for an emergency Caesarian; she settles herself on a bar-stool, burying herself intensely in the *Swan* magazine and an old-fashioned. The Four Pillars lift their hats to her, respecting as they do the dignity of the magazine she carries. Caraway recalls that he has seen her some weeks before whacking a well-known abstractionist with an umbrella in the benign shadow of the Jefferson Market jail shouting "Stalinist!" at the top of her lungs. Rover says she is a Character on the Cape, but rich. They are willing to accept comradely overtures from her (name of Hammerley, Rover recalls) but the lady is absorbed, in fact, blind. Things are dull at the Florida tonight, and it seems advisable to penetrate further into the interior of the Square. With a grave nod to Hank, the four pull hats firmly down over their ears against the light rain and file out like decent pall-bearers, heading with one accord for the America's Bar where they order four rye and waters (five cents cheaper than with fizz) just as the bartender, in one of those inexplicable spasms of bar tender morality, is throwing a customer out of the place for drinking and using a profane word in his temple.

The Four Pillars digest the new scene with quiet pleas-

ure, have a word with the manager at the back, a drink
on the house, a wink at the manager's wife who patiently
sits over the cash register as if she expected to hatch a
brood of gold eagles. They exchange further queries and
answers as to events of the evening previous, and what
happened to each after they separated. Sometimes it is
necessary to consult the bartender for accurate data on
Last Night. The Florida bartender, Hank, is a gloomy man
for six hours but curiously vivacious from then on to closing time, describing customers and situations that he,
with his almost psychic powers, has "sized up." He can
size up at a glance, it seems, particularly if he mops up
the counter steadily in front of the customer listening to
what is being said. He freely gives the Pillars the fruits of
his uncanny research. On the other hand, the bartender
at the New Place, where they next pause, is something of
a snob in his way, enjoying the spectacle of Names making
fools of themselves in his place; and he shares with the
Pillars his satisfaction over having "told off" a certain big
shot last night, of having refused to serve you-know-who,
saying "I don't care who you are, I'm trying to run a
decent place here."

It is here that the leading man from that play *Summer
Day* came in stinko last night, drinking rye Presbyterians,
waving hundred dollar bills till he passed out and that
good-looking girl from A. A. stepped up and took him
home, either for sex or reform or both. This elicits from
Marquette the news that he saw Allan Gaynor, *Summer
Day* author, twenty years ago in his own stock company, a
good actor but a chaser. Got mixed up with a banker's wife
in St. Louis—Marquette's home town, hushed up, of
course. Caraway used to see Gaynor's wife, Lyle, when she
went to Stokely, the girls' school in the Connecticut village where he spent summers. Talented kid, quite a
beauty, her family and the Beckleys ran the Beach Club.
Naturally, with that background, the school had to give
her all the prizes, especially in their dramatic affairs.
Seems Gaynor's company stayed at the Beckleys' where

Gaynor met her and first thing they were married, she being stage-struck and he being society-struck. Not much dough on her side but solid. The collaboration started with her writing a play, Allan doctoring it, then along comes his accident and he has to give up acting. She's smart and gets him to concentrate on writing. And now look at them—half a dozen hits, well not big hits but carriage trade, prestige. Rover complains that his wife had auditioned unsuccessfully for *Summer Day* but it was her dog who got a job at thirty-five bucks a week to sleep on the sofa during the second act. It burned up Clarice to have her theatrical career end as stage mother for a dog, and she blamed the Gaynors. Marquette wonders humorously how Gaynor casts his ingénues, now that he's crippled up, and the Doctor chuckles that maybe Mrs. Gaynor has to do double-duty in casting, now. Caraway remembers having idly observed the lady ordering a lot of plants, philodendron, he thought, at George the Florist's sent to a Bank Street address. It was nothing to him, heaven knows, but he could not help remembering that he'd seen her going in Murray Cahill's apartment over there once, and since Murray was out—"Must be that professor that Murray lives with," agreed Marquette. The bartender of the New Place is as indifferent to the Gaynors' private affairs as are the Pillars, and the subject yielding no more fruit in spite of intensive concentration on their individual wishing wells, he finally observes, "Everybody's got to come from someplace, I don't care how big they are. They can't always have been up there in those top brackets. It ain't the way of the world. And in the long run you'll find everybody's only human."

At each bar the Four Pillars act as quasi-owners, frowning on newcomers who do not behave, who complain of portions or ask for extra olives; they stare fixedly at bounders who try to engage lone ladies in conversation, they report dubious activities to the manager in a low voice, demonstrating that they might by chance drop in a bar for a refresher once in a while but they are by no means habitual drunkards, they are gentlemen, by George, and accustomed to behaving like gentlemen in all circumstances.

It is a pity that tonight Dr. Zieman succumbs to his tendency to fall asleep in unexpected places, obliging his friends Marquette and Caraway to give up further work and drag him across the Square long before closing-time, their six rubberlegs so desperately involved that the friendly policeman could not tell who is taking whom home. Rover stays on at the bar. The incident is not anything to be ashamed of, he explains to no one in particular. Dr. Zieman happens to be troubled with insomnia, that is all, and has to take his naps whenever they come. On this particular evening he had fallen smack off his stool dragging down a lady writer who had been pinning on material so long that she fell into a grateful doze herself as soon as she hit the floor and had to be removed before the Doctor, snoring peacefully, could be extricated.

"Boy, he sure had insomnia bad tonight!" the bartender exclaimed.

Someone had laughed, but Rover restored the group dignity by stating in a clear Barrymore voice that rebuked the entire bar, "Insomnia is a terrible thing, let me tell you, especially for a professional man like the doctor. You never know when it's going to hit you."

"The bald-headed old boy is a worse lush than the doc," the bartender said. "He fell down himself going out."

Rover was roused to further defense of the dignity of his friends. "The bald-headed gentleman happens to be a very close lifelong friend of the Allan Gaynors," he said haughtily. "It wouldn't be a very good thing for this bar to have it get back to the Gaynors that their friend was called a lush. They certainly would never let him come here again or at least *they* wouldn't come."

"Oh, forget it," said the bartender. "How about the match game? And this time let's play it right! No funny-business."

7

. . . the hide-out . . .

*W*OMEN were always infuriated at the Murray-Frederick establishment for it hinted of a permanent stronghold against marriage. "You lucky bastards!" married men friends always cried enviously. "What a hide-out!" The apartment on Bank Street was ideally arranged for keeping out of each other's way, yet each could use the other as protection against encroachments of ladies. They had separate entrances on the first floor of an old house; bath and kitchenette were off a connecting hall between the two large rooms so that days could pass without sight or sound of each other. Frederick kept his outer and inner doors locked except in summer when his access to the garden was used by Murray. Murray's doors were usually open to any number of friends and chance acquaintances, whether he was in or not. The two men had no friends in common, no joint social engagements, and only the most meagre idea of each other's private life. This did not prevent Murray's ladies from wondering how much Frederick Olliver knew of their secrets. His ex-wife, Gerda, was so sure Murray had told Frederick all about their troubles, that she made elaborate confidences to Frederick when she met him, asked intimate questions, and took umbrage at his silence, thinking he was being cagey and hostile instead of embarrassed. Murray's regular girl, Judy Dahl, had more complicated reactions to Frederick, certain that he was responsible for Murray's elusiveness, though she managed to maintain a superficially friendly attitude. She had a habit of wandering around the place naked in summer, and Frederick was often disconcerted to find her in the raw casually frying her lunch in the kitchenette or painting at her easel when he came out from a shower. Murray allowed her to use his big room for work since she had only a tiny hall bedroom at a girls' club on Abingdon Square. Frederick wished Murray would ask her to dress when he wasn't around, but the encounters were seldom and he finally perfected a technique for ignoring her. The presence of the telephone in the middle hall and the fact that Judy always answered it, when possible, gave her a few clues to Frederick's habits. Mr. Stalk had called and would be at the *Swan* office at three to discuss the new article; Mrs. Gaynor had called and would be free at six; the League office had called and was transferring his class from Room 20 to 28 this week.

The night after the Beckley party Frederick was working in his room, trying to concentrate in spite of recurrent stabs of guilt at his foolish quarrel with Lyle. He wrote a note to her. "Darling, it must embarrass you as much as it does me that I have never been unfaithful to you and never will be. Do forgive this blind spot." He thrust it in his pocket, decided to telephone instead, then frowned on hearing Judy moving around next door, which prevented him from going in to telephone in privacy. Usually Judy went home at night if Murray failed to return, but this night he heard her answer the phone when it rang, and then she knocked on his door. She was clothed, fortunately, and busy building up the fire by the time he came out in his dressing gown to answer. He hoped it would be Lyle but instead an operator asked for him and then he heard Murray's voice, low and guarded.

"Don't say it's me if Judy's still there. Look, Gerda is back in town. She told somebody she was on her way down to my place, but if Judy's still there, there's bound to be fireworks so I'm keeping out. See if there's anything you can do to get Judy out before things happen. Tell her you want my room for a friend. I'll call later to see. Right now I'm by way of getting plastered."

"I'll do what I can," Frederick said, and hung up. He knew quite well this was no situation he could handle and Murray must know it too, but he hesitated a moment. He saw that two women were sitting on the day-bed in Murray's room, with highballs and he heard one of them whisper, "Judy, ask him if he wants a drink." When Judy paid no attention to this suggestion, he realized he must have established himself long ago as a hopeless snob or boor to her, someone she had finally given up inviting, certain of his customary refusal. If she made no move to speak to him he did not see how he could find any deft way of asking her to go home, no matter what excuse he could invent. He assured himself that Murray was merely nervous and the chances were that Gerda would not appear at all. The sight of Judy's square, uncompromising back made him sorry for her and he wished he had made her believe in his friendliness. He did not know why he wanted Judy to understand him, and he knew she would be astonished to discover he had ever given her more than a passing thought. Even a slight knowledge of Murray indicated that the ex-wife, Gerda, was still top woman and that Judy meant probably no more to him than a boiled dinner. Patient, stolid, and devoted, Judy at twenty-four seemed older than either of the men, more like a mother in her pride in Murray's waywardness and success with women. Frederick saw a mirror of his own withdrawn proud misery in her, and seeing the mistake of it he wanted to show her how to be otherwise. He wanted to say something that would show he was friendly no matter what might happen but as soon as he heard the other woman's voice murmur, "Judy, make him stay. If you don't I will." He gave up and hastily went in his room and locked the door. Let Murray figure it out himself. He had his own rift with Lyle to worry about.

"For heaven's sake let him alone!" he overheard Judy

say to the others, and that settled it. "Murray won't stand for anybody disturbing his highness."

While Frederick tried to retrieve his ideas at his desk, the two ladies who had called to see Murray became intrigued, as was always the case, by the idea of an Extra Man wasting away on the other side of the hall. They were confident that here was a lonely male Cinderella wistfully hoping the beautiful ladies would invite him to join them. Judy curtly dismissed this idea with the authority of five years' experience during which dozens of Murray's guests had been rebuffed by this Cinderella. Murray had defended his partner with the statement that if Frederick was decent enough to ignore their noise, they should be decent enough to respect his privacy. Judy now took grim pleasure in protecting the laws of the house. After all, the ladies were Murray's friends, not hers.

"You can't tell me he's a stuffed shirt when he's lived with an old rounder like Murray Cahill all these years," said Miss Drake. Caroline Drake had come in at seven, swearing that Murray had invited her to dinner at the Barrel and had never showed up. She was a silverware stylist and had met Murray when she was organizing a fashion show at Marshall Field's and he had been running a trade magazine. She had known his ex-wife, too, and gloomily decided that maybe Gerda had been right to leave him if he broke dates this way. Judy provided Caroline with high-balls while she waited and meantime Lorna Leahy, who lived next door, walked in to ask why Murray had not called for her as he had promised. Both ladies, being old friends, after the initial awkwardness of running into each other in these circumstances, settled down for a good time cutting up Murray. Caroline was a hearty, big boned woman, groomed to the last follicle, and not at all flattering in her assumption that Judy's position in Murray's life could have nothing to do with sex. Judy was used to this and bore no grudges. She was secretly pleased by the arrival of Lorna Leahy, commercial artist, who declared loudly that she, too, had a date with

Murray, and Judy listened to the two ladies out-do each other in possessive anecdotes about Murray, who, when all was said and done, had stood up both of them. For this small favor Judy thanked her absent idol. Nevertheless, she was offended that they were more than ready to pounce on Frederick as a substitute.

"He's so distinguished looking!" Lorna Leahy exclaimed.

"I could go for that proud-faced hard-to-get kind," Miss Drake stated, stretching out her large, beautifully manicured hands as if one wrench from them would finish the hapless prey. "There was a fellow in Santa Fé like that on my Western trip. A cowboy. Same blue eyes that look right through you. Never said anything but one look and you turn straight to water. He joined the rodeo and once in New York I ran into him at the Ringside, drunk as a coot. A wild horse had thrown him and he was punch-drunk but he still had those sad eyes. He sure looked pretty in those tight pants and that fifty-dollar satin shirt."

Lorna Leahy, ruffled that Murray should have made a date with her best friend and not appeased by the joint stand-up, said that of all people in the world to compare with a cowboy Mr. Olliver was the last. She considered him aristocratic looking rather than handsome, with that faint fleck of grey at the temples, sensitive face and those blue eyes. She said it made her laugh to think of Caroline's cowboy, when Frederick Olliver was such a—well—such a highbrow. His essays were published abroad and in the *Swan* and the last book of his was out of this world. As for asking him to join them she wouldn't dream of it; that click of the key was enough for her. She'd learned something about men from her marriage, mistake though it had been. Caroline, quite humbled by this rebuke, asked eagerly for more information on Frederick's work, admitting generously that travelling around the country so much made a person a terrible dope.

While they discussed this subject Judy reflected bitterly

that Murray kept Frederick as a protection against herself more than anything else. The only comfort was that it protected him against other women, as well. She silently went on darning Murray's socks, resolved not to leave these callers to wait for Murray. She could outstay anybody. She was a self-contained, honorable young woman, who had no hesitancy in admitting she had been the pursuer, dogging Murray's footsteps, earnestly trying to prove her usefulness until he allowed her his bed and the privilege of forgiving his other affairs, looking after his clothes and room and hangovers, cooking for his friends when he permitted, and waiting for his anecdotes about parties with other women. She was sure Murray needed her and she thought he loved her in a way without knowing it. She might have a baby for him someday and then he would give in to her completely. Or maybe not. He had not liked her painting any better for her winning a prize last year; he hadn't liked it any better than he had when he met her sketching on a Maine shore and stopped to kid her about her color. He thought she was foolish, spending her salary from clerking nights at the stationery store on lessons and art supplies, and he said she ought to marry some farmer and have a dozen kids. But he was kind to her and let her use his room. She thought that if Frederick Olliver did not have the back room it would be easier for her. She could live there and look after him. The way it was now Judy blamed Frederick for Murray's trouble with his ex-wife; if she had the back room she could throw out Gerda. She knew she was unfair to Frederick. She was not even sorry for him, as Murray was, that he was tangled up with a rich married woman, and with all his brains could barely make enough to eat. He was the one obstacle in her stolid pursuit that patience and perseverance could not conquer. She thought about him as much as she did about the women in Murray's life, for it was his presence there that gave them full sway. She thought he must be comparing her to the others whenever he looked at her. She was a country girl and didn't care who knew it. She had a round, scrubbed blonde face and white pigtails hanging or else wound round her head, a square peasant body and a deep agreeable voice. Everybody liked and trusted her; push-cart merchants and shopkeepers gave her the best at smallest prices; dogs and babies leaped to her lap; women were never jealous of her; and fellow-painters liked her to pose for them even though they could not praise her painting. Judy did not mind their silence since she had never heard painters praise each other, anyway; moreover she knew she was slow. It would take years for her to do what others did quickly. She was content with small consolations along the way. Murray's open pleasure in a well-dressed woman did not incite her to any effort to compete. She never went anywhere fancy, so why should she? She wore her brown slacks, ski shoes and sheepskin-lined jacket in the city as she did in the country, a blue butcher's apron over her sweater to paint or cook. Murray used to laugh at her, suggesting an occasional change to more frivolous dress, then he got so he never mentioned it. Once, when Frederick came into Ticino's with Mrs. Gaynor, Judy had suggested that they might share a table with them but Murray had looked pointedly from Mrs. Gaynor to Judy's dirty fingernails and shook his head, laughing. Judy blamed Frederick for that, too. Mrs. Gaynor's life was complete without Frederick just as Murray's life was complete without hers. Frederick, too, was a silent lonely person waiting for crumbs, but it was no bond between them. She scorned him for the patience and silent acceptance of little that was like her own. When the telephone rang once again for him she recognized Mrs. Gaynor's voice and despised him for being in to receive it. Why wasn't he out in bars with mysterious other women the way Murray was, instead of always waiting for this dry crust? How much better to be like Murray, having the other person always worried while he laughed in bars with his private friends, unless he was being shoved into some scented boudoir by one of his stylish ladies! Judy was so disgusted with Frederick that she asked Lorna to rap on his door, fearing her scorn would show in her face.

Frederick came out to the telephone, stalling for time by lighting a cigarette, guessing that Murray was checking up on what he had accomplished. From the silence in the living-room he knew that the three ladies were waiting eagerly to hear whatever he had to say, and he knew he was helpless. But this time it was Lyle and before he could make a discreet suggestion to meet her somewhere she startled him by demanding, "Frederick, where were you lunching today that you had to break your date with Stalk?" The tone, accusing and peremptory, was not at all like Lyle and for a minute he could not answer for sheer bewilderment.

"I didn't have time for lunch today," he began, and was about to say he had taken a part-time job but stopped, feeling three pairs of interested female eyes boring through the walls at him. Lyle knew where the telephone was; she knew a personal conversation was impossible when Murray's room was full of people. The pangs of guilt over his silly behavior last night vanished in his exasperation.

"Darling, I can't get it out of my head you were seeing that Dodo girl again," now Lyle's voice sounded high and strained, and pleading. "I simply had to know if it was true."

"I said I was too busy to go out for lunch," he kept his voice low and casual because of the listening women, but he was really angry. He had sometimes been piqued that Lyle was never jealous of him in the fierce exhausting way he was jealous of her—of her marriage, of her all-absorbing work, of her suitors, of her simple joy in living. But now that she was acting like any ordinary woman, accusing him of secret meetings with a stupid girl he never expected to see again, and all in the presence of three curious friends of Murray. Frederick was genuinely outraged. Wild horses would not make him admit now that the girl was an unavoidable accident, someone whose very name, crazy as it was, he had forgotten until she brought it up.

"Supposing I telephone you around noon tomorrow?" he suggested.

"Do forgive me for being a fool," Lyle gave a breathless little laugh. "I just turned silly, that's all. I only needed your voice. Pretend I never said a word, darling, will you?"

"Of course," Frederick said.

When he hung up the receiver his cheeks felt hot and burning, either at the inferior object of Lyle's suspicion, or at her apology for having suspected at all; he was not sure which. In either case he felt too embarrassed to face the three ladies who must have gathered, judging from their smug smiles, that some misunderstanding had been going on and withdrew again to his room, too disturbed to work or to remember the little diplomatic task Murray had asked of him. He fumbled in his pocket for the note to Lyle and crumpled it up.

Caroline Drake and Lorna Leahy seized the telephone as soon as Frederick left and made telephone calls to several bars, local and distant to locate Murray, not guessing that Murray's motto, known to all bartenders and likely to be engraved on his tombstone was: "If a lady calls, I'm out." To disturb a man in his bar was as bad as to walk in on his bath. Women ought to be gentlemen, he had often complained. Judy knew this and did not enlighten her companions. She could not forgive their disloyalty in switching from Murray to gushing praise of Frederick. She thought all women ought to be true to Murray. She was too grateful for Murray's irregular favors to risk being jealous, though she knew he liked Lorna Leahy. He often mentioned his admiration for Lorna's magazine covers and illustrations, saying rather cruelly that at least Lorna knew how to make the most of a clever commercial gift without kidding herself into being a bad

Cézanne. Judy was not at all offended, admitting that she did not know enough about commercial art to appreciate Lorna's work. Moreover she did not think Murray, her wayward darling, knew enough about art to know whether she herself was bad, but she did not say this. It might hurt his feelings.

"Let's get Frederick to go over to The Barrel with us," proposed Caroline.

"You all go and I'll wait here," Lorna Leahy said.

Judy gave her a measured look but said nothing. She had no intention of leaving the place, regardless of appearances. Subtlety had never gotten her anywhere and certainly would not with these purposeful women.

"Let's have another gag first," said Miss Drake, pouring herself a generous slug. "Here I am, stood up by a dear old friend I just located after years. Of course I felt a little guilty dating up Murray, having been such a close friend of Gerda's. But you always stick up for the man in separations. I do. I always adored Murray anyway. I did, anyway, till he stood me up. Have a gag, ladies. Cheer ourselves up."

"What was Gerda like? I'm always curious about ex-wives?" asked Lorna.

"Gerda," said Caroline, weighing her words judiciously, "was an absolute fool. She looked clever and talked a lot of intellectual, arty claptrap but she had a kewpie brain."

"What made her so mean to Murray?" Judy could not help asking.

"Gerda wasn't mean. She wasn't smart enough to be mean," Caroline answered. "Intellectually and morally she was a mess, but you couldn't say she was mean. Just a fool. Good God, I should know. She was my best friend, wasn't she?"

When the doorbell suddenly rang Judy was against answering it, but Miss Drake had high hopes of the unexpected and leaped to the door. Judy and Lorna heard her astonished exclamation in the hallway.

"Gerda!"

"Why, Caroline Drake, what in the world are you doing here?" cried a fluty voice.

This was the moment Judy was always dreading, the return of the ex-wife with baggage. It was the only thing that could shake her stolid calm, and all she could do was to stare stupidly at the door, paying no attention to Caroline Drake's shrill squeals of introduction.

The latest caller was a tall, thin, olive-skinned woman with radiant, heavily mascaraed eyes, a spangled green scarf wound round her head, massive white mouton coat flung over paisley blouse and green slacks, gold-painted toe-nails protruding from metal-trimmed sandals, and as vibrantly intense in her movements as if she had been sprung from a bow into the room. Her heavy make-up, bracelets, huge rings, and glittering appurtenances securely camouflaged whatever reality might lie beneath and made even Caroline Drake, in spite of her meticulous grooming, seem a blowsy milkmaid. Judy looked at her with deep distrust and a sick sense of defeat, noting the small red leather bag that was ominously larger than a mere jewel-case.

"A party! How marvellous!" cried Gerda, in a throaty theatrical voice that trailed final syllables and last words like veils in the wind. "I'd adore a spot of sherry. But where's the host?"

"There isn't any sherry," Judy said.

"The host's gone to bed," Lorna said with a brilliant inspiration, pointing toward Frederick's door. "We couldn't keep him awake."

"Murray's out, of course. Not that we care. Come on, Gerda, have a gag."

Caroline's voice was crassly Middlewestern compared to Gerda's, and it was elaborately folksy now. Lorna tried to exchange a sly look with Judy but Judy remained coldly unresponsive.

Gerda directed her bright eager eyes toward each of the ladies; her near-sighted concentration gave an impression of ingenuous curiosity.

"All I really care about is that extra bed there," she sighed. "I'm dead. Plane, train, bus—and then I can't get into my apartment till goodness knows when. My subtenants. I was so clever to think of Murray, wasn't I?"

"Yes," Judy said as she tied her jeepshawl under her chin.

"And how lucky to find my old chum here, all in one stroke!" Gerda said, dropping the coat on the couch, then turning to Caroline she said in a tone of mild inquiry, "I had no idea you were in New York, Caroline. But of course it's been years. Five years, yes."

"Gerda, do you know how long it's been? Five years and six months!" Caroline exclaimed, pouncing on any detour around her hot embarrassment.

"Five years and six months!" marvelled Gerda. "I can't believe it, Caroline, it can't be! I must have had my mink then."

"You did!" enthusiastically agreed Caroline. "You had the mink—and of course Murray."

"Of course. But five years and six months without so much as a word between us!" Gerda turned to the others with a helpless shrug. "I simply can't believe it. Caroline and I were best friends, you see."

"We were!" Caroline affirmed. "It was a honey-colored mink."

"You must have lots to talk over," Lorna said politely, and received a suspicious glance from Caroline.

"Caroline testified for me in my divorce," Gerda laughed reminiscently. "She said Murray was a confirmed alcoholic and was mentally cruel. She said he was always asking where things were when they were right under his nose, until my sanity was jeopardized."

"She did?" Lorna asked, again seeking and receiving no sympathetic support from Judy.

"She simply couldn't endure poor Murray!" Gerda pursued. "He wasn't that bad, Caroline, even if he *was* my husband. Does he know you're in New York?"

"I'm having a night-cap if nobody else is," was Caroline's answer to this, pretending not to notice Lorna's slight attack of coughing.

"I think it's about time," Lorna said, holding out her own glass.

Judy tucked her sketchbooks under her arm and marched to the door.

"So long, everybody," she said, and walked out, not really minding that none of them suspected or would even believe she was Murray's girl, the only one of them with a right to the room, and the right to wait for him. She did not care that they were chattering at such a pace they did not bother to call her back, but she did mind the thought that Murray would be glad to find Gerda there, trouble and all, and she did mind the prospect of his sarcastic irritability when Gerda would leave, as she always did. He would be upset all over again at having lost her and angry at Judy for just being herself. He would get over it as he had the other times but it would be bad for a while. That was the only thing that hurt Judy and made her clench her fists turning the corner of Greenwich, longing to kill Gerda. There was not even a mischievous consolation in the thought that Murray, blithe as he might be in some tavern at this moment, was sooner or later coming home to a hornet's nest.

8

. . . the banquet-beagles . . .

*F*REDERICK may have learned a technique for
ignoring Judy in the apartment, but there was no possibility of ignoring Gerda. She assumed the role of charming
hostess who must urge the shy houseguest to join them on
all occasions. She insisted on bringing a tray of rather bad
coffee and a brioche in to him in the morning. She borrowed his victrola to play her new Mexican dance records.
When Murray went to his office she chose to sit in Frederick's room, sitting cross-legged on the floor sewing up
her costumes for dance recitals never to be given. "You
look so lonely," she explained. He did not dare invite
Lyle to visit him because Gerda knew too many of the
Gaynor friends. He was increasingly anxious to clear up
the misunderstanding with Lyle for she represented his
whole outside life, apart from his work. He knew she was
still hurt and knew also that they needed only a quiet
evening in each other's arms to banish their wounds. He
began to hate Gerda as the obstacle to this peace of mind,
just as Judy hated him for the same reason, and when
Gerda finally did depart for her own place he could barely
bring himself to say goodbye. The minute the door closed
on her—gayly ordering a subdued, unhappy Murray to
carry down her Mexican drums—he telephoned Lyle to
come over. They rushed into each other's arms as if their
separation had been six years instead of six days, and in
a little while both were laughing helplessly over the Dodo
incident. How naïve Lyle had been, for all her worldly
wisdom, not to have known his horror of the type!

"A pooh-on-you girl!" he reproached her. "You might have known how scared I was of her. Good God, darling, give me credit for choosing a more worthy rival for you than that."

"I was an idiot," Lyle freely admitted. "It's what always happens when I try *not* to be an idiot. Forgive me, darling."

It was a pity their reconciliation had to be cut short by Frederick's classes at the League for this was the night when he taught from 7 to 11. He would have to come to her apartment off Washington Square around midnight if he was to see her again before tomorrow, and this would be unsatisfactory because the Beckleys would be there. Allan Gaynor, being an invalid, had company around constantly even if Lyle herself was not entertaining. Lyle's home was never anything to Frederick but a reminder of all the barriers between them, and particularly when filled with the Gaynors' joint friends, emphasizing the indestructibility of marriage and the hopelessness of love.

Shying away from this basic problem as he always did, Frederick chose to direct his irritation at the League which had prevented him from enjoying at least an hour more of Lyle's company. It had depressed him almost from the very start but there had been nothing else for him to do. Now, on his way there, it occurred to him that he no longer needed that money. He pondered over the possibility of getting out of his contract and the nearer he got to the building the more odious everything it represented seemed to him, and the more imperative it was for him to leave it. "League for Cultural Foundations," he found himself muttering aloud savagely. "That's America for you. Words. Meaningless words!" The League seemed suddenly the whole basis for his quarrel with Lyle. It was the barrier between them. It was a dragon to be destroyed, though he was obliged to admit that leaving Lyle out of the question, it was a mighty monster in its own right.

It was as lecturer in the English Department that Frederick Olliver was connected with the League, receiving his rent-money in exchange for classes four hours a week in Contemporary Novel, International Literary Progress, Classic Reading, and Poetry. Four hours had seemed a small price to pay for a roof over his head with the rest of the week free for his own work, but after a while he had a desperate feeling that he was being bribed to distribute cancer. The only assuaging thought was that no one in his classes would have known the difference between cancer and culture anyway, and if they had had the hazards of achieving the latter explained to them would gladly have chosen the former.

The League for Cultural Foundation occupied a brownstone house in the West Twenties, specifically to the west of the feather belt, an area where the Hudson Dusters had appropriately enough once dominated. If the neighborhood's Polish bars rang out with slivovitch cheer far into the dawn, there was the cultural balance of Lily Langtry's historic residence and of a great poem ("Twas the Night Before Christmas") having been penned almost within blotting distance of the school. Distinguished members of the faculty might have to wade through truck-loads of aigrettes, plumes, coq feathers and peacock tails to get to their missionary tasks, but at least they were within walking distance of a Cavanagh steak and could pay calls after class on pleasant little couples in London Terrace or on eccentric celebrities flapping their bat wings through the monastic stained glass corridors of the Hotel Chelsea. If visiting savants occasionally paused to wonder exactly what they were accomplishing by the exhibition rather than the sharing of their intellectual wealth they were reassured by the knowledge that New York's most publicized cultural leader, Tyson Bricker, was the nominal head, the thing that made the League tick.

And tick is what the League did. It had begun ticking long before the war backed by an anonymous millionaire, with small classes of ambitious under-educated young office-workers who craved a conversational mask for their deficiencies without the labor of basic correction. During the war the classes bulged with middle-aged students anxious to get an idea of what it would be like to have an idea; servicemen's wives resolved to be prepared in case their warrior husbands had learned something suddenly; out-of-town teachers on brief cosmopolitan vacations anxious to thrust one toe in the ocean of fine arts. There were courses in Radio Appreciation, Radio Gag Writing, Radio Advertising; Contemporary Art Appreciation (involving the memorizing of names and addresses of art galleries, art critics, current exhibitions, and review quotes). In the Music Department business men, who had found tone deafness and absence of musical sense a handicap in salesmanship, were taught self-control during concerts and the names of composers. Students who could read music took courses in arranging, learning to disguise familiar songs by contrapuntal twists, since it was typical of the age that actual creative composition was impossible and therefore undesirable. In the field of literature were short courses in ghost-writing, short short writing, serial suspense, and contemporary novel-writing. The last-named involved a careful survey of the Sunday book review magazines and keeping up with guest authors on radio programs for inside information.

It was during his ten o'clock Novel class that Frederick made up his mind to see Tyson Bricker that very night and ask for release from his contract. His new duties at Straffords' took up his time, he intended to say, and between the League and *Haw* he foresaw himself being driven to either mass murder or suicide. He looked around the classroom objectively, feeling better now that he proposed to leave it, but marvelling afresh that so many grown-up, self-supporting people should be eager to spend time and money studying not a subject in itself but methods to conceal their ignorance of it. Some of them travelled hours on the subways from far-ends of boroughs for this evening of Books, but so far as he knew not a one of them read anything but *Lil Abner* and *Bruce Gentry*. To open a book with intent to read was as preposterous as to actually go into the Metropolitan Opera House instead of happily standing outside watching the suckers go in. Frederick had soon given up any effort to change this state, merely giving assignments and conducting symposiums. Listening now to the discussion which he had cleverly put in the hands of an ambitious young salesman, he discovered that one man did read at least enough to interfere with the others' pleasure in learning.

"Now what did you think of that new book *The West Waits* by that fellow Nackley, Miss Corey?" Frederick heard the chairman ask.

"It was long-winded and not what the public expected of Nackley," Miss Corey stated. "It didn't live up to the promise of his other book, *The Nevada Moon,* at least not to me. That's what the New York *Times* said."

"I agree!" declared a solemn young man in dark glasses. "I read the *Eagle.*"

"I liked it," said the fat overgrown ex-sailor from Sunnyside. "I liked it fine. I read the book."

Chairman and class glared at the interruption.

"It was pretentious, too, the style," said the chairman severely. "The New York *Tribune* said Nackley evidently was not aware what has been going on in the West today. Nackley's no Kenneth Roberts, either. The *Tribune* and *Times* both said that."

"I liked it," said the fat boy placidly. "I read the book. I read Kenneth Roberts, too. I liked him fine."

"I suppose you'd set up your opinion against the nation's leading critics," the chairman said sarcastically. "I don't need to read the book to know it isn't up to standard, at least not to us studying here at the League."

It was clear that the book-reader was throwing a monkey wrench into the literary discussion of review-readers, and it was equally clear to Frederick, if it had not been ere this, that there was nothing he had to offer these earnest seekers. If the bluebird of happiness were offered to them they would still be searching for its prefabricated duplicate, forever prizing the mechanical simulation to the unpriced, unmotored, therefore cheap reality. Unable to endure more, Frederick stole out into the hall and lit a cigarette. On the stair-landing a door had been cut from the League's house into the adjoining loft-building where larger classes were held, and he saw on the door a placard announcing that Tyson Bricker's class, "Motion Picture Criticism," was in progress. He might catch him at the close of this class. He wondered how Bricker "packaged" his motion picture culture, decided to listen in on him, and stepped inside the class-room. This course being Bricker's only class, was such a favorite that the room was packed with standees—some using their neighbors' backs as desks for note-taking. Tyson, trim, gray-haired, well-dressed, gray pinstriped suit, black tie, black cigarette holder, was giving his class an example of critical ease by lounging in a large red leather easy-chair, coffee-table with silver pot and cup beside him and a disarming absence of textbooks or notes. A young lady in a stupendous pompadour, was summarizing a current picture.

"So she thinks if that's the way he feels about it she'll just drop out of his life, so she takes a job in the department store to support herself and the child. All the time he doesn't know the child is his, he doesn't even know where she is and he's through with her anyway because he thinks she's bad after he saw her in the nightclub with Ricky Moller, the gangster; so he throws himself into his work and never will have anything to do with any women because the way he feels is that they're all no-good. Finally, the head of the department store falls in love with her but she won't have anything to do with him because she still loves the father of her child, but he doesn't know he is. Finally at the airport a call comes to rush some serum to a sick child, a dying child, and he is supposed to fly the governor personally to some big affair but instead he gives up the honor to another pilot and he jumps into the only plane left and the fellows all say, 'You can't fly that old crate,' but he says, 'A child's life is worth taking a chance,' and he flies the old crate with the serum and all the time it's his own child and she forgives him and quits work in the store."

"Your summary has occupied just twelve minutes longer than the picture itself," Tyson said in his pleasant Hoosier voice. "And you offer no criticism."

"I didn't read any," explained the student. "You didn't tell us to read any this week."

"You can take mine down and then read it," Tyson said, smiling. "Write down 'A touching story of a mother's sacrifice and of a man who found himself. An old story, but perennially true, perennially moving.' "

Frederick wondered whether Tyson was only kidding his class or whether an occupational disease derived from dusty clichés had affected his brain. A bell rang dismissing the class, and Frederick backed into a corner to allow the earnest pack to follow the scent through the halls to other troughs of wisdom. Just then he felt a hand tugging at his sleeve.

"Hello, there, you," said a girl.

He did not recognize the child in orange sweater, brown corduroy slacks, beaver jacket carelessly hanging over one shoulder, tight pigtails swinging. But the tilt of her head and the mocking half-smile and twinkle were familiar. Dodo, of course. He was surprised to find himself almost relieved to see her, perhaps because she seemed a normal note in a phoney world. She smiled up at him impishly.

"You're mad at me because I went off with those other men that night," she accused him. "I think you're mean. I've got to have a *little* fun, haven't I, when I may have to go back to Baltimore any minute?"

To assure her that her departure that evening had been a pleasure would have served no good purpose, so Frederick countered by asking how she happened to be at the League.

"I'm trying to get a job in a broadcasting studio and Tyson thought this would be good for me," she said. "But I haven't met a soul so far who could do me any good. The students are all *terrible*. So tacky, honestly. Tell you what.

You can take me to the Barrel for one teentsy night-cap but no more, not unless you'll be fun."

Frederick politely explained that he was to discuss a business matter with Tyson Bricker and would have to forego the privilege she suggested. At that moment Tyson saw him and came over.

"How do you like our little school-girl, Olliver?" Tyson asked, lightly spanking Dodo. "Pretty sharp-looking, I think. One of these days I'm going to keep her after school. How about a minute's chat, Olliver? Let's just step in my office a sec and then we'll go."

"I did want to see you," Frederick said.

Frederick had been wondering how Dodo could be disposed of, fearing her ability to attach herself, but it was evident that Tyson knew how to handle these problems. Tyson must have to brush off eager students every day.

"Darn business!" he exclaimed ruefully. "Why do we have to work, Olliver, when we ought to be taking this sweet kid out for a good time?"

"Can't I talk business, too?" Dodo asked plaintively.

"With that pretty little puss?" Tyson chucked her under the chin. "We'd bore you to death, sweetie."

"Pooh on you," said Dodo merrily, and wagged a finger at Frederick. "You too, Mr. Stuffy. Be seeing you."

She scampered down the hall, blowing impudent kisses at them. Tyson handled that neatly, Frederick thought enviously; Tyson could handle anything. Everybody could handle simple problems better than Frederick Olliver.

The two men came to the general offices behind the lecture room to the door on which was the name "*TYSON BRICKER*," as it was on the door of at least a dozen other offices in the city, for he was publishers' consultant, broadcasting adviser, promotion director of universities, newspapers, magazines and liberal organizations. On banquet menus the name TYSON BRICKER was as familiar as fruit-cup. Colleagues, without his gift for "mixing," declared that Tyson could smell a business dinner with its opportunity for a speech and publicity a thousand miles away. He was, they claimed, what Ben Jonson called a banquet-beagle. Since the ambition of the League's students was to become small-time banquet-beagles he served a special purpose as model. Uncertain as to what was his prime qualification for this career but having sublime faith that it was all exterior, some students copied his vocal inflections, some followed his example of black or orange ties with gray suits, and some gave up the natural lethargic shuffle of youth for his jaunty middle-aged swagger.

Frederick had noticed a dozen Bricker imitators in the halls as they went into his office. Although it was after ten a desperate looking elderly secretary was frantically typing in the outer office, and handed Bricker a sheaf of messages as he came in.

"That's a nice kid, that Dodo," Tyson observed, glancing carelessly at the notes as if they were the usual fan mail. "Money running out, so she's trying to get some kind of foothold here so she won't have to go back to her folks in Baltimore. Lives in dinky hotel room, drugstore lunches, beaux buy dinner, you know the struggle. Must be from pretty good people or she wouldn't have been invited to the Beckleys'—that's where I met her. I've tried to be nice to her on that account. Like to know Beckley better myself. That's right, I met you there, too."

"I think I remember the evening," Frederick said. Obviously, Lyle had been right insisting that he come to the Beckleys'. It must have been the reason for Bricker's sudden interest in him.

One memo roused Tyson's interest, and he begged Frederick to have a seat while he made a call. Nice kid waiting for him to telephone, didn't want to disappoint her. He slicked back his gray hair, adjusted tie and quizzical smile as he picked up the telephone.

"Hello, sweet thing," he said into the transmitter. "About time you called me, young lady! Now let's see when I can take you out to dinner—wait a minute, Miss Wells is right here. What about Wednesday—no, I'm talking at the News Editors Banquet at the Waldorf that night." (Miss Wells handed him a notebook which he leafed through rapidly, stopping abruptly at something the sweet kid was saying.) "What's that? You can't go out to dinner anyway? You're married now? Oh, you mean that nice kid in the Marines is back? Well, hooray for you. . . . Why, honey, I don't know of anything at CBS that he could do right now. Let me think it over. Nice of you to think of me, Gertrude. So long."

Tyson was fifty-two and had been spoiled by the war into believing that young girls really adored him. It still baffled him that the sweet kids who used to rhumba and jump for balloons with him at the Stork Club now called him up only to get jobs for their returned soldiers. It made him throw his weight very vigorously on the side of bigger armies and more wars. He had been such an industrious fellow all his life that he had only begun having fun in his forties, and the best part of it was taking sweet kids out dancing or sipping champagne, laughing at old codgers on the dance floor being made fools of by young girls. He disliked heavy drinking but did not mind getting a little tiddly over champagne, providing it was in gay, youthful company, and he found naughty stories, if broad enough, utterly irresistible. His essays into domesticity had not been successful. He usually had one wife packed up ready to go and one ready to step in. Since his official ménage was an estate far up the Hudson he saw it only seldom so that his marriages never interfered with the gay bachelor life he led in New York.

The little telephone interchange brought a little wrinkle of annoyance to Tyson's brow and he pored busily over papers on his desk to cover his momentary deflation. Frederick thought he detected a slight venomous smile on the thin lips of the elderly secretary, a smile that vanished the minute Tyson recovered his poise.

"Those darn kids!" he laughed, looking up at Frederick with a rueful shake of the head. "I love 'em, I do, I love 'em, but what a lot of trouble they can be! Ah me! Just another sec here, Olliver, and I'll be with you. Get out that Olliver manuscript, will you, Miss Wells?"

With considerable surprise Frederick saw Miss Wells place on the desk the red-bound manuscript of his own book. He knew that Strafford had spoken of having outside readings of it by learned authorities but he had not thought that even Strafford would deem Tyson Bricker a competent medievalist. Evidently Bricker was all things to all learning. Scornful though he was of the man's opportunism Frederick did believe in his beagling ability, and his being able to nose out quarry in any terrain no matter how unfamiliar. He accepted and lit the cigarette Tyson handed him.

"A fine job you've done here, Olliver," Tyson now stated gravely. "Strafford called me in for a consultation on his spring list, you see. I doubt if anyone with the possible exception of Helen Waddell could have handled your subject more sensitively. It's an outrage that you're not more appreciated. The years you've put into this sort of research, but who knows it? I was telling Strafford what a crying shame it is that a man of your caliber can do fine work all through life and never be recognized, while any little flash-in-the-pan with only one-hundredth your ability but with the human touch, let's say, is all over the place."

Nothing is more nettling than to be told you are unappreciated, and likely to be so all your life, so Frederick made no response to what his colleague seemed to feel was a pretty compliment. He restrained an impulse to retort that it was only Mr. Bricker's own lack of appreciation that made him think it universal, and that there were thousands far better equipped than he to appreciate Olliver. So far as that was concerned Olliver had admirers in far places where Mr. Bricker's own glossy name could never penetrate. But Tyson had meant well, as his warm friendly smile indicated. He beamed at Frederick with the honest affection one could feel toward a man who will never be a rival, a man one is sure will never be anything but a distinguished failure, a man one can praise freely and honestly without danger of sending him zooming up the ladder ahead of oneself. Frederick read all this in the fond smile and thought he would be able to feel encouraged about his future only when such people as Bricker snarled at him. He had misgivings already concerning the publication of his book, picturing the grave conferences between Strafford and Bricker, the repeated protestations of reverence for such scholarship, such fine prose; the lamentations over the vulgarity of the reading public, the noble statements that the dissemination of such work would constitute their life work had they only their own tastes to think of; then the solemn reminder of their practical duties as publisher and as teacher-critic to the underprivileged public (which had a right to "escape reading" regardless of literary standards), and to the masses whose tastes must be fed; finally, the mournful decision that the luxury of pandering to their fine personal predilections must be denied them; the Olliver book must be put aside if not abandoned altogether to some more selfish and fortunate firm.

"It struck me that a foreword in a popular vein might help a little to put it over," Tyson went on. "I'd be glad to do what I could in view of our association together here at the League. We can come to some arrangement if you like the idea."

Frederick was mystified by this offer, as well as embarrassed. He needed no foreword but would have felt bound to have one, if any, by Edward Stalk in whose magazine some of the material had been printed. As Stalk and Bricker were firm enemies he did not mention this but murmured his thanks evasively.

"I only wish I could take time off and do my own book, my Jane Austen," Tyson sighed, picking up his hat and giving a final wave which combined Miss Wells and his cluttered desk as if the two would merge magically into order. Tyson was famous for his passion for Jane Austen whom he quoted in every possible connection,

though he had not read her for twenty years and if he
ever should do so again would be astonished at what he
did not know about her, and at the number of sagacious
things she had never said. However, it was a dignified
harmless passion and entitled the distinguished fan to
write introductory paragraphs to many works on the lady.
These volumes were all listed as "Bricker's Austen,"
and the card catalogue in the Forty-second Street Public
Library had a dozen Austen and Bricker cards cross-
filed quite as if he had already made his definitive study.

"What I was about to suggest, Olliver," Tyson said
as they came out on Eighth Avenue, "was that you take
on a few more classes at the League, to tide you over.
That sort of book won't ever sell, as you know. Mrs.
Gaynor was saying to me the other day . . ."

"I couldn't possibly," Frederick answered. Had Lyle
been trying to help the poor failure again? He had not
told her yet about his job on Strafford's magazine because
he was half-ashamed, but now he told Bricker about it
defiantly, suddenly proud that he could be considered
as cleverly corruptible as the next one and not too un-
worldly to do some purveying to the masses on his own
hook. A little wildly he informed Tyson that *Haw* was
a certain success judging by the first issue he had gotten
out, that he expected to make a great deal of money out
of it inasmuch as Strafford was giving him an interest in
it, and that he had no need of being "tided over" in
spite of Mrs. Gaynor's thoughtful suggestion. To Tyson's
exclamation of astonishment that he could do such work,
Frederick replied that he enjoyed it very much indeed,
that it was a satisfaction to be giving the reading popula-
tion the sort of thing it craved, and that with due deference to Tyson's idol, he doubted if even Jane Austen
could give the joy that *Haw*, with its murder stories,
raffish jokes and raucous cartoons, was giving. He expected Tyson to resent the veiled sarcasm, but instead
saw a look of awe in the other's eyes.

"That's the stuff! You've got your feet on the ground,

old boy!" Tyson said approvingly. "I had no idea you had that much common sense. By cracky, Olliver, I knew we would get on if we got to know each other. Why, I feel as if I knew you better in these last five minutes than in all the time you've been at the League! Look here, I have to pick up a dame at the Plaza at one-thirty, but I've got an hour or so to kill before then. What say we chop over to the Barrel for a highball first? I'd like to hear you talk more, Olliver, by George, I would."

That was how well he managed things, Frederick thought hopelessly. He wanted to insult someone and the fellow was entranced; he wanted to resign and was offered more work; he wanted peace and quiet with Lyle and was on his way to uproar at the Barrel. In a last spurt of protest he told Tyson he had to check on an engagement first. There was a bare chance that Lyle might now be alone. But when he stopped in the corner cigar store to telephone he was told by Pedro that Mrs. Gaynor had gone out. In a state of numb resignation he accompanied Tyson to the Barrel and there was Dodo, sitting alone at the bar, sipping a stinger. She was watching the door and waved eagerly as they entered.

"I just knew you two would come here!" she cried, patting the empty bar-stool beside her imperiously. "I told Al here I wasn't alone, didn't I, Al? I said I was waiting for someone. Wasn't I bright?"

Tyson lifted eyebrows toward Frederick in wry amusement.

"You were, indeed, you sweet thing," he said and motioned Frederick to a seat on the other side of Dodo. "Two Scotches and another stinger, Al. Say, it's pretty gay here tonight."

An old gentleman in a checked suit with a bowler hat and spats, handlebar moustache pasted under his nose, was dancing around the piano, wheezily singing *A Bicycle Built for Two.*

"New talent," Tyson said.

The bartender leaned forward confidentially.

"Know who that is? Rich old crackpot. Always comes in with a big party. Likes to rig himself up like that and pays the pianist to let him carry on. Let's see—what's his name, now?"

"I wish he'd stop," complained Dodo. "I want *Day by Day*. Go make him shut up, Freddie. Make him go sit down at his own table."

"Beckley, that's it," the bartender said. "Lexington Beckley. Quite a character around town."

"Beckley?" repeated Frederick with a vague premonition.

"Look, he's with Mrs. Gaynor's party over in the corner," Tyson exclaimed. "I think she sees us, Olliver. Let's go say hello."

In the bar mirror Frederick could see Lyle's eyes fixed on him with an expression of hurt bewilderment. Of course it looked queer for her to find him with the very girl he had explained away a bare four hours before. But she would surely believe it was an accident even if she might not see the humor of it. He followed Tyson over to the corner booth where Lyle sat with half a dozen of the inner Beckley circle. She barely spoke to him and his case was not helped by Tyson.

"Just the person I wanted to see, Mrs. Gaynor," he exclaimed. "Olliver and I have a little pupil from the League with us over there and I'll bet you know how we can get her a film job. Anything at all, just to get a foothold. Maybe a word from you at Paramount. I'm not in good favor there myself now. Dodo Brennan. That's the name."

"I'd be glad to speak to Evan about her," Lyle said sweetly. "I'm sure she'd make a good receptionist."

"Anything," Tyson said. "The poor kid just wants an in, isn't that so, Olliver?"

"I'll mention to Evan that you and Mr. Olliver cannot recommend her too highly for any position whatever," said Lyle.

"Good!" Tyson laughed. "Lucky for all of us we know

a big shot or two so we can help out some of these sweet kids."

"Lucky for them, too," said Lyle.

She was flushed with anger and her flashing eyes refused to see Frederick, and as she addressed herself in a low voice to Tyson there was no opportunity to explain that Dodo's presence was not part of a mischievous plan. Dodo was beckoning from the bar and Lyle pointedly called Frederick's attention to this. Desperately he leaned over Cordely Beckley's head and said to her, "Perhaps I can walk home with you when you're ready to leave."

"My goodness, I wouldn't dream of taking you away from your little protégé," Lyle answered brightly. "She'd never forgive you."

"Tomorrow, then," Frederick murmured, growing hot with anger at Lyle's unfair condemnation of him on circumstantial evidence.

"Tomorrow?" Lyle repeated, frowning, and then exclaimed, "Oh no, I'm flying down to the Beckleys' in Carolina with Allan for a couple of weeks. We're considering buying a place down there."

One of the younger Beckleys clapped her hands at this.

"Lyle's changed her mind! She's coming with us!" she cried.

Knowing why she had changed her mind Frederick could not speak for indignation. She was punishing him, in a high-handed, arrogant way that permitted no defense. She was strong in the midst of her special satellites, the people who protected her from him, the people who came first. She was reminding him again that the "we" in her life meant Mr. and Mrs. Gaynor and that they were about to cement this invincible fort even further by new plans and home-buying that showed the indestructible harmony of their union and the insignificance of any intruder. She was revenging herself for his having, as she thought, deliberately chosen Dodo's company, and so far as that went why shouldn't he? She had her fine separate life with Allan, why shouldn't he have Dodo? Tyson had crowded into the seat beside Lyle but Frederick was still standing. He bowed goodnight stiffly to Lyle and ignored the others just as rudely as they were ignoring him. Lyle looked icily past him without response, and he stalked back to the bar. He made no move when Dodo tugged at his sleeve and squeezed his hand. She hung her head looking up at him sidewise, mockingly, thick black lashes quivering like legs on a green spider.

"You're a bad boy leaving me all alone," she pouted. "Don't you know you can't run away from me like that, you old naughty?"

"I'm afraid that's true," he said.

After Lyle's injustice the little dove hand in his seemed friendly and consoling. It was Lyle who had forced this situation on him, he thought bitterly. Tyson had helped, but it was primarily all Lyle's fault. Not his. Not Dodo's. He and Dodo were the wronged ones.

"Let's get out of here," he said explosively.

"Let's," agreed Dodo, jumping off the stool eagerly.

As they went out the door he felt a rush of mingled elation and fright as if his ship had just lost sight of land.

9

... young Olliver ...

"**L**ET'S go to someplace like the Stork Club," said Dodo, "Let's celebrate."

She sat on Frederick's day-bed combing her hair as casually as if nothing had happened. With her bare legs thrust in high-heeled black sandals and her tight black satin dress accentuating whatever curves were not exposed she looked like an *Esquire* picture, Frederick thought. What on earth is an *Esquire* picture doing in this somber, book-lined room, he wondered? And very much at home she was, too, full of suggestions as to changes in furniture and curtains. He laughed indulgently over her criticisms of the Bracque drawing over his fireplace, allowed her to boast of a cousin of hers in Salisbury, Maryland, who was the best artist she ever knew and who had had things in the school paper that everybody said were better than anything in New York. Everything she did not understand, such as the Bracque and his article in the *Swan* magazine made her feel personally affronted. But Frederick only chuckled, for she was a mere child, after all. For the same reason he did not refuse sarcastically her desire to celebrate, as he would have, had the suggestion come from Lyle. After all, he had to remember that Dodo was young, and an outsider, with the natural curiosity of both. It occurred to him that an excursion into the night world he loathed might have a certain piquancy if one was in the role of guide to a naïve stranger. He had been forced to accompany Lyle on some occasions and his position as nobody in the wake of a glittering group was no pleasure. The experience had its value, however, for at least he knew his way around, that was something.

"Turn your back while I dress," he commanded Dodo.

"Why should I turn around?" Dodo wanted to know. She twisted her hair over her neck with one hand, and pulled the spangled net over it. "You have a terribly nice body, much better than other men your age."

Never having thought about his body, and never having anticipated compliments on it from a young woman he knew only in bed, Frederick smiled. The implication that Dodo was familiar with many other male bodies, far from disturbing him, made him feel safe and even flattered, for it showed he was not unique in surrendering to this particular temptation.

"I'll have to find a decent shirt," he muttered. Lucky he had his salary in his pocket, shirt or no shirt, for Dodo took for granted that he was a man of means. Oddly enough he liked this, too, for the misconception was more flattering than Lyle's thoughtful consideration for his poverty.

"You're so poky! It's midnight already!" Dodo scolded.

She smoothed out the bed, arranged the red corduroy couch cover. While Frederick was pulling out one drawer after another she impatiently searched through the clothes closet. He could not help an inward amusement at himself for his pleasure over what would normally seem an invasion of his privacy.

"You silly man, here's a whole box of shirts!" she cried out. "All brand new and expensive! I should think that a man who went to all the trouble of buying shirts like these would certainly remember them! Honestly, Freddie! Just look! They must have cost you plenty!"

She had found Lyle's gift and it was no time to explain that he had intended returning them as soon as Lyle got back. But Dodo's awe over his possession of such luxuries changed his mind. It would only have added insult to the injury he was already doing Lyle, he reflected. Rejecting them would be a disagreeable and unnecessary gesture, he thought, the sort he could never control. He was always ashamed of the angry pride that was his curse, that always hurt himself as much as it did Lyle. Now he experienced surprised gratitude to Dodo for saving him from another humiliating expression of his weakness. Of course he would keep the gift.

Dodo had on her coat and had fastened the gardenias he had bought her at dinner in her dark hair. She was all impatience to be off and skipped out to the hall. While he tied his tie—a present from Lyle—Dodo attempted a tap dance before the hall mirror. He knew Murray and whoever else was in the front could hear her and would know it was not Lyle. This pleased him. He wondered why he had always been so secretive, almost ashamed, of his one great love, and now so proudly exhibitionistic of its betrayal. He wanted everyone to know he was not that vulnerable figure, a faithful lover, but a normal, regular fellow unhampered by any civilized emotions—carefree, uncapturable, faithless. Instead of tiptoeing out discreetly he made no effort to lower his voice. "Haven't you ever been to the Stork Club, Dodo?"

"Oh yes, Larry's taken me everyplace," Dodo answered impatiently. "But he always passes out. Besides I want to go with someone that knows who's who, like you do."

In the vestibule he pulled her to him and kissed her cool cheek.

"Let's go back," he whispered.

"Oh, Freddie, don't be silly!" Dodo expostulated, drawing away. "You promised we could go someplace and have fun!"

"Then come back afterwards and stay for breakfast," he urged.

"Maybe," Dodo shrugged. "Don't crush my gardenias, please!"

It was one of the amazing things about the new self Dodo had awakened in him that he was not at all embarrassed to be caught by Caroline Drake who came out of Murray's door at that moment. He was grateful again to Dodo, for release from his idiotic shyness. Caroline inordinately redolent of Shalimar and fine Bourbon, was so surprised she looked twice.

"Why, Mr. Olliver, for goodness' sake!" she exclaimed in bewilderment. "I didn't recognize you."

Aware of having been clumsy she dashed out to the street in great confusion.

"She heard you ask me to stay for breakfast," Dodo said resentfully. "You shouldn't say things in front of people. They might talk about me."

"Nonsense!" Frederick laughed.

It struck him that he laughed a lot for a man whose great love affair had crashed a bare two weeks ago. He had always felt that if Lyle were ever to forsake him he would die, but instead he felt as if he had just come to life. It was as if he had suddenly been admitted to The Club, and was from now on privy to secrets of which he had never even dreamed, secrets that all other men had always known. The first time Dodo had spent the night with him had revealed a new world and a new self and had shocked him with the awful thought that he might so easily have gone on forever without this simple knowledge. All his years with Lyle had given him not the faintest desire to be unfaithful. The very handicaps to their complete relationship—his all-absorbing work, her untouchable marriage, and her social and professional life, had made him want to keep perfect what half-portions he did have. But now he saw that he had been badly nourished, and it seemed to justify his surprising lack of conscience. Here at last was an affair that need not be hidden—he was a free man; Dodo was a free woman.

It was as if chains, gags, and blinders had been removed. He had no duty here to be respectful of her husband's name or her own public reputation, no need to conceal every natural feeling. He could ask her to take a trip with him, stay to breakfast, have dinner publicly with him every night since she had no husband or superior friends to be constantly appeased. With Dodo it was he who called the tune. He knew well enough that it was her picture of him as a person of importance that had made the easy conquest, but that bolstered his vanity even more. He scarcely thought of Lyle in the wonderful excitement of his new game, and when he did think of her it was to be glad she was away, glad she was angry with him, glad of anything that delayed the necessity of a decision. Above the marvel of discovery there was a wild jubilation of senses in merging with youth, a girl eighteen years his junior. He would have laughed scornfully at such a cliché until it happened to him. Actually the extraordinary delight of their love-making had nothing to do with physical or emotional fulfillment, being more tantalizing than satisfying. For Dodo it was a sexual triumph over Fame, for Frederick it was a triumph over Youth. It left him exhilarated for days afterward, eager to get up in the morning to begin savoring the memory and the anticipation. Everything had new vitality and flavor. The sun shining, the taste of coffee or cigarettes, the sound of a song in the street, the simplest sensations elated him. He had always had a detached literary curiosity about strangers he passed; now he was moved to ecstasies of appreciation of all mankind. The lethargic, gloomy janitor of the block saying, "Looks like the government is having its troubles same as us common folks," made Frederick ponder with delight on the exquisite rightness, the absolute Americanism of the working-man. When he crossed the Square at Eleventh Street, usually a hazardous, infinitely annoying venture, he paused now to contemplate with something approaching glee the stately disorder of the street arrangements, the possible mischief in the minds of the city planners. He saw his own street and his own apartment as if for the first time, with admiring surprise. It was odd that his heady glow had no effect on his original picture of Dodo, as he had seen her that first night with Murray at the Barrel. It was odd that he could be so enchanted by her yet retain his reservations complete in a separate compartment of his consciousness. He found her conversation as commonplace as on first meeting, and speculated (with amusement now instead of with impatient hostility) on how she was able to fancy herself an irresistible wit. It surprised him mildly that the vibrant youthful nervousness of her physical movements should be combined with such a rusty mental machinery. Though any sudden glimpse of her gave him quick delight it did not persuade him of her superior beauty. Her breasts were too sharp and close together, he thought, her hair too coarse and sleek, her trimness a cause for approval without admiration. Whatever effect she had upon him had nothing at all to do with her qualifications. She could have been plainer and far more stupid without lessening her attraction for him. Yes, her very ignorance was flattering to him. It implied that his appeal to her was a basic male superiority which overshadowed the handicap of mere academic virtues. His new injection of youth made him notice girls on the street for the first time, contemplating the possibilities of adding even further to his new knowledge. His blood pounded when he thought of last night; he went through his day's work thinking of making love to her again. How curious, he thought, to have thrown open every door to this stranger when he had kept so much of himself from Lyle! Dodo boldly pranced from Murray's quarters to his, and Frederick sensed that he was going up in Judy's estimation as a result. He was a regular fellow, now, like Murray. The news, relayed to Dodo by Judy, that Frederick had a serious secret affair made him all the more valuable to Dodo. The third time she stayed with him she hinted of marriage, and it pleased Frederick to be laughingly evasive, as other blades were, on this sacred point. From his pleasure at her pouting hints he realized how unhappy he had been at having the mere idea of marriage closed to him for so long; he could not marry Lyle, he could not marry any one else. He wilfully kept Lyle out of his mind quite aware that there would come a day soon enough when decisions must be made. He felt that each minute until then must be devoured greedily and in a vague way hoped and feared that perhaps the delirium would have vanished before the day of reckoning could come. Had the memory of his first meeting

with Lyle faded or was it really true he was now happy
for the first time? Dodo's dates with Larry, her coy allusions to mysterious other suitors did not stir him at all
for he seemed to feel no jealousy, just simple sensual
delight in whatever he gained. Her idea of being amusing
was to ridicule him in public but this, too, flattered him,
as if dignity was a chaperon well lost. She was irritable
after their love-making, for his immense delight made her
suspect she had given away something worth more than
she realized. But Frederick was not hurt by her peevish
jibes, his senses still singing of his triumph.

At the Stork Club—he must certainly be bewitched to
have consented to such folly—he saw that the producer
of Lyle's play was entering behind them. If he had been
with Lyle he would have kept haughtily aloof, seething
with resentment at having to share her with these professional admirers, contemptuous of the respectful flurry
their presence made around other diners. Now, he was
relieved to be recognized by the man for he was awarded
a good table on the strength of the association.

"Why didn't you introduce me?" Dodo whispered, as
they followed their waiter across the floor. "You're so
mean, Freddie!"

Everything about the place reeked of the life Lyle
led, the people she knew, of the things he had never
understood and therefore disliked which meant so much
to her. Tonight, however, he was glad to be able to name
the figures Dodo pointed out.

"It's just like being at a show—especially when you
know who everybody is!" Dodo exclaimed and squeezed
his hand gratefully. It suddenly struck him as strange
to be sitting on the outside enjoying the show instead
of being part of it and bored. For a second he was not
sure he liked the new role but Dodo's hand persuaded
him.

"Look!" Dodo cried out. "Do make him come over
here!"

Frederick saw Tyson Bricker, resplendent in the gayest

of evening sportwear with a group nearby. Tyson's reverent manner indicated that he was with very valuable contacts indeed and his smile of recognition was of the vague preoccupied sort usually intended to keep lesser lights at bay.

"Tell him to come over with us," Dodo insisted. "He's an old friend of yours, isn't he? He likes me, too. Waiter, tell the gentleman at that table I want to speak to him."

"No—" Frederick interrupted hastily, then stopped. Why not? Dodo had as much right to express herself as Tyson Bricker did. But Tyson merely smiled evasively at them and appeared absorbed in some compelling discussion. Very different, Frederick thought sardonically, from the times when Tyson spotted Lyle Gaynor. Then he would have attached himself to her table for the evening. In a fit of petulance at the slight Dodo was ready to get up and accept a drunken stranger's invitation to dance, till Frederick remonstrated.

"I don't see why I can't have some fun even if you don't dance," she sulked. She was further aggravated by being absent in the Powder room at the time Tyson chose to come over to their table.

"I'm with Cham Bellaman, you know," he explained. "Just bought the Barton publications. By the way, they say the Gaynors are expected back Saturday. Give them my regards, will you? I see you're taking charge of our little student. Sweet kid."

But he was gone by the time the sweet kid got back, and she was only appeased by being told Cham Bellaman himself had been with Tyson.

"He was all over last week's *Life*," she marvelled. "And I didn't even recognize him!"

The mere mention of fine names had subdued her. When her old friend Larry, from the K. G. R. Agency started toward them Dodo was feeling so superior that she murmured, "Let's not let Larry join us. He gets so noisy he'll spoil everything!"

"Hey, you people!" Larry called out, pushing past

tables toward them with a determination that knocked chairs and glasses to the floor. "What are you doing here?"

"I don't have to wait for you to take me places, Larry," Dodo said haughtily. "I know other men, plenty of them."

"So I see," Larry amiably replied. "Where's old Murray? Is he here too? What say we tool down to the Barrel for a night-cap?"

"Too tired, Larry," Dodo said. "Why don't you go on home, yourself? You're really disgusting!"

"So my wife was just saying," Larry agreed and shook Frederick's hand a second time fervently. "Not so disgusting as I'd like, hey, fella? You know, Dodo, I like this guy. He's alright. I like that deadpan of his. Shake, old boy."

Frederick shook.

"So that's your wife," Dodo observed, frowning across the room. "I notice you didn't get as good a table as we did. Freddie knows people, that's why. Come on, Freddie, let's go home. Freddie don't have any wives to keep us here, thank goodness."

"Good deal!" Larry laughed genially. "Well, so long as they keep us, hey, fella?"

"Pooh," said Dodo coldly. "I wouldn't advise you to be humorous, Larry. Goodnight."

When they got into the taxicab Frederick discovered that the outing had made Dodo highly pleased with him. He was glad now, that he had been trained, however reluctantly, by Lyle to know the way around in such places, since it had set him up in Dodo's eyes. She hummed happily for a while, then snuggled into his arms and fell asleep like a kitten, her gardenias drooping over one eye and her arm tight around his neck. Frederick gave the driver his address with an exultant feeling that in his arms was something entirely his own, dominated by him, awed by him. It was a delicious sensation, unmarred even by Tyson's words flickering dimly in the back of his mind, "I hear the Gaynors get back Saturday."

10

. . . lesson in acting . . .

*T*HE joke was always on women, Lyle thought. Their lives have become too complicated to be managed either by reason or instinct. Each path blocks every other path and goals are reached only by blind luck. It seemed to her that all the problems of her own life were rushing together in a wild dance, riding her like trolls, their clamor drowning any single voice. Whenever Frederick had hurt her before, she had been glad of the refuge of hard work and the impersonal frivolity of the friends he despised. But this time, it was different. It was not only another woman, but the fact that he had cruelly and deliberately mocked her. He had made a fool of her, made her laugh over her suspicions as if they constituted a preposterous joke between them, and this was monstrous. It hinted at deep wells of sadistic evil in him; it tainted their entire past, made her doubt that love had ever existed. Bitter as she was towards her lover the weeks spent away from him at the Beckleys' Carolina place did nothing to restore her. All her worlds were shaken at once. Nature itself, turned enemy; the silence of country nights was sinister, made her fears roar the louder through her brain, and sleep was won only by nembutal, even that magic deserting before daybreak. Outside her window the forests of elms hoary with Spanish moss shuddered with windy prophesies of lovers betrayed, lovers dead, woe and desolate age to come. At the hour of dawn

103

there was a terrific tuning-up of song birds in tree and
barn but it was as meaningless as a press-agent's drum-
beating for the sun never really appeared. After the fan-
fare of color in the sky, the rose and orange clouds parted
for the favorite's entrance, but, like a spoiled star, one
peep told the golden one there were no photographers on
hand, no crowd really, so she retreated sulkily, drew the
bat-gray shades, let it be known she refused to go out in
public, was a recluse really. Gray days and chill mists
drove the Beckley guests to the idle pleasures of the
interior, but this was even more unsatisfactory than the
outdoors for at this moment when Lyle was so anxious
to find consolation with her own friends she was bewitched into seeing them as Frederick saw them. Ephraim,
making ponderous pronouncements on art once outrageously funny to her, now appeared as Frederick saw him—
a vain, stupid man presuming that an inherited fortune
entitled him to intellectual authority. There was Mrs.
Ephraim, so steeped in her Boston antecedents she had
needed no further education, coasting on her harmless
belief that the earth was pear-shaped, the Beckleys and
Boston at the big end, Art at the little stem. How could
she have tolerated them! And how right Frederick had
been in estimating their hollowness!

Their group of guests—talented folk since Ephraim
supported his father's belief that talent around meant free
and guaranteed entertainment—seemed only the lucky
gamblers Frederick had declared them to be. If Barlowe's
opera had not had Koussevitsky to make it the season's
talk who would have deferred to his banalities on politics?
If Everitt's novel had not been a best-seller who would
have considered his insults a sign of wit? Her lover had
stabbed her, Lyle thought, and had taken away her
anodyne besides. He had taken away, worse yet, the sense
of guilt which had given her patience with Allan. She
was suddenly tired of pretending Allan's perpetual jeers
at her conventional upbringing were an amiable family
joke. She hated their game of being Happy Couple. Allan

seemed now a selfish, egocentric burden, a burden that
Frederick, she realized now, had made possible for her
to bear. Angry at Frederick, disgusted with her husband
and her friends, Lyle stayed in her room pretending to
be working over the new play Sawyer was expecting from
them, but there was nothing in any corner of her mind
but speculations about Frederick. How many weeks,
months, maybe years, had he carried on with this girl?
And before that how many others were there? Always so
smug, she mocked herself, always so certain that it was
the same with him as it was with her. How did she know
what went on in his apartment when she was not there?
Murray, his companion, had dozens of women around.
No reason why Frederick might not have shared them.
It was true as Frederick had often complained, she recalled remorsefully, that they had had little time together actually. Her fault. Their moments were what was
left over from her full life, she forced herself to admit;
time she could spare from rehearsals, Allan's requirements, the things she put first, relying on Frederick's
taste for solitude since it convenienced her to do so. It
was convenient to be blind, convenient to believe their
love needed no reassurances, their understanding needed
no words.

Thinking of the person Frederick was revealing himself to be, Lyle wondered what else was to be found out,
how long had he despised her own talents for instance,
as he did those of her friends. He had always admired—
or *pretended* to admire—the way she made the puppets
in Allan's bare outlines into real people. It delighted
him, he had said, the same way improvisations on a musical theme delighted him. He had often urged her to
do a play entirely her own, but that would be the supreme
disloyalty to Allan. Allan had been her teacher. He had
opened every door to her, he had made her discover her
own self, he had applauded each step, staged her, plotted
her happiness the same way he plotted a play. When he
cracked up physically, and then for a frightening interval,

mentally, she had been able to repay him, never allowing him to give up, assuring him that his confinement did not lessen his value to their collaboration, though the worry of rehearsals, revisions, try-outs and casting was now entirely on her shoulders. Actually this was the best thing that could have happened, and resulted in their increasing success, for Lyle was thus given opportunity to humanize and twist the rigid conventional framework of Allan's plots. She always insisted on the superior importance of his share, however, and saw now with her newly disillusioned eyes that she had convinced him that almost any amateur could take over her contribution. It was Frederick's fault, she thought, during the cocktail hour with the company grouped around Allan's bed, that she noticed for the first time Allan's constant reference to *"my* last play," the play *"I'm* working on now." Of course he had said this for years, but now it seemed significant, part of the plot against her. Every one knew she did most of the work, of course—or did they?

"I must never take anything for granted again," Lyle thought.

The longer Allan delayed their return on the basis that they were working just the same as if they had been at home, the more her long-buried resentment towards him rose, the more detestable the Beckleys seemed, and the more dim her lover's guilt, until wild jealousy melted into mere sorrow. She could scarcely wait to see Frederick and tell him she forgave him, that she understood at last the loneliness of his position, the position in which her loyalty to Allan had placed him.

She knew these affairs were only trivial, she would say, and he could rely on her understanding because she was the one at fault, the one who had failed him. Then, on the plane coming up it occurred to her that again she was taking too much for granted. Perhaps this Dodo business was serious. Perhaps he would even admit as much. Unable to face such a possibility, Lyle decided to act as if nothing had happened. She would telephone him

for lunch and keep up a gay, friendly front, demanding
no explanations, leaving their course completely up to
him. That is, providing he did not suggest that their
paths separate. Facing the chance that he really might
want release, Lyle determined to show him that she asked
nothing, that everything would be conducted his way.
She would be casual, and if his manner revealed the
dreaded wish to be free she would plan a next meeting
with others present, his own friends, Edwin Stalk, say,
to reassure him.

The program was not so easily carried out. She telephoned him the night she arrived, thinking that he
might have been as wretched as she and want to see her
at once, all things forgotten. But there was an ominously
long pause between Murray's answer and Frederick's
voice. He sounded cool and enigmatic, as if he had taken
time to prepare a defense against her.

"I wanted to catch up on all that's been going on,"
she plunged. "Did you give up your League job the way
you planned?"

No, he had decided to fulfill his contract, Frederick
answered, and went into detail as to Bricker's new plans
for the League, and the advantage of seeing them through.
Lyle made haste to agree completely with the wisdom of
his decision, and Bricker's need to back his opportunistic
inspirations with other people's brains, as Frederick had
often said——

"Oh, Tyson's got brains, alright," said Frederick, all
contrariness, and Lyle quickly amended her remark,
changing the subject to the boredom of Carolina and
her discovery that the Beckley set was fully as dull as he
had said. Frederick appeared to relax at this concession,
and then struck a blow to her heart by saying, "You must
tell me all about it. What about having cocktails tomorrow?"

"Tomorrow?" she echoed stupidly. Tomorrow. Not tonight. Not this minute. But it was even worse as he went
on.

"What about meeting me at the Ritz, say, around six. You probably have a dinner somewhere later."

The Ritz. Not at his apartment, but in public so they must be casual. And at six instead of five because she might have a dinner date relieving him from enduring more than an hour or two with her. Very well, then.

"The Ritz is so quiet!" she protested. "If we're going to be so grand let's go to the Savoy Plaza. I've just spent three weeks in the quiet!"

She would out-do him in casualness.

"Very well," he said and was about to ring off but she could not let him go without saying, "I'll have to leave early because I've asked crowds in for dinner."

There! She thought, as flushed and breathless as if she had been boxing. There! She had not begged him to come to her dinner as she always had before, with invariably sarcastic or wry refusals from him. She had not told him who was coming so that he would have the opportunity to ridicule them, either amusingly or jealously. She had shown no surprise at the unprecedented extravagance of his invitation, nor asked what success had come his way to warrant the change of habit.

It was serious, she thought, and her heart seemed to rock in broken glass.

"I'll invite Edwin Stalk and Benedict Strafford to dinner," Lyle thought fiercely. "I'll invite every one he admires so he'll wish he had been here. I won't have any of the people he thinks I'll be having. He'll be surprised."

It was such a silly little consolation that she found herself laughing hysterically.

11

. . . the revenge on love . . .

AFTER living together for seven years and keeping a gentlemanly distance, Murray Cahill and Frederick Olliver were suddenly intimate friends. The reason for the new relationship was as justifiable as that for some marriages between antipodal personalities—that is, those involved had one major experience together: they were in the same hurricane, the same war, or the same spotlight at the same time. Murray was in a jam with women and conscience; so was Frederick. Murray was changing his routine; so was Frederick. Murray's difficulties made it necessary for him to avoid his usual midnight cronies but not his midnight habits. He found new bars, and sometimes sat around Umberto's or the Jai Alai bar, neither place being on his usual agenda. Frederick's habit had been to work in his room nights, but after his rebirth he had an aversion to returning to his cocoon. He looked back on his years of self-imposed isolation with wonder, and he did not want to be alone remembering the cause. Sometimes, when Dodo was punishing him for a few days, he wanted to stay home to await a possible call from her, but there was the other danger that Lyle might find him and he was still unwilling to face the issue. He could not bear to be cruel, he could not say no, he could not say yes, nor could he bear to promise renouncing Dodo. He wanted reckless flight, but he wanted no bridges burned. To postpone definite decision he kept out of his apartment at the hours Lyle used to

call and took to coming into Umberto's directly from
his office, lingering over some wine and a dinner. In the
usual manner of men sensitive to intrusion, he and
Murray pretended at first not to see each other in the
little restaurant. After four or five encounters, during
which they warily circled each other like strange dogs,
they found themselves at the same table, speaking of
general matters together, in due course approaching the
remotely personal, and after awhile having night-caps together in their apartment, tacitly ignoring door-bells or
telephone, providing alibis for each other. Men are
understood to be absolutely silent with each other on
personal matters but this is only when they are asked
direct questions. Then they remember that men never
talk, men never gossip, men never betray a friend—certainly not for such a small audience. But, unquestioned,
they are apt to reveal their own secrets as well as those
of their friends, and are goaded on to all sorts of incrimi-
nating revelations by a look of indifference in the listener's
eye.

Since Frederick showed no interest Murray revealed
that he was attempting to relieve himself of Judy's overwhelming devotion, and win back his wife, for no other
reason, he confessed, than that Gerda had been on his
mind so long he couldn't have any peace until he'd gotten
her back.

"I'm not in love with her any more, I don't think,"
he said as they sat before the fireplace in Frederick's
room with a cold winter dawn breaking outside, and hot
rum drinks thawing out their secrets. "I know she only
wants me around to bolster up her ego, and I've an idea
she sleeps with anybody that's around but maybe not.
But she got her hooks into me twenty years ago and
every time she takes them out it hurts so that I want
them back, that's all. I run around with other women
but it never leaves a dent. And Judy's a damned nuisance.
Damn it, I want an adult woman. You know when you're
a kid and playing around with the other guys, somebody's

always got a little sister tagging along that's always losing her didy or having to have her nose wiped or falling out of the tree so nobody can have any fun? Well, that's the way I feel about Judy. A young girl's a hell of a responsibility and when you try to pry 'em loose it's like getting chewing-gum off your shoe."

Frederick did not say that for his part it was more like trying to catch an eel in the open sea without even liking eels. He was the more sympathetic of Murray's predicament since he saw no beauty in either Gerda or Judy. And Murray was the more sympathetic towards Frederick since he regarded Dodo as a little tramp and an affair with a married woman of Lyle's professional preoccupations as very small pickings indeed. Frederick obligingly reassured his friend that he was not treating Judy badly by trying to ease her out. She was young, he said, wrapped up in her ambition, and it was doing her a decent service to make her free for marriage and a family. Murray was glad to hear this angle, which coincided with his own and hoped Judy would some day appreciate what he was doing for her. He made a point of having other people around the place as much as possible, and contrived to have Judy leave with them or faked an errand outside himself, but these tricks couldn't go on forever. As to Frederick's situation Murray persuaded him he need feel no guilt toward Lyle.

"She can't expect you to go through life waiting in a corner drugstore for her to finish her parties or her family duties," he declared. "You say she was shocked to hear you'd taken over that *Haw* magazine job. Hell's bells, she ought to know a man's got to make a living. You can't go on living on a little critical prestige all your life. It shows how little she understands what you're up against. I'll say this for Gerda, she was the first to make me get out of feature writing into something that made dough."

It was a relief to Frederick to think of Lyle as thoughtless and blind to his interests. Indeed her behavior since

her return to town bore out the accusation. She did not
mention their quarrel when they met. She appeared engrossed wholly in writing her new play, asking about his
own new work with perfunctory politeness. After her first
outburst about his job on *Haw* she made no comments.
After a while her thoughtful questions as to how the magazine was succeeding, and her considerate "How nice to
be in work you enjoy" made him angry that she never
asked when his book was coming out or how his new
series in the *Swan* was being received, or why he avoided
seeing her alone. Yes, Murray was right, Lyle had failed to
sympathize with his work and he should not feel the dull
weight of remorse when he saw her. Curiously enough, he
felt most hostile and righteously aggrieved with Lyle at
the times Dodo was eluding him. Why shouldn't he have
other loves, he argued; Lyle never considered getting a
divorce for him! But when he had just spent the night
with Dodo he was able to call on Lyle or lunch with her
with a detached pitying appreciation of her qualities. He
was happy; she, whom he had once loved deeply, was not.
He found the new pallor emphasizing the contrast of
brown eyes and red-gold hair and the aura of secret sadness
made her extraordinarily beautiful. It excited him as
something he had caused and it tempted him to comfort
her but there was no comfort to give without committing
himself again. He confined himself to complimenting her
on her appearance, the wisdom of whatever she said, the
value of her work and the great future open to her. One
day Lyle sat very still as he repeated the favorable remarks being made at the next table about the Gaynor play
and the great charm of Mrs. Gaynor, an opinion that was
universally held, Frederick assured her, else why would
she have so many distinguished friends and satellites?
Lyle's rigid silence made him uncomfortably conscious of
the strangeness of his attitude. He had never called her
friends distinguished nor had he been given to delivering
obvious bouquets when he had been in love. He saw Lyle
staring at him, clutching her purse as if it was a life

preserver. Then she gave a choking gasp that turned into a hard little laugh.

"Your flattery will break my heart," she said. "It's like the compliments exchanged by nations just before the declaration of war."

He pretended not to understand, and retreated into a pose of wounded feelings. He had been puzzled at first by her silent acceptance of their new status but then he thought bitterly that it showed how little his love had meant in her busy life. Finally, a wave of remorse would engulf him that the light by which he had lived for years should have been quenched and replaced by a will-o'-the-wisp.

Frederick and Murray had fortified their stronghold by a program of joint engagements. Murray explained to Judy on these occasions that Frederick was using the entire apartment for a party, and finally said that they were planning a joint housekeeping arrangement which prohibited Judy's free use of the place. She patiently moved her properties back to the little room on Abingdon Square.

"That little moron of his seems to be making Frederick human late in life," she observed, adding hopefully, "it might be a good thing if he married her."

"Good Lord, no!" Murray exclaimed. "It's nothing but an affair."

"Nothing but an affair," Judy echoed mechanically. "Oh."

The "housekeeping arrangement" consisted of occasionally having morning coffee together or uniting in the expense of a casserole of *paellae valenciana* from Jai Alai for intimate little home dinners either for Dodo and Gerda or other ladies. After each man had confessed his attachment to one love, and had revealed how cavalierly he was treated by his lady, he felt the contradictory necessity of demonstrating his independence. Certainly, each boasted, nothing would induce him to seek consolation from his older love, when the present one was recalcitrant, but neither was he one to be inconvenienced by such

female capriciousness. If Gerda was chilly, as was usually
the case, or Dodo mysteriously occupied for days, Murray
did not resort to Judy nor did Frederick to Lyle; there
was Lorna Leahy next door or Caroline Drake, or person-
able ladies encountered in Umberto's or elsewhere. Sometimes men are tremendously set up by cementing a new
friendship, more than they are by a new mistress, and since
Frederick had never had an intimate friend, he found his
new life a continuous adventure. This was the way other
men were, this was the way they lived. Murray's acceptance
of him as a regular fellow, not a highbrow or stuffed shirt,
was wonderfully gratifying, and his assumption that Frederick was not allowing his infatuation with Dodo to spoil
his pleasures elsewhere was flattering though not quite
true. Murray slept with Judy once in a while "to keep
from hurting her feelings" and obliged other ladies indis-
criminately for the same reason. His fixation on Gerda
had very little to do with sex, anyway, he said. For his part,
Frederick could barely bring himself to touch Lyle's hand,
partly because of the dreadful pang of guilt over a passion
gone dead, fear that it hadn't gone dead, and would flare
up compelling him to end his adventure. He wanted to
go on anticipating or remembering Dodo's electric effect
on him as long as he dared. This state of excitement,
though it deliberately short-circuited Lyle's appeal for him,
made him for the first time find all kinds of women desirable, although his old shyness kept him silent even when
they made all the overtures, as he was astonished to find
was frequently the case. When he saw Lyle he took satisfaction in mentioning numerous engagements and new
interests. She was not the only one whose life was full. He
felt almost viciously triumphant as if he had conquered an
enemy instead of a love. He was no longer the orphan
lover, he wanted her to know, waiting for what crumbs
she could spare him, a man whose simple habits she could
always count upon, and whose preference for solitude in-
sured her his faithfulness. No, he was a man she had
subtly prevented from being himself as he now was. He

had been a guest of Bennett Strafford at a broadcast—("I thought you detested radio, Frederick!"); he had been to a gay cocktail party at Tyson Bricker's—("A cocktail party, Frederick?"); he had been to the theatre and enjoyed it—("But you always said you hated the stage, Frederick! You never will go with me.") It gave him a cruel pleasure to report having visited or encountered friends of her circle, implying that he did not require her sponsorship, and exaggerating the degree of intimacy to such an extent that Lyle felt they were no longer her friends but wholly Frederick's. She felt the sly reproach when he said, "I've heard you speak of your friends, the Bellamans, and so I was especially interested in being invited to dinner there last night." She had selfishly refrained from taking him there, his tone hinted, but he was welcomed there on his own merits, nonetheless. He had refused so often to go all the places he now went or to mix with the people he now praised that she had given up asking him, long ago. They were hers and Allan's friends, anyway, and she used to reproach herself for being a little relieved that Frederick's interests seemed elsewhere. One day lunching together (at her suggestion), she seized upon his new taste for the theatre to invite him to join her that night in the Beckleys' box; but he declined. The pleasure, she thought sorrowfully, was in the company not the event, and his quick refusal stung her. Would he like to see *Billion Dollar Baby,* then, tomorrow night? She had just gotten tickets, and before the doubt in his face could crystallize into a negative she deliberately tortured herself by saying, "I can't go, but if you could use the tickets—" His face brightened. Splendid. He thought at once of Dodo's passionate desire to see that show, and her childish delight if he produced tickets.

"I've wanted to see it," he said brusquely, pocketing the tickets Lyle thrust at him.

"Since when?" she inquired, smiling to cover her disappointment. "You said you hated musicals."

"I understand this is different," he said impatiently. He

could scarcely wait to call up Dodo and report what seemed a personal achievement on his part and not at all connected with Lyle. Dodo was always boasting of other men taking her to the theatre, and now she would see he was just as obliging.

"I'm beginning to believe you're taking a Dale Carnegie course, Frederick," Lyle said with an effort at lightness. "In another six lessons you'll be such a good mixer, you'll be running for office."

Frederick saw a welcome excuse for a quarrel in the remark and stated that he had been reproached for unsociability by Lyle for years and now that he was profiting by her criticism to come out of his shell he was being unjustly attacked. He had been buried in work for years, as she must have known, and he was surprised she begrudged him the natural reaction from such gruelling concentration.

Placed in the wrong, Lyle nervously tried to placate him. He was surely joking, she said, and perhaps she was tactless from the strain of the new play which was not coming on right at all. Indeed, she secretly hated the theatre now for its stern demands that prevented full attendance on one's love life. Frederick allowed himself to be calmed, and Lyle tried to talk of neutral subjects. She had a misgiving that admission of her work faltering pleased him as if he were a rival playwright. She was aware that he wanted to find her at fault in dozens of minor ways as an excuse for leaving her, and she was angry at herself for accepting the guilt—she was the unfaithful one, the one to ask forgiveness. She knew he was waiting and dreading the underlying questions, "Don't you love me any more? Why won't you see me alone any more except in public places?" But then she suspected from his uneasy glances that he was beginning to wonder why she did not ask. Mystery, then, was the only protection for her pride and she was stubbornly determined to tear her heart out rather than accuse him or try to woo him back, or comment on his new behavior. Each morning she woke with

the sinking thought of nothing to live for. Everything else
in her life seemed hateful. She could not work. Allan's
sarcasm, forgiven before in her guilty love, now made him
seem a galling burden that had caused her present plight.
She had no heart for the curtain of banter they had maintained to hide the crueller truths of pain and sacrifice. She
had once felt that in spite of everything, at least she and
Allan had always been able to laugh together. But, she
wondered, had they really laughed at the same jokes?
After some fleeting hint of an abyss of icy hatred in him
she wondered if he had only laughed at the naïve folly of
her own laughter; he was enemy laughing at captive. She
had other moments, as Frederick did, of considering her
lover the real enemy, for whose present triumph she must
be revenged. The strength of her pride enabled her to
baffle him by an apparent indifference to his coolness. It
was her weapon but it could be used against her. Finding
no expected reaction to his hints of new friends, Frederick
made his allusions more definite, spoke of mysterious private plans, referred to feminine names she did not know,
determined to have her wince or explode in anger that
would restore his advantage. Lyle submitted to the sharper
wounds, managed to agree that Caroline Drake was a most
interesting woman without inquiring how Frederick happened to see her, but finally she was goaded to venture on
the thin ice between them.

"By the way, Tyson Bricker reminded me to get some
kind of a job for that friend of yours, the Baltimore girl,
Dodo something or other," she said, looking intently into
her coffee cup. "He thought she'd be happy doing anything in any kind of theatrical or film office. I believe
Kerry is going to take her on. I must tell Tyson or perhaps
you will."

At her first sentence Frederick had stiffened himself for
the big scene, but as she finished all he could think was
how helpful he was about to prove himself to Dodo. His
friendship for Lyle Gaynor was winning Dodo her long-
craved job. He was able to do more for Dodo than her

advertising big shot from K. G. R. or any of the beaux who merely took her dancing. He couldn't dance but he could get her a job in the very office she most wanted. And he had tickets for the show she most wished to see. Frederick was in such a glow of satisfaction that he forgot Lyle's part in it. He wanted to find Dodo as soon as he dared leave, and savor her delighted gratitude. It was a delicious thing to be able to grant heart's desires to the one you loved. There had been so little he could ever do for Lyle.

"I'll be calling you," he answered Lyle and made an absorbing job of paying the check, refusing to let her pay her share as she used to do. She was going across the street and he got on a bus to go back to his office. He caught a glimpse of her from his window and before he was conscious of it the old aching rush of love for her swept over him. He saw how thin she was, how sad her face, and as he watched she made a troubled gesture toward her eyes. He wanted to cry out to her, to beg her to wait, only wait—but for what? Tears came to his eyes as the bus carried him on.

12

. . . cats out of the bag . . .

*T*HE ménage of Murray and Frederick was a never-failing source of discussion to those two bosom friends, Caroline Drake and Lorna Leahy. They kept a ready file of information on the activities of both gentlemen and used it as a sort of reference book for all masculine behavior, professional or personal. Lorna, living next door to them as she did, could report on encounters with their guests, chats with their mutual janitor, and the conduct of the servant they had just acquired. Caroline, as a figure in the business world and lady about town, heard tidbits here and there about Frederick's connection with Lyle Gaynor. (Like columnists' gossip, the news of the affair broke after it was all over.) Caroline was in Gerda Cahill's misguided confidence, too, so she could describe to Lorna the efforts of Murray to win back his wife, and Gerda's counter efforts to win every other man as a lover.

"She even took on some twenty-year-old poet or other," Caroline declared. "She said to me, 'My dear, you must try him. Marvellous! He stayed with me eighteen hours straight!' I said, 'Goodness, Gerda, how did you do it? You must have had a yo-yo.' "

"You were mean," Lorna beamed.

"She doesn't get it," Caroline said. "Gerda is so nuts about herself it never strikes her that anyone can be mean.

I give her a good crack now and then about Murray having affairs of his own, but she just sighs and says, 'Poor darling, he's so unhappy!' "

"Sweet," Lorna said. "Maybe, if you and I had been as dumb as Gerda we'd still have our husbands."

"God forbid!" Caroline exclaimed sincerely. "I'd rather put the money in a business of my own."

Ever since their marriages had exploded Caroline and Lorna had been in each other's confidence, sharing a bottle of an evening in Lorna's studio or Caroline's penthouse. In fact they had been telling each other everything for so many years over their cups that they'd never heard a word each other said. When Caroline's marriage was breaking up— (he was jealous of her superior success in the same store) she was kept going by Lorna's understanding support. Lorna had been in the same spot herself, in a common-law arrangement with another artist, George Leahy, who had no push and was ungrateful to Lorna for turning over her surplus jobs to him. Eventually, Caroline's Arthur left and she happily resumed her maiden name; Lorna, not having enjoyed the legal right to it previously, adopted her mate's name as soon as they parted. In spite of their relief at getting their freedom the two women in their endless confidences were increasingly sentimental over lost love. They told each other of their years of fidelity— (if only they had Gerda's frivolous nature!) and each lamented the curse of being a one-man woman. Men always took advantage of this virtue and Caroline agreed with Lorna that honestly, if it could be done over again, she'd sleep with every man who came along instead of wasting loyalty on one undeserving male. After a few drinks, Caroline finally said she *had* slept with maybe forty or fifty men but only because she was so desperately unhappy. Lorna said she didn't blame anyone in Caroline's domestic situation for doing just that, and many times wished she had not been such a loyal sap about George, but except for a few vacation trips and sometimes being betrayed by alcohol she had really never—well, anyway, she didn't blame any one.

Caroline liked to go straight from work to her modernistic Murray Hill apartment, fling off her smart office clothes, and after a brisk shower settle down in handsome house pajamas for leisurely home drinking. In winter she refreshed herself and callers before her huge living room fire or had friends gather around the great white bed in her bedroom where she lay with a tray, a polar bear rug thrown over her and cannel coal sparkling merrily in the fireplace. In summer the setting sun found her on her terrace—(she raised corn and tomatoes as well as flowers and grain spirits there). She always wanted Lorna to visit her but Lorna was annoyingly reluctant to change her working clothes to come up to Caroline's neighborhood and taxed Caroline's good nature with challenges to give up her comfort and come to Lorna's place for less and worse to drink. Lorna proudly confessed to being unable to afford the best (as Caroline could) and Caroline was obliged to declare heartily that hell, it wasn't the liquor, it was the intelligent companionship she was seeking. Lorna was selfish with her inferior beverages, too, filling her own glass constantly—(it was her whiskey, wasn't it?) with seeming absent-mindedness as she talked, then drifting off into a light doze when it was her guest's turn to reveal the mysteries of her secret nature. When she was uprooted and planted in Caroline's garden Lorna's dim resentment of the superior advantages made her keep her eyes fixed on the bottle as she drank, experiencing a sense of great achievement, even revenge, as the contents sank lower and lower, below the Canadian Club letters, below the label, down, down to the last dregs. "Maybe we'd better eat something," one or the other might say, but this seldom came to anything for they were solitary eaters, icebox snatchers, greedy to have that entire chicken all alone no matter how generous they were with liquids. Frequently they lost interest in dinner once they had descended below the bottle's label and then a remarkable inspiration would come to open a second bottle and repeat the revelations they had been repeating for years to glazed eyes and deaf ears.

"No, you don't mean it! Why have you never told me this before?"

"Didn't I? How strange! I was positive I had told you. In any case, now the cat is out of the bag you might as well know the whole story. Well, this dealer and I took the plane to Mexico City——"

"No! I can't believe it, Lorna! You actually——"

"I swear it, Caroline!"

"No!"

"Yes, yes!"

As the sun set and the stars and moon or for all they knew a typhoon came up the voices grew louder and shriller, neighbors listened by necessity and Caroline's colored maid, Johanna, was known to observe "Everybody listens to them ladies talk except theyselves."

Cats safely out of bags, the friends separated, either for private dinner or a tasty sleeping pill and oblivion till another working day.

As is often the case their indulgences kept them fresher and younger-looking than their hard-working, respectable contemporaries, since they spent so much more time taking care of their faces and figures than did their righteous friends who worked, spurned temptations, and foolishly trusted God instead of Elizabeth Arden to reward them with a complexion. Caroline was hard and fit, a trim size fourteen, with a fine jaw-line, carefully tinted dark-gold hair, and except for too pale near-sighted eyes and a wide mouthful of strong white teeth that seemed capable of crunching the bones of her human obstacles, she could pass as an attractive thirty-five instead of forty-two. Lorna was small, with a brown pixie face and a mop of curls that she ruefully termed "prematurely white." For years she had threatened to dye her hair but always yielded to her friends' obliging plea not to touch it! That white hair

is the most striking thing in town! Of course the only
person who sincerely liked the white mat was Lorna herself, but she was happy in her conceit and seldom wore a
hat, shaking her curls like a restless pony until someone
said "Do you mind my saying you have the most individual hair I've ever seen?" In spite of their years of intimacy
the two friends belonged to different sets. Lorna, the artist,
sometimes went to Caroline's parties and sat aloof with an
extremely mean pixie sneer for Caroline's wholesale job-
bers, visiting silverware buyers, and department store
heads. When Caroline tried to bring good-natured guests
over to Lorna's corner Lorna snubbed them curtly. Sometimes when the party was at its gayest with no one noticing
her aloofness Lorna would pass out just for spite and
whatever gentleman was being the life of the party would
be called upon to walk her around the block, take her
home, or do something for her that would disrupt the
general gaiety. In spite of her own commercial success,
Lorna's friends were mostly poor or pretentiously Bohemian, loudly literary or artistic, and at her own rare
parties one of them invariably managed to make some
crack about Caroline's expensive get-ups which would
either send Caroline home in a rage or keep her apologiz-
ing to them for hours for her superior earning powers.
"Caroline can be such a Babbitt," Lorna told her friends.
As for Caroline she had taken to making bets at her own
parties on just how soon Lorna would "do her stuff" and
just who would be drafted into service. She knew Lorna's
moment for vapors was bound to come when some talented guest was about to take the center of the stage by
song or dance; she knew, too, that having spoiled the
show Lorna would revive suddenly if the wrong man was
pressed to take care of her, holding out for the party's
key man with extraordinary genius, passing out, reviving,
and fading again until she'd gotten the man she (and
usually Caroline) wanted.

Both ladies talked in confidence of their frustrations in
the quest for love, but the truth was they had gotten all

they wanted of the commodity and had no intention of making the least sacrifice of comfort for a few Cupid feathers. The men with whom they occasionally dined had a way of needling them or as Caroline said "getting her ego down" because men were jealous of a woman's financial success. Men forgave genius, or a *succés d'estime* in a woman, but her financial advantage infuriated them. Women forgave success in business but never forgave success with men. One thing Caroline and Lorna had in common was an overpowering reverence for high-brows, no matter how obscure. Each had met friends' friends of great erudition who dazzled them with thoughts and phrases gloriously beyond their own intellectual means, something they could wonder at with neither envy of the possessor nor the desire to buy. Since they were able to afford what material objects they craved, they missed the innocent female joy of window-shopping, admiring something without the disappointment of possession. On their rare opportunities to worship an articulate Brain they listened raptly; the facile conversation on politics, philosophy and particularly scholarly facets of literature they rubbed in their scalps as earnestly as if it was a new tonic and tried the phrases on their mouths like the latest lipstick. They were as proud of their respect for learning as if their awe in itself was a credit to them, an achievement close to magic. They were both gratified to have made the acquaintance of Mr. Frederick Olliver and lived in an enjoyable state of suspense as to whether he would recognize them, snub them deliciously, or have one of his darling moods of Old World charm. Caroline had been so impressed by his arrogant sarcasm whenever she had met him that she bought his last book and read five pages of it every night before sleeping, no matter how tight she was. Cozily embarked on her own fortune hunt she thought it was enormously chic of Frederick Olliver to scorn commercial offers—Murray reported he had been urged to accept large sums in Hollywood as research expert on an historical film. "Privacy is the only luxury essential to me," he had said, "and I see no logic in giving it up in order to make money to buy it back."

In spite of being awed by the unfamiliar elegance of Frederick's mind Caroline's natural aggressiveness usually rose to the fore and she invited him to call many times until he surrendered. At first he consented out of courtesy to a friend of Murray; at that time they were becoming such great chums. Later he found a stubborn satisfaction in a life neither Lyle nor Dodo could enter or could even imagine. He talked of parties at Miss Drake's to Lyle in order to mystify and annoy her; when Dodo eluded or tormented him with talk of marvellous engagements it was consoling to call on Caroline and be welcomed with such obvious pride. Once Caroline frightened him by becoming amorous over old-fashioneds. Her fingers clutched his thigh with the iron determination of a medieval torture device— (he was literally black and blue for days) and she pulled him toward her by the coat-lapel so relentlessly that he was in great fear for his worn suit, and also of being devoured by the competent big white teeth. Just as he was resigned to a mighty kiss fragrantly concocted of *Fabulous* and *Old Granddad* Caroline released him and burst into tears. "Oh what's the matter with everything?" she moaned. "Everything's so horrible. There ought to be something. Something ought to be right. For God's sake, get me a drink, before I go absolutely nuts." In his relief and surprise Frederick was very kind and gentle, and after getting her a drink, a compact and cigarette, he held her hand for a while and kissed her lightly on the forehead, when he said goodnight. Caroline, he was amused to see, was too solidly realistic to be in the least fooled by this demonstration.

"That means a hell of a lot, now, doesn't it?" she said gloomily, lighting a new cigarette on the one he had just lit for her. "You think I'm a lady Babbitt and that's all you do think of me—if you ever did think of me, and the hell with you."

Frederick thought about this episode in the middle of

the night and several times next day and each time it made him chuckle. He was so taken with this evidence of Caroline's essential hard shrewdness contrasting with Lyle's subtlety and Dodo's coquetry that he called on her the next day with a small Victorian corsage of violets and sweetheart roses. Caroline was too astonished to be grateful but she told Lorna that he must have meant it as an apology for trying to "make" her.

"But I never thought of Frederick in that way!" Caroline explained dreamily. "So when he started making passes naturally I——"

"Well, how was it?" Lorna rudely inquired but Caroline didn't think that was a bit funny.

13

. . . the octopus named Virgil . . .

FREDERICK'S worst fear was that Lyle would find out somehow the sorry chase that Dodo was giving him. The depths of his humiliating defeats were in proportion to the heights of his raptures. Cautious of money by nature or rather frightened of insolvency he was goaded to extravagant gestures by Dodo's loud complaints of stinginess. As soon as he had agreed to take her to a "gay place," the Barrel or uptown, he offset his first sense of panic by inner arguments making the cause of his folly seem worthy. Then, having surrendered gracefully enough, and anxious to disguise his unbecoming poverty from a young lady who thought all men over thirty-five made twenty-thousand a year, he was given the privilege of sitting alone at a table while Dodo made friends at the bar, or else engaged in merry repartee with occupants of the next table. Sometimes she invited a few strangers, mostly men if possible, to their table where she edified them by stories of men in Baltimore who were crazy about her, silly fellows who never got onto the fact that she would let one take her home and go right out with another one. On rare occasions one of her listeners would have heard of Frederick Olliver and praise some essay. This was the moment for Dodo to interrupt petulantly, "Honestly, I can't understand a word Freddie writes and I don't think he can either. Nobody wants to read that sort of bunk."

Frederick only laughed indulgently.

Now that she had the job in the Paramount office Dodo

was constantly thrilled by proximity to wonderful actors, writers, producers, all crazy about her. Frederick's reward for what he considered his service to her was to be denied her favors, because of her superior new opportunities. He was tormented by her callous boasts to him of new conquests, but even more by her elusiveness. He knew his only advantage over his rivals was her conception of him as a social superior, someone mysteriously regarded as distinguished by others. It was therefore up to him to build up this advantage in order to hold her interest. He must never admit that the days he could not find her were hopelessly empty. He accepted invitations from any quarter especially any that might sound desirable to Dodo, aware that Dodo's idea of a successful society man was one whose book was full, no matter with what. It was dimly consoling to discover that his years of comparative isolation made his company prized the more highly. To Lyle he found it diplomatic to give the impression he was discreetly interested in many women instead of in one, and he mentioned every feminine name but Dodo's. Naturally, Lyle must guess there was someone else but he could not bear her to think that all was over between them, nor for her to know who her successor was. On the other hand he freely spoke of the Gaynors to Dodo because she was much impressed by them and tolerated him more because he knew them. Dodo's complacency did not give way to jealousy but rather to envy of his opportunities. If she voiced the familiar suspicion of other women Frederick was ready to reassure her until she would pout, "Well, if you aren't sweet on her why can't I go visit Caroline Drake, too? I like penthouse parties, too."

He saw that she was contemptuous of his bondage to her and he knew that she respected masculine infidelity just as Judy did, but he was congenitally unable to pose as a Casanova. His greatest advantage was his stubborn silence when she spoke of marriage. Other men she'd liked were already married but he had no such excuse. It mystified and piqued her that an old bachelor so excited

over her should be so cagey about marriage, and once she
made this surprising discovery she nagged about it constantly. She didn't want to marry him but she wanted to
be asked. It showed he was not really subjugated and that
kept up her curiosity even while she was annoyed. Frederick suffered a shock of horror whenever Dodo hinted at
marriage. The only idea of marriage he had ever had was
with Lyle and he was astonished that circumstances didn't
alter this desperate conviction. Lyle was the only woman
he could ever marry, and the feeling persisted in the bottom of his being like an underground river, fathomless,
eternal. The mere word on Dodo's lips seemed a violation
and he was as puzzled at his reaction as was Dodo. He
couldn't make love to Lyle, but he couldn't marry Dodo.
He admired Lyle and wanted to hurt her for the unworth-
iness of her rival; he despised Dodo and wanted to be hurt
by her. He knew he must seem a ridiculous figure in
groups where Dodo jibed at his age and shouted out the
small sum he got for the essays a few admired in the
Swan. She compensated for this by carrying a copy of
Haw around to show strangers, explaining that her escort
was editor but never got credit for it. She pointed to
Frederick's embarrassed face, giggling, "He's ashamed of
doing anything that everybody else likes, he's such an old
stuffy, but *I* think *Haw* is wonderful. Everybody likes
jokes and murder stories and comic strips. Wouldn't you
think he'd be glad to give the public what it wants?"

She still enjoyed attending the League class where she
could display for other students' envy her familiarity with
members of the faculty. She had not gotten over her first
impression of a League course as a badge of intellectual
distinction, and wanted everyone to know she was not only
enrolled there but was on cozy terms with the League
heads. Whenever she was impressed she betrayed it by
deriding the object of her awe insistently, unable to leave
it alone or disguise her awe by simulated indifference.
She wanted to bring whatever it was down to her own
level so she could dismiss it. Frederick could not reproach

her for lack of perception concerning the League since he
had himself been taken in by its pretensions at first. Now
his distaste for it was numbed by its service to his love-
life. Dodo liked it. Dodo liked to exploit her intimacy
with him, and walk past the less fortunate students with
Dr. Olliver, and if possible Mr. Tyson Bricker. Frederick
was glad he had not resigned. He was glad he had the
Haw job too, not only for the money to oil his new court-
ship but for the defense it gave him against any accusations of pedantry. Dodo was vaguely irritated by his serious writing and baffled by its effect on other people. She
was therefore exhilarated to have him humbled by an
ordinary job. She teased him by demanding why on earth
he took such a silly job as *Haw* anyway, then switched to
the statement that at least it was better than making a fool
of himself writing for magazines that never paid anything.
There were moments when Frederick was inclined to
agree with Dodo, particularly as it became clear that
Strafford was postponing publication of his book on the
flimsiest pretexts. Other times he found himself longing
for Lyle's reassurance after a long spell of Dodo's nagging.
He needed consolation after Dodo's strategic attacks of
headaches that prevented love-making but were miraculously alleviated by visits to gay spots where other men
could be found. Frederick wished there was some way of
having Lyle's sympathy for the wounds he received from
Dodo but he dared not make an overture, now that their
relationship was so conveniently casual. A false move
might mean too much and then he would not be free
when Dodo was in the mood to be kind. He had been
relieved to have Lyle telephone less frequently and he
thought it fair not to make any gestures but to leave her to
suggest meeting. He had avoided her house and it was
some time before it dawned on him that she no longer
invited him there. She had spent years pleading with him
to join her parties and evidently gave up just at the time
he was changing into a social person. It was only logical of
course. He tried to justify his twinge of envy whenever he

heard Dodo talk of someone who had dined at the Gaynors. It marred his standing with Dodo to be neglected by the Gaynors.

"But I thought you were *in* with the Gaynors," Dodo said many times. "I'd just love to go to their place and meet all those people. I don't see why they don't ask you. They ask Tyson Bricker."

Frederick consoled himself by reflecting that even for Dodo's esteem he could not go through an evening that would remind him of the countless unhappy hours of looking across a crowded room filled with the distressingly permanent-seeming belongings of the Gaynors, waiting to meet Lyle's eyes as his only reward. But there should be some other way of regaining at least the benefit of the understanding and deep admiration that had been underneath and seemingly apart from their physical relationship. At the first of his new social life he had braced himself for running into Lyle, but when the situation never occurred he began seeking it deliberately, and finally wondering, with a sense of panic, if the door was really shut. He pictured chance meetings in crowds which absolved him of intimate words but permitted a continuation of the old sympathy. The door must not be entirely closed. So he went with Benedict Strafford to one of the Beckley Thursdays but Lyle was not there and he heard that she seldom came. "Lyle seems to have buried herself, completely," he heard, and was curious as to whether this meant misery or unknown celebrations. He followed the openings of art shows where the artist was an old friend of hers. Murray mentioned having seen her at Gerda's and he accepted Gerda's invitation to a supper in the secret hope of exchanging a few words with Lyle, pretending to Murray that he dreaded such an encounter. But Lyle was not there and he dared not bring up her name. On two Sundays Dodo's evasiveness drove him to Friends of Music concerts, knowing Lyle had season tickets. But he saw no one he knew except Edwin Stalk, the *Swan* editor. After the second time he walked out with Stalk for dinner

at the Blue Ribbon. Frederick was surprised to hear that
Mrs. Gaynor had presented Stalk with her own tickets.
Lyle knew the Stalks only through him and Stalk had
always professed a scorn of the Gaynor theatrical and
social set. Frederick felt childishly jealous of Lyle's en-
croachment on his former private life. After all Stalk was
his special property, part of the meager private life he
used to have to offset Lyle's full one. He expected to discuss the *Swan,* and his own contributions during dinner,
for Stalk had always been completely preoccupied with
literature. But Stalk was moodily silent, barely answering
Frederick's attempts at their usual exchange. He was a
thin, dark, tragic-faced young man, brilliantly self-edu-
cated, and oblivious to everything in the world that was
not printed, so oblivious that women of all ages pursued
him, flung fortunes at him for his literary projects, presented him with theatres, houses, honorary degrees and
fitted bags. He lived with a White Russian woman, older
than himself, who was kept in a constant agony of jealous
insecurity never certain when Edwin's professional needs
might require the exchange of his body for some financial
backing, never certain how long his indifference to worldly
pleasures would protect her. Frederick had been so tortured by troubles of the flesh that he was relieved at the
idea of an evening with Stalk, discussing abstractions,
literature, anything that provided surcease from love. But
tonight Stalk stared into space, crumpled breadcrumbs
over the red-checked tablecloth with delicate long fingers,
neglected his sauerbraten and drank three seidels of Mich-
elob, an unprecedented dissipation for him.

"People ought to go to concerts in individual sunken
bells," he said fretfully. "They interfere with music. They
want to compete with it. Did you see that woman standing
in the aisle beside me? All during the second movement
she was scratching her bare arm, as if she was tuning up a
fifth instrument. I heard nothing else. And the man beside me. Moving his lips as if Wolfgang Amadeus himself
had commissioned lyrics. I couldn't look away. I wanted

to say, 'Louder, please, if you have a secret libretto to this quartette, in the name of God, out with it and no mumbling!' "

"The anesthesia wasn't strong enough for you," Frederick suggested. "You should have had a full orchestra and been blindfolded."

"Maybe. Maybe. I'm immunized now to chamber music," Stalk admitted. "I begin to notice the musicians and pick out a favorite by his mannerisms. Like an amateur at the races. I picked the cellist today because he wagged his foot." He shrugged his shoulders and fixed his eyes with sudden intentness on Frederick.

"You've known the Gaynors a long time, haven't you?"

"Several years," Frederick said, "why?"

"How did you come to know them?" pursued Stalk.

Surprised at any display of interest in personalities from Stalk, Frederick answered that he had met Lyle when he was attached to an Eastern university and she had come to the town to stage a try-out of one of the Gaynor plays. When he returned to New York he had called at the Gaynor home, the play having become their first success.

Edwin listened carefully, selected a cigarette from a ruby-encrusted silver case— (gift of some lover of *belles lettres*)—and tapped it thoughtfully.

"I remember it was you who brought her to the *Swan* luncheons some time ago. It seemed to me I'd seen you with them, and I wondered why I never run into you at their house."

"I didn't know you went there," Frederick exclaimed surprised. "Personally I don't care for that circle. Broadway and Hollywood tangled up with Wall Street and Park Avenue. Not in my line."

Edwin lifted his eyebrows.

"I never see that element there," he said. "Mrs. Gaynor has too much discrimination for that sort of thing. I daresay Gaynor himself would like it. He's a disgusting beast."

Frederick was astonished first at Stalk expressing such interest in any human beings who had nothing to do with either the *Swan* or his own mental processes, and second that any one should refer to Allan Gaynor as a disgusting beast. Allan had the invalid's immunity from criticism, and in all the years he had been the barrier to Frederick's happiness the latter had never judged him as he would have an ordinary rival. Allan was invalid, a middle-aged person whose conduct and tastes were dictated by his misfortune, a person to be pitied and excused if not liked, an unanswerable argument against Lyle getting a divorce. But here was Edwin Stalk of all people violating this unwritten code.

"Beast?" Frederick repeated.

Stalk shrugged thin shoulders and lit a cigarette.

"Why doesn't he bump himself off?" he said coldly. "He's nothing but a burden to her."

"He's a great favorite in their group." Frederick found himself in the extraordinary position of defender. "They tell me he knows more about the theatre than any one except Nathan, and he's still able to write damn good plays."

"She writes them and pretends he helps," Edwin Stalk said, then he asked abruptly, "You're not letting Strafford's have your new book, are you? Haven't they forfeited it by postponing it?"

Frederick did not think so. Besides Strafford's had the best name for his sort of work.

"Not any more," Stalk said. "That *Court Lady* best-seller didn't help them any. I hear they're making pots and pots and are going to specialize in that sort of trash. They're cleaning up on some cheap magazine, too, *Haw*. Won't do you any good to have the Strafford imprint, I would say."

Frederick was glad Stalk did not know his connection with *Haw*, although he doubted if it would affect any opinion of his *Swan* writing.

"How's *Swan* doing?" he countered.

"Ups and downs as usual," Stalk said carelessly. "Attacked for being non-political, political, academic, revolutionary, reactionary, dirty and squeamish. Your piece on Hrosvitha struck some as a recommendation of chastity for women dramatists. I was telling Mrs. Gaynor. As a matter of fact, I find her exceptionally helpful regarding the magazine. I never dreamed she was so brilliant outside her own field. Extraordinary woman."

"Very," Frederick agreed, nonplussed, wondering what had brought about the change in Stalk, shrewdly suspecting that Lyle had put money in the magazine. He was about to suggest a brandy but Stalk had reached for his black Homburg, an affectation, Frederick thought, to make him seem the continental artist. They walked toward Sixth Avenue and Frederick anticipated the usual visit to the Stalks' upper west side apartment and an evening of discussion. Instead Stalk hailed a south bound taxi at the corner and got in.

"You go down, don't you? I'll give you a lift. Or perhaps you're going to the Gaynors too."

"No," said Frederick, getting in the cab beside him. "I'll get off at Eighth Street."

"I've arranged to meet a Mexican poet at the Gaynors'," Stalk said. "I can't talk to any one in my own apartment. Solange always wants everything translated for her so she can argue too. She thinks every person of talent is my enemy and she must defend me, by insulting them. Mrs. Gaynor feels she's helping the magazine by letting us use her apartment from time to time. It's a godsend, of course."

Frederick murmured something. He had always been careful to take no liberties with the Gaynor home and was taken aback by Stalk's words. He was annoyed at the empty evening ahead of him as well and further bewildered when Stalk said meditatively, "Love is curious, isn't it? You could go through life thinking you know all about it but when it really happens you realize you have never really known it."

Frederick was on the verge of laughing at this gem issuing from a young man who had hitherto seemed adult enough to mock at such profundities.

"You won't come on down?" Stalk said when Frederick got out. "I'm sure it would be alright. After all you've known the Gaynors much longer than I."

Frederick shook his head and waved goodnight. He was conscious of a sense of injury that he was not free to call at the Gaynors'. He decided that Stalk was getting to be a bore and was sure Lyle must find him so, too. He recalled her having remarked about the doleful young man on first meeting him, "But he looks like a ham Byron, a stock company heavy. Is he really just solid brain as you say?"

He would like to have repeated to her Stalk's sententious thought on love but was suddenly struck by the implication that Stalk was in love with Lyle. The idea amused him tremendously and he was sure it would amuse Lyle if she knew. He bought cigarettes in the drug-store, smiling to himself and then amusement gave way to a smouldering indignation. Lyle was deliberately wooing the few old friends that belonged to his private life. She had no interest in them before, now she courted them and shut him out, her little revenge for his change toward her. It was only through him she had met such people as Stalk and the *Swan* intellectuals. Now she took advantage of her charm and professional standing to woo them away from him, to show they were as easily bought as the friends of hers he had ridiculed. He could almost see the *Swan* group lounging comfortably about Lyle's huge living room, Stalk, if you please, lolling back in Lyle's pleasant little study with the one object of his interest (Stalk could talk to only one person at a time); Allan Gaynor somewhere in a corner with his usual special little audience, smiling inscrutably at the somber discussions over the *Swan* problems. Frederick walked along Eighth Street, scowling, glancing in open bars unconsciously to see if Dodo might be there. He could walk over to the Americas and see Murray, perhaps, but he didn't want Murray to suspect the disadvantage of his position. Their masculine solidarity was based on the mutual difficulty of avoiding importunate females, not on sympathy for being abused by them. Frederick felt his bitterness toward Lyle rising; he thought of his wasted years of loving her, and now her undermining of his only intellectual support, making Edwin Stalk fall in love with her so that he preferred an evening with her to an evening with himself. He felt that he hated Lyle, and it soothed his conscience to find new justifications for his unfaithfulness. When he looked through the door of the Barrel and saw Dodo at the bar with Larry he was so filled with bitterness toward Lyle that there was no room for jealousy over Dodo. He felt only relief at finding Dodo again under no matter what circumstances, and had no hesitation in walking in to join them.

"I wasn't lying when I said I was going to Baltimore for the week-end," Dodo said defiantly, then giggled, "I guess I meant I was going to *Barreltomore!*"

"Can you bear this?" Larry asked Frederick, nodding toward Dodo who had buried her face in her hands in a convulsion of merriment. "It must be those double Scotch Mists she's been eating."

"I'll have one myself," Frederick said.

"Tell Freddie about the octopus!" Dodo cried. "Go on, Larry."

"Well, these people found an octopus in their swimming pool and it took such a fancy to them that they made a family pet of it, called it Charlie," Larry obliged. "Listen, this time I'll call it Virgil. Well, Virgil was a great help around the house—squeezed all the oranges, made all the beds at once—hey, you have to have another drink for this. Waiter!"

Frederick woke up the next morning with a frightful headache, fully dressed, but with a vague conviction that he had done something wonderful. He had gotten blind drunk for the first time in his life and now he remembered why. It was to show Dodo he was no more stuffed shirt than Larry. Her shrill giggle still rang in his head and he had a fleeting memory of her cry, "Larry, Freddie's ordered another Scotch Mist! Isn't he terrif? Come on, Freddie, now *you* tell about Harry, the Octopus. Come on! Show how he played the bagpipes again, go on!"

His hand was sore and bleeding and it took a long time for him to remember why. It had happened when he got out of the cab at his place and had tried to pull Dodo out with him. She had bit his hand till he let go and he could still hear her giggling as she drove on with Larry. He had stood dizzily hanging to his gatepost listening to the bagpipes. They were in his ears for days.

14

. . . voyage through the sky . . .

ALTHOUGH he had had a part in only a few hits Allan Gaynor was numbered among the city's leading theatrical figures for he had been a successful actor-manager before his accident had confined him to writing. The fact that he had never done a creditable play by himself was nothing against him since most of his colleagues required at least one collaborator unless they were shrewd enough to merely purchase plots and hire a stable of hacks to do the actual work. Allan knew his theatre, kept up with the new names, knew the traditions and was actor enough to hold that the manner of the great man was more effective than the proof in attracting a following. Lyle had nourished his ego and attended so carefully to his affairs that he had come to regard her contribution as nothing more than an extension of his own brain. He recognized the quality she brought to his collaboration but it never occurred to him that she had the major task of production problems nor that she might have succeeded all alone. He was comfortably unaware of managerial suggestions that she do her own play, or that it saddened more than flattered her to be told that his obdurate technical pattern handicapped her fluid approach to modern problems. He was impatient with her, lately, for the new play seemed to be getting nowhere and he had no intention of facing his own inadequacy when he could conveniently put the blame on someone else. What was the matter with her, he was finally stirred to demand, whenever reviews of a new

play reminded him that they had none to offer? Didn't
she realize that desirable actors were taking other jobs,
theatres were being sewed up, new names were crowding
them? Questions on plans from the theatrical columnists
irked him with the vague reminder that he could promise
nothing without Lyle. Lyle pleaded time to work at a kink
and he consented, but he had an apprehension that the
trouble might be more than a kink and that there might
be serious danger to the arrangement that gave him a luxurious idle life and yet full credit for worthy work. He
became more observant of his wife's habits, looked for
reasons for her apathy, criticized and accused her of faults
he actually did not believe in the least. In his irritability
at a possible hitch in his smooth life he often hit the target
without knowing it. You would think she was a lady
crossed in love, he mocked. She must have had her feminine vanity badly hurt, he said, by having old Olliver no
longer mooning around. Maybe it was too much for her,
hearing that one of her swains preferred chasing some little
cutie from Tyson Bricker's school to her mature charms.
Or maybe she couldn't work because she was spending too
damn much time with that *Swan* crowd, talking abstract
art, existentialism, Marxism, surrealism, instead of theatre.
It seemed ridiculous that his play, all ready to be put in
rehearsal except for the routine business of writing it,
should be held up merely because a pretty woman was
finding her court dwindling. Without the armor of guilty
love Lyle found herself seething with murderous indignation after such attacks. It was Frederick's fault for
making her thus vulnerable but it was her husband she
hated. She hated him for being a cripple and binding her
to him; she hated him for the revelation of his underlying
cruel self-interest. The graceful façade of their life together cracked daily. He was apt to be politely sarcastic to
guests whom he felt were flattering her and distracting her
from her duties. Lyle, in self-defense, met her friends in
bars sufficiently inconspicuous as to run no risk of en-
countering the Gaynors' joint friends who might tell

Allan. What was there to tell except what no one could guess—that she was desperately trying to reconstruct a life that would allow her to forget anguish for perhaps twenty minutes?

Every morning when he woke, Pedro brought Allan his breakfast, dressed and bathed him, wheeled him to the elevator and thence Allan proceeded to his study on the roof, where he remained till two o'clock undisturbed. The study was a small one-room shack originally used by the janitor but the Gaynors had begged for it, pleading Allan's need for sky and fresh air as well as his professional need to "get away." He could sit outdoors and get the grimy city sun and see far over the town, and in these brief hours alone Allan relived his life, rebuilding past triumphs to support him against the active world of downstairs. Some days he sat in the little cozy room where no one else was allowed to enter except the maid, and looked over old photographs, files of old programs with his name scattered all through them, letters from admirers, notes of play ideas, a genealogical chart of the Gaynor family, souvenirs of ladies, histories of the stage. His "concentrated work" here was pure fabrication as Lyle surmised, for all working conferences were held in her own study downstairs. But well men went to offices away from their home and so must Allan, and it was here on the roof that he really lived completely, not in the drawing-room below, as people thought, conducting his famous conversations, graciously accepting cues for his reminiscences, rewarding an epigram with his quick nod, basking discreetly in the respectful admiration of his chosen company. Here was a special world, swung like a great cage over the city, ten stories above the walking, riding world. Here he could lie back in his chair and see smokestacks on the East River, avenues of roof tanks advancing or retreating like giant chessmen far toward the downtown canyon, northward to the Chrysler tower and castle ramparts of mighty skyscrapers brought low by distance. When he wheeled to the east or west walls he could look down on the little

streets of tenements and shops, their flat or gabled roofs
raised or slanted for skylights protecting the asparagus or
art beneath. Across the northern areaway he could see
into the window of a loft sweatshop where fluorescent day
lights showed girls at looms winding red and blue cord
over giant spools. On warm days the girls brought their
sandwiches and cokes to the fire escape barely a dozen
feet away from him; he loved this proximity to alien life.
Sometimes when a girl crawled out of the loft window all
by herself he called to her softly or smiled a greeting, but
none ever smiled back or did more than stare indifferently.
They could not know who he was or that he could not
walk; he might be anyone taking a sun-bath for all they
cared, a wax dummy. He did not like to think their coolness was due to any other factor but the unfairness of his
infirmity; he did not want to think that even if he were
strong, he would still be a baldish man in his fifties, with
little remnant of the good looks that had won him so
many favors years before. Impatient with his failure at
mild flirtation he pushed his chair to the opposite wall,
watched the wind chase ashes and smoke over other roofs;
he followed cloud shapes trailing after passing planes, idly
composed melodies on the intricate radio wires that scored
the sky. In a high wind, the buildings swayed like ships,
the tanks and towers were smokestacks of great liners and
Allan carried on imaginary conversations with other pas-
sengers, strangers in whom he confided as one only could
in strangers. On vivid days, the sun had a way of spotlight-
ing a balcony or distant terrace that brought old associations into sharp focus; long ago events played again, cos-
tumed by memory, dialogued and emphasized by re-
flection. A suddenly illumined dormer window must be
where he had once lived; he could almost look in and
see himself making love to a girl named Carrie who was
always afraid that someone perhaps on this very roof
might be watching. He described Carrie to his imaginary
shipmate, he described his room as a struggling young
actor at Madame Blanchard's (long since torn down) and

Carrie's husband whose jealousy was so innocently appeased by being given a bit part in Allan's company. Allan was reminded by the charming imaginary stranger's sympathy of all the places whose chimneys he could almost identify, where he and Lyle had first sought apartments, each trying to suit the other's taste. There was the penthouse hardly a block away (he was sure he recognized the latticed wall and garden) which the woman wanted to sublet because "her husband left her alone so much at nights." Lyle had not liked the place, but that very night Allan had been impelled to go back to see the blonde Polish woman who was too pretty to be left alone. Call it rape, if you like, for she did struggle, but afterwards she was only ominously silent. Baffled by the tacit scorn he had defensively said that she was not a virgin, after all. The woman had frostily replied, "Certainly not, but I like to choose." He had gone back again to erase the unpleasant sense of defeat and fathomless contempt, trying to make it over into a gay sophisticated adventure, but her cold, scornful face reduced him to babbling helpless apologies. He had been strong and good-looking, then, too, but the girl had looked at him with the same cool indifference of the girls from the sweatshop, so that there was no triumph, nothing but angry shame in the victory even now, fourteen years later.

In his life on the roof he seldom thought of his physical handicap or of his life with Lyle but of everything far back, before the year of his affliction.

He sometimes napped, putting himself to sleep counting or trying to count, the women he had slept with and it pleased him to have a forgotten name or incident bob up each time. His taste had been for the bizarre adventure rather than for romance, quantity more than quality, and he regretted that the demands of his fame had forced him to surrender to ladies of social and financial value to him, renouncing the gambling-sport of chase and capture to be had only in servant quarters and territories that might have jeopardized his position. He spoke of this to his invisible shipmate and sighed over the waste of his energies.

"Rape, good God, it's the man who is raped. The actresses, heiresses, hostesses, I've had to make love to in order to save a play. The ugly women, old women, lonely women I've had to sleep with to save their feelings! The women I've hated that I've had to go on with to keep them from breaking up my marriage! A man in public life like myself is always raped or blackmailed into bed. His own lusts are a luxury he can't enjoy without terrible cost. Like refusing an autograph. He's always being backed against a wall and being had. He can't be the hunter—he doesn't have time or energy for the pure sport of normal sex, once he's arrived. He can't go foraging in strange iceboxes—everything is brought in on a tray, like it or not, —cold when it gets there, never what he wants at that moment."

Allan had grown accustomed to having his end of the roof to himself through all but the summer months. Even the maid who cleaned his room was allowed to do so only at night when he was downstairs. He was startled, therefore, to have one of his intimate discourses with his shipmate applauded by a tinkling laugh.

"Don't mind me, mister. I talk to myself, too," said a woman's voice. "Everybody says it means you're crazy but I say it's just that they're so crazy you can't talk sense to them like you can to yourself."

The woman was shaking one of his rugs over the wall, and the door of the shack was open so Allan concluded she must be a new servant from his own household. She was a buxom little mulatta with a soft moon face, an oddly babyish mouth with baby teeth and a prim baby voice. Servants were hard to get or her indifferent fluttering of the rug would have proved her inadequacy at once. Allan was on the point of scolding her for daring to approach his room during the hours he had expressly forbidden it but she forestalled him.

"Mrs. Gaynor said I was to come up at night to do you

but my husband won't let me go out at night. I guess it
don't matter if she don't know. She ain't around anyways.
I'll just drop in when it's handy. Just so long as it ain't
dark because my husband's awful upset if I'm out after
dark. Don't tell Mrs. Gaynor on me, please."

Allan hesitated, irritation melting into curiosity at her
impudence.

"What's your name?" he asked.

"Mrs. Bender. I don't usually work around but my
husband's the furnace man next door and your Pedro
asked me just as a favor. Just one room I don't mind. Of
course I wouldn't work for Jews or foreigners but I don't
mind this. Only I can't come nights . . ."

"Alright," Allan cut in, impatiently. "Come in the
afternoons after three, then, when I'm not in."

The girl's futile manipulation of the rug stopped. She
appeared to ponder for a moment then she shook her head
with a gentle smile.

"I'd be afraid to come to a place all by myself here all
alone, mister," she said. "It wouldn't look nice, me being
a married woman and then, too, anything missing you'd
blame me. And my husband'd get mad. He's from Trinidad. Wouldn't you rather I was around for company? You
act kinda lonesome lying up here nobody but yourself to
talk to."

She gave him another bland smile and Allan looked at
her more carefully, a little puzzled.

She might be thirty or she might be much older, he
couldn't tell. She was not pretty and her figure was stolidly
matronly though her legs were long and shapely. Allan was
mentally reproaching Lyle for permitting this intruder
on his privacy but then it struck him that for the first
time in years something was happening to him and only
to him. For Lyle and other free people days were filled
with dozens of little adventures, little trivial brushes with
tragedy or romance, exchanges with strangers, fleeting
glimpses of unknown worlds. But his day held no sur-

prises, his hours and even his friends were arranged carefully beforehand. Nothing as remarkable as a strange Negress addressing him on the roof had occurred to him in ages and Allan felt a sudden excitement out of all proportion to the episode.

"It's kinda chilly out here, don't you think, mister? Maybe now would be a good chance for you to show me just how you want things done inside. You just explain everything, because not working around I may not do it your way without your telling me. Don't it get on your nerves anyway those girls over there in the shop spying on you? People ought to mind their own business." Before he could answer she was pushing his chair toward the door of the shack and he was silent with inner amusement at her boldness. He was almost invariably annoyed by loquacious servants and certainly this one had said nothing extraordinary, yet the plaintive cajolery in her voice gave vague other meanings to her words. She was certainly a petty thief for she said, pushing his chair through the door, "If you weren't right here, see, you might think I took that brandy over there but being as you're right here you can see the bottle's almost empty anyway. And don't you worry about leaving your wallet around because I never take money from anybody. I never take anything that ain't freely offered, especially from a gentleman, because my husband wouldn't let me."

There was nothing to explain about tidying the room, nothing more than the usual admonitions about leaving papers as they were and taking care of breakables. Mrs. Bender, in fact, did not appear to listen as he began to tell her, but seated herself on a leather hassock before him, her soft opaque eyes fixed on him with her vaguely knowing smile. He could not disguise his surprise when she lit a cigarette, but she misconstrued the cause and said hastily, "No, I didn't take yours. I always carry my own cigarettes, no need to worry about that."

She had finished the room, evidently, but made no move

to go. Allan wondered uncertainly, if she was waiting to be paid or if she was under the delusion she was to act as a companion.

"I like it up here, you know, off by ourselves this way," she said, comfortably blowing a ring of smoke. "Living in a basement like I do this is a nice change. Quiet and private. Not like working in a regular home. I guess you and I can get along alright. Of course my husband wouldn't let me work for anybody unless it was a perfect gentleman."

Allan could hear himself imitating the baby lady voice for the benefit of Lyle and his evening's guests.

"Would your husband allow you to accept the brandy?" he asked.

Mrs. Bender considered this, he was amused to see, with great seriousness, blowing several smoke rings into space and finally studying the bottle as if the answer would come from some genie within.

"Tell you what," she decided, "he might not like it if I brought the bottle home, but it would be alright to drink it here. I guess you'd like some, too, kinda brace you up after being outdoors in all that wind."

"The glasses are in the little corner cupboard," he said, smiling openly now. "Very little for me, please."

"Now you're talking," Mrs. Bender said, quickly stamping out her cigarette in the tray and producing bottle and glasses with unexpected alacrity. She sat down with her glass, drawing her chair nearer to him, and looking at him with her odd, watchful smile.

"I'll just kinda relax and take my time if it's all the same to you," she said. "If I got home too soon my husband would think I hadn't done my work right and he wouldn't like that. He wouldn't want anyone going around saying his wife didn't do her work right."

It was too amazing, and so basically feminine, Allan thought, in its peculiar way—shuffling chivalric husband and standards of etiquette for her own curious purposes.

He was exhilarated by something—no matter how trivial —happening to him now instead of always in the past, or in his reading. He felt alive again.

"You're too fine-looking a man to be wasting away up here all alone, mister," she said, sipping her glass.

It would make a funny anecdote at dinner; he was particularly good at imitating odd accents, and it would show he had a life of his own in a way, still open to the unexpected. But for some reason Allan did not mention the episode at dinner that night. When Lyle asked him how he came to spend so long a time on the roof, he answered that he had happened to find himself in particularly good form for working.

15

. . . the trade analysts . . .

*W*HAT do we mean by the name "Strafford's?"
Or rather, what do we think when we use the word "Strafford's?" What flashes across the mind—the very first association, that is—before we have time to think? What does
"Strafford's" *stand for,* perhaps I should put it that way?
Without stopping to connect it consciously with publishing do we think Permanence, Quality, Usefulness, Luxury, Escape, Jewelry, a style of dress, perhaps . . . ?

These were the solemn questions under discussion in
the conference room of Strafford's increasingly affluent
company when Frederick, at the urgent behest of Mr.
Strafford, reluctantly appeared. He had been aware of
the brainstorm that had recently visited Mr. Strafford,
resulting in carpenters, painters, new faces and great
batches of important inter-office memoranda all over the
place. Miss Jones, the wizened young-old firm fixture who
handled the routine details of *Haw* with one hand, while
brewing a canned stew over a sterno with the other, had
informed Frederick some time ago that Strafford's was
being "stream-lined."

At first the process revealed itself in the form of millions
of memos in triplicate (one for your desk, one for your
files, one for checking and returning to the sender) snow-
ing over the employees warning against paper wastage, and
appraising all of changes in personnel which they had
already noticed. The memos stated that hereafter, as part
of the firm's progressive policy, the receptionist was to be

149

called Contact Manager, the switchboard operator was Traffic Co-ordinator, the file chief was Chief Co-ordinator, the salesmen were Traction Engineers, the office boy was Intercommunication Chief, all clerks were Junior Executives, stenographers were Communications Executives, and Mr. Strafford himself was Operations Chief or "O.C." if you wanted to save the company's time and paper and indicate a cozy familiarity between boss and workers. Accustomed to Mr. Strafford's periodic attacks of business genius (coincident usually with a splendid hangover, remorse and resolutions) Frederick paid little attention to these manifestations, expecting them to blow over in due course. The changes did not affect the *Haw* office, since the firm's connection with this seedy sheet was still a secret. But after a few weeks it became apparent that this revolution was something out of the ordinary; heads were rolling, brisk new chiefs and executives replaced what the memos referred to as "deadwood;" desks whizzed through the halls, a loud speaker croaked out messages and calls to conference from the O.C.'s office and the Intercommunication Chief rushed from office to office in this busy bedlam pinning up large placards saying "THINK." Frederick was not to escape participation in this, for after his ignoring dozens of peremptory calls to attend Policy Change Conferences, Miss Jones informed him that his presence was now obligatory, not as *Haw* of course, but as one of the book department's Editorial Advisers.

"Strafford's is being analyzed now," Miss Jones gloomily stated. "That woman who's always flying around here with her hat on and types memos standing up with one glove on is doing it."

"Mrs. Caswell," Frederick remembered. "I thought she was publicity or something."

"She's from Berghart and Caswell, Trade Analysts," corrected Miss Jones. "They analyze institutions and stores. They did Beckley's Jubilee Year and it seems its the talk of the trade. So of course the boss had to have them, too. Her name's Eva Caswell."

Frederick glanced idly at the latest memo on his desk, ignored up to that point.

"Mr. Olliver, *please!*" read the dashing handwriting in green ink. "What happens to Strafford's concerns you just as much as it does everyone else. In order to get a clear picture of Strafford's as a whole we need your help. *You* as much as anyone else *are* Strafford's. Now that we've cleared out the deadwood and gotten focussed on our objective, do let's work together on the new structure. Four o'clock today in the new conference room, then, for our final week of crystallization. P.S. Dear, dear Mr. Olliver, I know very well you're busy, but this is the big moment in our firm's life, so big we're inviting our most important friends in for today's conference. I know you will come. Yours, Topsy."

"Topsy?" repeated Frederick.

"She signs her personal notes Topsy," Miss Jones explained. "It's just a cute way of saying her name's Eva."

"I see," said Frederick. "Why do I have to go?"

"I guess to make a show for the editorial department," Miss Jones offered. "There is so much sales and promotion and advertising that I guess it doesn't look right to have hardly any editors. Ever since *Court Lady's* been a bestseller Strafford lets the sales-force pick the books. He always goes a little nuts when he makes money or goes on the wagon. We just humor him."

Frederick was in a dour state of mind since the *Haw* job, which was to be such a casual affair, was requiring more and more of his time due to its outrageous success. It seemed to prove that a magazine with no staff, no taste, no conferences or danger of improving the reader's mind, could run on greased tracks. He spent an hour or two every morning in the office then left the routine with his instructions to Miss Jones and the make-up man. He was free to ascend the stairs to Strafford's proper and devote the rest of his day to his own work, but what use was it? It disgusted him that he could handle *Haw,* which he hated, with belligerent efficiency, but was powerless to promote his own work. He checked and polished his own manuscript, planned his work for *Swann*, commented on works of other authors, but was corroded with the bitter conviction that he was victimized. His worst obstacle was his success with *Haw*. Strafford, he knew, realized that publication of his book with no more than his usual laurels, would ruin the golden goose. Frederick was too proud to push his own cause, relying on his haughty modesty to elicit eventual justice. Moreover, the disturbed condition of his private life made him fear a direct showdown with Strafford. He mocked himself by sudden bursts of studying *Haw's* success with the seriousness of Larry attacking a cigarette slogan for Hazelnut. That morning he had found sardonic amusement in discussing a new comic strip with an ex-convict's ghost-writer. He described the moral value of a serial about a two-cent crook who was always caught and he spoke of the great artistic merit of such a project. He dictated a note to Miss Jones on obtaining a strip to popularize the adventures of Candide. He added a pompous editorial foreword on the intellectual beauties of the comic strip, the international good-will engendered, the crimes prevented, the seeds of social conscience planted through sheer economy of articulate or literate thoughts. He smiled inwardly when Miss Jones, who had her own opinion of a man whose books contained no conversation suddenly looked at him over her notebook with the dawn of reverence. At last, her expression said, you have seen the great light, you really aren't such a dope after all. You can learn . . . "Mr. Olliver," she breathed, "you're a genius." Art is a cigarette ad, then, Frederick mused, literature is a soap opera, integrity is getting your claptrap done by pay-day so you can take some trollop to some clip joint where she can double-cross you.

It seemed to him that Dodo's capricious treatment of him was somehow responsible for the dismal confusion of his life. The effort of justifying his infatuation was tainting his whole reasoning processes. He blamed Strafford for taking advantage of his weakest moment; he blamed Lyle for allowing him to fall in love with another woman and again for not consoling his vanity when Dodo injured it; he blamed Dodo for keeping him in such spasms of uncertainty that the affair had no chance to burn itself out. (Where had she been last night and the night before? In what gay place had she been gay with what stupid rival? Had she forgotten it was he who had gotten her that movie job that offered her such splendid pastures? He dialed her office. "Freddie, please don't bother me when I'm at work," she said primly. "I'm terribly busy. One of our West Coast producers just got in and I have to show him around . . . Well, for goodness' sake, you must have heard of Eddie Fargo! . . . No, I can't meet you at the Barrel, I'm going to La Rue with Eddie. It's business and besides I've never been to La Rue . . . Oh Freddie, stop being such a silly goon. We're not engaged!")

And now, smarting under all these wounds he must be further tortured by attending an asinine seance concerning the "stream-lining" of Benedict Strafford's business. Yes, and there was no use blaming anyone else for his fix, disagreeable as this admission was. He was furious with himself for being the gull, for lacking the offensive capacity for personal promotion. He was the nice little fellow who was always the scapegoat in the school prank, the respectable gentleman who always got snow-balled, the good husband who always got the horns. Always the target, never the archer, he berated himself. Frederick tore up the note signed *Topsy* and flung it viciously in the waste-basket. Only six months ago he had been a free man—now look at him!—so tarnished with compromises that he dared not demand his simple rights. He could not free himself from Dodo but at least he could resign from *Haw*. He would, yes he would resign; moreover he would insist that his manuscript be published without further delay. He would have an understanding with Strafford at once, today, and give up once and for all the naïve notion that one gentleman behaving with modesty and forbearance induces another to recognize his undeclared rights.

"Trade analysts," he mocked as he went up to the conference room.

Berghart and Caswell had evidently been at work on every phase of Strafford life, for the once dank, mission-panelled old room was now air-conditioned red-lacquered and glass-bricked, artificial daylight oozing from the happy walls illuminating with impartial precision the doodlings on every memorandum pad. In the diffusion of false sunshine Frederick saw a complete wax works conference set around the long center table—the university president, the magazine editor, the venerable explorer, the refugee professor of note, faculty brothers from the League of Cultural Foundations and behind them, a dozen departmental figures and other gloomy countenances of undoubted leaden weight in the world of letters. Mr. Strafford motioned him to a vacant chair with an air of grave responsibility.

"Mr. Olliver, of course you know," he whispered loudly to the gentleman beside him. "A special editorial consultant for us, distinguished writer as well."

"Extinguished, he means," Frederick thought.

He observed with distrust Mrs. Caswell and her assistant at the head of the table. You would know them anywhere, he thought, as the robot engineers of a vast machine, oiling and guiding it to work with the speed and tireless futility of an exercise horse. Mrs. Caswell's bisque face, electrically-controlled twinkles, dimples, smiles, frowns, and laughter were phenomenally and impressively unlife-like—the business mama-doll, call me Topsy for business camaraderie, Eva for formal intimacies. Business mama-doll, Iron Virgin, chromium Lorelei, the camouflaged Vacuum Cleaner ready to clean any vacuum. Her assistant bore similar traces of terrifying robot leadership—a keen-eyed young man in chalk-striped business

suit, black-rimmed spectacles, a well-exercised, well-Turk-
ish-bathed, well-groomed, well-disguised steel model for
success, who slipped notes under the nose of big chief
with mechanical regularity. Mr. Strafford, directly between his two experts, looked winningly apoplectic and
human, even juicy, and Frederick speculated on how
much juice the two Fruit-masters could really squeeze
out of him. He would be popped in the lady robot's jaw
of Hollywood-capped teeth and come out the male robot's
jaw of powerful porcelain, all canned and labelled for
distribution. Mrs. Caswell acknowledged Frederick's arrival with a flashing smile and wagging of a pink-gloved
finger.

"Our truant," she said. Faces of salesmen, and other
departmental furnishings of Strafford's turned to Frederick with a dull apathy engendered by six weeks of daily
pep-talks. Frederick thought he caught a flicker of scorn
from the Traction Engineers who must be recalling the
difficulty of selling his last book.

"Mrs. Caswell is giving us our final analysis today,"
Strafford announced in a solemn voice. "We want to restore the firm's name to its original significance. To do
so we have had Mrs. Caswell, our expert, analyze our
conception of the firm's original status and then compare
with its present one. We have slipped, boys and girls, if
Mrs. Caswell's report is to be trusted and of course it is
or she wouldn't be here—we have gone far off our proper
course. All very well to be making more money than
ever before but what of our seventy-year-old reputation
as intellectual aristocrats?"

Mrs. Caswell graciously allowed the publisher to have
his say, then tossed aside the wisps of pink veil over the
gay, crazy hat that showed she was woman first, executive
second according to the latest robot rules.

"Like any private analyst we make no definite suggestions. We only help you to help yourself. We add up
what you yourselves have said and show you the final

figure. In this case, after six weeks of study and daily get togethers we submit our findings. Do you know what the name Strafford's now stands for—or is beginning to stand for? Tell them, Vincent."

"Sex," said her assistant and Frederick heard a stunned voice behind him murmur "Good God!"

"Ever since the novel *I Was a Court Lady* has rocked the country and incidentally put our company in the black, we have been attacked from pulpit to lecture room as purveyors of obscene literature," Mrs. Caswell continued. "Mr. Strafford himself actually admits he has been refused membership in a very fine club because of his connection with the book. The quality of manuscripts submitted to us has dropped to the level of pulp fiction. We have censors after every book we put out as if we were in the erotica business. Since this is the first major success in forty years the firm has many enemies to help capitalize on the unpleasant reputation. Mr. Strafford realizes that he owes a great debt to the ancestor who founded the firm, and must repay it by restoring the original prestige at any cost. How? Let's hear from our distinguished visitors."

The university president, well known as a guest on Invitation to Learning pitting his er-er-ers against those of the most erudite, now obliged with the famous clearing of throat that blew the cobwebs from his mental wine-cellar, and declared hoarsely that the answer was obvious. Strafford's must counter their errors by publishing treasuries of profoundest significance and give them promotion equal to the *Court Lady*. Mr. Strafford looked vaguely distressed, thanked the doctor, and said hopefully that he was sure Tyson Bricker, the well-known molder of public opinion might have an even better, more definite solution.

Mr. Bricker, never one to be caught napping, sprang to his feet.

"I would suggest getting hold of something—say like

Nietzsche or Shaw—something new and controversial, something with bite, then push it to the skies. I agree with the doctor that now is the time to show you dare be an intellectual. Furthermore . . ."

Jingling his keys with his right hand and stroking the back of his gray hair with his left, gazing dreamily at the ceiling, Mr. Bricker was the picture of a man-thinking-out-loud, a feat for which he was famous.

"The original Strafford dared publish many uncommercial books," he pursued in a gently musing bed-side manner, a manner that allowed him to switch to the opposite view if it seemed more advisable. "Why not recapture that old spirit of daring? Dare to be long-hair, as the saying is." Looking about among the impassive faces for a sympathetic response his eyes lit on Frederick and he went on more urgently, "Olliver, there, ought to have some ideas. I'm sure he'll agree with me that if Sex is dragging you down on the one hand you need Brains to bring up the balance. Start an intellectual revolution, Benedict. Let Strafford's be our leaders, show us the way out of materialism and nationalism, give us a new philosopher or a poet—something to build a new culture upon. Come on, Olliver, a seasoned scholar like you ought to give us a definite lead to work on. What about some hook-up between the Renaissance and today —you know that field better than I do. Who's our man—what's our angle?"

Frederick felt the blood rushing away from his body, veins and arteries being filled with a torrent of tears, hot and searing. This was the time when he should have robot molten steel coursing through him, this was the time he should rise and say, "Gentlemen, this firm has the answer in your safe at this moment, a work by Frederick Olliver on the seeds of thought planted in ancient and medieval monasteries, the roots that grew in the earth when the flowers were scorched by wars and tyranny, the roots that produced tranquillity and beauty after cen-

turies of despair, the tree that never dies that bears peace
and salvation forever. The book you want is mine, gentlemen, and the man you want is Olliver."

For a fleeting moment the thought seemed to communicate itself to Tyson on whose face a sudden light dawned.
He pointed at Frederick, then snapped his fingers triumphantly, in a gesture of inspiration. It could not be,
Frederick warned himself, trying to hold back the wild
hope. Was there possibly a chance that his hour had come
at last?

"By George, Olliver, you *are* the man," cried Tyson.
"That manuscript of yours gives a hundred and one lights
on this very problem. I swear, people, that if any one
man can give us a definite lead on the kind of book we
want it's Frederick Olliver. Obviously, if we've gotten a
reputation for vulgarity we regain prestige by throwing
our weight behind some classical work of high aspiration.
Let's look into Olliver's work for suggestions."

Mr. Strafford, looking increasingly red and uneasy,
asked, "Have you anything to suggest, Olliver?"

Frederick rose unsteadily, gathering steel from the
bright glitter of the eyes of Mrs. Caswell and her assistant.
He was weak with a helpless rage of which he had not
dreamed himself capable. The hopes he had buried each
year deeper and deeper had risen shamefully to the sur-
face at Tyson's first appeal to him, betraying him again,
weakening him to cruel disappointment, making him
once more the eternal gull, vulnerable, prey to every false
dream.

No, he would not hope, he would not be party to any
hope, no one could say he was open again to despair.

There was an exchange of notes between Male and
Female robot as he rose to his feet. Before he could speak
Mrs. Caswell leaned forward to ask with great intentness,
"What about this manuscript of yours, Mr. Olliver? Per-
haps that's the very thing we're after."

"Hardly. The money to be offended at failing prestige,"
Frederick said, smiling coldly, "was obtained by publish-

ing an offensive novel. I suggest that Strafford's publish as many such books as they can find until their integument is gilt-proofed against shame."

There was a ripple of laughter, a reproachful shake of the head from Tyson, and then the Traction Manager got up applauding Frederick's suggestion. Frederick felt as if he was choking to death, as if his familiar enemy, himself, had burnt his throat with the mocking words. The only power over his life that he had, he thought, was the power to ruin whatever meant most to him, to show he had discarded hope before hope had left. It was impossible to stay in the room any longer not knowing what fresh damage he might do himself, either by his mockery or the folly of new hope. He pushed out the door, glad of the voices raised in argument that cloaked his exit. He ran downstairs to the *Haw* office to snatch his coat and hat. On the street he started to hail a cab, but, after all, where was he going? Some place, where he could cry out. *But I didn't believe them, you see, I wasn't fooled this time, I was smart enough to know it was a trap and I didn't fall. But wasn't it a cruel joke?*

I have no one, no one, he thought more with surprise than self-pity, and the fault is in me because I have always hidden myself, because I never learned the secret of communication with human beings, because I have always been afraid and have worn armor and a foil on my rapier, never trusting treaties, my friends, enemies or myself . . .

Lyle was the only person in his whole existence before whom he had laid down arms, whose identity with himself was safe and implicit, but now that was gone . . . You rejected me, she would say, and now you are rejected and you expect me to console you for this justice? There was Murray, at this very minute in all probability standing at the bar in Bleeck's for his first five o'clock exhilarator, but how could he describe to him his fierce self-defeat without first explaining who he was, what the real self beneath his Murray-self was? In a crisis there was no one who even knew you—there was no eye that would not cloud with bewilderment if not contempt that what meant nothing to him should mean everything to you. I have no one, Frederick thought—even if I were sure of seeing Dodo there is no language between us, she would understand only that something had defeated me and she would rejoice as if in some way it exalted her. In a way he felt the elation of complete destruction, himself, just as Dodo would. He was as much his own enemy after all as was Dodo. He was conscious of walking toward Times Square, hurrying, as if he were late to a definite destination and realized he was on the way to Dodo's office in the Paramount Building. He suddenly wondered what bribe he had for her favor, as busy parents wonder, coming home late with no toy for the spoiled child. He was ashamed for himself and for his love that he should immediately think of promising her an introduction to Edwin Stalk of whom she had recently been hearing, or he would take her to the night's opening and point out, even introduce her to important people. He would not talk of his own desperation, but he would have the consolation of making love to her. That much, at least, he thought. Dodo was standing at the reception desk, her hat on, green sport coat jauntily over her shoulders, absorbed in painting her lips when Frederick came in. (She was hoping for someone else, he guessed, but he might do.)

"How'd you know I'd be here this late?" she wanted to know. "I always leave at five but Carter Tenafly, you know, the English writer that wrote the book of the month is in with J. B. so I waited to see if they needed me for anything."

"Come down to my place for tea," Frederick said, trying to sound casual, knowing that a hint of his urgency would put her out of reach at once. "We can celebrate later."

Dodo looked at him curiously.

"You look sort of funny, did something happen?"

"Yes," Frederick said wildly. "I've just come into some money, in fact a small fortune. Of course it's a secret."

Dodo's eyes widened. With a squeal of delight she slipped her hand under his arm.

"Freddie! How wonderful! Oh do let's celebrate! Oh I wish you'd let me go in and tell Mr. Tenafly and J. B. Oh Freddie, do let me tell them . . ."

"No, no, it's a secret!" Frederick said, pulling her toward the elevator, his hands trembling and his whole body shaking with the shame of his lie and the necessity for it. Dodo looked reluctantly back toward the door where the great men were conferring. Frederick knew she had been waiting, as she always did, for the men to come out, find her alone there, and in a burst of after-hours geniality, perhaps invite her to join them, drink with them, sleep with them—whatever would seem the greatest social honor to her. But he didn't care. He didn't care what monstrous lie had won her sudden change of heart, making her snuggle tenderly in his arms in the taxi all the way downtown. Once there, shades drawn and door bolted, nothing mattered, but the marvel of her happy complaisance, her return to her original role of eager seductress, flinging off her flimsy garments, pouting naughtily over a difficult fastening, kicking her slippers across the room to land on his hat. I do have this, this much at least for this minute is mine, Frederick thought, his head throbbing fiercely. But after a little while he lay with his head in the pillow, aching with the agony of further defeat, and Dodo swiftly and ominously dressing herself, face flushed with rage.

"Dodo . . ." he murmured. "Wait . . ."

"For what?" she said harshly, putting on her hat without even looking in the mirror. "Life is too short to wait for a miracle. I'm going out with a real man."

He heard the door bang viciously. He had no one, no, no one and he despised himself fervently.

16

. . . the black magic . . .

*G*ERDA CAHILL had a knack, everyone said and she admitted it herself with perfect candor. She was a born salonnière. She could, she laughingly confessed, turn a seat on a Greyhound bus or a roomette on a train into her own salon at the drop of an olive. She could move into the most barren cellar in the dreariest alley in Europe, any place from Telegraph Hill to Savannah— (you should have seen her place there on Factors Row), toss a scarf over a broken box, simply fill the umbrella jar with fresh green branches or possibly claret cup, cover the rat holes with Aubusson scraps, and in no time everyone who was anyone for miles around would be drawn there magnetically, crying out that there was no one in the world with such a knack as Gerda. It was a knack that had annoyed and fascinated her ex-husband, since he understood neither her motives nor their rewards. For years she had maintained an attic at thirty dollars a month in a condemned building far over by the East River, in the Thirties. Inconvenient of access as it was, the minute she was back in town guests came and went, found the key to the mailbox if no one answered their ring, brought their compositions for her piano, their poems for her desk, their tears for her shoulder, their friends for her supper. Gerda accepted each new talent at its owners own appraisal with the good-natured tolerance that comes of ignorance and serene indifference to

162

everything outside one's self. Her little geniuses sometimes found that her seeming appreciation was merely a mirror giving back no more than it received. At least she was never disillusioned or angry when they arrived at a position to drop her, and often in more discriminating salons they missed Gerda's amiable unanalytical applause.

She had the easy self-confidence of having renounced high society in her youth, preferring the bohemian life, and she still spent a great deal of time assuring everyone that she would never, never go back or ever regret the place in Tuxedo. As is usually the case with those who throw away titles or position to champion the peasantry she had trouble convincing these chosen friends that she was even an equal; they suspected her of coming up from even lower depths, fruit of the most depraved miscegenation. However, Gerda was blind to this, and would scarcely have understood such skepticism in any case.

Auctions at Flattau and Park Bernet had yielded her a dozen tremendous pieces of formidable furniture, bargains because no respectable home was large enough to house them. A great square piano and a gold-painted sedan chair were lavishly useless but impressive; in the corner tottered a huge rococo wardrobe closet decorated with life-size Cupids chipping off like old love itself, the loose doors popping open at the sound of any bell or automobile horn as if to allow refuge for half a dozen secret lovers instead of for the gaudy costumes packed within. Chairs were never less than thrones and quite as precarious; divans were sumptuously pillowed to atone for dead springs; rugs were deep-piled, ancient, choking up with dust as if with tears, at the least footfall. Caroline Drake thought everything looked frightfully buggy and usually gave herself a thorough brushing the minute she got outside, but then Gerda privately thought Caroline's own glass house was very Gimbelish looking. One good thing was that there were always lots of men, new men, at Gerda's, though Caroline said it was no wonder; any woman who stayed home all day, kept the latch open and always had a pot of soup on the stove and a thimble of liquor could have the place teeming with men. Caroline herself usually managed to bring home from Gerda's parties some young choreographer, poet or percussionist willing to forget his sexual preferences in exchange for her Scotch. There was always the fun of seeing poor Murray trapped there, too, glaring around to see what people liked about this sort of thing, prepared to take a poke at anyone who might be making fun of Gerda when she began speaking foreign languages or discussing world affairs.

"Gerda doesn't want him there and he hates it but he just can't stay away," Caroline said to Lorna Leahy. "I think he comes because he's a frustrated martyr. He wants to be in a bar bellyaching to the fellows about his wife nagging, making him come to her parties and damned if he will. It baffles him horribly to have her beg him to stay away, so of course he has to come."

Caroline thought she might inveigle Murray out if the crowd stayed on, but there was an even better prospect today for Gerda had sworn to produce Frederick Olliver, always a prize to be fought over with Lorna. Frederick had started out by mocking at Gerda's artificial postures but had ended by discovering an admirable basic sincerity in the tremendous to-do she made over him. He was almost sure to be there. This was the reason Caroline waited half an hour in the pouring rain for a cross-town bus, unable to get a cab, her brand-new brass-gold curls wilting by the minute. She was sure Lorna would be there even if she had to swim because she was so damned afraid Caroline would grab off Frederick. First it had been Murray Cahill, now it was Frederick. Silly to find yourself practically breaking up an old friendship over a man who didn't care, really, about either of you and whom, for that matter, neither of you really wanted. It was all Lorna's fault for being so underhanded. When Caroline asked Frederick to dinner she used to ask Lorna too, until she discovered that whenever Lorna rounded him up she kept him smugly to herself to crow about later. The result was that Caroline was unwilling to pass up a chance to get ahead of Lorna. In addition to bucking the storm she had to carry two bottles of rye under her arm (Gerda wouldn't have anything but wine and everybody had to chip in on anything else), and by the time she had gotten off into the flooded gutter and her umbrella had blown inside out, Caroline was in no mood for carnival, longing to step into a vestibule and swig her bottles all alone. The rain was coming down in torrents, a garbage can had overturned and was shipping grapefruit rinds down the streaming street, people with sense were darting under the El posts or into shops, newspapers over their heads; no one would dream of being out on such a night except a woman looking for a man.

"Even Lorna won't come," Caroline thought. "It would be too obvious."

She struggled with hat, bottles, and umbrella across the street, dodged the careening garbage-can lid as it sailed past her, and blinded by the cutting rain was almost felled by a taxi-cab skidding to a stop before Gerda's address. Caroline muttered a sincere oath as she reached the door of the battered building and was discomfited to see that the occupant of the taxi-cab was following her and had heard her. Anyway it meant that there was another fool besides herself today—a woman too, of course. To her surprise she recognized Mrs. Gaynor, no one she ever expected to see at Gerda's and who probably wouldn't remember having met her once in a restaurant with Murray Cahill, but this was no day for coy reserve and Caroline reminded her at once of their former encounter. Mrs. Gaynor was openly grateful for a kind word in this unknown world. Almost in the same breath they apologized for having braved the tempest for such a slight occasion, as if their presence was a shocking confession of loneliness and scarcity of opportunities. Caroline suddenly remembered that this was rumored to be the woman in Frederick's life, and thought happily, well

if she gets him away today she'll be taking him from
Lorna as well as herself. They climbed the four flights
of stairs—good heavens, what fools! Tornadoes, four flights
of stairs, anything for a man! They passed the show-room
for artificial limbs on the first landing, the chemical
laboratory with its mysterious smells on the second, the
photographer's studio on the third. The contrast of rot-
ting stair-case and feeble light on mottled walls only
intensified the seedy grandeur of Gerda's carpeted, in-
cense-filled hall, her door gaily hung with sleighbells.

As they waited Caroline studied her companion furtively, reflecting that she was losing her looks, thank God;
that radiant red-haired pearly-skin glow did wear out
faster than less sensational types. (Mustn't be too critical,
though, the rain had probably washed out her own looks
as well.) She still had a figure, *faux-maigre* as the copy
called it, feathery light but curved. Having no bones
helped, of course, Caroline reflected enviously, wishing
some magic would melt down her own rawboned hips.
Lyle, for her part thought here was one of the women who
now figured in Frederick's life, here was someone who
was closer to him than she was and she wanted to cry out
"What was it he wanted that I couldn't give him and you
others could? Where did I fail? What made him change, or
was he always looking for something else and I didn't
guess?" She wondered if the reason for her unusual presence at Gerda Cahill's was completely obvious, if the
other woman guessed at once that her life, without her
lover, was spent in tracking down remnants of him, taking
up whatever person was said to be now in his confidence,
gathering mournful solace from merely hearing his name
spoken, piecing together a Frederick she had never known
from scraps of strangers' talk. Analyzing, rehearsing accusations and then apologies, puzzling over the change in
him, she thought the truth must be that one never
changed, one was merely found out. She had been blind,
that was all, cruelly blind. She had reproached him for
his resentment of her kind of life and his unwillingness

to take part in it or wait on the outskirts for her spare moments; but she herself had never made an effort to enter his life, beyond the confidences he offered, until he was gone. Only then did she comprehend the vast ocean between them, the ocean she always expected him to overcome. At every step of her road backwards to reconstruct a man she had never known she found new cause for penitence. No wonder he disliked her circle! No wonder he hated the Beckleys, the nightclubs, the parties, the first nights. It was easier to admit her own cruelty than to bear the burden of his. Lyle only hoped that her new knowledge of him would not cause her to fling herself at his feet for forgiveness if they should be left alone.

How sweet of them to come on such a day, Gerda cried, spectacular in a sea-green velvet robe, both hands reaching out to them through twin cylinders of tinkling bracelets, while the eyes of both guests leapt past their welcome into the dark corners of the room to see if He was there. Lyle could see the *Swan's* Mexican poet lying on the floor playing with Iamb, the cat, pulling its claws over his thick black hair, laughingly inviting bites and scratches. Lorna Leahy, in gray slacks and tight purple sweater, emerald bow in white curly mop, was very much at home as hostess-assistant, stirring up the great vase of wine and fruit mixture with a baton.

"I put rum in it this time," she whispered loudly to Caroline. "After all it's a celebration, isn't it?"

Frederick was not here but this was part of the life he liked, Lyle thought, and looked eagerly around. In a corner by the Franklin stove she saw a little pallid blonde with the intent vague expression, coronet of braids, high cheek-bones and firm calves of the dancer, earnestly demonstrating some sort of Oriental contortion to two fragile young men in plaid wool shirts.

"It's the story of Ramajana, the Demon King of Sanka," Gerda explained to Lyle. "Then she's doing something perfectly extraordinary on the Krishna dances during the

Monsoon Rains. I want Miranda to show them to Frederick Olliver especially."

"He's coming?" Lyle asked involuntarily. Gerda slipped her bracelets up and down her arms and Lyle was not sure the sound of bells was from them or from the sweet syllables of Frederick's name.

"Of course," Gerda said. "I had to coax him but by this time I know he adores parties; he just wants to be coaxed."

Another thing she had never guessed in her cursed complacency, Lyle reflected.

The windows shook with the lash of rain, fog-horns bellowed from the bowels of the earth, the long narrow room in candle light with the giant furniture and fluttering draperies seemed a vault for musty treasures and guests from beyond. Yet the sleighbells on the door quivered with newcomers, the reality of the tempest was admitted by the growing mound of galoshes, proof that there were dozens of foolish citizens who were glad to give up lonely security in their own rooms for danger in company, the bare chance of finding the lost love or the new. Years of war were sponged off, those who must have been involved avoided its mention as if they were on probation for a crime they hoped would be forgotten. But then these were days when the gift of forgetting was a treasure in itself.

Caroline Drake was obliged to greet Lorna Leahy with exaggerated joy, and Lyle, left alone, saw no one she knew. She was ashamed and frightened that no one, except Padilla, the poet, recognized the name Lyle Gaynor, or if they did there was none of the respectful murmur she had not realized she took for granted as her due. She regretted that she had not taken more pleasure at the time in the critical praise for *Summer Day*, whose advent last year was overshadowed by the success of half a dozen subsequent hits. But she had been too cautiously cynical in her theory that the press had only the power of veto. Drama critics in the city, she often said, were like an old married couple; they had lived together so long they looked and thought alike, they disagreed only on the details of the funeral—burial or cremation? They compared plays with other plays, never with life, for they sent the second-string reviewers to that; a play was true to "life" if it conformed to other plays on the same subject. Life, in fact, was a lady in front asked to remove her hat so they could see the play. Sometimes they took a sabbatical year but only to travel; a theatrical gesture in itself. The Gaynor plays, they chanted, were gay, bitter, revealing studies of sensitive moderns, true pictures of modern society. How would they know, Lyle had queried, except that they recognized the sets from the last play of modern society? But she had profited by their dream world and knew she had received far more applause than she deserved. At least she had *thought* she knew that, even when she was most contemptuously ungrateful in her mind. But now that she seemed in danger of being obscured merely for an hour or two she was dashed, even hurt. If she was to see Frederick again here she must have her usual, undeserved, court. For the first time it came home to her how comfortably she had counted on reputation to make up for minor personal disappointments. A crutch, a cushion, a veil, a safety net for all missteps, that knowledge of work recognized and admired whether she was old or young. Without it she felt vulnerable and exposed, a woman in her thirties whom no one knew, an everyday woman with no protection of love or fame, with no banner to bear but that of pleading mistress begging for a crumb. Left standing unnoticed for a moment it struck Lyle how soft and spoiled she was, never venturing on any path that was not especially paved for her, innocently astonished that the paving could wear out and torches on dark corners would not be lit. And she had been hurt because Frederick was no braver than she!

"I didn't get the name." Someone was repeating Gerda's introduction, but even when it was repeated there was no sign of recognition or interest. How perfectly idiotic to expect any, Lyle thought, but, after all, she had been spoiled and Frederick had been too kind to tell her even when he knew it was a wall between them. It was as silly as an old romance where lovers separate forever because, incredibly enough, she has not explained to him that she is a duchess or pregnant, and he has not explained that he has tuberculosis or a mad wife.

With a wave of relief she saw that Tyson Bricker had arrived and with his usual quick appraisal of the contents of a room had elected her as the one of most importance. Accustomed to being the aggressor, if not the intruder, he must have been surprised at the cordiality of her greeting, not realizing that he was rescuing someone from a desert island of self-analysis.

"Who would dream of finding you here, dear lady?" he exclaimed, drawing her hand under his arm and stroking it fondly. "Gerda's is the place for promising talent, not for the already-arrived."

"Should I be offended or flattered?" Lyle asked, warmed with mere recognition. She had long ago accepted Frederick's disparaging opinion of the man as a relentless, if shrewd, climber, but at least he was familiar.

"Not yet published, exhibited, heard or seen are the entrance requirements for membership here," Tyson murmured in her ear. "We grown-ups are allowed only on sufferance and must expect certain youthful insults. I never find you at home any more, you cruel creature. Everyone says the Gaynors have begun to lock their door to the old friends. Where does one find you these days?"

"Here today," answered Lyle. "How do you happen to be here, yourself?"

Tyson squinted at his wrist watch after another lightning calculation of the room's value in human possibilities.

"I promised to pick up Frederick Olliver here. No taxis and I have the car outside unless it's floated down the river. Interesting chap, Olliver. I remember now you used to try to sell him to me."

"What finally sold you?" Lyle asked.

Tyson produced cigarettes and a lighter with a thoughtful frown.

"I already had him at the League, of course. But it was what he did with that *Haw* magazine that really sold me on the man. Phenomenal. Not many know he's at the bottom of it, of course."

Lyle said nothing. Poor Frederick. She should have understood how the ironic success of *Haw* had only pointed up his other failures and made him dash with almost suicidal frenzy into anything new or different.

"I only know his other work," she finally said. "You must admire that, of course."

"Admire it?" exclaimed Tyson. "My dear lady, I've finally succeeded in putting it over! I must say it's been a tough job, too, when you consider how difficult Olliver himself is. When you hear about it I'll bet you anything you'll have to credit me with one of the sweetest deals in my whole career."

"You've persuaded Strafford to publish his book?" Lyle guessed.

Tyson looked pained.

"Strafford! Oh yes, of course he'll want to take all the credit! But I'm sure Olliver realizes who is responsible. Don't ask me any more questions because it's not to be told yet. But it so happened I was in a position to pick anyone and I put my money on Olliver. I wonder where he is. Coming here was his idea, confound him."

Lyle wondered how it had come about that Frederick should be a frequenter of this environment. His Pooh-girl was no part of it, clearly. She was tantalized by his name leaping out of conversations around her and tried to trace which one had said it and what there was about him or her that fitted into Frederick's present tastes. Which ones had he made love to, what did he talk about when he was alone with Caroline Drake or Gerda or the pixie-faced woman passing out glass cups of whatever it was? Tyson gave her a warning shake of the head as she took the cup, and ever mindful of his expensive stomach he inconspicuously produced a flask for her to share, but Lyle thought this would mark her as an outsider and drank the punch. She saw Murray Cahill in a corner, backed there by Caroline Drake who appeared to be serving her own whiskey to him and other applicants. At least Murray made Frederick seem more imminent, but she was afraid he'd come in and find her standing around like Alice Adams, fixed smile on her face, all too obviously waiting for him. She had two more quick drinks to give her courage to talk to these strangers who ignored her. But one had no right to feel offended at the snubs of the poor or unsuccessful. What?—the hostess failed to introduced you, someone spilled wine on your gown and stepped on your toes? Why not, you are sufficiently famous, as much in public domain as if you were a civic institution. But mind your own manners, let's have no reprisals from you. The Spanish poet, holding the cat around his shoulders like a furpiece with its bushy Persian tail flicking his cheek rhythmically in delicate protest, came over to kiss her hand and speak to Tyson. He was incredibly handsome as well as gifted, and Edwin Stalk had occasionally brought him to her house. Lyle wished she had dared let him make love to her but the memory of love stood between her and any consoling surrender like the Church itself. She was becoming more and more impatient with her body's stern fidelity that remained like a perfume long after the vial was empty. In her old age, she warned herself, she would look back on this continence with regret. No, she thought again, the nuns had something; there was more voluptuous satisfaction in having been desired and withholding than in indifferent squandering and unhappy quests for something beyond the immediate gestures. The real cause for regret in old age would be that one had met no love great enough to command fidelity.

"Padilla refuses to be translated," Tyson said, amused.

Padilla stroked the cat's mouth. (He would be the kind of lover, Lyle thought, who was happier in the exhibition of his skill than the quality of his conquest.)

"Because everything becomes sinister when translated into English," he complained. "Edwin Stalk tells me he will do it very painlessly but it frightens me and I am not going to consent. The Anglo-Saxon poet is always possessed and I am not ready for the devil. Supposing I am translated into a poet who cannot go three blocks from my own door? In Spanish, I am always safe. Maybe I fear that fourth block beyond my door. Never mind, in Spanish the people of the village would have a sweet pepper here, some wine a mile further, good morning, here's a new baby, good-day professor, advise us on philosophy and the weather. Presently I am miles from home, maybe drunk, but at least not Anglo-Saxon. No, I stay Spanish, I tell Edwin Stalk. I am afraid of translation into English."

"The fear itself is a good Anglo-Saxon neurosis," Tyson Bricker said briskly. "Maybe you're already translated, young man. The worst is over."

Lorna Leahy was beside Lyle with a fresh glass, part of Gerda's knack for hospitality being in letting the guests provide for each other as well as for her.

"He was for Franco, you know," Lorna murmured in Lyle's ear. "Can you imagine Gerda sleeping with him? I think we should shave her head, honestly, but of course no one cares about that sort of thing now the war's over. So long as we don't sleep with the French or English or Russians. Really, Mrs. Gaynor, doesn't it seem absolutely mad? We don't know ourselves or anyone else from one day to the next, things are changing so fast. I'm so glad to have this opportunity of meeting you. Will you have a new play for next year?"

"I'm afraid not," Lyle said eagerly, amazed at her childish pleasure in being noticed, almost as if she was through, an old-timer long forgotten.

Lorna watched Caroline's corner jealously and confided

to Lyle that Murray was getting absolutely rigid, thanks to Caroline, and Gerda certainly wouldn't take care of him, throw him right out in the teeth of the hurricane, like as not. As a matter of fact, she, Lorna, thought it would be a good thing to have him take her home where she could look after him before Caroline got him too plastered to move. Not that she expected any thanks, either, for looking after him. The chances were he would probably walk out on her and go see that Judy girl, that little square he always had hanging around. Did Lyle know her? Judy Dahl, new winner of the Hazelnut Cigarette prize, God knows why.

"Obvious," Tyson explained with intent to console. "Like all lady artists she uses her sex to get ahead in her profession, don't you agree, Mrs. Gaynor?"

Lorna was not entirely gratified by this explanation, implying as it did that she herself did not have proper sex appeal to get ahead, and Lyle murmured that women had as much right to use sex to get ahead professionally as men had to use their professional success to get ahead sexually.

"Thinks she's a genuine artist just because she knows the difference between the canvas and the brush," Lorna went on indignantly. "Of course I'm just a hack, you see, that's the idea, because I'm good enough at it to make a living. But she's the real thing, a regular Picasso, because she can't make money! Disgusting! Second prize, mind you! Two conch shells on a table with a doll's head and an alarm clock! Will somebody tell me what that has to do with art or cigarettes? When Hazelnut gives *me* an order I have to make the cigarette look like a cigarette, of course, but little Miss Judy Rembrandt gets a prize and two thousand bucks just to leave out cigarettes. How chic! Yet even Murray himself says she's lousy. Honestly, is it any wonder we drink? Here, let me give you another. God knows it's not champagne but at least it's got rum in it today. I couldn't have stood claret lemonade on a day like this. Excuse me, I have to mix some more."

This was the way Frederick must have felt all these years at her parties, Lyle thought, grateful for an occasional kind word, then left alone thinking, "I'm really an idiot to expose myself to this kind of embarrassment." She tried to detach herself and see everything as Frederick saw it. Obviously he must be the best-known person in a group like this, more than Tyson since his work was elegantly free of mass appeal. They made him feel as young as they were, too, for there was youth in an insecurity with the world ahead; she and Tyson were established and had only the toboggan ahead. That is, if it was for appreciation of his work Frederick came here. She pushed her reservations back in her mind resolutely, attempting very carefully to study every angle of this picture for what it gave him, and she told herself it was unfair to say this was an inexpensive reprint of a Beckley evening, the flaw for him in the latter being that she was central figure and the virtue in the former being that she was not. She saw that Tyson was already bored with the number of guests arriving whom he did not know and who did not know him, or if they did, seemed to regard him as a merely respectable representative of an older, stuffier order. He was not at all pleased when Padilla said to her, "Do you think we could get Edwin Stalk to come to Gerda's sometime? She would be so flattered, but then he doesn't like crowds. If we could get him, it would be amusing."

The punch was making her feel dizzy and a little sick but conscious of Lorna's apology for its not being champagne she felt obliged to drink it whenever it was passed. She must show she could be gracious with Frederick's friends in spite of his making no effort with hers. He had criticized her friends relentlessly and in the end she was seeing them as he saw them—smug, dead, selfish, opportunistic, hollow . . . She tried to see the superiority of these friends of his with his eyes as well, doing her best to keep down the impression that she had seen, heard and discarded all this before in her life-time. In the ballet-lovers group which had grown steadily a lean dark snake-headed girl in a Mexican sweater, velveteen dirndl and thick gaucho boots, leapt to the piano bench every few moments as if to settle some verbal argument by an instrumental rebuttal. "Isn't this the sort of thing you mean, Miranda? Isn't this it?"

Tinkering over the treble chords hopefully, waiting for an invitation to play that never came she presently slipped willy-nilly into a Chopin prelude, head bent submissively over the keyboard, lips moving until she got the right connection when she rolled and gyrated on the piano bench in a pelvic ecstasy, eager to conduct worthy phrases over the doubtful rocks and rills of Gerda's bargain piano. She bent over the tiny runs with a tender smile, letting the smaller Pomeranian chords have the run of their leash, then bending back suddenly as if to keep the big bass hounds from jumping on the grass. Throughout she was the fond, responsible disciplinarian conducting the doggish romp—down Towser, down—come on Peewee, jump, Peewee, down Towser, down, down, down! "It's that mood you want, isn't it, Miranda—" but Miranda wasn't listening.

"Frederick Olliver said Renée—" of course her name was Renée, Lyle thought, overhearing—"made Gerda's old Beckstein sound like a harpsichord."

So there was something else Frederick found amusing, though he had found nothing rewarding in creditable compositions played by experts of renown in her company. Maybe the mere fact that a person or talent was properly appreciated spoiled it for him, reminding him of his own failure; these inferior demonstrations built up his pride of superiority. Poor darling, oh poor darling, she thought, how unhappy he must have been to have been comforted by such modest fires.

Outside, thunder and the rumble of the El rolled like breakers in a stormy ocean over the tinkling music and shrill beat of voices that carried only the skeletons of words, though Lyle could hear someone crying repeatedly for the medieval Breton whaling song—"the one Frederick liked so much." Who said that, she wondered? She went to the window and drew aside the moldy green velvet draperies which Gerda used to shut out the days. Gerda's costume, belted in silver, she realized was contrived from the same fabric, probably once in Isolde's own chamber, along with the baronial furniture and Gerda herself. The rain was coming down in a fine, almost invisible curtain now, veiling the street, throwing up spray from the gutters, giving wavering lights the look of lanterns on ancient fishing boats. A strange glow from somewhere above or below transformed the street outside into the lonely sea itself with a dim moon rising in dim clouds above it, far away, long, long ago. The high choir-boy voice she heard behind her was followed by the twanging of a lyre and she was Isolde herself, waiting for the lover's ship, or was she a maid on the Breton coast peering through the fog for the lost fisherman? She felt a hand on her shoulder.

"Look," she exclaimed. "Do you see it, too? It's like black magic! . . . Now it's gone, of course, the street is back."

"When you say the words, whatever you saw goes away," Tyson informed her, concisely. "You ought to know enough about black magic to know that, dear child. It's probably that black magic punch you're drinking, frankly. At the moment, you look like a slightly drunken angel—adorable, of course."

"Thank you for the 'slightly,' " Lyle said, following him back into the room.

"Come over here by the door," he urged her in an undertone. "I always like to have a foot outside in a party like this. What's keeping Olliver, for pity's sake? By George, I'm going to run him down. I want to leave. I don't know these people, really."

"I heard someone say there's a telephone downstairs," Lyle said. He looked dried, and tidily insignificant, it struck her, as if air and life went out of him in a foreign element where he was not an important personage. (Was she affected this way, too?) He would telephone Strafford's, Tyson said, though it was long after six, and the office was only a few blocks away.

"If you can't get in the booth downstairs there's one in the bar next door," Gerda cried out, and then as he left, "But why is Tyson Bricker so nervous? I want him to hear Victor sing some more."

"He's nervous because he stays up all hours without drinking," Caroline Drake loudly stated. "I know because I tried it once. And last night I saw him—he never sees me, of course—at the Stork Club. It cost him a forty dollar check for the little drip he was with to win a bottle of California sherry out of a balloon. No wonder he's nervous today."

"I prefer the pet shop next door to the Stork Club," Padilla said, thrusting a macaroon at the cat on his shoulder. "It's more exclusive. There is the same rope to keep out the wrong people, and you stand there waiting to be recognized by some celebrated bird or dog in a cage. You wave and sometimes they bark back and you are allowed inside the rope. I am *persona grata* there because my *chihuaha* lives there now. I find no place to live, of course, because I am only a poet. But Manuelo has a whole cage to himself because he's of royal blood."

Lyle stole a look at herself in the fly-blown mirror by the door and was surprised at her flushed, disheveled appearance—red hair kinked up out of its careful coiffeur by the rain, one earring gone, lipstick awry.

"Why, I do look drunk!" she thought in consternation. "Blowsy!" Like Tyson, then, part of her good looks came from the knowledge of belonging. But no sooner had she fumbled for her compact than she saw Frederick entering the door behind her and there was nothing for either of them to do but shake hands politely. He looked remarkably well, of course, even with the rain dripping from his hair and his shabby old raincoat trailing puddles over the floor. Six weeks and five days since they had met, she recalled, in a crowd at the Museum opening of course— six months since they had lunched alone.

"It's been awfully wet," she said tentatively.

"Awfully," he replied, shaking himself.

So long as she could smile when he greeted her. So long as she could keep from crying out, "Oh darling, at last you're here. See how nicely I fit into your new life! See how much your friends like me. See me drinking this stuff and not minding it at all. See how little I miss the things you thought were so important to me!"

How glad she was to have Padilla come back with Gerda at that moment, Padilla bringing a hassock for her so that he might sit at her feet! That, at least, was some indication of her right to be there. But Frederick could not even take off his raincoat, he explained to Gerda; he had only time to pick up Tyson and get on his way. At first he avoided looking directly at her when he spoke, but when the others came up his eyes rushed to Lyle's, unable to look away, and she felt herself drowning, unable to save herself. She knew well enough that he would not have dared sit beside her on the hassock, when she instinctively moved over, if Padilla and Gerda had not been there to make the gesture safe. She knew he would not have pretended to support himself by an arm half around her if he hadn't been certain of immediate departure. But she knew, too, that he must feel the need again to be near her, no matter how he covered it with talking to the others, and she could not speak for joy. She moved slightly so that she felt his heart beating against her back, his very breath on her neck. She was afraid to look at him for fear a conscious contact would frighten him away.

"But everyone has been screaming for you!" Gerda protested. "Murray swore you would come! I'll have to punish Murray for making everyone come out on such a day for nothing. If it's a sweetheart why didn't you bring her here? Never mind, you must stay for one drink. A toast to the book. Besides Tyson may be gone for hours, hunting for a telephone."

"Then the book is coming out?" Lyle murmured over her shoulder. Their hands, unexpectedly touching on the leather seat were held together as if by an electric current.

"I thought Tyson had told you," Frederick said, flushing. He had not been able to find an easy way of telling her, though he knew he should have. "It's the International Award——"

"Frederick!" She glowed with triumphant pride in him and he drank it in thirstily.

"Strafford's are using it to square themselves for that *Court Lady* success," he went on. Telling it to Lyle made the fantastic news seem true to him for the first time. "They've been scouting around for something like it. International usually picks a European or Englishman. It was just luck Strafford's needed my kind of thing and International needed to make up to America."

Their hands tightened silently, each pretending to be unaware. He's happy, now he's won, Lyle thought, and it seemed that his reward was all she had ever wanted for either of them. She reminded herself that he had not sought her out at once to tell her this sudden culmination of all they had dreamed. This was the hour they had dreamed of but the dream was all she was permitted to share. The reality excluded her. She must not let herself think he was hers again. Gerda was clapping her hands, insisting that everyone toast Frederick's success and the ladies all rushed up to embrace him. Everyone knew about the award except herself, Lyle thought. This was really cruel. She thought of the nights they had spent going over each chapter, a part of their love-making. The fact that she shared her own work so completely with her husband and a public made her the more loyally absorbed in Frederick's. Was there no kindness in him at all that he must bar her from even the smallest compensation?

"It's the most important work of our generation, oh by far," Renée shouted and pulled Frederick into the center of the room.

" 'Our generation'?" Tyson repeated sarcastically in Lyle's ear. "I declare I hadn't expected that. No wonder he wanted to come here."

He folded his arms, scowling at the young ladies fussing merrily over Frederick.

"This amuses me, it really does," he drawled, with an attempt at a smile. "The man hasn't done anything different than before when they paid no attention to him. Then I knock myself out to put him over—I could have picked anybody else, mind you—with absolutely no co-operation from him, as you might expect. And now he gets the credit. I hope he realizes how funny it is."

He must have known it was funny, Lyle suspected, not only the sudden female adoration but Tyson's ruffled envy over the tributes from youth. He flashed her a half-smile, as Miranda and Renée tried to comb his wet hair. This was the last straw for Tyson who called out impatiently, "Come on, Olliver, we'll be late, let's go."

"He doesn't seem to realize what it means to be asked to dine at the Beckleys'." he complained.

Lyle could not believe she had heard aright. It could not be that Frederick was surrendering to the Beckleys of his own accord.

"Beckley is out to get him away from Strafford's eventually, I suppose," Tyson said, with another glance at his watch. "You know how they always like to claim every new fish, after somebody else has proved them. I asked myself along because, by Jove, I deserve some thanks after all the time I've put in building him up. No help from him, either—excuse me, I forgot he used to be a friend of yours."

"Yes, he was," Lyle said. "I think I will have some of your flask now if you don't mind."

Tyson whisked it out of his pocket.

"Here, keep it. I was here once before and knew I'd need it. Look here, you're an old friend of the Beckleys, why not nip along with us and barge in?"

"No, I wouldn't dream of going without being asked," Lyle said, thoughtfully. "I really don't care about their parties any more. I like it better here."

She was pouring Tyson's flask into the punch when Frederick came up to say goodbye to her.

"Please!" Tyson expostulated from the doorway, waving Frederick's raincoat. "Olliver, for Pete's sake, hurry. It isn't everybody who gets asked to the Beckleys' for dinner. A small family dinner, mind you, at that!"

"What luck!" Lyle said smiling at Frederick brightly. "Nobody there but the morons as you used to say."

"Come, come, they're not that bad," he reproached her without thinking. "When you get to know them—alright, Tyson, I'm coming."

Lyle picked up the baton and stirred the punch.

"Now why did that monster make Frederick go to the Beckleys'?" Gerda cried, throwing up her arms in a theatrical gesture as the door closed on the two men. "He hates that sort of thing."

"Does he?" Lyle's lip curled.

"He must hate it to drive up there in this tempest," Padilla called out from the window. "Cats and dogs! Look!"

Lyle walked over and looked out as he held back the curtains. Once more she heard the roar of the surf on the legendary coast and she saw the spume of the stormy sea, black and lonely, with the moon in mourning above. Far out, the lantern on her lover's boat bobbed up and down and was lost.

17

. . . the foul weather friends in fair weather . . .

"**I** SUPPOSE you'll be pulling out of this joint any day," Murray said, without looking up from the *Tribune* comic section.

"Me?" Frederick asked, startled. "Why?"

Murray rattled the page and raised himself on an elbow to sip at the cup of coffee on the end-table by the sofa. He had not been dressed for days, nor shaved, and now at five o'clock was still in striped purple pajamas, feet slipping out of sandals. The apartment had not been cleaned for some time so that the spring breeze had the opportunity to chase a herd of ghostly floor "pussies" back and forth across the bare floor. The part-time maid had not been in and, Frederick feared, was gone for good, since Murray refused to get up to let her in. The paucity of rugs and furniture in the front room kept it from appearing really dirty, but the sink in the alcove was full of cups and saucepans in which dregs of coffee or canned soup had ossified. Frederick kept his own room tidy but he was afraid to touch the other end of the apartment after over-hearing Murray's indignation at Judy's attempted inter-ference. If he and his room-mate needed any goddam housewifely supervision they would ask for it, he had shouted; the reason they didn't was that they hated bang and clatter when they were trying to think. Since then Frederick had been cautiously tiptoeing around his friend's jitters, aware that he was in some way responsible for them.

"I'm surprised Strafford doesn't make you put up at some fancy uptown hotel. He could get you in," Murray went on. "Fellow in your position can't afford to live in a fleabag like this. You gotta give 'em a show for their money. Ought to get some new clothes, too, old boy."

Frederick was in the hall between their rooms, brushing his suit with a whisk-broom. He decided, after a moment's uncertainty, to treat this as a joke.

"Do you mean to insinuate that peg-top pants have gone out?" he laughed. "No, Murray, I'm no good at 'shows' even if they wanted one. This isn't my show anyway."

"Take all these saps busting in here for interviews," Murray said. "Half the time I have to throw them out. God knows I'm not trained to be a gentleman's gentleman. Wish I was. Telephone ringing every minute. They all figure you can pay for a snappier set-up than this."

"I realize it's a nuisance," Frederick answered awkwardly, not sure what Murray was driving at but the word "saps" and "pay" hinted at adulation dishonestly come by and honest poor folks deprived of a humble abode by a stingy rich man. "I'm waiting for a private phone. Or do you mean you want my room for someone else . . ."

"Who, for instance?" Murray laughed mirthlessly. "No, I'm thinking of the position you're in right now. I'm trying to say you wouldn't be letting me down, so far as your rent is concerned, if you wanted to move. I've got unemployment insurance and plenty of prospects."

This was the kind of tension between them ever since the papers had announced Frederick's good news, and Frederick was at a loss how to handle it. Their loyalty had been cemented by difficulties in common, but now Frederick was removed to unknown heights, an unconscious betrayal of friendship, since Murray was in depths of trouble. Murray could not deny it was his own fault but this did not keep him from blaming others. He had gone on a week's binge as was his annual post-Lenten habit, but this time he had lost his job, a thing that simply never happened and certainly should not happen at a time his creditors were pressing him. It meant he could not go on with the quiet arrangements for the summer cottage at Pomfret Gerda had wistfully admired. He had counted on renting it for her as a quixotic way of compensating her for Judy's prize (a matter about which Gerda neither knew or cared). Judy's silent satisfaction over her Hazelnut Cigarette triumph struck Murray as vaguely unfair to Gerda who had the womanly grace to win nothing but what he gave her; now that he could make no gifts she did not complain, nor, for that matter, had she ever thanked him, being under a hazy delusion that one casually reached into whatever pocket was nearest just as others reached into yours. If he could not be of use to her he had no right to hang around, she felt and he knew. Usually an amiable fellow the recent twists of fate kept Murray with a constant supply of chips for his shoulder and plenty of time to keep them polished. His room-mate's bright prospects made him feel even more wronged.

Frederick was discovering that no matter how generous friends are in your failure, they do not easily forgive your success. He found the only way he could mollify Murray was to feed him delectable tales of hard luck everywhere and he made the most of every possible shadow in his own glaring sunshine. He turned into a veritable papa robin industriously bringing home jucier and uglier worms to cheer the fledgling. Let's see, he would think on the way to the apartment, what lovely bad news had he heard today? Ah yes, Strafford was said to be drinking again and had, in fact, been tapped for A. A. instead of the club he wanted; Umberto was selling his restaurant because the OPA and his family were conniving to ruin him; the *Swan* magazine had a nasty run-in over rights with the English *Horizon*, Lorna Leahy had a calcium deficiency, bones turning to pure water or worse, someone had cancer, someone was fired, sued, dead, arrested, caught frightfully unaware in a hydrangea bush one night at the Botanical Gardens. Eagerly Frederick plied his friend with these choice proofs of human incompetence until Murray relaxed into a state of modest satisfaction, and even looked on Frederick with a return of the old fondness when as a final frosting for his cake Frederick generously confessed that his love life was in a desperately unhappy state.

"Ah, you're lucky, getting out of that Dodo mess, from what I hear," Murray consoled him. "Of course, I don't really believe she's a nympho as they say; she just thinks she's got enough lollypops for everybody. I could have told you at the start all about that baby but you were in too deep."

Frederick debated whether to give his friend further comfort by an all-revealing question as to why women were always being nymphomaniacs for everybody but you: however Murray might be just touchy enough to think he might mean Gerda. No, there was no use trying to regain the old camaraderie after the crime of good luck. Bad weather friends were as undependable as fair weather friends in a crisis, the relationship in both cases being dictated by conditions of fortune instead of mutual tastes. How could he possibly have imagined himself close to a man who followed the funnies, Frederick asked himself with a touch of irritation; a man who used the book section to gather up a broken highball glass? There had been a perfectly good reason for their having kept discreet distance all those years; the peacefulness of their relationship had been in acknowledging no common ground. He had always known that Murray shrugged his shoulders over the eccentricity of a man who read or wrote anything but detective stories; therefore his demonstration of practical success in an unpractical field was in itself a kind of insult to a man's common sense. There would have been none of this veiled hostility if they had only stayed in their separate corners. Now the very air was charged with the blackmail of confessions soured, wounds foolishly exposed; each looked vainly for the door marked *private* which they had so blithely unhinged. When Murray dropped and broke his cup he looked reproachfully at Frederick as if even his hangovers were no longer his own secret. I'd better get out, Frederick thought, but where could he find companionship that would permit him to be his old self, without the strain of consideration for rivals, enemies, flatterers? He longed to be able to speak his natural tongue instead of the diplomatic idiom of success, the false humility, the pretense of gratitude for ignorant praise, the tactful turn of the other cheek to unfair attack.

"Have you seen the Hazelnut Exhibition yet?" he asked, seeking to deflect Murray's attention. "How was Judy's picture?"

Murray flung the paper aside with a gloomy sigh.

"I took a look at it a couple of times while she was painting it, but she knows my opinion by this time. The kid's no artist, she's a little farmer—ought to be cooking for some fisherman back there in Maine. I've told her so, but seeing all those phony bohemians vacationing up there in Rockport every summer gave her the art bug. She thinks a couple of prizes means she's good. Hell, there's more sheer art in this *Penny* strip here. Judy hasn't got the temperament. Take Gerda. Gerda's never done anything, but just the way she fools around with music or dancing shows the real temperament. I'm glad the kid got the prize, of course, since it means so much to her, but I hate to see her wasting her life on a pipedream."

The airing of this point of view seemed to relieve Murray and he sipped his coffee quietly for a minute.

"You feel alright?" he asked suddenly. "Seems to me you've gotten pretty skinny. Color not so good."

A little surprised at this solicitude Frederick admitted he did not sleep well.

"Too much celebration, too much running around. People always did wear me out," he confessed. "Just an hour or so trying to talk to strangers goes right to my stomach. I drink more than I ever did and I don't enjoy it particularly."

"Cracking up just like me," Murray said gloomily. "Old age. I used to think old age was a kind of feather bed you gradually sank down into, but it's not. It's a goddam stone wall you butt your head into till it cracks. Ever think about dying? I mean, who would you want notified in case it happened? Here we are, living together all these years and we wouldn't have any idea what to do with each other's body."

"Don't go to any trouble with mine. I'll just take pot-luck," Frederick said but a spasm of childish terror struck him. What to do in case of death? Who would care? Who would grieve? Not Dodo, he guessed. What was he heading for—Murray, too? Two old hermits, perhaps, starving together; loving privacy all their lives they have it for bride in death.

"I think about it sometimes now with a hangover," Murray said. "Maybe we ought to exchange cards. I have a brother in Wheeling. That's the only things relatives are for, isn't it—to look after remains? I don't think we could trust each other to handle a demise properly. You're too thin now to lift me and I have the shakes so I'd probably drop your cadaver in the gutter. Well, cheerio, there's still Schenley's Black Label. Stick around."

"I'm late for a date," Frederick answered, knowing he was offending Murray by rejecting his overture, but he had to see Dodo if he could possibly find her. He did not want to give away the uncertainty of his engagement by telephoning her where Murray could witness a possible rebuff. He would go outside to a booth.

"Give Judy my congratulations," he said.

He left Murray silently pouring himself a slug of rye.

18

. . . the brick in the bouquet . . .

$\mathcal{F}$REDERICK liked to think that no matter how much she ranted against him Dodo did enjoy sharing the outward aspects of his rise. The headwaiter bringing a pencil with the check as if his picture that week on a magazine cover had transformed him at once into royalty too fastidious to have pockets soiled with vulgar cash. Such touching tribute necessitated his paying for whatever friends Dodo brought with her, and his shock over a two hundred dollar bill from one restaurant, was almost compensated by her excited approbation. It was something, he thought. It was something that she boasted about him, too, and carried newspaper clippings about him to show to strangers, even if it did make him blush. The poor child, at least, was being her natural self. It was something that she called him "Freddie" and teased him with intimate possessiveness in public, even though, alone with him, she went into sulks and accusations that left him hopelessly defeated. He found it faintly ironic that she must remind him not to be kidded by compliments, it was only because he was in the papers. She could not have understood his horror at the salaams the city made, not to Mind but to the negotiable evidence of it. The shameless reverance for notoriety of any caliber, criminal or cultural, was frightening, the more so because he could so easily not have been its object. It was his luck not his work that was esteemed; his horse had paid off, the slot machine had showered him with gold, and such robot honors magically changed the man. It seems he was a wit, a genius, a beau; though no one knew exactly what wonder he had performed. The exaggerated sum of money declared as his mental weight was wonder enough. He could not imagine how he could maintain a decent ego when it was his luck not his work that was admired. But it helped justify him to Dodo. Sometimes he marvelled at himself in public whenever Dodo spotted a Name and artlessly introduced herself, showing clippings of her escort as a ticket of admission, explaining the finer points of Mr. Olliver's work, what someone at Harvard had said about it and what she — (very merrily)—privately thought about it. He was pleased to be of such use to her, glad to make up in some way for the emotional confusion that affected his whole body, glad even to suffer her sudden reversions to vindictiveness.

"You think you're so smart when you're just dull, dull, dull!" she had cried only the night before in the Barrel, "Larry has more brains in his little finger than you have with all you're luck. He knows what people like and that's more than you do. You just get all the luck because you know the right people and he doesn't."

It was as if his good fortune had been at the expense of half a dozen worthier rivals and he must atone for it or be accused of pure arrogance.

The night before his penance had been to listen to Larry's idea for the new Hazelnut campaign and to simulate Dodo's enthusiasm over these remarkable inspirations. He did not disagree with Dodo's assertion that he had all the breaks whereas Larry had to fight the whole K. G. R. Agency and the entire tobacco business before he could come into his own. Hadn't Larry originated the idea of an art show, the Contemporary Masters series (*"There's art in cigarette-making, too, gentlemen!"*), yet some guy at B. B. D. & O. took all the credit. Lone dreamer that he was, unappreciated by his firm (you couldn't call thirty thousand a year appreciation)—he had to go ahead fighting, bravely solacing his wounds with a friendly bonded Scotch, watching the other fellow always get the gravy. As he was about to go, Dodo, moved to tears over the world's injustice to genius, pointed her finger accusingly at Frederick:

"You see what some people have to go through while someone like you gets away with murder just because you know the right people? You ought to be ashamed of yourself acting so smug and superior when Larry has such a hard time."

"Don't go, old man," Frederick urged in desperation, sensing the punishment he would receive if left alone with Dodo. "Stay, have another drink."

Wherever he turned it was the same—the winner must feign humility, thank fools for praise, maintain a sweet temper in the face of bores and insult, expect the brick in the bouquet as his just desert, struggle to conceal his natural shyness and undemocratic tastes. He was obliged to admit to himself that the only place he could relax was at the Ephraim Beckleys' among wealthy dilettantes amiably eager for any new kind of lion. Tyson Bricker, when they met at the League, was too self-assured to acknowledge jealousy, but took a quizzical, patronizing attitude of you-know-and-I-know-old-man-this-is-just-one-of-those-amusing-flukes-and-we-won't-let-it-turn-our-head. Benedict Strafford looked upon him more as bank collateral than person, a testimony to Strafford publishing shrewdness. ("I had such a fine tribute from Lindsay of Chase National," Benedict boasted to Frederick. " 'It's men like you, Strafford,' he said, 'who carry the banner of our American traditions of clean mind, and clean body. Let's have more books like *The Treasure*.' And you should have heard the ovation I got in Hollywood!") He rather wistfully hinted at the possibility of siphoning the censored sex in the *Court Lady* film into the abstractions in Frederick's book and making it more of a "property." *Lady*, as the much discussed chronicle of madcap love and youth was now familiarly called, was being filmed with the youthful lovers played by Hollywood's leading off-screen grand-parents, their heady raptures sternly leashed by the Johnson office and arthritis. He spoke of high praise offered everywhere to the talented publisher of *The Treasure* and congratulated the world for perspicacious bestowing of credit. In his brand new sartorial splendor — (a man carrying the banner of American tradition had certain obligations to fashion)—Mr. Strafford was busy as the White Rabbit, consorting with the press, bankers, brokers, politicians, and Palm Beach widows. Olliver? Frederick Olliver? Oh yes, an excellent property.

No wonder Fortune's favorites took to speaking of themselves in the third person, Frederick reflected, for it was the masquerade costume that won the prize, never the person beneath, nor did one ever dare to remove the mask and breathe again.

After Frederick left Murray pouring himself a shot of rye, he hurried over to the Greenwich Avenue drugstore to telephone Dodo. She had told him she had a breakfast date at the Plaza with an actor from Hollywood who thought she was much too smart to be just a receptionist, and she ought to be in Hollywood where a good head was really appreciated. It was now five o'clock and Frederick wondered bitterly on what pillow the good head was resting that she hadn't gotten home yet? But next minute he was thinking the poor child wasn't really responsible, she deserved what pleasure she could find. His nickel brought a response this time and he was relieved that she was in a gay humor.

"I've had champagne all day, Freddie," she giggled. "Now Tommy and I are looking for a party. Look, he says a friend of his is invited to the Gaynors' today and I said you knew them and you could take us there. Will you, Freddie? I promised him you would so you've got to."

"I'm not invited myself," Frederick said. "I . . ."

"Now, listen, Freddie, you're such an old friend you could take us there without asking! Don't be such a stinker!"

He was relieved that rumors of his affair with Lyle had never reached Dodo's ears, suspecting she would be more apt to claim social privileges from the facts than revenge.

"I really wouldn't dare presume—you see I . . ."

"Alright, don't!" Dodo was angry again. "You're in a position to do anything you like and you're being mean. Alright, Tommy and I will go some place else! Pooh on you!"

She hung up and he mopped his forehead, in a relief that he was saved from being pressed into some horrible situation, even if rescue had come from her wrath not his own courage. He walked eastward toward Washington Square, his feeling of humiliation giving way to an unexpected elation. At least he would not have to suffer a threesome dinner, acting the part of hell-of-a-fellow, decent extrovert, always happy to share friends and mistress with any plaid coat and suede footwear from the West. Good God, what a desert he'd been in, he thought, how thirsty he was for merely adult minds, what a world of perpetual juvenilia he had deliberately elected!

He found himself looking in the direction of the Gaynor apartment, musing that at last he was in a position to enjoy the kind of company they kept for he had proved himself one of them, hadn't he? There would be no need to appease or make apology for others' frustrations; here would be people seasoned and humorously knowledgeable in the ways of worldly approval, banded together, you might say, against the savage enmity of the hungry mob. He wished there was some plausible way of re-opening that door. He longed to exhibit his innocence to Allan, as well as to the group. "My dear fellow, I no longer resent you; in fact I appreciate you fully for the first time and see why your wife could not leave you for another man. See how splendidly I can look you straight in the eye, more honorable than any man present for I am innocent of intentions toward your wife (all the nobler for having been a sinner once)—and am ready to help protect your home against any lusting stranger." To the friends he could indicate his freedom from all the old jealousy—"of course you love her and no reason she should

not enjoy your company for she deserves every happiness."
And to Lyle he could pay the compliment of asking only
for her sweet friendship, adding himself to her list of
devoted, undemanding worshipers. He saw himself already in the big, friendly living-room being at ease at last,
but the vision of a Frederick gaily chatting with the
Gaynor guests faded quixotically into the new Frederick
facing the old unhappy Frederick and growing hysterically
genial to offset the chilly scorn in the latter's eye. He
almost saw himself whispering to Lyle, "Why do you have
that fellow scowling around? He acts as if we were all
responsible for the doom of civilization, putting down
everything we say in his judgment book, he being self-
appointed judge just because he's no good at our games?
He seems envious of crowns we haven't even won, discon-
tented over failures he hasn't even had. I've done him no
harm and my ruin would do him no service." Frederick
tried to hold the vignette, tantalized by the picture of the
person he once was, inwardly chagrined that it was so
grim, hoping for a stranger's glimpse of some grace he
never knew he had. All he got was a nostalgic stabbing
sensation in his chest, an echo of the ache of desire for
Lyle—or had it been only the desire to prove himself
superior to her friends and work? He *had* proved superior,
come to think of it, but had he proved it to *her?* For a
moment an idea tempted him, then he turned his head in
the other direction. The whim to test his strength might
lead him into embarrassing pitfalls. He would call on the
Stalks, instead, he thought, and a moment later was telephoning and being urged by Solange with unexpected
warmth to come up at once.

The Stalks lived west of Central Park not far from the
Hotel des Artistes in an apartment of sufficient rococo
gloom and space to accommodate relations of Solange as
fast as they arrived from various corners of Europe. Bald
and frowsy heads of all ages popped out of doors down
the long corridor as Solange admitted Frederick. He
caught the aroma of many diverse highly spiced dishes

being stewed or roasted as if many quarrelling palates must be appeased. If Stalk had been any other kind of man the encroachments of his mistress's relatives would have indicated female domination of the worst sort, but his utter preoccupation with affairs of the mind and treatment of his co-household as if they were subway strangers gave him a pedestal not to be assailed. Guests from Russia, Paris, and Germany had crowded him into the front parlor which he occupied as bedroom, study, and reception room. Here nightly political arguments took place, complaints of betrayal by their leaders, the betrayal consisting in tyrants refusing to confine their oppression to minority groups. If Hitler had only pursued his purge of radicals and the unprotected instead of threatening the great middle-class, taking away *our* property—*our* very ideals as it were—the whole war could have been averted. Here Solange led Frederick, two miniature toy poodles and a huge Siamese cat padding along behind. A refectory table, covered with fine yellowed lace, stood in the bay of the ceiling-high front windows, and on it were samovar, percolator, and chafing dishes quietly bubbling beside platters of smoked salmon, kippers, herring salad, red caviar and pastries. This was what he disliked about Europeans (he meant Solange's Europeans)—the obscene worship of food, the groaning tables of indigestibles at all hours, the conviction that full mouth and stomach make for love, gaiety, peace and mutual understanding. Bars inspired brotherly goodwill because there was the implicit sharing of vice whereas the unctuous assumption of saintly virtue in pandering to the belly and storing up juicy treasures for worms made for individual complacency positively dangerous to fellowship.

Solange enjoyed the role of hostess but could not conceal her jealousy of all Edwin's friends and enthusiasms, feeling perpetually cheated that he (as well as all her family) could not be swallowed whole by her. She encouraged his hypochondria as her ally, and her happiness would have been complete if she could have kept him under sedatives in bed, dependent on her for everything—food, opinions, and carefully rationed friends. She was eighteen years older than Stalk and had managed to capture him simply because he had been unprepared for danger from such a quarter. Aside from her relatives she brought to him a *dot* of intimate literary lore gleaned from famous men she claimed as lovers. She candidly boasted of having stolen the young man's virginity while he was under the spell of an extremely absorbing story about Annamites frolicking in Jean Cocteau's closet. She used her reminiscences as the children's photographer uses the birdie and had unpacked her trunks in his apartment, chattering steadily and hypnotically before he realized what was going on, and then he was too indifferent to struggle. She freely confessed that she talked to keep people from noticing her ugliness, though she made up for this disarming modesty by frequent assertions that she could get any man she ever wanted, competing with Hedy Lamarr or any beauty you could name because as Wells (or was it Bennett or Shaw or Stalin or Heinrich Mann or Picasso or Molnar?) had said, she was not mere woman but absinthe (or was it aphrodisiac, marijuana, ambrosia or Dr. Pepper?) Frederick found her more than a little terrifying and wondered if even death would loosen her passionate clutch on Stalk. She had a thin treacherous clown face, long self-absorbed upper lip, narrow wolfish head, thin nose, suspicious black rat eyes set close together betraying a routine of madness and secret hysteria. Light showed through the crevices in her elaborate hairdo, its red far redder than red hair, perhaps, he thought, because she adored blood, its color, perfume and texture. He thought of her as totally dead, needing a lash to feel a feather, vibrating rustily only to Inquisitional tortures, smelling of graveyard flowers, indeed carrying herself like a newly embalmed corpse wound up to live motion by some secret devilish drug. She had mummified herself with self-worship and was forever infuriated that no one else recognized her god, so her black eyes (doll's eyes that clicked back in her head when she lay down, he thought) bubbled and glowed with hatred. He was repelled, even while admitting to a queer drug-like fascination about her, and the luminous opalescent sheen of her skin did give her a ghoulish beauty. He saw with dismay they were to be alone, that not only was Edwin absent but that she shouted down the hall something in Russian that must have meant "Stay out" for the heads immediately popped inside their cells, doors hastily banged shut. He was not reassured by her long ringed fingers remaining on his arm, guiding him to the Victorian loveseat in the darkest corner, where she bade him sit beside her, motioning her pets to sit quietly at her feet, and insuring their obedience by flourishing a box of dog-biscuit.

"I want to see you alone, Frederick," she stated in her hoarse bronchial voice. "I don't want Edwin to know because it is about him I wish to speak. You think I do not like you, perhaps. It is not true. I like you very much. I *wish* to like you much more if you know what I mean. As a friend. Now! Allow me to tell you in secrecy that Edwin is in great, great danger and you must help me."

Frederick fixed his apprehensive gaze carefully on the opposite wall wishing a door would suddenly open and kind demons snatch him off to some safe hell away from what was certain to be embarrassing confidences. And shouldn't he have said, "I like you too or at least about as much as you like me?"

"You are a man of the world, a man of many love affairs, perhaps, while Edwin is a child," Solange said, forcing his eyes back to her with the ferocity of her willpower. "I know him better than he knows himself. I have made him what he is, whether he says it or not. He is a child and a genius. I make him eat coffee and cake when he doesn't know he is eating. If necessary I open his mouth and feed him with the spoon. I have put the very clothes on him when he might forget he was in pajamas in his concentration. I keep the world from nibbling at him. I am all around him, inside, outside, fighting his enemies

—he could not reach out a hand without finding me there to help him. It is a terrible struggle for me, Frederick, against everyone, even Edwin himself. And now comes this disaster that I have only discovered lately. This is how I first knew. Look."

She produced a small volume and held it open at one page for him.

"The Satirical Epigrams of the Greek Anthology," Frederick said, glad to find any remark that did not commit him.

"Yes. We are both very fond of this particular volume and pick it up often. I was reading it only a month or two ago. Now, let me make one thing clear. Edwin has such regard for books that he never underlines a favorite passage. He has notes, perhaps, clipped to the pages, but never does he pencil a line here and there. Never."

Should he say he was very happy to hear this, Frederick wondered?

"When I picked up the book a fortnight ago I found this," her long forefinger indicated a heavily underscored paragraph. "What would you think if you were a woman almost eighteen years older than your lover, Frederick?"

Frederick read the words of Parmenion: *"It is difficult to choose between famine and an old woman. To hunger is terrible but her bed is still more painful. Phillis when starving prayed to have an elderly wife, but when he slept with her, he prayed for famine. So the inconstancy of a portionless son."*

"Does it mean something?" he asked uneasily.

"Two nights later this too was underlined," Solange went on in a choked voice, leafing to another volume. " 'And what is the evening of women? Old age and countless wrinkles," Macedonus the Consul. Am I really so wrinkled and in my evening, Frederick? Of course, I knew at once there was someone else younger and made it my business to find out who it was. This time, I tell you, it was dangerous. So I ask your help. You must go and explain to her that Edwin Stalk cannot exist without me. This woman must not ruin his life, all his hopes for his future. I am his future. I am Stalk! Edwin is with her this very moment—perhaps in her arms. He seldom comes home till morning, so I am not at all deluded. You know her. You must beg her to give him up, for without me he will have nothing. Her name is . . ."

Frederick had a desperate last hope that he would be spared definite information but Solange was relentless. ". . . Lyle Gaynor."

He seemed to be falling through space, and surely someone had kicked him hard in the stomach, numbing him momentarily to the knife in his chest. Lyle! What in heaven's name had he expected, after all? Was his male vanity so colossal he had actually fancied a woman would be forever true to him through all his other loves? As if he were examining broken bones after the wreck he tentatively put his hand on his heart, trying to diagnose his sharp pain—was it jealous love, unquenchable, or was it shock, outraged ego, perhaps an unsuspected priggishness offended by word of female promiscuity? Whatever it was Solange's next complaint, accompanied by weeping, came to him from some far distant planet. Death, that was what he was experiencing, he decided; he had been on a voyage but the harbor had always been there. Now harbor itself was gone, and he was no longer voyageur but exile.

"Edwin has never believed in marriage," Solange's voice beat against his unwilling consciousness. "I know, because of course many women have tried to get him and I've not been afraid because his ideas are too fixed. Now I am told she is planning to divorce her husband, and marry Edwin."

If the first news had numbed him the last shocked him back to consciousness, and wild anger. Lyle could do this? What about those years of loneliness he had spent, believing in the impossibility of her divorcing Allan? How miraculously he had escaped a whole life under such a delusion! How lucky to have gotten out before the brutal awakening when she would have found no barriers to marrying someone else! The weight of remorse he once experienced at thought of Lyle was blasted by Solange's words and the harsh laugh that echoed through the room seemed to come from that other Frederick, now mocking him.

"You don't believe she wants to marry Edwin?" Solange asked, startled. "You laugh at the idea?"

"I believe it; that's why I'm laughing," Frederick bitterly replied. A thousand horns from Dodo could not have made him burn with outraged pride as this news had done; he could not recover calm to study its authenticity. He wanted to dash out of the house straight to Lyle and accuse her, not of unfaithfulness, but of thieving from his life, deliberately seducing from him his stout armor of cynicism the better for him to suffer, traducing him into belief in her so that pleasures away from her were poisoned by conscience. His indignation mingled with a savage joy in vindication. See, he wanted to cry out to invisible accusers, this is the very treachery I anticipated unconsciously! Can anyone blame me for fortifying myself against it? Solange's ringed hands clung to his hand like a chained falcon's claw and reminded him that Lyle had wronged this splendid woman, as well as Allan and himself.

"Edwin admires and respects you, Frederick," Solange said, her voice rasping with tears controlled. "I would ask you to speak to him but I think it best you go to her. She is so interested in him and in the *Swan*—tell her the best way to help both is to give up, go away. She is a woman of the world—he's not used to anyone like her. An infatuation, if you know what I mean. She has dozens of other lovers. She can turn to them."

"Of course," Frederick agreed, amazed at the fatuous complacency that had never before permitted a doubt of Lyle's fidelity. Being obliged to admit such peaks of masculine vanity heightened his anger, drove him to the other extreme of suspecting a thousand other deceptions.

"Then you will go see her?" asked Solange eagerly, oblivious to the poodles which had leapt to her lap and were tearing at the box of dog biscuit.

"Yes," Frederick said. What was he promising, he asked himself, his head swimming with rage, confusion and Solange's own mesmeric gaze.

Solange gave an exclamation of delight and rose to her feet, the dogs tumbling to the floor.

"And now we'll have a little supper. Hermann! Katya! Natasha! Frieda! You've met them all." He could hear the cages down the hallway opening with happy cries in many languages and reached hastily for his hat, a little afraid that Solange might move him into one of the rooms, lulled into subjugation as Stalk had been.

"But you must not leave now that we are such friends, for we are, aren't we?" protested Solange, her hand still clutching his wrist and her little eyes searching his face avidly for some clue to his feeling.

"I want to plan how best to help," he explained, lamely. "I agree that Edwin is too valuable to risk his going off the deep end this way. I want to think for a little while."

He ran out of the house as if he were scrambling out of a pit and started walking at a furious pace through the Park. At first he had a burning desire to face Lyle with her crime which grew uglier whichever way he looked at it. He had credited her with loyalty to Allan, a loyalty he had been obliged to bear, too, but the truth was she had only been waiting for the right man. He, Frederick Olliver, had not been considered as worthy as Edwin Stalk, that was all.

"Stalk, good God!" Frederick mocked. "Stealing him from the dead, you might say. What kind of man is he, anyway, to be dominated by that witch for years? So Lyle thinks a zombie is worth getting a divorce for!"

How gullible he had been not to have seen all this as inevitable! Thirty-seven years old and as naïve as a child. He asked himself if there was any hope of his ever learning, if age and experience could ever teach one anything but to pretend they did.

19

. . . Sunday-School for Scandal . . .

*T*HE coolness between those bosom friends Lorna Leahy and Caroline Drake was a great inconvenience to both of them and stemmed from nothing more than a fortnight on the wagon which gave them the opportunity to dispassionately observe unpleasant traits in each other. Caroline had listened with seeming sympathy to Lorna's tirade about Judy Dahl's Hazelnut prize, the injustice of an amateur (call it Fine Arts, if you liked, it was sheer Communism!)—getting more kudos than a hard-working professional—the years Lorna had worked to perfect her technique only to be by-passed by a clumsy whipper-snapper with pull!— (Judy Dahl had slept with the judges, of course she had!) At the end Caroline had said with a maddening, dreamy smile, "You know I always liked that kid!" which sent Lorna off in a dumb rage. Then Caroline had staged a series of silverware demonstrations at the Waldorf, hiring actors and stage directors to put on luncheons, cocktail parties, buffet suppers and so on to demonstrate the proper use of silver and glassware. She had suggested Lorna sketch these affairs for the trade, with the horrid result that Lorna Leahy got all the credit with her picture looking like Freddy Bartholomew printed in *Home Styles,* and not a word about Caroline Drake.

"I expected that," Caroline said to Gerda, "but imagine her never even thanking me for the publicity!"

She gave a large party for the express purpose of leaving out Lorna, and when Lorna made grieved reproach later she replied heartily, "Oh, but you hate my friends so much I was sure you'd be bored silly!" Lorna retaliated by telephoning a glowing report of her box party at Carnegie and laughing, "I would have invited you but I know how you *loathe* music!" They were too civilized, thank goodness, for open quarrels, contenting themselves with a little friendly candor about wrong choice of hats, food, doctors, dressmakers, and words, when they did meet ("It's *regardless*, Caroline, not *irregardless*," Lorna said gently. Caroline huffily replied that *regardless* was a footless, weak word and got you nowhere, that on the other hand you threw in the word *irregardless* and won any argument hands down. She added that there were a lot of people going around New York saying *regardless* who couldn't make the living she could with all her ignorance). Tacitly they agreed on the definition of the word "climber," which as they now secretly applied it to each other meant "a person enjoying the company of others besides one's self."

Between unsatisfactory meetings they telephoned each other of small triumphs;—Lorna had lunched at *Le Pavillon*, Caroline had moved up two on her firm's vice-president list, Lorna had four marvelous invitations for this week-end in the country, Caroline was buying a Packard black-market, Lorna had a terrible time with a total stranger telephoning obscene proposals to her (she couldn't imagine where he'd heard about her!)—Caroline had drunk *fundador* all night with that gorgeous Spanish poet and goodness only knows what happened. Naturally nothing was as annoying as the preference each exhibited for insincere flatterers who praised her virtues to an honest friend who could point out her faults. Lorna described the thrill of going to Sammy's in the Bowery, how really sordid she found it personally but "of course *you* would have loved it!" Caroline retired for a few days' rest after this *coup,* explaining when Lorna eventually telephoned that she'd been doing the town with Benedict Strafford, the publisher, having been inspired to tie up his *Court*

Lady book—you know the one the censors fussed over—
with a *Court Lady* silver design.

"You *would* think of that!" Lorna replied plaintively,
adding in a voice close to tears. "I've wanted to meet
Benedict Strafford for ages. Honestly, Caroline, I don't
see why you don't let *me* meet people like that?"

Caroline was familiar with this reaction, but determined
not to be taken in by it this time. "Why don't you let me
meet So and So," from Lorna indicated no interest or sympathy but was a sort of animal cry, meaning "Why aren't
these people thrown to me for nourishment? I want to see
how different they are from your unperceptive description.
I want to see what there is about them I wouldn't like. I
want to see how wrong you are in believing they like you.
I want to sit with my lip curled preparing my future
criticism while they do the awful things I was positive
they would do. Oh, do let me meet them that I may tear
them to pieces!" No, Caroline thought regretfully, she
would not be wheedled by her clever friend into giving her
such advantage, but on the other hand nothing was much
fun without the mulling it over with an old friend later.
Supposing it was true that Lorna, regarded soberly and
dispassionately, was a vain, hypocritical, super-rayfeened
bitch; had these shortcomings prevented them from having twenty years of good times together? Maybe it was the
difference in their faults rather than the similarity in
their virtues that bound them together. You seldom noticed good qualities in a close friend anyway; you took
them for granted and used your eyes to pick out the flaws.
Caroline, finding the maintenance of a grudge much
against her easy-going nature, and having accumulated a
cumbersome stock of secrets, threw caution to the winds
and invited Lorna to come over and meet Mr. Strafford
for Sunday breakfast. Lorna at once demurred, most
aggravatingly, saying she was booked so far ahead and for
this Sunday had promised to go driving out in the country
with Gerda and a wealthy friend, but—well—she did hate
disappointing Gerda's friend but—well—since she had

only accepted *tentatively*—yes, she would do her best as a favor to Caroline to come for breakfast. Now, pondered Caroline, how could she produce Mr. Strafford, for their relations were not nearly as cozy as she had led Lorna to believe. Being a sound business woman, however, Caroline set to work on the technique of promotion and contact. She telephoned the business manager of a magazine which was waiting eagerly for her store to enlarge its advertising appropriation and asked ("this is purely social, Tom," she explained) if they would not be interested in a future article on Benedict Strafford, the great publisher. Tom declared nothing gave him more pleasure than to do her this personal favor, showing he liked her as a human being not just as a prospect. He was astonished that the magazine's editorial department had been too dumb to think up the idea, and he would push it right through. Murray Cahill had once done features for them so Caroline suggested the interview be assigned to him. This also seemed a perfect inspiration. Caroline then contacted Murray, advised him to contact Tom, then contacted Mr. Strafford with the flattering news that *People* wanted to feature him as Man of the Week, and wouldn't it be pleasanter if he met the interviewer at her apartment for a quiet little Sunday breakfast? Mr. Strafford was enchanted at the fresh evidence of public appreciation, thanked her profusely, and Caroline with a sigh of satisfaction laid in enough Bourbon and sausages to accommodate the greediest Sunday school class. She had looked forward to propitiating Lorna by providing an intimate little foursome, just the two ladies and the two beaux but at noon Murray called up and asked if he might bring Judy Dahl, the reason being that she was coming down with flu and apparently would be enormously improved and cheered by passing around the germs.

"That fixes it!" groaned Caroline after polite cries of pleasure. "Lorna will be furious to see Judy and will catch the flu from her besides!"

She provided herself with an invigorating ounce of

medicinal spirits before adding a fifth place to her attractive table, wondered whether she dared telephone Lorna and confess the dilemma, decided that the best thing was to round up another man as buffer for possible quarrels, telephoned several Extra Men, extricated herself as deftly as possible on finding that each Extra Man was inevitably equipped with two or more Extra Women, all happy to come, decided to let bad enough alone, and hoped at least that Lorna would descend from the wagon long enough to be human. The lateness of her guests gave her time to think about Benedict Strafford, and she speculated on why he had never married. Either he had a convenient little nest somewhere in the wilds of Staten Island (some peasant type unsuitable for marriage), or was a confirmed sporting-house type (probably sneaked up to Harlem or Chinatown the way so many of those intellectual men did, never guessing that any lady of their own class had a similar apparatus), or he might be as Padilla insisted, a well-integrated fairy. She could question Frederick Olliver about this except that she sometimes had similar suspicions about him. Padilla, of course, suspected everybody, proclaiming that it was not the fighters but the Four F's who had won the war with their five years to slip into the absent 1-A boss's shoes. Padilla declared that our boys had returned to find the whole Horatio Alger democratic system of economics shifted;—the bright young man no longer got the job by marrying the boss's daughter but by sleeping with the boss himself. A funny idea, Caroline had to admit, and that led to wondering if Padilla's own excessive lady-killing wasn't a sign of "protesting too much"? A pity amusing men were invariably on the wrong side socially or physically or financially—Padilla being possibly all three. Good heavens, she thought in consternation, what kind of an age is this anyway where a woman suspects a man of disguised homo tendencies just because he wants to sleep with every woman he meets? Those big football-playing he-men must have started that sort of rumor to justify their own disappointing performances.

The arrival of Benedict Strafford at half-past one put an end to these maiden reveries and introduced a new problem for he had taken the liberty—he was sure Miss Drake would forgive him—of bringing a lady friend, none other in fact than little Miss Dodo who had heard so much of Miss Drake's wonderful parties he could not refuse her plea to be brought along.

"Of course we have met before but only in crowds," Dodo cried.

Caroline vaguely recalled the new guest as someone who was always being brought places by men who didn't know her last name, and other guests were always stumbling on her hugging their husbands in back hallways, giving her telephone number to gentlemen without pencils, or emerging from dark terraces demurely soignée with bewildered gentlemen all tousled and rouge-smeared. The young lady was darting eagle eyes about Caroline's apartment as if memorizing the terrain for future strategy, and Caroline determined immediately to keep all possible hiding spots locked. There was something ominous, Caroline thought, in the business-like way the girl stripped off her long black gloves in the bedroom, removed her large black crownless hat deftly, tightened the wide fancy belt of her rose-printed black silk, and patted her sleek black hair, as if "*Now!* Get in there and start punching!" Damn these cagey bachelors, Caroline thought, always so scared to go anyplace alone!

"This young lady is a friend of the chap who's coming to interview me," Benedict explained, rubbing his hands happily at sight of the large room with the May sunshine glittering over breakfast table and fine bar. "My, what a beautiful view you have here!"

"I've known Murray Cahill for just ages!" exclaimed Dodo. "He's one of mother's oldest friends in Baltimore! They graduated together."

"How sweet!" Caroline said, wishing with a burst of the old affection that Lorna could have been there to hear about Murray being "one of *mother's* oldest friends," and

giving a quick critical survey of Baby's neck and chin
with the satisfactory conclusion that Mummy must have
graduated at the age of nine to have a daughter this
mature. It appeared that Dodo had just accidentally acquired Mr. Strafford an hour previously at a public broadcast sponsored by the League for Cultural Relations, (Mr.
Tyson Bricker, presiding) where he had discussed "Can
the Post War Generation Be Taught to Read." As publisher of *The Treasure* Mr. Strafford had voiced an en-
thusiastic affirmative and highest hopes for the young
people, only shaken in the Question Period by Dodo's
asking what made him so sure any member of the Post
War Generation had ever read or purchased *The Treasure.*

"She had me there," Mr. Strafford confessed to Caroline,
chuckling ("He would have strangled any female his own
age piping up with that" Caroline thought), "so I had to
bring her along to think up an answer."

It was refreshing to see that the arrival of Judy Dahl
with Murray eclipsed Miss Dodo temporarily. Mr. Strafford had a literary man's curiosity about feminine workers
in the graphic arts, and Judy looked her part. The childish lack of make-up, careless blonde hair, stubby nails,
scuffed shoes, faded "Levis" and blue sport shirt struck
the right tone for Artist-Too-Successful-To-Give-a-Damn,
hinted at many summers on fashionable beaches snubbing
the Bourgeoisie, and made Dodo and Caroline look like
suburban respectability. Naturally, the impression Judy
made might have been less interesting if no one had heard
of her prize, but this gave her curt manners the charm of
a royal snub and her monosyllabic replies the weight of
epigrams. Lorna will be positive I invited her just for
spite, Caroline thought, and began wishing the phone
would ring saying Lorna was on her way to the country
after all. Still she did need Lorna to hold her own against
these too fortunate younger women. If she was to be
forced into the Chaperon's corner it would be less morti-
fying if Lorna were there alongside her. Since she had

been mistakenly inspired to show off her own cooking
the maid Johanna was not present and the extra guests
obliged Caroline to stay in the kitchen stretching the
omelette with more tomatoes, watercress, mushrooms,
while Murray acted as bartender. Very happy he was, too,
in these duties, for he could drown out with fierce rat-
tlings of the shaker Caroline's tactless shouts about Gerda,
and Strafford's pompous compliments to "our charming
little artist here." One of the most sordid demonstrations
of masculine opportunism, Murray found, was the way
men clustered around Judy Dahl now, and he was put to
it as an old friend to keep her head from being turned.
If he had not reluctantly invited her to come along today
a couple of other guys would have asked her out and he
couldn't get it into her thick little head that all they
wanted when they flattered her about her painting was
to get her in bed. Judy did not worry at all over their
sincerity; at least it blackmailed Murray into taking her
out with him as if they were any married couple. Maybe
Caroline Drake was one of his women and probably Dodo
at one time or other, but at least she, Judy, was the one
he had brought today. Quite content, Judy folded her
legs under her on the white leather sofa and applied herself earnestly to a perusal of *Life* magazine, emerging
from this trance only when Murray shouted with cold
exasperation, "Judy, you're being spoken to!"

"I was merely asking if you saw the Peter Blume exhibition at the Durlacher Galleries," Benedict Strafford was
saying, so taken with the charming little artist's no doubt
typical artist ways, that Dodo felt aggrieved and flounced
over to tinker sulkily with the small ivory piano.

"No," Judy answered, adding loquaciously for Murray's
benefit. "I don't go to exhibitions any more."

Mr. Strafford was enchanted.

"You make it sound as if you'd outgrown dolls!" he
chortled. "Delightful!"

"Judy only means that now she's a big enough artist to
ignore her contemporaries," Murray said, adding morosely

as he poured a daiquiri into the publisher's greedy goblet, "They always get that way. It's 'Me and Michelangelo but not Me and my rivals.' "

"A wonderful career for a lady," Mr. Strafford said, beaming paternally at the young lady's healthy bosom as emphasized by her open shirt. "Painting is so much more suitable for them than writing, pardon me for saying so. Women who write all day have a theory they have to talk all night, and of course the training in finishing their sentences absolutely spoils them for any interruption. Oh, I have many brilliant women on my list but I've often thought how much pleasanter for everyone if they'd just gone off in the woods and painted quietly. However did you begin, dear child?"

"Representationalism," Judy answered, biting into an apple from the table's centerpiece since she was very hungry and the sizzling of sausages on the kitchen stove had only just begun. "Like everybody."

"Of course, of course," Benedict nodded sympathetically.

"I'm in my intermediate period right now," Judy amplified not sure whether Murray's frown meant she was talking too much or too little or merely to the wrong person.

Dodo had been revenging herself by poking out *"Cha Ta"* on the keys with one finger as if she was prodding a drowsy trick elephant that might bellow satisfactorily with due stimulation. This display of musicianship failing to attract attention she added vocal power not at all deterred by ignorance of the lyrics.

"She had 'em, she had 'em," she chanted, "Dum dum dum de dum."

"I hate to bring up business before breakfast," Caroline shouted from the kitchen, "but why don't you two boys decide on what angle you want in this article?"

"Any suggestions, Strafford?" Murray inquired in a hostile voice, significantly frowning at the arm the gentleman had casually placed across the back of Judy's seat.

"What—oh—er—" Strafford closed his eyes to down his third daiquiri at a gulp. ("A lush," thought Murray with the stern contempt of one drinker for another.) "I—let me see, now. To be quite frank with you I'm sometimes referred to in the trade as a human dynamo."

"Oh, Murray, that's *cute!*" cried Dodo, quite bowled over by the expression and jumping to her feet. "You *know* it's cute, Murray, it's so absolutely right! Admit it, now!"

"Can't you leave that damned magazine alone?" Murray answered, snatching *Life* and her apple from Judy's hands. At this moment the shock of the door-bell ringing caused a sudden crash in the kitchen, Murray's gesture knocked Judy's drink into the publisher's lap, and with a silvery sweet halloa Lorna thrust her gray curls coquettishly in the door.

"I'm late—I know I'm late," she crooned, allowing Caroline's warm kiss to fall somewhere midair, "but look at the wonderful surprise! Look, Caroline, Lyle Gaynor! She was going to drive Gerda and me out to Cobb's Mill for the day but Gerda's sick so here we are!"

"They'll all have to eat on their laps," decided Caroline with a rueful glance at her beautiful table, and began her introductions. "Lorna, this is Dodo—er—anyway she's one of Murray's mother's oldest friends, and Mrs. Gaynor—that's right, you two must know each other through Frederick Olliver—and this is Judy Hazelnut—oh dear, Mr. Strafford, let me mop you up, did something get upset?"

20

. . . the baby skin . . .

*A*S CAROLINE told Lorna later she was so rattled by the way her party was going that she didn't know the difference between Lyle Gaynor and Eleanor Roosevelt. All she did know was that the wrong people were being thrown with the wrong people at the wrong time and there was nothing she could do about it, so she simply decided to have a good time and the hell with everybody else. She was grateful for her divine gift of making her mind a complete blank which she did as soon as she grasped the full horror of the Dodo girl (of course, now she recalled she was Frederick Olliver's private cutie) —flinging herself upon Lyle Gaynor (what was that tale about Lyle and Frederick she'd heard?)—and squealing, "Lyle Gaynor, just the person I've wanted to know better! I'll bet you don't remember the time Freddie Olliver introduced us at the Ephraim Beckleys' party. Did Freddie ever tell you how thrilled I was at meeting the author of *Summer's Day?* I've been dying to know you ever since. Do let's sit over here and talk."

Lorna, for her part, later recollected that at this moment her great prize, Mrs. Gaynor, had looked desperately around for help, had backed toward the door and then had given her, Lorna, a look from those lovely hazel eyes of such profound reproach that Lorna couldn't think for the life of her what she had done. Mind you, Lorna had not had to urge her to come along; she had just had a funny hunch there at Gerda's that Mrs. Gaynor was blue. God

212

knows a woman like that wouldn't be leaving her own crowd for Gerda's crazy set-up unless she was in a pretty low state of mind about something. Lorna hadn't known Dodo would be there and all she knew about Lyle and Olliver was that there had been whispers, but no one was sure. So she hadn't noticed what was wrong at first. Anyway she had been too amused at Murray's trying to keep Mr. Strafford away from Judy, at the same time dying to find out who was staying with Gerda and if she was really sick this time. Trust a man to never want anything to fall through his mitts! Of course Lorna had been a little disappointed in Benedict Strafford, she told Caroline, for he was not at *all* what Caroline had described; much older than she had imagined and utterly and completely bald.

"I love him for it!" Caroline had cried. "Men getting bald is the only thing God ever did for women. It evens things a little bit."

Strafford being acquainted with Lyle had saved the situation for a moment and kept Dodo from jumping right on Lyle's lap. Without realizing what was going on, both Lorna and Caroline could see (hours later) that Lyle was in the awful position of fending off that always unwelcome deference to age from tactless youth. You would have thought from Dodo's manner that Lyle was grandma in a lace cap, and no matter how she tried to duck her the kid clung to Lyle like Death itself. It was because there wasn't any man for her to grab. She was going to get something out of this occasion, Dodo was; if it wasn't a new man it would be a new name.

"You should have heard our broadcast this morning, Mrs. Gaynor," babbled Strafford. "Do you know Tyson Bricker told me afterwards I had a first-rate microphone personality? There was some talk of being on a regular weekly program, literary quiz sort of thing. You theatrical people aren't the only ones, ha ha!"

"Tyson said he was much better than Ephraim Beckley," Dodo eagerly contributed. "And Freddie Olliver was simply awful when he was on—he hardly said a word and you couldn't even hear him. I'll bet you get hundreds of fan letters, Mr. Strafford."

Mr. Strafford stroked his left cheek, reflecting on this with judicious modesty.

"I don't know. I confess I had a moment or two of what you call 'mike fright.' I'm afraid I committed the unpardonable sin of ending several declarative sentences with prepositions," he confessed, ruefully. "I may be caught up on that by the radio audience, eh, Mr. Cahill?"

Mr. Cahill sourly assured him that the radio audience did not care whether a sentence ended in a preposition or a rout. He added, shaking up a fresh batch of daiquiris, that the speech had probably made a pleasant obbligato to all the nation's papas spelling out the Sunday funnies to their howling young. Mr. Strafford decided to consider this very amusing, exclaiming to Judy that here was a most delightful chap, certain to be a crackerjack journalist if he took up residence in New York, and how strange he had not met him before.

"He's lived here with Frederick Olliver for years," Judy said, reaching for a pear but giving up at Murray's coldly disapproving eye. "Olliver never introduces people to other people, that's all."

"Will you pipe down?" Murray muttered menacingly.

Mr. Strafford looked again at Murray, this time with less enthusiasm, concluding with an old New Yorker's cynicism, that anyone around for years that he hadn't met after a lifetime of circulating was probably not worth meeting anyway. Murray's pointed statement that Lorna Leahy, too, was an artist, made Mr. Strafford affirm once more his interest in the brush. He asked Lorna, poised elfishly on a footstool before him, if she, as an older professional, was not excited over the fine new talent turned up by Hazelnut's art show? He gave Judy's knee a fatherly pat, absently allowing his plump hand to rest there as he waited for Lorna's considered opinion.

"Don't let's pay any attention to them. They're talking art," Dodo urged Lyle, conducting her to the piano bench.

"You know that suit is awfully smart, I really mean that. You know I hear lots about you from people at Paramount, people from Hollywood. Do you know Tommy Ramus? Do you know Alfred Sutter? Do you know Archie Bleisher? I've heard about those wonderful parties you have."

"Thank you," Lyle said helplessly, feeling herself reddening under Dodo's curious inspection, suspecting she must be looking badly to have Dodo compliment her, for the girl was no one to make up to a more alluring female. Had Frederick confessed his former love, Lyle wondered nervously, and was Dodo trying to be nice to a defeated rival? Or had he never told and was her pointed attention sheer coincidence? Either theory hurt.

"You and I are the only ones that don't care about art," Dodo whispered, and to demonstrate their solidarity she applied her kerchief to dusting an infinitesimal speck from Lyle's shoulder. "I'm going to get myself a suit, too. I think nothing looks nicer. Where do you have your hair done? Do you see why they're making such a fuss over that artist girl? If I'd known this was going to be such a dumb party I wouldn't have come at all. I just came to spite a boyfriend of mine. I just want him to find out I don't need to wait for him to introduce me to his friends. Is your apartment modern like this?"

Now that she was caught in this jam Lyle had to face the fact that she had secretly wanted to meet Dodo during the shameless year of pursuing Frederick's new life. Yes, she had to admit that she had prayed for a chance to see the girl away from him so that she might study what magic she herself had lacked. But Dodo's unexpected overtures left her confused and speechless. The girl had no business appealing to her, she thought hotly. If she didn't guard herself she would be advising Frederick's preference in clothes and perfume just because she was a fool in love, ready to accept anyone the lover (even decamping) loved. She stiffened, however, at Dodo's presumptuous hands twitching, tweaking, and clutching her in friendly possessiveness. After all she was not old or plain enough to be liked by a rival! She steeled herself to hate Dodo. Everything about the Pooh-girl was repulsive to her—the pointer's nostrils, the sleek, taut little body squirming proudly in its sheath, the coarse pomaded black hair and tiny ears, the indefinable animal quality, an invisible hairiness about her, the even white squirrelish teeth, the slender, long-nailed hands, forever caressing her hair, hips, waist. The sing-song nasal Southern baby voice offended her even if what it said had not done so. These unfavorable observations should have a tonic effect, Lyle told herself, and should help her to forget a lover with so little discrimination.

"I wish my hair was red," Dodo was saying generously, belying the compliment by complacently stroking her own smooth black coiffure. "It wouldn't suit me the way it suits you. I don't see why Murray and Mr. Strafford pay so much attention to that goon when you're a lot better-looking. I really mean that."

Lyle thought this would be cruelty in a clever woman but must be pity in Dodo's case. She gave a start at the unexpected touch of Dodo's little hands at her throat.

"What a marvellous scarf—!" Dodo gushed. "I've been looking for that shade of turquoise; it looks like a spider web."

"Do keep it," Lyle said, loosening the gossamer material, as if it already choked her, "I never liked it."

"Oh, really, now, Mrs. Gaynor! I *love* it. Even if it doesn't go with my dress! What *is* that wonderful perfume?"

"*Je reviens*," said Lyle.

"Murray, why don't you take Benedict into the bedroom for your interview," Caroline shouted, pushing a teawagon of breakfast remains into the kitchen. "If you wait too long you'll both be too high and don't forget, I'm responsible for this piece. It'd better be good so I can get special rates out of *People*."

"So I'm part of a deal, well, well! Glad to be considered so valuable," laughed Benedict.

"With these career-women everybody's part of a deal," Murray growled, unable to keep from snapping at somebody even though Caroline was the only one present who did not annoy him. "God, how I hate them!"

"I beg your pardon, Mr. Cahill?" his hostess remarked frigidly.

As Caroline had loaned him hundreds of dollars over a period of years and had only half an hour before slipped two twenties in Murray's pocket she felt justified in giving him a fruity wedge of her mind. She stated icily that nowadays men wanted a woman to work but not to be too good at her job—just good enough to pay her own way and not bright enough to add up what men owed her, not bright enough to see when she was getting a bum deal; they wanted her clever enough to admit his brains and ability when he shot his trap over world affairs but not bright enough to realize it was the liquor bought by her salary that was loosening his tongue. In fact men used the term "career-woman" to indicate a girl who made more than he did and who was unforgiveably good at her job when he was not able to hold one. Having thus cleared the air Caroline rushed over to Murray contritely and kissed him for she knew he couldn't help being a porcupine when he wasn't working, the old dear!

"Now you two get in there and get to work!" she ordered, ashamed of her outburst. "That leaves us a hen party but all the better, isn't it, girls?"

The belligerence of her question made Lorna declare that she loved nothing more than a good old hen party, and besides it was the first chance she'd had to talk to Judy since her prize. ("Good Heavens! Now what?" Caroline groaned apprehensively.) There were so many things they had to talk over since they both had studied with Miller and both knew Larry Glay at Hazelnut, a darling as ever was. Lorna said roguishly that she, for one, was not at all surprised when Judy got the prize because she had heard Larry rave about Judy's figure and complexion. Dodo's face had brightened at the first mention of Larry Glay, and she leaned forward ready to shine with inside information if knowing Larry was the key to popularity. But Lorna's "tradelast" for Judy made her sink back with an expression stricken and incredulous. Lyle, observing the change, looked around for the cause. Dodo sat frozen, swallowing the rum collins Caroline now produced as if her throat hurt her. Staring fixedly into space she said presently in a strained voice, "Everytime I go around in any old thing then everybody else is all dressed up so I feel silly. Then when I'm all dressed up nobody else is. New York is so funny that way. Sometimes I wish I'd never come."

"Is that the only thing you have against us?" Lyle asked, thinking how strange that she could not repeat this minor tragedy to Frederick who would have found it amusing, once. The girl's lip was actually quivering.

Dodo stared balefully at Judy who was sitting cross-legged on the sofa, streaked ashen lock falling across her face, stolidly munching an apple as she listened to Lorna. Occasionally she grunted an answer.

"Larry Glay simply raves over your baby skin," Lorna was again declaring.

"You never can tell what men are likely to go for in this town," Dodo burst forth, her brows knitting unhappily. "There just isn't any point. You could read *Harper's Bazaar* and *Vogue* all day long and still you couldn't tell. I just hate men. New York men, I mean. This dress cost eighty dollars but I might as well have come here in shorts. I wish I had."

She whipped out her compact and painted her lips savagely, pausing and slowly replacing the unnecessary lipstick as if reproached by the sight of Judy's pale mouth. She tied Lyle's scarf carefully in a new bow, and this appeared to restore her confidence. Caroline, having efficiently placed her dishes in the washer with loud protestations of needing no help, came back in the room and seeing that the hen party was pairing off poured herself a drink and nipped slyly into the bedroom to join the men, raising her voice from time to time in such happy howls of glee that the ladies looked up jealously.

"Caroline just loves a hen party," Lorna tinkled, "for other women, that is."

The suspicious quality of the ladies' merriment reaching Caroline squashed her own glee, allowing her a good guess as to who the victim of the unheard joke might be.

"You see what I mean," Dodo went on to Lyle, endeavoring to sound calm. "A man takes you to a party and then starts making passes at somebody else. If you call *that* a baby skin! I just don't get it."

Quite mystified Lyle followed Dodo's jealous eyes again to Judy who had risen and was blowing her nose with artistic fervor. What could Dodo be talking about? Whatever its cause there was no mistaking the sincerity of her emotions for she had difficulty controlling her voice and her twitching lips. Certainly it had nothing to do with Frederick Olliver or even Strafford. It must be, Lyle concluded, that Dodo was pathologically jealous of every other female any man admired. She studied Judy too, wondering why Judy gave no sign of having met her before, then remembered they had never exchanged more than a cool nod, even though they knew all about each other. She watched furtively for some sign of astonishment on Judy's, Lorna's, Caroline's face at seeing her and her successor in a confidential huddle and felt a pang of dismay that they showed no surprise. It was one thing to have conducted an affair with such discretion that no one knew when it was over, and she had been grateful that Frederick had meticulously observed the rules she had laid down. But now she was the only person who could remember that there had been love and for her would always be. She should have mistrusted a love that was not stronger than a gentleman's code; she wished with all her heart that he had shouted her name in all the bars, confessed his love to every passing stranger. It would have made the memory less a dream, and she would not be cursed with the dreadful doubt that she had ever been important to him. Waves of shame for her own stingy caution came over her, for it had been she who dictated the terms, and the day had come when she wanted heavenly forgiveness for cowardice in her sinning more than worldly approval of her virtue. There was a stinging implication, too, in Murray Cahill's casual treatment of her, that he considered her only one of many women in Frederick's life. Ominous above all was Dodo's singling her out for special friendship. A woman in love could always sense a rival, predecessor or possible successor—when it was important. She had not been important, face it, that must be it. Dodo, if she sensed anything, evidently dismissed her. How humiliating to inspire no jealousy in a rival—and how bitterly revealing!

"I have a friend in Baltimore who's a better painter than anybody around here, and everybody who knows anything about art says so," Dodo confided in a low tone. "Of course he's a man so I don't suppose that old lecher in there would like him. That's another reason I hate men. You're the only person here I like. I knew I'd like you but Freddie Olliver would never take me to any of your parties. I came here today just to spite him, he's always going on so about Caroline Drake's apartment but oh no, I can't come here. And oh no, I can't go when he's with his old editors. I can't wait to see his face when I tell him I came to Caroline Drake's with Benedict Strafford and met you here, besides! I think I'll call him up right now. Only then I'd have to have dinner with him and I'd never get rid of him. You know how he is, always wanting you to himself, so you can't have any fun."

"I've always admired his work," Lyle said weakly.

"Oh, that! I'll tell him you said so," Dodo said, glumly, and then clapped her hands in inspiration. "I know what. I'll pretend you made me jealous then I can have an excuse for ditching him. I feel too blue to be stuck with him all Sunday evening. If he'd take me to a party, it would be all right, but oh no he thinks he's so interesting I have to have him all alone! Don't you hate men like that?"

For this Frederick had left her, Lyle thought, with mounting fury. No wonder he hid from her, knowing as he surely must, how wasted his new love was. She could not listen longer to the little monster who had elected her ear for confession. She was afraid she might cry out in indignation. ("How dare you not love my lover who loves you more than he does me?") She was saved by Benedict Strafford suddenly springing out of the bedroom door looking on the verge of apoplexy. He had his hat in his hand and made a stiff, unsmiling bow in the doorway, carefully avoiding a direct look at Judy.

"Thank you, thank you very much, Miss Drake," he said formally. "Thank you all and good day!"

"I'll drop you," Lyle said, leaping up.

"But—" began Caroline. He sidled out the door skittishly as if he expected or had just received a sound kick in the seat. Lyle followed him exclaiming, "I'm sorry but I must drive Mr. Strafford home. Do excuse me."

The flight left Caroline's jaw agape. "What'd I do to her, for God's sake," she wailed. "Murray, what happened?"

"I told the old goat off," Murray said, coolly as the outer door banged. "Who does he think he is, anyway? Human Dynamo! Caroline, for God's sake, where do you find people like that? I'm damned if I waste my time building him up, even if I do need the dough. Pawing women!"

"If Judy ever buttoned up her shirt he wouldn't have pawed her," Caroline shouted, exasperated. "Blame her for not wearing a brassiére, don't blame me. *I* didn't ask her here to put her dirty little shoes on my white sofa!"

"Come on, you little idiot, don't you know when you've

been insulted?" Murray yanked Judy to her feet and
toward the door, his round boyish face flushed with indignation. "Let's get out of this."

"Take the service elevator or you'll run into them,"
Caroline called out, furiously, then turned on Dodo who
was looking wide-eyed. "What? Haven't you been insulted
yet? Am I losing my grip?"

"What did she say to Mrs. Gaynor?" Lorna wailed.
"Caroline, I feel so *responsible!* Did Dodo say something
to upset her?"

Dodo rose.

"Listen, Lyle Gaynor is a friend of mine," she said
haughtily. "If she goes I go. Besides, I don't want to get
mixed up in other people's fights."

"That's just fine! Here's your hat," approved Caroline
shrilly and barely two minutes later she was pouring a pair
of very stiff ones, indeed, handing one to Lorna. With a
huge groan she kicked off her shoes, collapsing on the
sofa, hand over eyes. Lorna sprawled cozily in a big chair
with an equally weary sigh.

"I don't know why it is men never get insulted till
they've finished your dinner or your liquor or your pocketbook," Caroline whimpered, and suddenly tears streamed
down her face, making white ruts in her thick tropical
make-up. "We're just a pair of soft-headed old career
women, Lorna, you and me. Well, here's to us!"

In no time at all they were embarked on four weeks'
worth of pent-up confidences. Lorna told Caroline what
she liked best about her was her marvellous flair for
parties. Alright, supposing guests did quarrel, it was
never boring, and she almost died laughing when Caroline came out with that crack about not having invited
Judy. Of course the girl was alright, Lorna had nothing
against her. Caroline generously replied that she thought
Judy was awful and never the artist that Lorna was, but
since Lorna liked her she would try not to be too hard on
the kid. She added that as far as she was concerned the
only nice thing about the party was Lorna being so sweet

as to bring Lyle Gaynor. Lorna insisted that she deserved no credit, and furthermore, in her opinion, Lyle Gaynor acted stuck-up. Lorna wished to apologize here and now for not asking Caroline's permission first to bring such a wet-blanket. Caroline would not listen to any denigration of any friend of Lorna's even if Lorna herself did the denigrating. She only wondered if Lorna would ever forgive her for introducing that old bore, Benedict Strafford, into her life. She only hoped he wouldn't start persecuting her. Lorna promised that if he ever presumed on the slight acquaintance she would not hold Caroline in any way to blame.

What a satisfaction to have the place to themselves, letting their hair down like old times, clinking glasses, and passing judgment on the recently departed! There was nothing like old friendship, no matter how tried or trying it often was. Naturally you couldn't love anybody twenty-four hours a day; in fact it was during the periods of coolness that you appreciated your friend the most, and returned with all the more pleasure. Lorna dashed off some sketches of Mr. Strafford that seemed to Caroline at the moment the most brilliant works of genius she had ever seen, and whether Murray did his piece or not she was certain she could sell these drawings to *People*. Lorna said she valued Caroline's artistic criticism more than anyone's, and she would rather appear in *People* than in the Metropolitan Museum. At seven o'clock that evening they were deep in familiar confidences and Lorna had cured Caroline's hiccups by efficiently fixing up a magic concoction of lemon slices soaked in sugar and Worcestershire sauce.

Caroline's amazement and admiration of her friend's unexpected domestic lore was boundless.

"Lorna, what I like about you is you have so many sides to your character," she said with deep feeling. "Who would guess you could cure hiccups! I never even dreamed you were such a home body!"

21

. . . variations on a juke-box theme . . .

*T*HE Four Pillars of Rubberleg Square sat at the bar in the Americas viewing their future in the bar mirror and drinking up their past and present. The juke-box was aglow and bursting with joyous booms of *You Won't Be Satisfied Until You Break My Heart,* and whenever it heaved into silence a fragile girl with a Veronica Lake blonde bang drooping over one eye and a blonde fur coat over her shoulders got off the bar stool with great care to extort more jubilation from the obliging instrument. The nickel always dropped on the floor, the coat slipped down, and the bang had to be thrust back in the ensuing search before the same song boomed out again with the girl replacing herself on the bar stool with suspicious care. The Four Pillars had contemplated this routine with placid enjoyment for some time as nothing else had happened since a Labrador retriever brought his master in for a drink then dragged him out precipitately when challenged by little Queenie, the bar cat.

"Don't let that dame horn in on you, ever," warned Rover addressing his friends in the bar mirror as was their custom since they always sat side by side at bars and probably would not have recognized each other face to face. "She drinks beer when she's on her own but stingers when it's on anyone else. I've seen her around. Came from some whistlestop down East to go on the stage."

"Maybe she thinks this is it," said the doctor.

Instead of their usual custom of keeping separate accounts, tonight Dr. Zieman had insisted on being host to the other three and for persuasion produced a remarkable roll of bills with elaborate casualness. Caraway whispered to Marquette his guess that the doctor's wife must have finally sold *Wootsie the Bad Cricket* to Walt Disney for a fat sum; but Marquette had read somewhere that *Wootsie's* little sister, *Betsy the Good Grasshopper* had just been published and Schwarz's toy shop was bringing out the two lovable little insects as a Twin-Toy sensation. This reminded Rover that his own wife's talents produced no profit, her present assignment as walk-on or dance-on, in the Ballet rewarding her (and him) with only a free backstage view of three productions weekly. ("What do I get out of watching her get pushed around by a bunch of fags?" he often complained.) He spoke wistfully of her artistic heyday when her cat made thirty-five dollars a week in the Gaynor play, and inquired of the doctor whether the story of a stage cat wouldn't make a wow of a juvenile book, if he could only deflect his wife's energies to such a task. This made Caraway reflect favorably for the first time on the advantages of having a wife and for a moment all four were silent, contemplating the pleasant prospect of being kept drunk for years by the kiddies. Everytime the doctor displayed his roll, gartered with a wide rubber band, Marquette was impelled to avert his face with the curious feeling that he was spying on Mrs. Zieman's intimate garments, a fancy that for a moment gave his rye and water a disagreeably woolly taste. In a little while, however, all three of the doctor's cronies experienced a pleasurably relaxed sense of riches and personal achievement and moved their stools closer and closer to the doctor the better to inhale the heady fragrance of folding money. They ordered Canadian Club instead of bar rye—only fifteen cents more, what the hell —and this automatically raised the level of their conversation; they spoke of art. Dr. Zieman quoted several lines from Gerard Manley Hopkins, graciously pointing out the sprung rhythm; Marquette gave an opinion on world affairs and mentioned India; Rover had new secrets from

Brock, Herman, Miriam, Jasper, and Bogey. The simple bar was transformed into a most exclusive club, and in compliment to the occasion Mr. Caraway, first trumpeting the hint that his own reserve had melted by much nose-blowing and coughing, revealed certain episodes from his past life. He mentioned summers in Old Cove, Connecticut, a quiet, healthy resort he could recommend to anyone needing a change of air; i.e. there was a vast difference in the air of fishingtown saloons from Greenwich Village saloons. He spoke of having watched the playwright, Mrs. Lyle Gaynor as a girl, driving her ponycart down the beach-road with her pale auburn hair flying and all the boys mooning for her. Prodded by the Pillars he gave the inside story of her romance with Gaynor. "I never have mentioned this and perhaps I shouldn't—" he began hesitantly. Naturally no one could reply that indeed he had mentioned it dozens of times. Besides the familiar anecdote sounded much finer and more intimate than it usually did under less affluent conditions. Mr. Marquette, as if for the first time, was then moved to divulge details of a scandal in Allan Gaynor's earlier life in St. Louis, while his friends exclaimed, "No, you don't say!" as if they had not been fanning their drinks with these same tales many times over. The repetition did serve, however, to bring the two Gaynors closer and closer to the Pillars' lives, and even Dr. Zieman, the only one who had no fingernail hold on these public figures, now referred to "Lyle" and "Allan" and tonight added to the script his opinion that Allan would probably end up losing his mind. At this point the sensibilities of all four were unpleasantly jolted by a mocking laugh from the jukebox girl.

"That's all you know about it," she said, tossing back the fair locks. "Don't you worry about Allan Gaynor's mind. Allan Gaynor happens to be alright. I happen to know Allan Gaynor personally and I can tell you right here and now that he happens to have more brains than you four creeps put together."

The Pillars could not have been more startled if Gaynor himself had popped up behind them, though the chances were that they would not have recognized him in spite of their boasted acquaintance with him. Rover catching the doctor's eye in the mirror, lifted a wry eyebrow, Mr. Marquette and Mr. Caraway exchanged expressionless glances and drained their glasses.

"Allan Gaynor!" the girl repeated with her musical laugh. "A lot you know about Allan Gaynor. Allan Gaynor's a genius. You wouldn't know that, naturally."

Ladies in their cups or forced by circumstance to do their pubcrawling solo were invariably outraged by the spectacle of four men free to enjoy themselves without visible feminine chains, and the Pillars were usually complacently prepared for illbred insults and reproaches. But this was different. The girl's hint of deeper and more recent connection with the subject of their conversation brought them down with embarrassing suddenness from their lofty reminiscences. They examined their empty glasses which seemed to chorus a suggestion to move on, but at that moment the advertising man named Larry Glay leaped jauntily through the door and the Pillars could not bear to miss whatever fresh drama he might bring. The advertising genius had not been around for a time and looked as if he'd been through the wringer, ears laid back, hair slicked to the bone and the general skinned and plucked appearance of a man who had submitted to purification by shower until all color and juice had been drained from him. He darted a swift look around the booths. "Looking for that Dodo kid," whispered Rover to the doctor.

"What's the matter, Spike, losing all your trade to the Barrel?" Larry asked the bartender genially. "Nobody around tonight."

"Suits me," was the curt answer. "Who you looking for?"

"Me?" Larry repeated evasively with a second glance around. "Well, who you got?"

"Your friend Murray hasn't been around," Spike, the bartender said. "I got a bouncer of his here. If you see him, tell him."

"I'll warn him to keep out," said Larry. "Say, I feel terrible. Can't you cheer me up?"

After a whiskey neat he was sufficiently refreshed to take an interest in the juke-box girl. There was the customary procedure (after another survey of the room to make sure nothing better offered) of merry remarks seemingly addressed to the bartender and accompanied by disproportionate hilarity, and sidelong glances at the girl who responded by smiling sardonically into her beer.

"Where would that little tramp get a fur coat like that?" Rover muttered to the bartender. "Last I heard was she couldn't afford any more diction lessons."

"Some Coast Guard boy friend gave her the dough to get a cure," Spike whispered happily, "but she decided she'd have more fun with a fur coat."

"Well, you can't have everything," Dr. Zieman reflected philosophically, stroking his beard.

His three friends laughed heartily at this, repeating it over and over with such unaffected enjoyment that the doctor felt justified in ordering another round at once. They were not too engrossed in their own fun to ignore the activities of the K.G.R. man and nudged each other as he ordered a stinger sent to the young lady. For her part the tribute to her charm made her increasingly haughty and very much the lady, dallying with her drink indifferently to offset any impression that it was of any consequence to her. Her lips curved in a quizzical dreamy smile suggesting private amusement at the idea of herself, of all people, being in this sordid spot with these sordid people.

"Haven't seen you down here, much, lately, Mr. Glay," the bartender said. "What's the matter, going Park Avenue on us?"

"His wife doesn't like his sweetie, that's all," spoke up the girl, pointing at Larry. "Isn't that so, Jackson?"

"Hey, now, you're talking to an old married man," Larry protested with a wink at the Pillars. "What would I be doing with a sweetie?"

"I bite. What?" said the girl, and after a moment of

concentrated thought added that whatever he would be doing with a sweetie somebody else was doing right now and serve him right.

"Serves everybody right," said Larry. "Service, that's what I like. One more for me with two chasers of the same."

"Now watch her get nasty," Rover nudged Caraway. "Get a load of this."

"I suppose you wonder how I happen to know so much," pursued the girl with a faint smile and (as the Pillars noticed) suddenly remembering to get her money's worth out of her diction lessons and becoming very pear-shaped indeed. "Naturally you happen to be the type that doesn't know what's under your own nose."

"Sure I do. It's *Old Granddad*," said Larry happily and downed his three whiskeys with accompanying incantations of "See no evil, hear no evil, do no evil."

"Oh, I could tell you plenty if I cared to, my fine simian friend," the girl continued in her best dowager voice. "I happen to know the world, myself——"

"I'll say she does from what I hear," Rover nudged the doctor.

"—and nothing amuses me so much as you married men thinking nobody else can get away with it. Oh, you're so clever! I could tell you a few things." She leaned her chin on her hands with a look of infinite sorrow for human error.

"What about more of the juke-box and less of the gypsy, honey?" suggested Larry uneasily, fishing for coins in his pocket. He selected an attractive fifty cent program divided fair and square between *You Won't Be Satisfied* and the *Anniversary Waltz*. After a brave attempt at a soft shoe routine, forefinger pointed skyward, while the juke-box burst with rosy apoplectic song, he edged toward the Four Pillars who were sternly minding their own business by staring fixedly in the bar mirror.

"Oh, please don't feel you must sit with me, Mr. Hazel-nut," the girl said huffily. "I'm sure your four ancient friends will appreciate your conversation more than I possibly could. After all, I happen to be used to Allan Gaynor's conversations."

"I can see you're a kid that likes her conversation alright and plenty of it," Larry gaily conceded, looking around hopefully for other and friendlier companionship. "Say, this place is dead tonight. What's the matter with old Murray anyway? Any you fellows seen him? What's he up to these days?"

"I haven't the faintest idea, I'm sure," Dr. Zieman said, gesturing to the bartender for another round on the kiddies. "I believe it may have been Murray I saw an hour or so ago with that Pollock girl, your prize artist. Having gin rickeys and a little quarrel in Barney's, as I recall. I just happened to glance in the door."

"The guy he lives with, he was here last night at closing time. Olliver, that's his name," volunteered the bartender. "With that kid, Dodo."

"See what I told you, Jackson?" cried the girl, nodding her head, at Larry. "And you married men are so sure you know everything."

"If I don't, you're insulting my wife!" said Larry. "She should have told me more."

"Frederick Olliver's a big shot now," stated Caraway. "Yes sir, he must be taking in a lot of dough right now. Smart fellow, I like him."

"I figured he must be rich, never buying drinks," meditated the bartender, polishing his nails on his cuff, "except when that Dodo kid runs up the check on him, and, boy, can she do that."

"See?" said the girl, triumphantly. "Sometimes a girl can get away with just as much as you can."

"Now what'd I ever do to this woman?" complained Larry. "Or didn't I?"

He appealed to the Four Pillars but their faces remained impassive. The girl burst into her most musical laugh and pushed her face close to Larry's.

"Snap out of it, silly boy, can't you tell when you're being kidded? I dare you to take me over to the New Place for a nightcap. I dare you."

As a gentleman accustomed to overcoming female reluctance by bold attack Larry Glay was obviously confused by counter-attack. The girl rubbed her cheek affectionately against his shoulder.

"Come on, let's get away from these creeps," she indicated Dr. Zieman and his guests. "Your girl-friend's out with other people, don't you worry about her."

"Honey, you're the only girl I'd ever invite to break up my home. I thought you knew that." The advertising man gallantly surrendered, clapping his hat on his head, and crooking his elbow for the lady. "Excuse us, gentlemen, we're off to a small, middleclass hotel where a lady can lose her good name in comfort. What *is* your good name, anyway?"

"You are clever, you know," the girl said, sweeping her cloak about her frail body. "Marianna Garrett. You remember Marianna."

"Isn't that something?" observed Caraway watching them through the door. "They're crossing the street. I guess she's taking him to the other bar. Funny seeing a wise guy like that get trapped. I wouldn't have missed it."

"What'd she mean she worked for Allan Gaynor? Was that on the level?" inquired the doctor.

"Say, I was just thinking," said Rover. "Maybe she was planning to meet that guy here all along and they just put on that act for our benefit."

"No, he was looking for somebody else," stated Marquette. "He was trapped, that was all. Serves him right. He thought he was doing so well when she let him buy that first drink. So trusting and so proud, it makes me laugh. Like sticking his head in the lion's mouth."

They were going over the incident with increasing pleasure when Frederick Olliver and Dodo came in and stood at the bar. Dodo was gotten up in a tight tweedy coat of purple plaid, a high stovepipe felt hat swathed in veils, magenta gloves, shoes, and enormous shoulderbag, her small neatly chiselled face shining under a smooth layer of gypsy foundation cream, her Fatal Apple lips pouting sulkily. The ensemble gave an impression of garish simplicity and still smelt of the shop in spite of the heavy sprinkling of Tabu. The Pillars sat back, expectantly. She ordered a Bourbon and sipped it in silence. Frederick Olliver looked gloomy staring at Dodo who looked haughtily away from him. Must have been wrangling, deduced the Pillars. You couldn't get a girl like that to keep her trap shut unless you managed to make her mad. She was annoyed, that was clear, and with reason, so Dodo felt. Here was the first chance she had to wear her brand new outfit and she had waited for a really exciting date, refusing Frederick, then no one else had called her and at the end she was obliged to fall back on him, for which naturally she would never forgive him. He had taken her to three or four places of her choice but no sooner were they seated than she was dissatisfied and wanted to leave; this too was unpardonable in him. Finally they came down to Rubberleg Square where surely someone could be found to admire the new clothes.

"What makes everything so dull tonight, anyway?" she demanded peevishly of the bar-tender. "Where is everybody? It's so dead."

"I wouldn't say it was bad as all that," Spike answered. "We been having fun, haven't we, fellas? You shoulda been here when Larry Glay and the blonde were going at each other. First I thought she was going to conk him, next thing she's out to make him. Funny, wasn't it, fellas?"

"Larry?" Dodo said, eyes widening. "How long ago?"

"They just left," the bartender said. "Five minutes."

"I told you we should have come here first!" Dodo whirled on Frederick, petulantly. "Where'd he go?"

"The blonde wanted him to go to the New Place at first," Rover offered. "But I don't know."

"You mean he brought his wife?" Dodo asked sharply, her nostrils quivering, like a mouse's moustache on the scent, Frederick thought with that detached scorn part of him always felt for his love.

"No, this was just a girl around here," the bartender said casually, squinting at the glass he was wiping. "They got to talking. She——"

But Dodo was out of the door in a flash. The Pillars forgot themselves so far as to turn around and gape after her. Frederick stood still, frozen.

"What's with her?" the bartender exclaimed, and scratched his jaw, the friction evidently producing inspiration for he clapped a hand over his mouth.

No one said anything. Frederick reached for his change pocket and laid the money on the bar. He strolled toward the door.

"I wouldn't go over to the New Place if I was you, bud," called the bartender. "Looks to me like you'd be running into bad news."

"Thanks," said Frederick stiffly, and the Four staring through the window, saw him hesitate outside then saunter in the opposite direction.

The Four waited a suitable length of time and then with one accord rose and filed out. Their discretion had betrayed them, though, for when they got to the New Place there was no sign of Dodo, Larry, or the juke-box girl. All that the bartender would tell them was that he was trying to run a decent place and some things he wouldn't tolerate. Give him a Bowery bum, sterno can and all any time, in preference to a drinking lady. The Pillars were grieved to get no more than that for their trouble.

It was days before they found out that Dodo had bolted into the bar and after a seemingly polite encounter with Larry and the blonde had slapped the blonde and thrown a highball in Larry's face. The blonde had run out in great dudgeon, Larry had disappeared out the back entrance, and Dodo after long conferring in the telephone booth, was finally called for by Mr. Olliver in a taxicab. What a pity Dr. Zieman's celebration had cost the Pillars their grand-stand seat at such a juicy show!

22

. . . the blue plate reunion . . .

$\mathcal{T}$HE SWAN Café had been ruined or made by the eminence of its patrons, your point of view depending on whether you were patron or proprietor. Created in the cellar of a Chelsea delicatessen during the prohibition era by the inevitable ex-Mouquin waiters, one a Swiss cellist, it managed to survive the depression by the unvarying plainness of its fare—lentil soup, sauerbraten, sulze vinaigrette, potato dumplings, apfel strudel and pineapple-cheese pie. New patrons were deeply resented by the old faithful customers. It was these faithfuls, after all, who had kept the place going all during the bleak days of prohibition and depression; here, as precocious undergraduates, they had created their little magazine, graciously permitting the proprietors to invest in it. Here they used tables as editorial desks, booths as conference rooms, the dark hallway and garbage-strewn courtyard as trysting ground. Their battered felt hats moulded in the dark cellar closet, forgotten; their bills, I.O.U.'s, and bouncing checks, yellowed and dignified with age, popped out of the dusty roll-top desk in the kitchen. They had seen Fanny, the kitchen cat, through a dozen litters, adopted her children, glorified her in cartoon and story. During the magazine's periodical slumps they were cheered by drinking coffee in the little cellar room while the chef took out his cello and played for them. When Edwin Stalk miraculously took charge, bringing distinction to their magazine and its restaurant home, they loyally continued their patronage and even paid an old bill occasionally. They felt justified in their indignation, therefore, when the faculty members of the nearby League for Cultural Foundations began crowding the place, ordering lavish meals, demanding "spritzen" instead of beer, demoralizing the waiters with tips, and referring to the seedy Prohibition *decor* as "amusing" or "quaint." The faithfuls had to wait for tables only to find the sauerbraten crossed off the menu, the lentil and sausage soup watered down to thin bean juice. True, their corner table was still reserved but it was no longer dominant. Workers from nearby lofts once entertained and bewildered by loud quarrels approaching fisticuffs over nothing more than a dainty problem in aesthetics, were more interested in watching for radio notables or queer bearded foreigners among the League diners. Talk of the changes over two decades made small impression on Edwin Stalk, the *Swan's* saviour, for he was rarely conscious of surroundings, never certain whether people or places were real or something he had read. Neither active in nor responsible to his own generation, the Swan Café and the Mermaid Tavern merged for him into one picture. His friends, with clothespin heads for all he knew, were pegged in his memory by the particular subjects he liked to discuss with them and he thought of them not by names but as Poetry, Ballet, Minor Prophets, Western culture, Russian Soul, Swedish Architecture and sought out one or the other as he would a special book, according to his mood, closing it at his will, and vitally disturbed if Subject did not stick to Subject. His memory of his own youth was not of foundling home, rich foster-mother, travel, doting women, and many honors but of the time and place he had first read Proust, Joyce, Pushkin, Freud and Spengler. Women had taken possession of him early, fought over him until the day Solange had established her firm clutch, and Stalk accepted the victor with passive indifference and even relief. The *Swan* was the first great reality—it was mother, mistress, child, past and future. He never admitted into his consciousness the fact that the magazine had been struggling into shape for some years under other hands before he had adopted it. Whenever anyone made reference to a poem by T. S. Eliot or an essay on The Word Revolution by Jolas in the old *Swan*, Edwin's handsome brows arched together in a look of pain as if: "You are not speaking of *MY Swan* and therefore I think you are being rude." He had the same grieved expression when someone firmly fixed in his mind as Southern Agrarian escaped his category and spoke of unrelated matters. Whatever appeared in the *Swan* seemed his very own, accidentally put into lucid even jewelled words by his contributors, just as carpenters and masons carry out the architect's dream without making it any the less his. Edwin was not aware of unreasonable egotism; he believed he was giving absolutely selfless devotion to a cause, liking and tolerating human beings in proportion to their belief in the *Swan*, interested in events and talk only where it might feed the *Swan*. Indeed he thought he was unconcerned with his pocket and the needs of his body; you might call him totally unaware, too, of the feminine dither over him except for the fact that he had always taken it for granted and would have come to sharp attention if a sixth sense informed him that women's eyes were not upon him. Already Edwin Stalk was credited with being a Great Editor, and if this réclame implied possession of antennae sensing and pseudopodia enveloping all varieties of spiritual caviar then the reputation was deserved. If it meant his profile and an unerring instinct for sponsor appeal had drawn capital into the wizening coffers, then it was twice deserved; if it indicated a royal faculty for getting other people to attend to the labor and steady grind of producing, then the term was merited even more. He was fortunate in having that convenience, familiar to Great Editors, the Magazine Mama, an enormous girl with a profound and hairy mind, a body so huge and unwieldy for general group arrangements in office, taxicab or theatre, that her steadfast anonymity was astounding. It was Josephine Carey who had been with the *Swan* from its feeble inception, even setting type at one time, paying its bills from her own modest allowance, trudging on messenger duties, keeping books, reading manuscripts, attending to correspondence, meeting lawyers and sub- poenae-servers, offering a memory stocked with encyclo- pedic information, keeping herself wonderfully in the background through all sorts of staff changes. Her services for Edwin Stalk were performed so unobtrusively that he was scarcely conscious of her presence, and often forgot her name, looking up sometimes from his desk with complete bewilderment at the shapeless hulk padding about, her billowing draperies wafting a smell of musty hay and soy sauce. Her garments were always the same—dark greenish black serges or crêpes with flowing bat-wing sleeves, al- ways mussed, always showing a cerise slip below the hem and chewed bits of shoulder-straps at the neck. She lived for each issue and on the occasion of its tenth anniversary number was caught by the printer in the act of pressing a passionate kiss on the gold-lettered cover.

Josephine was as sublimely unconscious of her great size and clumsiness as Stalk was of his beauty. If no one stopped her she was all for tucking herself up on the smallest footstool, attempting to squeeze dangerously into the child's chair or onto the arm of the frailest antique sofa, wedging into the most crowded bus or elevator, una- ware that anything beyond her wee whisper required ac- commodation. Though she spoke little during office hours, it was Josephine who answered all queries at the weekly luncheons, providing statistical ballast for both sides in all arguments, whether they concerned the Bolivian tin dynasty, European literary criticism during the *Sturm and Drang*, or the pet charades of the Goncourt circle. It was her habit to arrive before anyone else at the Café corner table and take her place at the remotest corner to avoid inconveniencing others, but since she drank gallons of coffee she was obliged to excuse herself frequently for the ladies' room, squeezing herself back and forth past the chairs of late arrivals with gasping apologies. The demands of the body embarrassed her dreadfully and she was only consoled by remembering that the great minds she revered suffered from similar interruptions. Her vast fund of general information saved her from trivial interchange and when anyone threatened to become too personal she had been known to deluge them with the figures on some ponderous subject, talking rapidly for what seemed hours, not as an exhibitionist but as a desperate defender of her own privacy. Some spy from the human race might spot her vulnerability, so barriers of statistics must be piled up like sandbags to protect the small shy bird within. It was a good thing that she did not suspect others of any more interest in the physical than she herself had, for it saved her from any inferiority; her evident impression that she went from head straight into winglets like a seraph resulted in astonishing displays of bare porky thigh and generous bosom. The unexpected treat combined with her majestic mind and soft creamy skin sometimes tempted neurotic young men to bury their faces in the cool buttery curve of throat, only to be chilled by the deadly flow of portentous information issuing from the face above.

On the occasion of the special Olliver issue of the *Swan* Josephine, armed with bulging briefcase and wearing a mangled brown moleskin cape of the Valeska Surat era, padded into the Swan Café before twelve and was surprised to find no one present but Editor Stalk who sat in her own special corner. He was lost in thought and did not even notice Josephine wedging her bulk heroically through improbable apertures. A pale lemon glow filtering through the barred cellar window behind him softened his dark, sharply chiselled face and gave it boyish wistfulness. Josephine was stirred with vague yearnings to cheer him with some rare offering, some little-known anecdote of Tallyrand's life, say, or a well-documented tidbit concerning André Chénier. Nothing of the sort occurring to her she resorted to office news.

"The International Committee is ordering ten thousand copies of this issue for foreign distribution," she said, and repeated it when Stalk looked up at her blankly. "That pays the printer. And the ads we got from South America will carry the Padilla poetry number."

Stalk lifted his shoulders indifferently and Josephine sought for other subjects. "Too bad nobody's here today," she said. "Padilla was coming but I guess everybody else has gone to the country. And Olliver's so puffed up nowadays he's forgotten we gave him his start. He never shows up any more."

"I don't care," Stalk said. "The only person I wanted to see today was Mrs. Gaynor. I hope she got my message."

A cloud passed over Josephine's face. She, too, had been questioned by Solange about Mrs. Gaynor. Josephine had been offended by the intimacy of the question as well as by the danger of Stalk's beautiful mind being defiled by normal masculine preoccupations. And she always shuddered when a wife's grisly shadow crossed the temple stairs.

"Do you think we can get money from her?" she now asked. "I read that her play folded on the road and there was no film tie-up."

Edwin brushed this aside as irrelevant.

"I don't want money from Mrs. Gaynor," he said impatiently. "All I was hoping for was the benefit of her kind of intelligence. We tend to get too academic. To expand we need someone with Mrs. Gaynor's experience with large audiences."

"She hasn't done anything for ages, has she?" Josephine murmured. She unlatched her briefcase and drew out a batch of notes with a certain setting of her round jaw that would indicate to anyone but Edwin Stalk her dismissal of the lady's intelligence and a quiet resolution to barricade her intrusion. An angry button in a strategic frontal position rebelled at the strain of duty and popped off as she sat down.

"It's our academic following that's built us up so far," Josephine contented herself with adding, oblivious to her calamity. The editor smiled radiantly. Not for her, it seemed, but at the sight of Mrs. Gaynor pausing uncertainly in the dining-room door, her marvellous intelligence being marked with interest by alert gentlemen accustomed to the *Swan's* drabber feminine trade. Not often had they seen mind so elegantly packaged in soft sables, rusty-feathered hat blending charmingly into rusty gold curls. Edwin Stalk, usually languid in motion, startled Josephine by bounding up like a boy and running toward the guest. He was pushed into the background by Tyson Bricker suddenly rising from a table and seizing Lyle's hands.

"What is this charming creature doing in this end of the world?" Tyson exclaimed, deftly managing to present his exquisitely tailored gray back to Edwin Stalk. "I never see you. No one sees you. Is this old saloon to be the background of a new comedy? *Are* you working? What are you and Allan doing?" His fine eyes assumed the grave accusatory look he was wont to direct at writers to remind them that he, as critic and teacher, was still boss, waiting to catch them up on tardiness and mischief.

"Perhaps I need a course with you at the League, first," Lyle countered, flushing at his keen gaze which might see through her flimsy pretext for being there.

"They have introduced a course in Fast Reading at the League," Edwin Stalk maliciously interrupted. "Bricker starts them off by showing them how to keep their minds a blank, and they can read like the wind, unless, of course, thinking sets in. How do you cure that, Bricker?"

"Ah, Stalk, how are you? Stalk has never appreciated what we're trying to do," Tyson acknowledged his enemy's presence with a curt nod, "any more than I appreciate what he's trying to do. For instance, he believes in keeping a Frederick Olliver just for his fifty or sixty readers. I believe in giving fifty or sixty thousand the privilege of reading him. Never mind, old chap, you'll learn just as

Olliver has. Saw him only last week out at Oak Ridge, by
the way."

"Oak Ridge?" Lyle repeated. "Not Cordelay Beckley's
country place?"

"The very same. They turned over a guest cottage to
Olliver to work in whenever he likes," Tyson sighed
enviously. "Lucky boy! Surely the Beckleys told you."

"I haven't seen them for a long time," Lyle said. She
was conscious of Edwin tugging at her arm like a spoiled
child and was glad to be excused from more questioning
by Tyson. She had come, she pretended to herself, because
the editor had urged her. Actually, it was only to hear talk
of Frederick even if he was not there. She was getting
shameless in her need, she thought, utterly shameless.

In the *Swan* corner the Spanish poet had just arrived
and insisted on placing Lyle beside him. He was in a
jubilant mood, freshly pomaded, manicured, and gaudily
sport-coated. He embarrassed Josephine by kissing her
hand passionately. "Thank you for the twenty dollars,
I hope," he whispered loudly in her ear.

"You must all be good to me today," he explained,
"because I am celebrating my metamorphosis. I am about
to become a breakfast food. In six delicious translations.
Stalk here brings out a Portable Padilla. At once Tyson
Bricker, whom I just saw, promises to bring out a Padilla
Omnibus. Stalk hates Bricker so he must come back with
a Padilla Treasury. Tyson retaliates with a Pocket Padilla.
What about a Pick Pocket Padilla, Edwin? Eh? Next will
come the Potable Padilla, the Edible Padilla, the Med-
icine Chest Padilla. I have not written a line since I found
out this secret of success. My fortune is as good as made.
I am already famous."

"Are you sure it's your fortune?" Lyle asked. "Tyson's
and Edwin's pictures will be on the cover, not yours. And
it will be Stalk's Padilla Portable and Bricker's Padilla
Omnibus, you know."

It appeared that Padilla had already considered this.

"They are good enough to let me have a small percent," he reassured her. "I have their word on that, bless their hearts."

"Only a verbal agreement?" Lyle teased him.

"Certainly," Padilla answered. "An ironclad contract would be too easy for them to break."

Suddenly Frederick Olliver had come in and slipped into the bench next to Lyle.

"What expert has been giving you such masterly advice?" he asked Padilla.

"A Miss Marianna Garrett," answered Padilla and seeing the blank expression of all he added, "She is writing a play with Allan Gaynor. Doesn't that make her an expert?"

"No. Every female budding playwright in New York thinks marriage to Allan Gaynor would fix up her career," Stalk said, impatient of Padilla's frivolity. "But Lyle's talent is what they need."

Lyle's joy in seeing Frederick and wild flicker of hope when he came straight to her side had vanished abruptly at Padilla's remark. The odd behavior of Allan and his barometer, Flannery, during the last weeks suddenly came to mind. The two men had long ago stopped arguing with her for a Hollywood season ("Everyone else goes there when they can't work and they clean up")—and in her relief at being left alone Lyle had not questioned why. She found it increasingly easy to keep to her own suite and was grateful for Allan's mysterious preoccupations whatever they were. Sometimes she ran into the little thin blonde in the hall looking smug and guilty but she was accustomed to his lady visitors making much of the great man's harmless flattery. That there was a conspiracy against her in the house, however, and a new writing collaboration under way had never occurred to her. Terror made her pale at the hint of secret enemies—Flannery, Pedro, the other servants, Sawyer, too, perhaps—traps being laid for her. ("So you are definitely against going ahead with the Reno comedy? . . . So you think it's better to wait another season to finish the musical version of *Summer Day?* . . . So you think we're both too used up to tackle the new idea before fall?") She had discovered an unconquerable aversion to every contact, even mental, with Allan, and her old career of decorating and concealing his stock company plots with her own lacy twists and feminine wisdom seemed actively nauseating to her. No, she could never endure the double harness again, but the news that it was not even offered, that she was being locked out of prison, disturbed her frightfully. Enemies, enemies everywhere, even here, she thought.

"Does that mean you are working alone at last?" asked Frederick in surprise.

"Evidently," Lyle said in a low strained voice that made him sense something was wrong and that it had to do with Padilla's word of Allan's new collaborator. The old habit of consoling her for outbursts of her husband's insensitivity came over him and he struggled against the instinctive impulse to take her hand, disarmed by the unexpected glimpse of Lyle at a disadvantage.

"I'm looking forward to Mrs. Gaynor's first solo flight," Edwin Stalk said, gazing yearningly at Lyle. "I think it's the best thing in the world that Gaynor has found someone else for his factory. He'll probably find dozens more in Hollywood, as Padilla says."

"Did Padilla say—" Lyle exclaimed, almost betraying her incredulity. So there were more and more conspiracies against her. Everyone knew about them. She was angry that Frederick should know, too, and deliberately drew back from the understanding pity in his eyes. She could not bear him to be kind or that she should need kindness.

"We'll do our best out there," she said.

"But Padilla said the other day you weren't going," Edwin said plaintively. "Olliver, we mustn't let her go."

"I doubt if anything could ever persuade Mrs. Gaynor to leave her New York," Frederick said easily, turning to her. "Of course it's not true, you're not leaving?"

Why couldn't she, Lyle thought wildly, her shattered

pride flaring up at his calm assumption of knowing all about her. The affection in his tone and manner wounded her, reminding her of the months she had longed for it in vain. That it should come because he found her betrayed by others as well as himself made her indignant. Why didn't it occur to him that her love could change as his had? Even if it couldn't, she would not want him to be so sure. She had never wanted to leave New York because of him, and he dared assume this was still true. She thought of how he had turned her against the Beckleys, then blithely accepted them for himself. Betrayal all around her, she thought.

"I think the atmosphere out there will be ideal for work," she said haughtily. "Not so chic as a Beckley guesthouse, of course."

"Which Beckley is it that has the seismograph in the cellar that shows where and how the guests have been sleeping?" Padilla asked eagerly. "Have you been warned of that yet, Olliver? Amusing idea."

Frederick's face had crimsoned at Lyle's sarcastic rejection of his overture. He picked up the menu and studied it silently.

"I could publish the magazine in California, couldn't I?" Stalk demanded. "That's exactly what I will do. Wonderful!"

"Ideal," agreed Lyle. She was suddenly crushed against the table as Josephine Carey wriggled out behind her chair with a hiss of "Sorry. So sorry."

"Must telephone," muttered Frederick and sprang to his feet.

23

. . . sweet kid on the make . . .

*D*ODO hated him, she would never forgive
him, she wished he would stop telephoning her, her dear-
est wish was never to set eyes on him again. This time it
was goodbye for good, she was going away, far away,
or back home to Baltimore; she might even kill herself
but she knew that would please him too much! As these
threatening words climaxed a quarrel lasting half the
night, through nightclubs, taxis, streets and bed, Frederick was exasperated into retorting, "For God's sake, go
then! I can't stand any more!" She did, and an hour later
he was trying to find her, telephoning her room and eventually her office, frantic for her voice, despising himself
for his weakness, arguing in excuse that the only cure for
him was satiety. If he could just see her when and where
he chose for just one week, say, then he would be free
again, but Dodo must have half-guessed this for she kept
him always wondering. He would have given up anything
to see her, even if only to quarrel again, but she was nowhere to be found. He remembered telling her that he
might go to the *Swan* luncheon, and he went there in the
faint hope that she might call him there, or even burst
in on it. His nerves were exhausted, he did not feel like
Swan talk; off-guard, his first instinct on seeing Lyle was
the old relief that here was refuge; the hint that she too
was in trouble stirred him, but in a few seconds he sensed
her coldness. In his disappointment at Lyle's unfriendli-
ness, and then at Dodo's not calling, he concentrated on
analyzing his luncheon companions as if they were to

blame. Clearly there was something between Stalk and Lyle; Frederick considered Stalk disparagingly, annoyed that he should be ten years his junior. Too young for Lyle. Was he such a remarkable editor, after all? He was definitely reactionary, ridiculously ivory-tower for the times, and childishly befuddled by infatuation, even if all one believed was his doting eyes apart from Solange's warning. The magazine would suffer. In fact its studious aloofness from present-day problems seemed dangerously political, even seditious, to Frederick, reminding him that its editors had almost always been only two or three generations removed from Europe. Yet they had no patience with the "melting pot" idea, snubbing any manuscripts that smacked of steerage, peasantry, or labor, pouncing greedily on Henry James, for instance, as if their approval elevated their own ancestors and granted them hereditary rights to elegant drawing-rooms. Obviously this style of literary social climbing was dated, Frederick mused, glowing with a democratic passion now that his own work was proclaimed to have a message for every class. He no longer needed hot-house protection and forgot he ever had. He disliked the *Swan,* its restaurant, its editors, and was sorry he had come.

He went out to telephone every few minutes all to no avail and Dodo's cruelty made him the more angry at Lyle. Now that he was ready to turn to her for forgiveness and renewal of sympathy she belonged all too clearly to Stalk. She had deliberately snubbed him. If Allan was taking on a new collaborator it must mean Lyle had someone else. Her slur about the Beckleys brought back all too vividly other difficulties only last night on the same score. And how dare she invade his private domain anyway? The *Swan* was *his* field, admitted so by her in the old days where everyplace else was hers. Even in the midst of their affair he would have resented her presence, and how much more so because another lover was responsible for her visit! Padilla's innuendoes proved that Solange was right, she had other suitors. It relieved him to find some cause besides Dodo for his restless misery. Perhaps this was a game Lyle was playing to punish him, quite apart from her interest in Stalk. Of course! Wherever he went nowadays, it dawned on Frederick, he came up against her sabotage, for it must be that. The more he thought about it the more he could see nothing but intent to injure in her adopting his old friends and interests. Why should she have been at Caroline Drake's except to make mysterious trouble in that small corner of his life? Why was she seeing Benedict Strafford and even Gerda Cahill except to harm him in some way? None of these represented her kind of life; they could not amuse her nor could she claim they were Allan's friends. Frederick thought of Allan with pity, a man admitted by Lyle as responsible for her career, yet here she was brazenly flaunting her hold on young Stalk, and flirting with Padilla, dominating the luncheon as if it was her own little tea-party. He thought of poor Solange, too, who had done so much for Stalk, and wished to do more but he would not have her interfere in his work; Lyle alone was allowed to do that. Frederick wished for his old advantage of proud poverty that he might punish her for presuming on her position. He had introduced her to this very table years ago; now she wished to edge him out in the subtle ways known so well to her, show that she could always have an ascendancy over him.

And to what evil end had she dressed herself for a *Colony* luncheon so that Edwin Stalk could not take his admiring eyes away from her? It affronted him for her to glow with that suspicious radiance of a woman in love or beloved. Her nearness to him, obliging frequent contacts, made him remember with bitterness old days of longing for just this proximity, old days when he had foolishly fancied himself her one love. He told himself that no matter how savagely Dodo treated him, at least it was direct, and his present pain was nothing to the long-hidden anguish of his years with Lyle. It was a pleasure to take the role of victim rather than offender. He welcomed the idea that it was actually Lyle who had caused last night's final vicious quarrel with Dodo. Lyle had plotted the whole thing and must be gloating over it. It might even be she who had suggested that Cordelay Beckley offer him the cottage, so beautifully equipped for work, friendly companions whenever or if he chose. Lyle must have foreseen how this would complicate his relations with Dodo! Why couldn't she go out to this wonderful spot, too, Dodo had immediately protested, making such a scene every time he intended going that he had to stay in town, only to have Dodo punish him by stubbornly denying him her company. If she wasn't good enough for his friends she wasn't good enough for him, thank you. He was thinking of her reputation, he lied. Thinking of his own reputation, Dodo had mocked. She chanced on revenge by acquiring her own Beckley, no other than Uncle Lexington, whom she met at the Barrel in an excessively amiable mood. He was old, and maybe he liked to do dumb things but at least he was a Beckley. A Beckley took her to the zoo, she could boast, a Beckley took her bowling, a Beckley gave her jewelry and an oil painting when she pretended it was her birthday. Some men thought she wasn't as smart as they were but now she had a Beckley beau, thank you, and a millionaire knew what was what. He was always borrowing money from her, but alright, a rich man like that had to keep all his money in trust funds and stocks and things like that. A rich man had funny ways, you had to take that into consideration, for instance the way he always carried a little bag with that checkered coat and false moustache and bowler so he could put it on in nightclubs and sing Gay Nineties songs. Sometimes he paid the orchestra leader a hundred dollars to let him do it, so you couldn't say he was stingy. Dodo's triumph ended when her discreet attempt to sell her gifts brought out the fact that bracelet and clips were false, the painting cut out from *Town and Country* and framed personally by Uncle Lex.

"Why did you do this to me?" she tearfully reproached him. "You took advantage of me because I'm poor."

"Just shows you don't need money to be happy, by Joe," Uncle Lex gleefully retorted, "if you don't know the difference in things. I had you fooled for a while, didn't I? You can't beat the Five and Dime. Why, I always give girls presents from the Five and Dime and they never know the difference."

"But coming from you, Mr. Beckley—"Dodo had wailed, and later blaming Frederick for the whole misadventure she complained bitterly, "And he isn't even crazy, that's the worst. Making me meet him at the Plaza just to go stand in the Zoo watching that Barbary sheep jump for nothing!"

Last night she boasted of Caroline's party. ("You weren't invited, I noticed!") He surmised she had crashed it by thrusting herself on Benedict Strafford, and was resigned to the worst. But he was unprepared for her trump card when she crowed that Lyle Gaynor was there, and had been simply darling to her, devoting herself to Dodo alone, in fact she couldn't have been sweeter; no one in the world had ever been as sweet to her; and their talk was so interestingly confidential that Dodo would not give Freddie the least hint of what it was about, no she wouldn't. Didn't he wish he knew, though? Why should he act to jumpy simply because an old friend of his liked her? The implications of Machiavellian strategy on Lyle's part maddened Frederick beyond all discretion.

"She couldn't possibly have liked you," he was stung into shouting. "She was just being bitchy. You should have seen through it."

"And why couldn't she possibly have liked me?" Dodo inquired, pausing ominously in the midst of unzipping her dress for she had finally been cajoled into his room.

Frederick saw defeat ahead already but his nerves were beyond diplomacy.

"Because she never likes people like you," he floundered wildly.

"What do you mean—'people like me?'" Dodo leapt at the phrase suspiciously, her slim body in the half-

unfastened purple jersey as taut as an arrow about to
whizz through him.

"I mean anyone natural and simple, anyone outside
her circle—." He saw with despair that she was zipping up
her dress with finality.

"So I'm simple! I don't know I'm being snubbed!"
Dodo cried. "Nobody could ever possibly like me, they
just pretend they do to be bitchy! That shows what you
think of me. You're the one that hates me! Well, I hate
you, too."

She was pulling on her jacket and he tried to stop her,
trying to appease her with kisses but she kept her face
averted haughtily, the green eyes glittering and the jaw
revealing its unexpected hardness as it did in these encounters. Why couldn't he learn to wait till afterward,
Frederick scolded himself, but even while he strove for
command Dodo tempted him to fresh folly by tying on the
cloudy blue scarf which was so unmistakably, significantly
Lyle's.

"Lyle Gaynor gave me this scarf," Dodo said proudly.
"She insisted that I take it!"

"It's not becoming to you and she knew it!" he could
not keep from retorting, furious at Lyle's revenging herself by such a devilish joke; she must have known in her
infinite feminine wisdom that Dodo would always wear it
as an excuse for boasting of her new friendship, that the
delicacy of its fabric and design and its familiar fragrance
would be reminders of another love. Whatever he said to
persuade Dodo to discard the scarf made matters worse,
seeming proof positive that he wished her to have no
friends and no pleasure.

"You think I'm not good enough to marry you!" she
sobbed. "Other men better than you want to marry me,
if they could get a divorce, but you don't even have to
get a divorce. You—you—why you won't even give me a
ring yourself yet you won't let anybody else give me a little
scarf. Pooh on you, Freddie Olliver, you wait!"

"I didn't know you wanted a ring," he shouted after her, not caring whether Murray heard or not, and hurrying into his clothes. But a taxi speeding away into the dawn was all he saw when he got down to the street . . . Lyle's fault. How diabolical a clever woman could be with a naïve rival, he thought, yet not so clever after all, for Lyle's victory steeled him with a fierce protective desire to avenge Dodo, who could never be a match for a woman like Lyle. He glared at Stalk and Padilla as if they had already made a slighting remark about Dodo, or perhaps were *thinking* one, comparing her unfavorably with Lyle, as of course would be the case. It seemed to him that they were the ones who tried to keep Dodo from her simple good time at Beckleys or even from this very luncheon. What right had they to sit in judgment on a poor child who merely lacked education and sophistication? He forgot that neither Padilla nor Stalk knew Dodo: their attention to Lyle seemed a tacit criticism of his own preference. He would atone for all this to Dodo, he thought, and when he went out to the phone booth he was resolved to beg her to come down there so that he might defend her from others corroborating his own secret opinion of her. He would tell them she was to be his wife, and he would really mean it! That was all she wanted, poor child. The resolution frightened him, revealing how firmly he still resisted the ultimate surrender. But the hour for it had struck and his reasoning process, after the first shock, rushed to perform its duty, contriving an argument that marriage would solve everything. At least it would solve the immediate problem.

She had not reported at her office yet; so he forced himself to telephone "Tommy," "Dick," and the young whippersnappers she always talked of, and he grimly accepted their veiled amusement at his query. No, they had not seen her. She had no girl friends but eventually a girl answered her room number.

"I've taken Miss Brennan's room," the girl said.

She had really gone?

"When will she be back?" he asked. "Did she leave a forwarding address?"

The girl could tell him nothing. He hung up the receiver, noting absently that his hands were shaking frightfully. He made his way back to the Swan dining-room, not wanting to go back but incapable of any other choice. Tyson Bricker stopped him as he passed his table.

"Have a drink with me," he urged. "You look as if you needed one. Hangover?"

Frederick sat down.

"What do you know about that sweet kid kicking up those pretty little heels all over the tabloids? You can't tell about these children, can you?"

Tyson pushed the newspaper toward Frederick. The photograph of a blonde Mrs. Lawrence Glay of Riverdale meant nothing to Frederick at first nor the news that she was suing for divorce. She was naming as co-respondent one Miss Dorothy Brennan, of Baltimore, identified by reporters as the girl on the plane for Bermuda that very morning. Mr. Glay was staging a Hazelnut style show in Hamilton, it seemed.

"Says it's been going on for five years," Tyson chuckled. "Claims the kid followed her husband up here, from Baltimore and made a hell of a row. I never even heard of the guy. I thought she was just another sweet kid on the make. Glay's his name. Ever know him?"

"Hazelnut Cigarettes," Frederick muttered idiotically. "You know. 'Let me give you a light?' Just the one line."

Tyson looked baffled.

"Just the one line, mind you," Frederick said mechanically, "but it sings."

24

. . . the calendar slogans . . .

*L*YLE rapped on the door of Allan's room but
there was no answer. Either he was asleep or staying up
on the roof late. It was too bad for any delay might make
her falter in her decision. Or *had* she decided? Nobody
ever decided anything. Situations were solved only by
other situations. She could take no credit. The sudden
light that had made her past mistakes and her future
correction so simple might fail any moment and leave her
struggling again in her eternal puzzle. She was strong
enough right now but there was no guarantee she could
hold out. She needed props—love, security, success. She
went into her study and stood looking at the work neglected for months on her desk. The notes clipped to
some typescript seemed incomprehensible to her, though
they were in her own writing. She must get back to
work. She glanced at the pages of dialogue and thought
how silly they sounded. In the folder were a dozen variations of this same scene; she might better have occupied
herself writing some copybook maxim a hundred times.
She crumpled up the pages and tossed them in the basket.
She would never write that play, or perhaps any other.
The thought frightened her. But why should it? Once she
had found out the sham of her profession she was no good
at it. The Show Must Go On. She laughed scornfully
remembering how Frederick had mocked the sentimental
phrase. "The Show Must Go On" so the old trouper

clowns on till he drops dead. No, it was *not* just for the manager's profit, she had argued, and was angry that she could never articulate her emotional reasons to match Frederick's crisp logic. But if you did not believe the Show Must Go On what did you have left?

The desk calendar was turned to a date weeks ago, evidence of her indifference. As for copybook maxims there was one printed on the calendar, "Thursday the 12th. Darkness Comes Before Daylight." She could not help smiling, leafing through the pad for further philosophic gems, but why smile when the Platitude was the staff of life, the solace for heartbreak, the answer to "Why" even though the oracle spoke in the priest's own hollow voice. Underneath the woes of the world ran the firm roots of the platitudes, the calendar slogans, the song cues, a safety net to catch the heart after its vain quest for private solutions.

"I must be old at last," Lyle thought, but she had known that before. A woman was old the day her lover left her.

To keep up her courage she decided to telephone a lawyer, but she could only think of those Allan had used. Cordelay Beckley was a lawyer but he was now Frederick Olliver's friend. She didn't want Frederick to know until the divorce was final. He might think she was getting it as a trick to win him back. But it was to prove something to herself, at no matter what cost to her. Before, it had been Frederick who paid. If it had not been for his love she would have left Allan years ago, paradoxical as the reasoning was. The more intense their relationship grew the more bound she had felt to make up to Allan in other ways for never having desired him. All the time it had been Frederick who was being wronged. No sooner had he withdrawn from the triangle than the two remaining figures fell apart, their whole security based on his presence. He had been used, and her blindness to it, and the fact that he had been willing to be used did not condone the crime, Lyle thought. Without him, her sense of obligation to Allan vanished; she felt dislike, even revulsion for him, and days passed when she could not bear to see him because it was he, not Dodo, who had devoured her happiness. Whether she ever wrote again, she knew she could never work with him, and this certainty with what Padilla had told her made divorce more plausible. She would not have dared come to the decision if it had not been for that.

Going through the halls the whole apartment seemed hostile and unfamiliar. Even the maid on her knees scrubbing the kitchen floor was one she had never seen before. The curtains had been drawn for months in the big dining-room, and the long dark room reproached her for neglect. No more gay dinner parties, no casual Sunday night suppers, no after-theatre buffets. One would have thought it was the host who had departed instead of the hostess's lover. Curious that the parties she used to love and defend to Frederick had turned tasteless and as boring as he had said when she no longer needed to defend them. She had enjoyed them, perhaps, knowing that when the last guest left she would find Frederick waiting for her the more eagerly. Curious that her sentimental duty to Allan was so unimportant without the argument over it with Frederick. As soon as she had made up her mind to leave him his independence of her seemed justification enough. He had his own social life, now. Hadn't Padilla indicated he was making plans without her help? She would give up this place, of course, and as soon as she made up her mind it was intolerable to spend even another week there. She would go to Reno or wherever she must and come back to a small studio apartment, like Frederick's, she thought. The thought of working without having to propitiate Allan's fixed notions excited her. But what would she do until she was ready to work? The question frightened her and she wavered. She had never been alone in her life. Everything had always been arranged for her—first there had been her father, then her maiden aunt, then her guardian, Cordelay Beckley, then Allan. Maybe she should wait—but she recognized her old sin of evasion. She must make her own decisions and clear everything with Allan this very day if possible.

The phone was ringing again when she reached her bedroom, and went on ringing, indicating that Pedro was out, and for some reason no other servants were in the house. Even the kitchen maid had vanished, apparently. Lyle let it ring on. She remembered that an actress from *Summer Day* was going to call about the prospects of a new play and there was nothing to tell her. This reminded her that she had helped the girl arrange for her own divorce last year, hiring a man Sawyer knew. The very person, Lyle thought, and rang his office at once. He remembered her, showed no surprise at her request, assured her of immediate action. As it was late in the day he was willing to meet her for tea whenever and wherever she suggested. Lyle named a hotel near his office and hurried out. As she stood before the house waiting for a cab, she saw the colored janitor watching her from the basement entrance.

"He ain't back yet," he said.

He stumbled towards her, and stood watching the doorman put her in the cab.

"He took the car," he said, grinning. "Your man took the car."

She understood then that he was referring to Allan. Allan found all travel so difficult he used the car only under necessity and she wondered why now.

"Be sure there's someone on hand to help him when he comes back," she said to the doorman, but the janitor spoke up with a disagreeable smile.

"That's alright, he's got somebody."

Flannery and perhaps the little Marianna, Lyle guessed. She did not like the way the man was smirking at her, and there was a definite insult in his mocking laugh as the taxi door closed. She would have Allan ask the agent about him, but right now she had more important matters on hand. She did not think about him again until three hours later when she returned, her mind filled with the ominous step she had just taken. The dark man was still standing on the basement steps as if he had been waiting for her.

"He ain't back yet, missy." His voice startled her into turning and seeing his mocking smile. "That's one cripple that ain't coming back, either, if he knows what's good for him."

The man was crazy, Lyle thought. Allan would have to—no, she would have to ask the agent about him herself. She would be alone from now on. She hoped someone would be in the apartment, for the madman might follow her. She was afraid of everything now. No sign of Pedro but the telephone ringing was encouraging. It was Cordelay Beckley. He had been trying to get her all day to tell her about Allan.

"Yes?" she said almost knowing.

"Lyle, you mustn't think I'm on his side in this. There was just nothing else I could do, considering his condition, and considering the jam he was in. Naturally, I couldn't tell you but believe me I didn't think he would walk out —good heavens, Lyle, how could I guess when he's been laid up so long? But then still waters as they say——"

The voice in the transmitter went on though Lyle had dropped it and lay on the bed staring at the ceiling.

25

. . . the buzzard is the best flyer . . .

WHEREVER he went that day and that night
he found people were either strangers or enemies and he
had no protection against them. Eyes everywhere appraised
his strength, plotted against his weakness, waited for his
surrender, as if his destruction was their salvation. Round
and round about the streets he walked swiftly and mechanically, heeding no traffic lights, fancying sounds of
smothered laughter and mocking whispers. Round and
round about, the Boyg in *Peer Gynt* had commanded,
go round and round about, young man, round and round
about. The awful loneliness and fear of his fellowmen
that had cursed him up to the day he had first met Lyle
was upon him. He could have wept with longing for all-
forgiving, all-excusing arms, and he muttered aloud alter-
nate pleas and reproaches to Lyle for having deserted him.
It did not seem unreasonable to expect comfort from her
for Dodo having left him. At every corner cigar-store he
paused with the old habit of trying to find Dodo, and he
was overwhelmed with memories to find his pocket filled
with nickels, a cautious habit he had formed of being prepared to telephone her any moment without the delay of
making change. In his notebook he had only yesterday
added a new telephone number where she might be
traced, a hair-dresser on Madison Avenue she had mentioned. It was a strange use for his research training, he
reflected, and a damning record of his insecurity—the
pages of names and numbers where she might be hiding
from him. Folded neatly inside the notebook were news
clippings of nightclub openings, musical shows, indoor

polo games, restaurants, every possible inducement for her favor. Carefully concealed in his wallet as safeguard against her scornful jeers was announcement of an honorary degree to be conferred upon him by an Eastern university. Frederick stood still re-reading the note which had arrived that morning and which he had immediately hidden as if it was evidence of some crime. His first feeling of satisfaction had been lost in hasty assembling of defenses against Dodo's jibes. "No, it really means nothing, no of course I shan't go, no, of course I don't care about it, and of course I realize it doesn't signify I'm any better than your uncle who is the best lawyer in Cumberland or your second cousin who is very high up in Washington." Now there would be no one to taunt him and he should feel relieved instead of bewildered and lost. He must keep on going, he told himself, as if he was frozen and only constant action would ward off the end. It fooled the enemies, too, into believing he was still alive. It surprised him to discover himself in the Strafford office at four o'clock, the exact hour of his appointment with the head, though he was not conscious of having remembered it. Benedict Strafford's door was slightly opened and Frederick pushed in. The Human Dynamo was fast asleep in his swivel chair, hands clasped under his cheek like a child, feet on desk. His three telephones were ringing simultaneously but he slept on.

"Oh dear, I'm afraid that's my mistake," a feminine voice cried out contritely beside Frederick.

It was Mrs. Caswell, black eyes gleaming full power through blonde veils, an extraordinary covey of lovebirds atop her menacing topknot of bronze braids. She slipped a beige-gloved hand into Frederick's, flashing him the special hundred percent porcelain smile.

"I thought I'd discovered Benny's D.Q.—" she said, adding archly, "Drinking Quotient. Two brandies at lunch. No martinis. I had it figured out that his brain is at its best around three-thirty if he's had two brandies, no more, no less, and he had such a wonderful inspiration to discuss with you. But perhaps it should have been three o'clock."

"Or three brandies," said Frederick.

The publisher sprang out of his chair belligerently.

"As I was saying to Mrs. Caswell," he boomed, "we haven't been on the best seller list for two weeks and something's got to be done. My idea is this——"

"I was right after all," Mrs. Caswell murmured, seating herself on Benny's desk, and adjusting the small silver-backed pad and pencil that hung from her wrist.

"I've done all I can to put you over, Olliver," said the publisher, earnestly, "and I know you appreciate it. That's why I feel free to ask your help now. I'm sure you'll agree that it's not fair for an author to make more out of a book than the publisher, and what with all these plagiarism suits on *Court Lady* I've been doing a lot of thinking. Our trade analysts here, Mrs. Caswell—Topsy, I mean,— has been analyzing best sellers with me and by George, I've finally got something."

Frederick heard the words but they meant nothing.

"Ever come across an old paper-back periodical called *People's Home Journal?* Or *Family Journal?*" Mr. Strafford lowered his voice craftily. "Used to run novels about lords and ladies and governesses and seduction in the old manorhouse. All unsigned. All like *Court Lady* and every other damned best seller period romance. My idea is to hire a stable of hacks here to bring them up to date with certain movie stars in mind. We create a firm author —say a Hazel Poysonby Dart—Mrs. Caswell's idea—. The stuff's in public domain so all rights are ours. No author trouble, no split profits. What do you say?"

"Isn't it wonderful?" Mrs. Caswell cooed.

Mr. Strafford chuckled and took out a cigar.

"By George, the idea tickles me, I must confess," he said. "I get a hunch now and then, they've got to grant me that, after what I did with *Haw*. This little lady helps, of course."

"Mr. Berghart and I didn't expect to go into the publishing business so intensively when we first took the

Strafford account," Mrs. Caswell confessed. "We've made it worth while, though, and I'm sure we'll be able to handle future publishers much better because of our investigations here."

Mr. Strafford patted her vigorously on the back.

"You bet you will. Olliver, not only have they analyzed best sellers for the past five seasons but they've analyzed reviewers, so we put in special features to attract each reviewer. None of them care about fiction, we've discovered, so we put in bits about gardening, cooking, baseball, sailing—whatever hobby they fancy. By George, I do think we've got something."

"It's confidential, of course," Mrs. Caswell warned, squirming out of range of Mr. Strafford's friendly grasp.

"Beckley's agent tried to buy stock in *Haw* and I'll venture they'd want to buy into this if they knew about it," Strafford chuckled, and then pointed his cigar at Frederick. "It's what you did with *Haw* that makes me know you're just the man for this job, too, Olliver."

Frederick's wandering thoughts came alert at the last words.

"Me?"

"I could hire somebody who would do what I told 'em, but no more." said Strafford. "You, on the other hand, can give a plain business idea class. The public is ready for class. You gave 'em Voltaire and Homer in comics and now that you're leaving the job don't be surprised if we feed 'em your own works in funnies, eh, Mrs. Caswell? You could set up the new enterprise in your own way, just the same. Give you a free hand. Show him the rough plan we worked out, Topsy."

"I'm afraid I wouldn't be interested," Frederick said.

Strafford held his cigar at a distance and examined it reproachfully.

"I know you didn't get the money out of *Haw* that you should have. I admit it," he said. "But this time it's different. Big dough. I should say at the outset we could pay——"

"It isn't the money," Frederick interrupted.

"Heavens, Olliver, you can't live forever on what you made out of your book!" Strafford said impatiently. "And if it's the extra work you object to that's where you're foolish. A little extra work never hurt anybody, does a man good. When you get to be my age you'll find work a damn sight easier for you than pleasure. Take the way you've been going in for night life. And the money it costs besides."

"That's over," Frederick said, embarrassed. "I can get along on very little when I choose."

"Shouldn't have to," objected Strafford. "A man ought to want more money."

"He doesn't feel it," Mrs. Caswell shook her head regretfully. "But what shall we do? We can't just have anybody."

"Try Tyson Bricker," Frederick said.

"He'd claim the whole idea was his," Strafford said. "He takes all the credit for *The Treasure* getting the award when everybody knows I'd had Olliver here under contract for years. No I won't cut Tyson in on this, damned if I do."

"Still—" mused Mrs. Caswell. "If Mr. Olliver definitely refuses——"

"Definitely," said Frederick. "I have two or three years of research ahead of me."

"A new *Treasure*, eh? That's splendid," said Strafford, his face lengthening. "Of course we can't expect a great whopping prize on everything you do from now on, you know, old man. Some things happen only once in a lifetime."

"I know," said Frederick. "I think I'm old enough to realize that now."

"Man of integrity, Mrs. Caswell," Strafford nodded toward Frederick with a deep sigh. "That's what I admire, —integrity. But it does make people hard to get along with."

"Think it over," implored Topsy, as Frederick rose to go. "Look how disappointed poor Benny is. Poor Benny."

Benny did look disappointed. Frederick had an uncomfortable impression overhearing a suppressed squeal that the publisher was forcibly pulling the trade analyst onto his lap for consolation as the door closed behind him. He walked down to the *Haw* office and collected his belongings in a brief-case. The numbness of losing Dodo gave way to elation, the false elation experienced sometimes in a bereavement, an uncontrollable animal joy in personal survival with a vulture glee in wolfing the departed's share of air and light and joy. The memos on his desk to call Gerda Cahill, call Caroline Drake, call Lorna Leahy, call Mrs. Beckley, made him think how strange it would be to have no battle with Dodo over each of these invitations, whatever they were. A copy of *Horizon* with an essay on his work reminded him that he would not need to grin indulgently while Dodo jeered at the respectful praise. He was so exhausted that he could not trust his sense of relief. It was the relief of the tired mother when the baby stops crying at last; the realization of its death comes much later. He could not trust his curious indifference to her relationship to Larry Glay. It seemed to him now that he had always known that. He tried to think back when it was he had guessed, and decided it was the very first night at The Barrel. Even when Larry had been at the other end of the bar and she had been between Murray and himself they had each stopped talking to close-harmonize sentimentally when the pianist played *Who*. He had never dared think about it before, but that was the moment. He could never claim to have been deceived. The mere sight of the telephone on his desk reminded him of the hours he had spent trying to find her, plead with her, explain, apologize, implore, bribe. He took out the tabloid from his pocket with Mrs. Glay's picture on page three and Dodo's on page four. Miss Jones, coming up behind him, startled him.

"Funny how often it's the wife who's the good-looking one," she said, critically pointing to Mrs. Glay's picture, and then to Dodo's. "This one looks like a weasel. Maybe she's got money, though. Honestly, *men!*"

It was not even necessary to start disliking Miss Jones for saying Dodo looked like a weasel, he thought. Larry Glay would have the chivalrous duty of defending Dodo from now on.

"Mr. Strafford says you're giving up *Haw*," said Miss Jones. "I suppose I can carry on by myself for awhile but I wish you'd give me some ideas."

"I haven't any," said Frederick sincerely. He could not imagine how he had ever had any ideas. He thought suddenly of an ancient Latin fragment called *The Pumpkinification of Claudius*. He wondered if this was what had happened to him, and if some classical Dodo had caused the process in the eminent Claudius. The idea amused him.

"You might try to get Al Capp or Caniff started on a dumb boy named Claud who has the best of intentions but always takes some wrong step that turns him into a pumpkin," he said, and then noting Miss Jones' blank expression added, "Never mind. Mr. Cahill will have plenty of new angles when he takes over. He knows a great deal more about this business than I do, I assure you."

Strafford had taken his word on Murray's capabilities for the job, agreeing to hire him before he remembered their former unpleasant encounter.

"But you'll come in from time to time, won't you?" she asked.

Indeed he would, Frederick answered, knowing that he would never set foot in the *Haw* office again if he possibly could avoid it. The mere sight of the bound volumes of the year's issues made him acutely sick, and he could scarcely bear to spend a minute more there. He hurried out with the exuberance of someone just rid of a monstrous burden. How had he endured it so long, he marvelled. It was a weight to balance the weight of Dodo, he knew. He could not have borne the one without the other. He was about to take a cab but he felt utterly incapable of any decision, where to go, whom to see, what to do. His chest felt empty, and he found himself touching it experimentally from time to time as if something was lost, though he was conscious of neither pain nor sorrow. His feet carried him along through the streets, in and out of bars, through daylight into night. Dodo and Larry were already in Bermuda, he thought, and saw them wrangling in some magnolia-shaded garden, Dodo with a scarlet poinciana in her black hair; he could hear her berating Larry for the handsomer costumes of the other women, and could see these beauties flirting with Larry while Dodo stormed and sulked, jealous that it was not she who was getting attention. He could see her furiously making up her face, repainting her lips, pitching her giggle higher, patting her nice little body invitingly, making raucous fun of Larry's latest advertising triumphs to rival ad-men at the bar, struggling belligerently to out-glamour the lovely creatures now surrounding Larry. She had her match, Frederick reflected; no pity for her child-ishness and ignorance would ever weaken Larry; he was as ready to answer any other call to love as she was. Frederick could almost hear strains of orchestras, juke-boxes, street-musicians and the pair of quarrelling voices blend suddenly into close harmony, *The girl that I marry*— He touched his chest again, curious that he still felt no woe, nothing but a detached wonder that he had ever been concerned in such a farce. He thought of Miss Jones' calling Dodo weasel-faced, and it struck him that his past year had been a year of destruction, of rodent gnawing away at everything he valued in himself. He had accomplished nothing on the *Treasure's* sequel, honor and pride forgotten in the delirium of his foolish chase.

It seemed he was in the New Place bar finally with chatter all about him and stately prints of old Knicker-bocker days dignifying the flyblown walls. A red-haired girl named Buffy was weeping loudly that she had been double-crossed by Larry Glay, but one thing she would bet her bottom dollar on, was that he would never marry that little tramp who followed him onto the plane, because he had told her personally that was all off. Anyway his wife had gotten divorced from him twice before and they always got married again.

"You'd think they'd get tired of the blood tests," she said.

A stout lady with iron-gray hair under a mannish felt hat adjusted her mighty rear to the frail bar-stool next to Frederick, and ordered a double old-fashioned. She raised a lorgnette to the pictures above the bar, stating to no one in particular that the proprietor was to be congratulated on maintaining the quaint atmosphere of old New York. The old-fashioned itself she pronounced a miracle of delicacy and superior to any mixture she'd sampled at the Florida or other bistros she had just renounced because of the offensive presence of those four old goats you saw everywhere. The bartender acknowledged his lofty standards, priding himself on always washing the glasses, meticulously removing all insects before serving a potion, throwing out any customer who had 'had enough,' and often refusing to serve customers who came in only because they had been tossed out of every place else in the neighborhood. However since few patrons appreciated his stern code, he hovered gratefully before the lady, his eyes searching the room for an opportunity to demonstrate his finicky ideals. A small newsboy entering with a few morning *Mirrors* was all that offered and the honest fellow ordered him out peremptorily, declaring that his customers were not to be annoyed in their pleasures and it was time every little bum was in bed, anyway. He ignored the obscene gestures of reprisal made by the wistful little chap from the street. A burly truckdriver declared that he would back the new place and Jack, the honest bartender, against every bar in town, and the test of a customer's loyalty was whether he came around to you for his belt before breakfast same as for his nightcap, a sentimental routine he hoped Jack appreciated. The stout matron winked at Frederick and produced from her armpit a copy of the *Swan,* which she placed on the bar before her.

"Interesting characters around here," she whispered, and then blinked at her magazine which bore a drawing of Frederick himself on the cover. She looked again at Frederick, then extended a sturdy hand.

"A real privilege," she said and vowed that she had read every bit of Olliver she could lay her hands on. Frederick gave a quick apprehensive glance around as if Dodo might suddenly materialize with shrill deprecations of the work admired. In his relief he thanked the lady fulsomely, even ordering her a drink. He looked at the red-haired girl, speculating whether Dodo could hold her own against her. The burly fellow construed his look as admiration for he nudged him, muttering, "No dice. I took her out the other night and boy is she dumb." Frederick nodded, pondering the grievous lack of brains in a beauty who refuses, though she becomes axiomatically brilliant if she surrenders. The girl was prettier than Dodo but all Larry cared about was quantity and variety. He wondered how Dodo could get along with a man even more irresponsible and unpredictable than herself.

"The buzzard is the best flyer," he heard the navy pilot at the end of the bar saying, and it seemed an answer to his own query. "You watch the buzzard and see how he picks his air-currents, makes his landings—beautiful sight, really. If a flyer could only learn the buzzard's secret——"

"He's always after something, that's why," ventured the pilot's companion. "Something for himself and nobody else. That steers him. A bird always looking out for himself can fly straight and fast and never gets lost."

Two ladies passing by stopped to peer through the glass and make mysterious gestures, but Frederick was idly listening to an argument on whether the Naval Ordnance manual on ballistics did or did not scan for one whole chapter.

"They're speaking to you," the stout lady said to Frederick.

Caroline Drake and Lorna Leahy gave up their efforts to attract his attention and came inside.

"We couldn't believe it was you," Caroline exclaimed. "I just can't picture you in this dump. We've been taking the new course in Fast Reading with Tyson Bricker over at the League. Marvellous! We decided you must be waiting for Murray too, or you wouldn't be in a place like this. We stopped by your house but beat it when we saw what was going on."

"Judy Dahl was helping unload something in front," Lorna said breathlessly. "Do you think Murray knows?"

"Do you know what she got with her prize money?" Caroline demanded gleefully. "A Bendix! And it was going into Murray's and your apartment, believe it or not. We nearly died."

"We couldn't have been more shocked if it was a baby-carriage," Lorna said. "I went right up to her and said what in the world do those boys want with a Bendix and she said, 'I don't have room for it at the Y.' We simply screamed."

Frederick was glad to see them, glad they clung to him, glad that somebody obviously liked him. He invited them to have a drink. Lorna cast a significant look about the bar.

"I wouldn't want to be seen in here myself," she murmured deprecatingly. "Of course Caroline doesn't mind but——"

"Oh shucks, let's go up to my place and get some good stuff," Caroline interrupted impatiently. "We can telephone around for Murray from there unless he's gone home and got caught in the Bendix already. Say, what do you know about Larry Glay?"

Lorna let out a peal of laughter.

"Go on and tell Frederick what we heard tonight at Nino's. He'll die."

"Somebody said you were engaged to that girl, Dodo Whatsername," Caroline obliged. "We nearly died. Imagine you marrying that!"

Frederick managed a sympathetic laugh that sounded so convincing he kept it up for several minutes, with the ladies joining in.

"Excuse my broken heart," he chuckled, and it really seemed to him that nothing in the world could be so preposterous as the idea of himself and Dodo.

"Larry's a fool if he marries her," Caroline declared. "She'll sleep with all his accounts and the wives will murder her. He might as well kiss his job goodbye, poor guy."

"Poor guy," Frederick said. The fantastic wish that it was he in the poor guy's shoes—if only for twenty-four hours—overwhelmed him. He was afraid to speak for fear the words might pop out so he kept on laughing as they went up the street together.

"That Bendix!" he repeated in the greatest glee.

"The joke is that Gerda's the one that's likely to use it," Caroline chortled. "We just left her and she says——"

"Caroline, that was confidential!" rebuked Lorna. "If you're going to tell about her psychoanalyst——"

"Confidential, hell," Caroline zestfully went on. "It's a riot. Gerda's been occupying her bird-brain with being psychoanalyzed and what does this Groper finally tell her but that she needs her husband."

"The Groper thought she was sex-starved!" giggled Lorna.

"Or else he thought she ought to be," Caroline amended. "Anyway Judy had better take her Bendix out of Murray's room because the Groper's sending Gerda down to take over. Wouldn't that kill you?"

They went into fresh gales of laughter. Frederick swore he'd never laughed so in his life. His heart was broken, Mrs. Glay's heart was broken, Solange's heart was broken, Judy's was probably about to be broken—in fact the world was so full of jokes the three friends were kept laughing far into the night.

26

... *more like sisters* ...

MURRAY and Frederick were friends again, since Frederick had graciously allowed Fate to reduce him to Murray's own state of cynical resignation. Once again they united in barricading the apartment against rapacious females, but as usual all nature conspired against their safety. Murray had borrowed a thousand dollars from Frederick to pay for Gerda's psychoanalyst, but immediately Judy announced herself pregnant and Murray had to deflect the money for her abortion, not at all sure but that the resolute girl would go ahead and have the baby anyway. The portion saved for Gerda was immediately lavished by that lady on providing a recital for a Voodoo dancer from Haiti who had taken up his quarters with Gerda. "I'm really disgusted with her for the first time," Murray gloomily admitted. "Gerda's always been a *lady* before, but this sort of thing looks so awful. And no one will believe it isn't sex unless they know Gerda as I do."

As the only man who had ever devotedly loved Gerda, Murray was the only one persistently rebuffed, but his delusions of her incredible frigidity were all that saved his pride. The latest episode really hurt, although it coincided fortunately with a counter-dilemma, namely Judy's marriage proposal from none other than Mr. Strafford himself.

"I'm being shoved into the old halter and nobody knows it better than I do," said Murray. "Of course I'm not fool enough to think Gerda and I could have hit it off on a second try even if that dumb doctor did put the

idea in her head. Still, I knew what to expect and when
a man's getting on in his forties that's something. Then
Judy pulls this *or else*. She wants to marry somebody
and she's perfectly satisfied to marry old Strafford and
palm off my baby on him. Olliver, I swear, there's no
limit to what an honest woman won't do to get a man or
a baby."

He'd marry Judy, especially since Gerda's hi-jinx with
the Voodoo man made the idea less grim. He assured
Frederick, however, that it would be merely a gesture
to pacify Judy; she was reasonable enough to demand no
change in their habits. She'd keep her room and he'd con-
tinue with his independent bachelor life. No sense in
a man getting in any deeper than necessary. He requested
that Frederick keep the wedding news quiet as Gerda
would get upset if she heard about it. Frederick did not
answer that Caroline and Lorna had already reported
Gerda's sublime indifference to the project.

"She's so darned sure he'll always come arunning no
matter how many other women he marries," Caroline had
said. "It couldn't be a better arrangement since Judy
doesn't care where he runs so long as she's got him nailed
legally and his twins under her belt. I give him six
months after the ceremony to find himself in a Ludwig
Baumann bedroom suite out in Queens all lined up with
the Parent-Teachers' Association for Friday nights."

"If he makes good at that job maybe it'll be a little
house in Rye," chortled Lorna. "I can just see Murray's
first night at the Dads' Club."

The ladies guffawed over their prophesies like a pair
of jovial witches, giving Frederick an uneasy suspicion of
their merriment over his own masculine bungles. Knowing from his personal experience that whatever he might
say would be wrong he carefully agreed with Murray as
to the common sense of his plans, showed no skepticism
when told that no matter what happened there'd be no
need to worry about Judy taking over their nice bachelor
quarters. He accepted Murray's comments on Dodo with-

out invitation, for he found himself needing co-operation
in the little unpleasant dilemmas that followed her flight.
Strange male voices on the phone claiming to be Baltimore cousins or family friends wanted to know if Mr.
Olliver could give them Miss Brennan's new address.
Frederick was not sure whether he was being made mock
of by his many unknown younger rivals of whom Dodo
was always boasting, or whether their concern was legiti-
mate. He was glad to have Murray relieve him of this embarrassment by brusquely answering that Miss Brennan's
activities were no concern of this telephone number; he
maliciously suggested inquiring at the K. G. R. Advertising Co., or at the Paramount's Hollywood office. The
worst happened when Dodo's mother came to the apartment in person, a calamity so much more painful than
any of Murray's that he forgave Frederick for everything, and after vanquishing the intruder the two men
repaired to Umberto's below and sat with the proprietor
discussing life in the large over a bottle of consoling
grappa. Dodo had often referred to Mama, a Southern
gentlewoman of such refinement and moral apprehensions
that Dodo could scarcely smoke a cigarette or apply a
lipstick without sighing, "Mama would *kill* me if she saw
me smoking. Of course, she's a terribly good sport about
things and is more like a sister than a mother but being
always idolized by Papa and brought up in cotton wool,
you might say, she does get shocked sometimes." Frederick had no delusions concerning the lady, surmising
that if she were any credit her daughter would have allowed her to visit her in New York. Three days after
Dodo's exit, Mrs. Brennan appeared at the Bank Street
apartment with a small handbag, arriving as Murray was
unlocking the door. Daughter had written her about her
distinguished gentleman friend, Mr. Olliver, and knowing Murray from Baltimore Mama could not resist the
impulse to talk things out, knowing Mr. Olliver must
be as upset as she was over a scandal in the family. She
was in the living-room, hat, white cotton gloves and silver

fox jacket off before the men could collaborate on defense.

Frederick had not been outside the house since his night with Lorna and Caroline. He could scarcely drive himself to get out of bed, exhausted as if by a long fever, oddly relieved of the burden of his infatuation, but ashamed of his defeat even though no one really knew how much he had been involved. It surprised him that he should experience only a wave of tired relief the moment Dodo's step seemed final. At last he need not fear offending the jaunty blades who telephoned for her, the ones who called her "Dee" or "Brenny" from some secret other life she lived, and spoke to Frederick with the careful respectful tones of thieves addressing the warden. Even if any longing for her remained the visit of Mrs. Brennan would have acted as a shock cure. The lady was a plump duplicate of her daughter, a cartoon of her mannerisms and defects. The small tidy features, half-moon nostrils enlarged as if by long practice in sniffing out valuable contacts, green marble eyes with the roach antennae lashes, pencilled brow arches, querulous bee-stung lips were all incongruously centered in a wide, flat face; the black hair was even blacker and coarser than the daughter's and drawn back to a thick knob at the back of the short bullish neck. The hands were soft and tiny and meaningless as Dodo's were, swelling into slender arms that swung curiously from the thick shoulders. She addressed her image in her compact mirror as lovingly as Dodo ever did, and seemed fully as confident of her power over men. She was nearing her fifties, according to Murray, but sighed regretfully over the tragedy of her approaching birthday.

"I can't *believe* I'm thirty-six next Tuesday, I swear, honey, I swear I just can't believe that old writing in the family Bible! Married at fifteen and all—well, I guess Dodo's told all about me. She always says I never grew up, just stayed like the day I was married, and excepting for putting on six pounds—but thank goodness I still wear a size twelve. I guess Dodo told you how we're al-

ways swapping dresses when we have dates, not that I go
out except when I get blue and Dodo says 'Mama, for
goodness sake, get out and enjoy yourself, you can't live
on memories, people will think you're stuckup.' So I go
to some of the real nice functions, exclusive little parties,
or maybe some high-class hotel. Always with somebody
like Judge Haggerty, or the Davenanty lawyers, gentlemen everybody looks up to so there's no talk."

Frederick sat helplessly as the lady prattled on, mentioning fine names of friends and forbears, her voice
sweetening and diminishing into a terrifying burlesque of
Dodo, and he brushed aside hastily the picture of himself
legally attached to these two gentlewomen. Murray handled the situation by pouring out several drinks for the
lady and thoughtfully telephoning for hotel reservations
in a distant part of the city.

"I just had to tell Mr. Olliver not to break down on
account of my little girl running off in that naughty way,"
said Mrs. Brennan, swigging her drink with a little finger
daintily crooked. "Us being more the same age we have
to understand how hot-headed youth can be, and I know
my daughter did admire you because she sent me lots
of clippings about you, knowing how crazy I am about
writing and books, especially historical, not just trash,
if you know what I mean. I don't want to raise any false
hopes, but from all I hear it isn't too certain she'll marry
Larry after all. Not that I don't think he shouldn't pay
through the nose, though, dragging our family name
through all this scandal—well, alright, I'll have a tiny
drop more, Murray. Murray's just like family to me, Mr.
Olliver, and that's why I didn't hesitate to come right
down here, because I knew if hotels were full as they said
Murray would want me right here."

"We got a room for you, though," Murray reminded
her with a look at Frederick. "Mustn't forget to check in
before eight."

Mrs. Brennan declared she was having such a good time
getting acquainted that she'd just as soon skip the old

hotel and make a night of it with the two gentlemen
which Dodo would tell them was certainly a compliment
as she was almost too fussy about making friends, probably her convent training and widowed so young with
so many important men courting her, and for the sake of
the little girl she'd had to be so careful. But she could
let herself go, seeing that her little girl wasn't there and
these were men of her own generation, maybe a little
older, but she thought the man ought to be older than
the woman, anyway. Sort of protect her like a daddy, and
speaking of daddies, no one had a nicer, sweeter daddy
than she had had, a cultured millionaire who lost everything to a less cultured partner but—my goodness, Murray
needn't be in such a hurry, they had time for a teentsy
night-cap, this time a real power-house, please, on the
rocks as Daddy used to say.

Murray's patience with the visitor was doubtless due
to his appreciation of Frederick's embarrassment, and an
undeniable delight in the astonishing similarity of mother
and daughter. For Frederick each moment of the familiar
baby voice and gestures, genteel boasting to an obligato
of lapel twigging, knee-patting and seemingly casual
brushes of her body against whichever man was nearest
was hideous burlesque of his recent love's tricks. He
dared not picture the two women together, nor think of
how near he came to a lifetime of defensively enduring
the double cross. When Murray peremptorily wrapped
the silver fox cape around her reluctant body, softening
the blow by a sly pat on her grateful hip, Frederick sank
back in his chair with a shudder. He heard the too-
familiar voice in the hall gurgling coyly over Murray's
simulated flattery. He heard her cry that her daughter
would simply kill her if she heard Mama had been in a
bachelors' apartment, but she'd simply had to talk things
over with Mr. Olliver, his being an older man of her
own generation, actually more apt to be a beau of hers
than her daughter's but don't let on she said that. And
they knew where to find her if they wanted to go to some

quiet little place where people with nasty minds wouldn't talk and they could have a few drinks and a few laughs because she loved a good laugh and had a memory for a good limerick—nothing off-color understand, but just a teentsy bit risqué—cute things the Judge had told her and what a story-teller he was to be sure! And sweet! Leave it to an older man to know how to be nice to a woman, that was one thing she'd tried to drum into Dodo's head, and when she first told her mother about Mr. Olliver it looked as if she had learned, but my goodness, now look what happened! If she'd guessed what was going on Mrs. Brennan declared she would have marched right up to New York City months ago, only Dodo had kept putting her off—honest to goodness she shouldn't be saying so but she honestly believed her Mamma would get her beau away from her—her own Mamma, mind you, but more like a sister, of course. Murray briskly reminded her that the hotel must not be kept waiting and Frederick heard the voice cry petulantly "If you're trying to get rid of me, Murray Cahill, pooh on you, I can get my own self a taxi, you just run right along—" then the hall door closed on Murray's soothing words and her coquettish giggle. Incredible, Frederick thought, trying in vain to shake off the nightmare. He went to the bathroom to turn on a tub with a desperate longing to be cleaned of the curdled musky atmosphere of Dodo's Mamma and all she represented. Judy's gray flannel houserobe hung on the bathroom door, two pairs of her white socks were on the towel rack, a can of turpentine with paint brushes in it under the bowl. No, there was to be no change in their bachelor arrangements with Murray's wedding, Frederick reflected sardonically, no change except that the bride was moving in. He pondered over some paint-smeared garment soaking in the tub, then gave up the idea of a bath as he heard Judy herself come in the door. She was laden with brown parcels and was obviously about to engage in some domestic enterprise involving the front half of the apartment. She greeted Frederick with unaccustomed warmth.

"Murray's bringing up some wine from Umberto's in a minute as soon as he gets that woman a cab. Why don't you have some supper with us after a while?"

The invitation made Frederick the more conscious of being an intruder, an outsider even in his own quarters. He saw that Judy was in a mood to talk and deduced that the procuring of the marriage license had evidently produced a simultaneous speech license. He foresaw a switching of roles with Murray the silent partner and Judy released by happiness into perpetual chatter. That she was happy, there could be no doubt, for her round, blonde face glowed with it, and her usually shy, almost sullen eyes were radiantly friendly.

"It was nice of you to turn your job over to Murray, Frederick," she said. "He thinks he'll like it even if he doesn't like Mr. Strafford. Aren't you going to keep any regular job? I heard someone say you resigned teaching at the League, too."

"I have to catch up on a year's research," Frederick answered, though each time anyone questioned him he was filled with fresh doubts of his future without a regular income, solitary, and now insecure even as to his living place. Even if he did have enough money put aside for three or four years of modest living, it had been rash to abandon both League and Strafford's as soon as Dodo left him. They seemed unpleasantly linked with the whole betrayal and since he could not revenge his own folly on anyone else he wanted to punish himself. If he hadn't taken the *Haw* job Dodo would have been out of his reach, and if he had given up the League job as he had first planned she would never have disrupted his life with Lyle.

"I'm doing some work near Boston this summer, where I can read, too," he explained, and reading Judy's eager expression astutely went on, "I may stay on the college staff all winter if I like, which would give Murray my room here, of course."

Unable to disguise her satisfaction at this prospect Judy changed the subject.

"I can't remember who that woman is I just saw outside with Murray. I know I've seen her and I remember
her voice but I can't place her. Oh yes, here's a telegram
for you I just signed for."

Frederick took the yellow envelope she extended from
under a bag of oranges and went into his own room.
The visitation of Mrs. Brennan made him feel physically
ill and he sat down on the bed, his hands over his forehead. Not only that but the feeling of being gently pushed
out of his home made him desperately lonely, his whole
being crying out for Lyle at any price—love, understanding, peace—home. Too late, now, to try to patch things
up. With all her kindness she would not accept the sorry
overtures of a man publicly rejected by her rival. She
would be foolish indeed to take him back on those humiliating terms when Stalk offered fresh, untarnished adoration. Frederick felt his head suddenly bursting with
jealousy and cold hatred for the young editor. He vowed
to himself that no matter what happened he would withdraw from the *Swan*. A new quarterly had appeared in
Boston under distinguished international auspices, and
there he would publish his new work—when he got down
to it—and let the *Swan* go its way with its too-clever
Padillas and young Western aesthetes.

The sight of the ruffled purple satin bolster which Dodo
had given him distracted him momentarily. He picked it
up gingerly between thumb and forefinger without thinking and pitched it out the open French windows into
the general region of the garbage pail. It made him feel
better and he tore open the telegram, half sensing what
it would be. It was a cablegram from Hamilton, Bermuda.
*"Freddie darling Please Forgive Horrible Mistake Please
Cable Plane Fare Back Will explain love Your Dodo."*

For a split second a wild rush of joy came over him
but it was lost in blazing anger. He tossed the crumpled
paper into the grate, wishing it were something that could
break with a thunderous crash. His temples pounded
with rage and he cast his eye around for further outlet.
There was her cute little collection of china and glass

monkeys to be swept into the empty fireplace, there was the moustache cup marked "Daddy" she had mirthfully gotten for his Valentine, there was the red satin nightie with pink chiffon jacket she liked to hang over his pajamas when she felt magnanimous, and liked even better to pack up to punish him. Frederick flung the mementoes into the grate, tore the nightgown off the hook into rags and tossed a lighted match into the fireplace after it. He could hear himself panting hoarsely as if he were pushing away some giant boulder, and perspiration dripped from his forehead. The flames were slow to start and he used the Cape Cod lighter and bellows on them till the pretty nightgown swelled out first like a Hollywood pin-up model. The smoke curled above it into a vague ghostly face, sharp nostrils, wolfish lips and then the smoke spread into the wide, flat expanse of head, features now a vague, tiny pocket in the middle, then lost as the flames covered them. The heat brought out the perfume and the room filled with the sickening poisonous incense of Dodo—or was it her mother? Frederick threw open the other window and the garden door. He heard Murray's rap and then a conspiratorial chuckle.

"How about a quick snort now the old girl's gone? A toast to Southern womanhood, suh."

"Thanks for handling her," Frederick managed to say. "I'll be right out."

He stood at the open garden door drawing long deep breaths of the June night. He looked up at the soft innocent sky and remembered the first time he and Lyle had stood in that doorway, admiring the surrounding gardens and sun porches, the budding ailanthus and scrubby ivy vines, exclaiming rapturously over the tropical beauties of Manhattan summer even in near-slums; the remarkable magic of the air, the stars, the view, but most of all their love, newly-minted and shining bright forever. He saw himself as he was then, wretchedly solitary, withdrawn, haughty, shy, carrying himself carefully secret as he had from childhood in a routine of polite helplessness, bursting through the prison only in his work. He remembered the joy of finding Lyle and his reluctant doors opening to unbelievable happiness. Lyle. After a little while he lit a cigarette, closed his doors and went in for the quick snort with Murray. Judy was busy defrosting the dinner, her drink beside her in the kitchenette.

"I don't know who keeps the old girl but she still manages to make 'em fork over," chuckled Murray with the usual masculine good nature over a friend's embarrassment. "Funny thing if you shut your eyes—no, by jove, even if you keep 'em open a little bit, you'd think it was Dodo. Dodo in ten years, anyway. You should have heard her when she got taken with family pride, all mixed up with being jealous of Dodo. Jealous of her own daughter for being younger, can you beat that? She said, 'I'm worried about her good name because Dodo's not a young girl any more. She says she's twenty but she's really twenty-five. You see I was only thirteen when I married!' Here's to our Southern belles, Olliver, you can't beat 'em."

"I guess women are the same all over," said Judy laconically, and Murray winked at Frederick with an approving nod. Judy made sense and had a funny, dry humor when you got to know her, he whispered to his friend. There were lots of things about Judy quite aside from her fine talent.

Even if there weren't, Frederick reflected pessimistically, you could always pretend there were if you were bound to marry her anyway. He did not trust himself to accept the dinner invitation but hastened out, wondering as he locked his own door how long before Judy would ask if he minded her keeping the baby in his room—just while he was out of course. He hesitated outside Lorna Leahy's apartment, hearing Caroline's voice inside, knowing they would welcome his call. But lonely as he was he didn't want to see the ladies. He didn't want anything in the world but Lyle.

27

. . . the mosaic . . .

*T*HE round-faced rosy little fellow waiting for a taxicab in front of the Jefferson Market looked familiar but Frederick did not recognize him as Sam Flannery until he eagerly saluted him.

"You've come up in the world since I last saw you, old man," Flannery exclaimed, pumping his hand. "Over my head, of course, that stuff you write, but give me credit for knowing my limitations. I understand you're coming out in a syndicated strip just like Knights of King Arthur. Congratulations!"

"How are the Gaynors?" Frederick asked.

Flannery's cherub face clouded and he drew Frederick aside, waving away a taxi just drawing to the curb.

"You mean you haven't heard?" he asked. "I thought everybody heard and was blaming me, on account of my being the manager and knowing the girl and all. But Allan Gaynor's a deep one, you know, nobody can handle that guy after a certain point. I covered for him, well, you know how a guy has to cover a client especially when the wife's somebody like Lyle—a lady and collaborator too, part of the picture in every way."

"What are you talking about?" Frederick asked. "Do you mind walking?"

Flannery had just been calling on Lyle, it seems, or trying to but she refused to see anyone. It must have been a shock to her. And Pedro had gone with Allan, there was no maid around, so Flannery didn't know really how she was taking it. She was in, alright, the doorman said, but she didn't answer the door. Fortunately she didn't know the whole story and if luck held it wouldn't get out.

"I still say she was a little to blame, letting things get out of hand," Flannery said plaintively. "She just took no interest in anything for months there just when I told them both they were hot and ought to be producing. I told them. I said—well, anyway, he thought he'd train a new collaborator on the side. He'd kinda got the idea he was like that guy in *Pygmalion*. This Garrett kid seemed willing enough, just a little tramp, but ambitious, ready to take anything. When this other jam came up, he lined up a private train, put it up to the Garrett girl, and they beat it to Palm Springs. He always wanted to go West and Lyle never would, and I fixed up a kind of picture deal—mind you, I don't consider I'm to blame. I just saw which way the cards were falling——"

"He was strong enough to do all that when he wanted to, then," said Frederick. "She—none of us needed to have been so sorry for him, evidently."

"It leaves me in a nice fix," Flannery complained bitterly. "After I stood by and sort of helped, then he doesn't even let me in on the other thing. Having that Trinidad woman up on the roof all the time until her husband— the janitor, mind you, came in and stabbed him! A frame-up if you ask me, but no fool like an old one! Mussed him up so he had to clear out, left me to pay off the couple and shut them up. Lyle doesn't know about that. All she knows is his running off with the other girl. I don't know how much she guessed about what a chaser he was when he got a chance. Any skirt, anything at all."

"I didn't know—" Frederick began.

"Nobody thought he could, of course," Flannery said gloomily. "A tart could always guess or someone like this janitor's wife. I'm telling you because you're an old friend and I'd like someone to appreciate what I've done, hushing up a juicy bit like that. I might know he'd try to doublecross me if he could, because he's got his own idea of what's funny. Lyle could tell you that but I guess you know. I'm kind of afraid she doesn't like me any more and I can't very well tell her what I've done for her. You might put in a good word. When all's said and done I'm the guy that put those two on the map. I deserve a break from one or the other and she's the one I could really sell, if I could get her to working again. He's through except for riding on the old name in Hollywood, maybe. He isn't kidding anybody but himself and maybe that dumb cluck."

They were approaching the Square and Frederick was no longer listening. His whole being ached and throbbed with the unaccustomed idea of Lyle in trouble, Lyle betrayed, alone, needing him as he had always needed her, but too proud as always to call for help. He could scarcely bear to listen to the peevish chatter of the rosy young man who had outsmarted himself by working against Lyle.

"Who helped him get away?" Frederick demanded, concealing his dislike as best he could. "A man in his condition must have had pretty powerful co-operation all along the line to be able to run away. Not able to move but able to make a getaway across the country."

"Your friend Cordelay Beckley," Flannery replied. "You were bound to hear it from him anyway, being down at his place as I've heard. I wouldn't have said anything if I hadn't been sure he would have told you, anyway."

Frederick stopped abruptly.

"I go in the other direction," he said. "So long."

He crossed the street, aware that Flannery was standing on the corner gaping at him, chubby choir-boy face dismayed and bewildered.

Poor Lyle, he thought, always protected but now with no one. He hurried down the street, and when he reached the apartment house he stopped and lit a cigarette, trying to think, but in a way it was better not to think. The fat white-haired Irish doorman recognized him and pushed the automatic elevator button for him.

"That's the way they'll do it tomorrow with the atom

bomb," he said, beaming. "Just press a button, they say. A wonderful age we're in, Mr. Olliver. Just press a button and blow up a whole country. My wife declares she's afraid to even listen to it on the radio. Says maybe the whole world will blow up, not just Bikini."

Frederick nodded impatiently. The car shot upward and he got off on the third floor in the Gaynor foyer. He rang the bell but there was no answer. After a few more attempts he rapped on it with his knuckles and called her name.

"It's alright, Lyle," he said softly, hearing a faint motion from within, and his heart smote him that he should have contributed to her terror of facing a visitor. I won't hurt you, this time, I will be very careful of the wounds I have already given you, you can count on me for that much kindness. . . .

The door opened and he saw Lyle, pale and defiant in a dark gray trailing negligee, eyes unsmiling, shadowed with purple from headache, weeping, or illness. They stood looking at each other, silently. Frederick tried to speak but only his lips moved and besides there was nothing to say. Slowly she opened the door wider and he took a step inside. She seemed smaller or it might be that he had never seen her helpless and bewildered before. It was like taking a child in his arms.

They had said all these things to each other a thousand times before. They had told each other over and over of the loneliness they had known until they met; they had confided often the half-life inadequacy of all experiences, joys or triumphs away from each other, the way nothing in their days was complete until they had told it to each other; they had marvelled for years that all pain vanished when they were in each other's arms, and they had told each other the little remembered woes of childhood for the other to console. Yet all Sunday morning they said these things again, listening eagerly even with amazement.

"Until I met you," Frederick said, "I thought of myself as a kind of spectator at all human antics, never a participant. You were like the beautiful prima ballerina who stopped in the ballet to pull me into the carnival."

"You taught the ballerina the meaning of her dance, my dear," Lyle said, and did not add that the lesson had gone so deep she could not dance again with the meaning gone. They did not speak of Dodo. Whatever they repeated now, however, was new for they were different people. Before, in the confidence of their love they had scarcely listened to words or meanings, hearing only the beloved's voice and delighting in his presence, certain of knowing and loving each tiniest wish or thought. Then, suddenly, they found they were strangers, each was capable of desires and deeds beyond either of their imaginations. Now they listened and fell in love anew at words they knew by heart. Frederick lay in her bed, and whether it was herself or the image of his lost Dodo to which he had made such violent love Lyle did not ask, knowing only that he was hers again, that it did not matter who found him here or saw their love, now that they needed each other so desperately. It was Sunday and they made their own coffee and talked of Frederick's new plans, of Lyle's first play, of an apartment in Boston for a while, perhaps, and he spoke of wasted sacrifice.

"The same things would have happened even if I'd divorced Allan years ago and we'd married," Lyle said. "I wonder now if I was sacrificing anything but you to Allan. Whatever it was, I don't believe anybody but the sacrificer really gets any value from the sacrifice. He always wanted to go to the Southwest and he's gone. I must have been unsure not to have faced the whole truth before. I must have. The way I never faced the fact that you were a young bachelor, in a woman's world so that any new face——"

"You created the face yourself," Frederick said. "You created your own enemy, not believing, suspecting——"

"Must we remember it?" Lyle begged. "Must we?"

Frederick drew a deep breath.

"Darling, I was unfaithful to you," he murmured, "but it was my own heart I broke. I could never stand it again. No, there are things I couldn't bear."

Lyle, combing her hair at the vanity table, smiled at him in the mirror. She could bear anything, she thought. There was never too much that a person could give or endure in love. Frederick was idly fiddling with the bedside radio and there was a sputtering of words and confused noises.

"It's the Bikini test—the atom bomb the elevator man's wife is afraid of," Frederick said.

"When you hear the words—'What goes here' that will be the signal—" said the faraway voice, and suddenly Frederick was filled with fear, too. He went over to Lyle and held her tightly. In a world of destruction one must hold fast to whatever fragments of love are left, for sometimes a mosaic can be more beautiful than an unbroken pattern.

ABOUT THE AUTHOR

Dawn Powell was born in Mount Gilead, Ohio, in 1897. By the time she was twelve, Powell was writing short stories and hiding them from her stepmother under the porch, only to have them discovered by her and burned (an incident later fictionalized by Powell in her 1944 novel *My Home Is Far Away*). With thirty cents in her pocket, Powell ran away to live with an aunt, eventually working her way through Lake Erie College for Women. Graduating in 1918, Powell headed for New York and joined the Naval Reserve. After the war she took up publicity work and met her husband, an advertising man. They were married in 1920, and a son was born in 1921. Throughout her life in New York, Powell lived in Greenwich Village, the setting for many of her later novels. Despite tragic family illness and severe financial hardship, Powell never stopped writing. Her first novel, *Whither*, which she later disavowed, was published in 1925. Fourteen novels followed, with the last, *The Golden Spur*, being published in 1962.

In addition to writing novels, two plays of Powell's were produced—*Big Night* by the Group Theatre in 1933 and *Jig Saw* by the Theatre Guild in 1934. Powell's short stories were published in such magazines as *The New Yorker*, *Harper's Bazaar*, and *Redbook*, and her book reviews appeared in *Mademoiselle* and the New York *Post*. Powell's regular circle of friends included Edmund Wilson, Dos Passos, Robert Benchley, Hemingway, and many well-known artists she socialized with at the Cedar Tavern. Unlike many of her literary peers, she did not court fame and tried to avoid publicity and interviews. Nevertheless her writing attracted devoted followers in both the United States and in England.

Although besieged by emotional crises throughout her life— "Somehow in the boom years," she wrote, "the boom was always lowered on me"—Powell still managed to spread cheer, wit, and charm, and was considered by her friends to be the funniest woman alive. By the time she died in 1965, after a long battle with cancer, most of her work was out of print. In 1964 Malcolm Cowley presented her with the Marjorie Peabody Waite Award of the American Academy and Institute of Arts and Letters.